ANTAF

STORM

An Aggressor Inc. novel

FX Holden

Map © licensed from Shutterstock

Contact me:
Join my mailing list for exclusive previews and freebies:
WWW.FXHOLDEN.COM

Write to me at: fxholden@yandex.com

Or come and chat at:
https://www.facebook.com/hardcorethrillers

Antarctica STORM is a stand-alone supplement to the Aggressor series.

With huge thanks to my fantastic beta-reading team for their encouragement and constructive critique:

Gabrielle 'Hell Bitch' Adams, Bror Appelsin, Juan 'Pilotphotog' Artigas, Mukund B, Robert 'Ahab' Bugge, Marshall Crawford, Ted 'Bushmaster 06' Dannemiller, Julie 'Gunner' Fenimore, David Firth, Harry Garland, Dave 'Throttle' Hedrick, Martin Hirst, Dean Kaye, Rob Kidd, Thierry Lach, Graham McDonald, Alain Martin, Paul J Neel, Barry Roberts, Chris Scott, Scott Sherrick, Andy Sims, C Gordon Smith, Thomas Smith, Mark Sreniawski, Claus Stahnke, Lee Steventon, JD Torda.

And to editor Nicole Schroeder,
alexandria.edits@gmail.com,
for putting the cheese around the holes.

Books in the Aggressor series in reading order:
1. AGGRESSOR
2. BEACHHEAD
3. SWARM
4. MIDNIGHT
5. FULCRUM
6. ANTARCTICA STORM

Also by FX Holden: The Future War series
(each is a stand-alone story, but the recommended reading order follows)
1. KOBANI
2. GOLAN
3. BERING STRAIT
4. OKINAWA
5. ORBITAL
6. PAGASA
7. DMZ

Contents

Preface

19 December 2024, Media Unit
Conseil Européen pour la Recherche Nucléaire / European
Council for Nuclear Research

CERN experiment takes a big step towards portable antimatter

The experiment successfully transported a box filled with unbonded protons across CERN's main site, thus demonstrating that the same feat will later be possible for antimatter

Antimatter might sound like something out of science fiction, but at CERN scientists produce and trap antiprotons every day. They can even contain them for more than a year—an impressive feat considering that antimatter and matter annihilate upon contact.

Antimatter is a naturally occurring class of particles that is almost identical to ordinary matter except that the charges and magnetic properties are reversed.

Yesterday, a team of scientists and engineers took an important step towards this goal by transporting a cloud of protons in a truck across CERN's main site. "If you can do it with protons, it will also work with antiprotons," said Christina Sonora, the leader of the CERN's PUMA (antiProton Unstable Matter Annihilation) project.

The goal of PUMA is to create an antimatter 'trap' that is small enough to be loaded onto a truck and can resist the bumps and vibrations that are inevitable during ground transport. The current apparatus—which includes a superconducting magnet, cryogenic cooling, power reserves, and a vacuum chamber that traps the particles using magnetic and electric fields—weighs 1 ton and needs two cranes to be lifted out of the experimental hall and onto a truck.

"Eventually we want to be able to transport antimatter to any laboratory in Europe," Sonora said. "People ask if it's safe, but the amount we are transporting, if it escaped, would only release the energy of a pencil hitting the floor."

The PUMA transportable trap should be operational by 2025.

Cast of players

Project Minerva / Concordia Station
Dr. Jake Bellings, Deputy Director Engineering, Project Minerva
Solomon Cohen, Deputy Director Operations, Project Minerva
Cath Delaney, Deputy Security Chief, Concordia Station
Leroi Fontaine, base security drone officer, Concordia Station
Donovan Grant, US Antarctica Program (USAP), meteorologist, Concordia Station
Dr. Henrietta Jansen, Deputy Director Science, Project Minerva
Dr. David Lau, Director of the US Office of Energy Research and Development
Logan Raleigh, Station Security Chief, Concordia Station
Colonel Victor Sandilands, Deputy Director for Military Operations at the Defense Advanced Research Projects Agency (DARPA), Project Minerva (attached)

US Navy/US Air Force
Commander Sincere Jones, USNS *HO Lorenzen*
Lieutenant Juan Perine, USAF CIC comms officer, USNS *HO Lorenzen*
Lieutenant Andrew Stiles, USAF kill chain specialist, USNS *HO Lorenzen*

Aggressor Inc.
Lieutenant Elvis 'Ears' Bell (USN retd.), Deep-Submergence Reconnaissance Vehicle (DSRV) Systems Operator
Lieutenant Julie 'Trigger' Brown (USN retd.), Deep-Submergence Reconnaissance Vehicle (DSRV) Lead
Commander Jules 'Two-Tone' Hamilton, (RAF retd.), Chief Operations Officer

8

Lieutenant Robert E. 'Uncle' Lee (USAF retd.), copilot, AC-130X 'Outlaw'
Captain Rory O'Donoghue (USAF retd.), pilot, AC-130X 'Outlaw'
Captain Karen 'Bunny' O'Hare (RAAF retd), FB-22 Nemesis Detachment Lead
Captain Brad 'Grinspoon' Rice, (USAF retd), FB-22 Nemesis Detachment Support

Russia VMF
Chief Engineer Lieutenant Akopian, Russian Navy (VMF Rosii), submarine *B90 Sarov*
Sonar Operator Mikael Alekseev, Russian Navy (VMF Rosii), submarine *B90 Sarov*
Lieutenant Commander Ivan Fedorov, executive officer, Russian Navy (VMF), submarine *B90 Sarov*
Captain Yury Komarov, commander, Russian Navy (VMF), submarine *B90 Sarov*
Captain Anatoliy Kutuzov, 22nd Separate Guards Special Purpose Brigade, 411th Spetsnaz Detachment, GRU
Lieutenant Andre Spivak, 22nd Separate Guards Special Purpose Brigade, 411th Spetsnaz Detachment, GRU

Russia Project Chay
Major General Tomas Arsharvin, Main Intelligence Directorate of the Russian Armed Forces (GRU), Project Chay (attached)
Dr. Artur Eizen, Deputy Director Science, Sluzhba Vneshney Razvedki (SVR, the Foreign Intelligence Service), Project Chay (attached)

Russia VKS

Captain Andrey Adamov, copilot, Russian Aerospace Force (VKS Rosii), 184th Heavy Bomber Aviation Regiment, Tu-190 *Envoy*

Colonel Roman Gusev, pilot and commander, Russian Aerospace Force (VKS Rosii), 184th Heavy Bomber Aviation Regiment, Tu-190 *Envoy*

Map of Antarctica

For a downloadable version of this map, go to
www.fxholden.com/blog

Clear conditions

December 27, 2041
J-Day minus 4 days

"The transponder codes indicate they're civilian aircraft, took off from Christchurch six hours ago ..." the Russian Envoy heavy bomber's copilot, Captain Andrey Adamov, said as he parsed the data from the tactical display.

His pilot, Colonel Roman Gusev, commander of the 184th Heavy Bomber Aviation Regiment, grunted in response. "Civilian my ass." He pointed at the display. "Since when does a 'civilian' cargo aircraft get escorted by a 'civilian' stealth aircraft?" He frowned. "What even is that escort anyway?"

Gusev twitched his flight stick, keeping their aircraft oblique to the Americans, and invisible. He had matched altitude with them, but they were descending, so he also trimmed the *Envoy* to follow them down from 25,000 feet. It looked like they were headed for the ice runway at America's Concordia Antarctica Station.

Adamov tapped the screen and had his AI run the contact through its database. "No ID on the escort," he said. "But it's definitely stealth. The AC-130 is an X type, owned by a private contractor ... uh, Aggressor Inc."

"Private *military* contractor," Gusev said, affecting disgust. "They can try to hide who they are, but civilians don't fly strike fighters."

"Or AC-130 gunships, which that 'cargo' plane is." Adamov ran his eye over their radar warning screen. "No sign they've seen us," he said.

"At 150 miles, I'd hope not, or the engineers at Ramenskoye lied to us." He checked the contacts' flight track again. "Destination Concordia, has to be, yes?"

"I'd say. *Something* is happening if a cargo plane gets a stealth fighter escort."

"And wherever something is happening …" Gusev said with a grin, reaching a fist out to Adamov.

"That's where you'll find us." He grinned back, bumping his fist against Gusev's.

No other aircraft in Russia's Aerospace Force could have detected and tracked the US flight at 150 miles, as Gusev's Tu-190 *Envoy* was able to—because Russia had only *one* operational Tu-190. Gusev's *Envoy* was the first production aircraft to roll out of the Tupolev hangar at Kazan, after a troubled gestation.

But she was a game changer. Five times the size of a typical sixth-generation fighter, it was a multi-role evolution of the Tu-160 heavy bomber. Most importantly, Russia had finally mastered stealth designs and used materials that made her radar cross-section about the same as a stealth fighter. What gave the *Envoy* the edge over any American counterpart, however, was its first-in-class quantum entanglement (QE) radar.

It could see the American fighters with real-time precision at great range, and they had no idea they were being painted by the Russian radar. The quantum entangled radar didn't broadcast radio waves, like a traditional radar; it fired quantum entangled photons in two streams. One was sent into the sky ahead of it, and the other was held back and used for comparison. When the first beam bounced back from a target, the return was compared with its paired photons, and the *Envoy*'s AI filtered the returns.

13

The *Envoy*'s QE radar could tell a butterfly from a bird at a range of up to 200 miles and could spot an otherwise invisible stealth aircraft against the background noise of the sky, and it couldn't be jammed.

Gusev's copilot, Captain Andrey Adamov, was the *Envoy*'s weapons systems officer, and over the last year he had become very, very proficient in the use of the QE radar. Trained against the crude stealth of Russia's Su-57 and China's J-20 fighters, he had honed his skills over the Pacific: tracking, but not engaging, American stealth aircraft without any of them realizing the *Envoy* was there.

There was, after all, a ceasefire in place between Russia and the US-led coalition forces since the debacle of Russia's short-lived Shanghai Pact alliance.

Which made their rules of engagement for this mission all the more frustrating. After an 8,000-mile journey from Vladivostok in the Russian Far East, requiring just a single tanker rendezvous, they had landed at Russia-friendly Chile's air base on King George Island, just 800 miles from Concordia, and put their aircraft under cover, waiting for the "go" signal for the coming operation. Knowing it might never come. Eager for the day it would.

Until then, they were limited to careful probing patrols like today's, never getting close enough to the Americans' flight routes to betray their existence.

***

Karen 'Bunny' O'Hare wasn't happy about her rules of engagement either. Her FB-22 was flying in Aggressor Inc. livery, not USAF, even though Aggressor Inc. aircraft and pilots were officially part of the USAF Reserve.

But military activities on Antarctica were banned by multiple treaties, so apart from supply flights, the USAF stayed out of the continent. Aggressor Inc. had been hired by the US Department of Energy to support its "Project Minerva" with cargo and passenger transport and "airborne security."

"Airborne security?" Bunny had shaken her head at Aggressor Inc.'s head of flight operations, former RAF Commander Jules 'Two-Tone' Hamilton. "That's a new one. I'll be a flying security guard?"

"A flying *armed* security guard," Hamilton said, "which is why you'll be flying out of the Royal Australian Air Force's nice new airfield on Macquarie Island, not basing out of Antarctica, where heavily armed strike fighters are frowned on."

"'You' being me and who else?" Bunny asked, since it wasn't normal procedure to deploy an aircraft and pilot alone.

"You being you and Grinspoon. He can be your reserve, and fly the Stingray refueling drone you'll need so you can shuttle back and forth. I can get you another aircraft if yours has issues, but we don't have another spare pilot anywhere, sorry."

Bunny had flown with Brad 'Grinspoon' Rice over China and they'd done their FB-22 qualification training together. "Grinspoon is good. And I assume I'm flying under the usual 'don't shoot until shot at' restrictions," she said. "Because you know how bad I am at that."

He frowned. "All of our long-range fighter aircraft are deployed to Korea for flight training. Your nice new FB-22s are the only aircraft we have with the legs to make the return flight without refueling. So you will need to moderate your impulses."

That made Bunny laugh. There was nothing "new" about the FB-22s Aggressor Inc. had rehabilitated from the manufacturer's boneyard. The recent war with the Shanghai Pact nations—in which Aggressor Inc. had played a considerable part as the USAF Reserve 68th Aggressor Squadron—had taken its toll on the private contractor's fleet of ex-USAF F-22s. But much of the technology between the F-22 and FB-22 was interchangeable, so Aggressor Inc. was able to cannibalize parts from its remaining F-22s, and the manufacturer still had a good supply of fresh F-22 parts because the type hadn't been retired from the USAF until 2038.

Bunny O'Hare had been given the job of getting the six airframes flight and combat worthy, which also meant upgrading weapons and avionics to modern standards so they could be used to train Aggressor Inc.'s partner air forces or support USAF combat operations if needed—official or unofficial.

Like in Antarctica.

The FB-22 had never been deployed by the USAF, so it had never received a type designation, like Raptor, Lightning or Eagle. It was left to the pilots of Aggressor Inc. to come up with a designation, and they'd held a beer-fueled vote to land on the winner. 'Raven II' was a close runner up, but the winner—as judged by the volume of its supporting voters—was 'Nemesis.'

For Project Minerva, the USAF was sparing no expense. Looking at the mission requirements and operating area—the huge Southern Ocean—O'Hare put in a requisition for AIM-260 and CUDA missiles, external fuel tanks, and air-deployed anti-ship and anti-submarine weapons.

The ordnance was approved without question. When Bunny saw she apparently had a blank check, she put in a second requisition. That one saw her called to Two-Tone's office for a "please explain."

"What, exactly, is a GAMBIT?" he asked. "USAF said they'll approve delivery of a GAMBIT system, but if we break it, we have to pay for it. Before I agree terms, enlighten me."

"Think of it as the Swiss Army knife of combat drones," Bunny said excitedly. She held her hand up like it was an airplane and put her finger on the back of her hand. "Comes in a shipping container, fits on hard points under the Nemesis. Fuselage, wings, landing gear, basic flight control electronics are fixed, but the entire center of the machine is hollow, modular. You want to rig it as a recon bird, you drop in a recon module with cameras and synthetic aperture radar. You want something for air combat, you drop in a combat module with AESA radar and centerline stations for six missiles or small diameter bombs. You want an aerial picket, you go with the electronic warfare module—it has a radar jamming suite plus laser infrared jamming and can carry its own decoys …"

"Your pupils are dilating," Two-Tone said. "It's unsettling."

"There's two airframes per GAMBIT system, and one of each module," Bunny told him. "I can't promise we wouldn't bend or break any, if things get kinetic."

"Things are not going to get kinetic," Two-Tone said with a finality that he apparently thought fate would hear, reaching over and clicking his mouse. "The request is approved."

Bunny was flying her Nemesis 5 miles behind and 5,000 feet above the Aggressor Inc. AC-130X 'Outlaw,' breaking off at irregular intervals to scan the sky around them for intruders. Because it was a strike fighter, the Nemesis was fitted with the latest scanning array radar that had equipped the USAF's F-15EX Eagle II, capable of seeing non-stealth targets out to 100 miles with ease, and stealth aircraft out to 30 miles.

During the recent war, Bunny had mostly flown the US next-generation air dominance fighter, the P-99 Widow. Converting to the older FB-22 hadn't been the step backward she'd feared, probably because Bunny O'Hare was an aerial street brawler at heart, and the Widow was designed for combat over

17

the Pacific and was more like a quarterback … great at calling plays and delivering long-range harm but completely vulnerable when the pocket collapses.

The Nemesis was only 20 feet longer than the F-22 Raptor, and it had a broader delta wing to allow it to carry more fuel and ordnance. Twin thrust-vectoring engines gave it an impressive thrust-to-weight ratio, and leading canards had been added in the later stages of flight testing to boost maneuverability, giving it an appearance and performance similar to the Eurofighter Typhoon, with a stealthier profile. It was more than competitive with any fighter Russia or China could put up against it.

Why hadn't it made the cut for USAF's next strike aircraft? Air Force already had a multi-role aircraft in development—the F-35 Lightning II—and was close to choosing a strategic bomber successor to the B-2. And it had just decided to keep its F-15 strike fighter fleet flying until well into the 2030s. The Nemesis was all of these but better than none of them. So the prototypes developed had ended in a boneyard until Aggressor Inc. liberated them.

Bunny hauled her Nemesis around in a circle and put it on Outlaw's tail again. And as she did, her radar warning receiver, or RWR, *flashed*. More precisely, the radiation indicator on her RWR flashed. Just for a millisecond. It didn't trip the threshold to set off a radiation alert, and if she hadn't been looking right at it, she might not have seen it.

OK, weird. She stayed in her turn, circling over the spot where the spike had occurred, dropping lower in case it was something on the ground that had triggered the radiation sensor. In the dying stages of the war with the Shanghai Pact, rebels in the Chinese military had detonated a tactical nuclear weapon in space. After that, radiation monitoring equipment had been added to the radar warning receiver on USAF fighters, including those leased to Aggressor Inc. *Nothing.* She wrote it off as a glitch, checked the threat environment again and got back on Outlaw's tail.

She keyed her radio. "Aggressor Two, Aggressor One on overwatch. Nothing but clear air all the way to Concordia, gentlemen," she said. "I'll leave you to your dinner of seal blubber and powdered mash. Me and Grinspoon with be doing T-bone and fries at Macquarie tonight."

The pilot of the AC-130X couldn't let that one lie. "Better blubber in Concordia in good company than a T-bone with Grinspoon and the penguins on some shitty rock in the Southern Ocean."

"Aw, he does love me," Outlaw's copilot said. "I knew it. But for the record, I'd go for the T-bone, too."

Bunny smiled and banked her aircraft, peeling away and pointing it northeast.

"Coming up on Concordia Station," the pilot of AC-130X 'Outlaw' said over the purr of the aircraft's four Rolls-Royce turboprop engines. "Aggressor Incorporated trusts you've had a pleasant flight with us today and hopes you will consider us for all of your future clandestine transport needs."

Wiseass, thought David Lau, director of the US Office of Energy Research and Development, looking out his window at a vista of uninterrupted snow and ice under a pale blue sky. He craned his neck, trying to see ahead of them to where the triple red and white cylindrical habitats of the US Concordia Research Station would soon be visible. He couldn't see anything yet.

As they'd come out of a satellite communication dead zone about an hour ago, their routine transit to Concordia Station from New Zealand had gone critical. He turned his deep-set, piercing green eyes on his deputy director operations, Solomon Cohen, trying to keep his voice level, though his heart was thudding nearly as loudly as the props outside the fuselage. "Have you got an update on the temperature escape?"

Cohen, a former program manager at the Israeli Directorate of Defense Research and Development, consulted a tablet PC perched unsteadily on his lap. "We just got in range for a download. Central containment module temperature has been heading toward 0°C at a rate of 1 to 3 degrees every 30 minutes."

"Current temperature in containment?"

"Uh, minus 16 Celsius," Cohen said. He was normally unflappable, but Lau could see beads of sweat across the top of his shaved skull. Which, considering the dual US-Israeli citizen had once been in charge of nuclear weapons research for the Israeli Defense Forces, didn't give Lau a feeling of great confidence.

Lau cursed. "Dammit, summer is the worst time possible for a field test. I told General Maxwell that."

"Actually, December or January is the worst, if you're thinking about temperatures in the ice cap," Cohen said. "From now until October, the ice gets colder."

"And yet our containment core is getting *warmer*, Solomon," Lau said. "The whole reason we buried the damn module in the ice here was to make sure this couldn't happen." Lau had a lean face with hollow cheeks, which struck people as "unforgiving" if they incurred his ire. There was plenty of ire being directed at Solomon Cohen at that moment.

Unfairly, in Cohen's mind. Yes, he was in charge of project operations, but not the day-to-day running of Concordia Station. "We only expected to be here two to three months, June to October last year," Cohen said. "We should have completed the test by now."

Lau looked away, trying to spot the approaching station again. "Should have built in more redundancy."

"The system has multiple redundancies. This is something else—a technical issue we didn't foresee. Or …" Cohen let himself speculate out loud. "Maybe a human one."

"There are several hundred personnel on this project. Any one of them could have screwed up," Lau said absently. "Human error is always a risk."

"I'm not thinking human error. I'm thinking sabotage," Cohen said bluntly.

Lau looked at him with hooded eyes. "Not this again."

"Yes, precisely this," Cohen said. "I warned you not to have so many personnel on-site. Half of them should be elsewhere, working remotely …"

"And we'd still be here this time *next* year if I hadn't," Lau said. "There's a 12-hour time zone difference Concordia to US East Coast. You want every discussion, every email, every message to wait overnight for someone to react to it?"

"No, but at any one time, 10 percent of the personnel on an Antarctic deployment are having personal, psychological or financial problems. That's three people if you only have the most essential 30 people here, but it's *30* with 300 personnel on the base. Any one of them could be the reason we are facing an 80-megaton event," Cohen said.

***

The "wiseass" pilot at the controls of the AC-130X gunship was Captain Rory O'Donoghue, and if you'd asked him, he wouldn't have considered his remark out of place. Everything about the project under the ice at Concordia Station was hush-hush, and while Rory had always had a healthy respect for security classifications—not least because, as a former pilot with the USAF 18ᵗʰ Flight Test Squadron, he had security clearances that even the US president hadn't heard of—he was never comfortable being kept in the dark.

And everything about Project Minerva was shrouded in a blanket of impenetrable darkness. For a lot of the Antarctic year, almost literally. But with summer came daylight, and on the horizon, he could see the triple white cylindrical habitats of Concordia coming into view.

"Got a ghost on RWR, starboard," Rory's copilot, Lieutenant Robert E. 'Uncle' Lee, said, pointing at their radar warning receiver. Outlaw didn't have an air search radar of its own, but it had a very sensitive radar warning receiver that could pick up everything from ground or aircraft radars to strong radio emissions, and a small blip was showing about 20 miles east of Concordia. As he watched, it disappeared.

Rory nodded to Uncle. "I'll log it; you can bring us in."

"Copilot has the controls," Uncle said. "You're just handing over because you know I land this beast prettier than you do."

"Beers are on me if you can get down on the ice without sliding off the runway this time," Rory said confidently. A message ticked in on their comms screen, and he read it, then reread it. "Look at this," he told Uncle, pointing at the screen.

Uncle read it. "Never a dull moment."

"I'll call Two-Tone." Still frowning, Rory switched his comms unit to satellite phone and dialed the secure number that would get him the Aggressor Inc. head of flight operations, Commander Jules 'Two-Tone' Hamilton, formerly leader of the air wing aboard the British aircraft carrier HMS *Queen Elizabeth*. Tapped to head up the creation of a new Aggressor squadron for the Royal Navy Fleet Air Arm, the Royal Navy had contracted Aggressor Inc. to assist in standing the squadron up. At the end

22

of the contract, he'd "jumped ship" after getting an offer from Aggressor Inc.'s billionaire owner, Mark Aaronson, that he couldn't refuse.

Rory O'Donoghue had a mixed history regarding his relations with the many and various commanding officers he'd served under, but the fact Two-Tone Hamilton was a pilots' pilot in every sense of the word went a long way with him. His Jamaican heritage showed in a relaxed demeanor on the ground, but in the air, he was buttoned up tighter than a hatch on a submarine. He set boundaries, of course, but Rory found that he could comfortably operate within them with a little mutual give-and-take.

"O'Donoghue," Two-Tone said, picking up Rory's call. His call sign was because of the differing colors of his irises—one blue, one brown. It was approaching 6 p.m. where he was, at RUS Navy Base Harewood, in Christchurch, New Zealand. "I hear engines. Aren't you down yet?"

"Headwinds," Rory told him. "Be on the ground in 10 mikes—earlier if Uncle screws up the approach and augurs us in."

"I haven't been able to find anyone willing to insure that bird, with all the hours on that airframe and the modifications it carries, so please don't even joke about that," he said. "What's up?"

"Just got a strange message," Rory told him. "Says that Concordia base is in lockdown, we won't be unloading cargo, and only our two very-high-ranking passengers are approved to leave the aircraft."

"I haven't heard that," Two-Tone said.

"Well, boss, I'm telling you what I was told," Rory said. "You might want to make a few calls."

"I'll do that. Stand by comms."

"Good copy. O'Donoghue out," he said. He put the sat phone handset back in its cradle on the instrument panel with a curse. "Goddamn secret squirrel BS. What kind of operation is it where your CO isn't even told what's going down?"

"You don't think he knows and just isn't telling?" Uncle asked.

"We'll see," Rory said, not wanting to distract Uncle with his conspiracy speculation. Landing any aircraft at one of the highest points on Antarctica required full concentration. Landing the highly modified, abused and tortured airframe of Outlaw on Concordia's single 10,000-foot ice runway without sliding it "into the rough" required a pilot who knew their aircraft better than they knew themselves and had a sixth sense for the weather that only hundreds of hours flying in dangerous conditions could teach.

The trick was to come down the glide path on the edge of a stall and drop onto the ice with all skids almost simultaneously, allowing the aircraft to start gently braking with the full length of the runway still ahead of it. As Uncle eased Outlaw lower, Rory could feel the aircraft balanced between flight and falling out of the sky. His hands were sitting lightly on his own controls … just in case. His eyes roved across her instruments, the indicators in his helmet visor display, out the window at the angle of the white and blue horizon, and ahead to the runway beside the three habitats, with the line of lights that was their aiming point.

Data from Concordia's weather station flowed across his visor display. "Wind 15 knots from the northwest," he said tightly. "Thirteen. Twelve. Back to 15."

"Roger that," Uncle said. He started going through the landing checklist and turned to Rory as they felt the landing gear thump into place. "Skis to retard."

"Aw, that's cheating," Rory said, reaching down beside himself and flicking a switch. "Skis in retard mode."

"There's a joke in there, but you didn't laugh last time I made it," Uncle said.

Flagged for the scrapheap after one too many mishaps, Outlaw had been purchased by Aggressor Inc. from the USAF not just restored to operational condition but also given new mods to allow it to fulfill its Antarctic missions. The first was the fitting of two JATO (Jet Assisted Take-Off) pods—solid fuel rocket boosters mounted on the fuselage, which enabled it to take off with half the runway usually needed. The second was a fat ski that wrapped around each wheel strut to stop the wheels sinking into soft surface snow, with the added benefit of providing significant additional friction on landing if the "retard" landing mode was engaged.

Uncle and Rory had been relegated to the career boneyard too, with commercial air services overrun with pilots quitting the USAF and Navy, until one Bunny O'Hare, who they'd met on Hawaii, had pointed out to Aggressor Inc.'s billionaire owner that buying Outlaw without putting Rory and Uncle in the cockpit was like a owning a racecar without a pit crew.

Rory quickly learned that Aggressor Inc. took on jobs the USAF couldn't, or wouldn't, and that suited him and Uncle just fine. Outlaw had earned its call sign while in their care for a reason. As they thumped down onto the ice, and the cockpit was filled with the sound of props batting the air and skis biting, he turned his attention back to the view out the cockpit—and the group of people huddled beside the runway in cold weather survival gear. Not a good sign. Even the airfield's dedicated ground crew didn't usually brave the cold until they had shut down their engines and the props had spun to a halt.

Uncle taxied them in without any drama, then powered the engines down. He looked out his side window to check the tracks his skids had made on the ice. Neatly down the centerline of the runway. "Like a mother kissing her baby," he bragged. "Beers are on you."

"You skidded," Rory said, releasing his harness and opening the intercom to the rear compartment. "Gentlemen, please wait until the rear ramp is opened before you unbuckle."

"I *trundled*," Uncle said, offended. "This runway is corrugated. There is a difference between an unavoidable trundle and a skid, which I didn't."

"Well, how about you get your furry jacket on and 'trundle' out there to help our passengers deplane?" he said. He saw a couple of civilians in the group from the station edging closer to the aircraft. "And tell those idiots out there to stand back until the props have spun down unless they want to get skittled across the ice by propwash."

When he was finished running through the shut-down checklist, he gave a signal to the small building beside the runway and helipad, where the ground crew sheltered from the elements. Two aviators and a crew chief ran out to lock down the wheels. Just because the winds were light now, and the forecast was optimistic, didn't mean the weather would stay that way. Antarctica had a reputation for weather as unpredictable as Rory's moods.

The crew chief climbed through a hatch and made his way up into the cockpit, standing behind Uncle's recently vacated seat. "Sir. My orders are to get you refueled and ready to depart on five minutes' notice," he said.

Rory looked out at the sky. "Is there a front moving in? I haven't seen any warnings."

The man didn't answer. "What's your maximum passenger load?"

Rory thought about the message saying that the station was in lockdown and assumed the worst. "Officially 100, but I can do 150 standing up and stripped naked. Why?"

The crew chief bit his lip. "We might need to evacuate. There's an Australian C-17 inbound McMurdo from Casey Station, but it wouldn't be able to get here in time."

"How many are on this base now?" Rory asked.

"More than 300, last I heard."

Three *hundred?* Rory had overnighted a few times in one of the three habitats, and though it was two levels high, and probably had underground storage, he had figured it could hold maybe 50 people, at most. In the last six months of ferrying personnel and materiel to Concordia, he'd lost count of the comings and goings, that was true. There had also been a constant stream of "traverses," or transport convoys, from McMurdo Station to Concordia, whenever weather allowed. And yeah, he'd seen the occasional C-17 transport parked up on the station's single runway, which he hadn't really paid much attention to. But 300 personnel? Where had they stashed them away? Were they all in cryogenic storage, like the crew of some kind of interstellar starship?

"What the hell is going on, Chief?" Rory asked.

"Information like that is hard to come by," the crew chief said. "You've been flying in and out for a few months now. What do you know about what's under the ice here?"

"Not a lot," Rory admitted. In addition to ferrying clandestine passengers and cargo from New Zealand Antarctica, Rory and Outlaw had conducted a series of surveillance and weather-watch patrols of the Southern Ocean north of McMurdo for the National Oceanic and Atmospheric

Administration (NOAA), all uneventful. They had also been making small cargo drops out to a NOAA weather monitoring platform 400 miles off the coast of McMurdo using 'Vigilant' tiltrotor drones. The Vigilants were launched into flight from hardpoints under his wings, and his job was just to get them within range of the platform so that NOAA personnel based on the platform could fly them in and then refuel and dispatch them to McMurdo Station. What their cargo was, he wasn't told.

He had been told very little at all about what research was being conducted at Concordia, but he had noted that a lot of the passengers he and Uncle were flying in and out were not your house and garden polar researcher. Like the two he'd just delivered, most were from the US Office of Energy Research and Development. When he'd asked about that, he'd been told they were researching "cold-temperature energy generation" under the ice, and had assumed it was something geothermal.

But any sortie that didn't involve someone shooting at you was easy money in O'Donoghue's mind, so he hadn't been too curious.

The crew chief looked pained. "I don't know everything," he said. "But what I do know? Whatever they're working on down there, if it gets out of control, it can kill everything on, under and above the ground for at least *50 miles* around. That's the safety perimeter we've been using in evacuation exercises."

"Some kind of nuclear reactor?" Rory guessed.

"If it is, we're talking the mother of all meltdowns," the chief replied.

That detail focused Rory's mind. He checked their fuel state—they had landed from New Zealand with just 21 percent remaining in their tanks. "The closest runway to Concordia we can put down at is 600 miles away," Rory told him. "And it's Russian. The nearest US base is McMurdo, 800 miles away. I can

28

fly out a couple hundred personnel, but if this is a time-critical emergency, by the time I get back, it will be over."

The crew chief looked pained. "Well, you're all we got." He threw open the cockpit access door, and a cold blast of air washed over Rory, blowing straight up from the open rear ramp. "Chief!" Rory called out. "Anything I can do except sit here with my thumb up my ass?"

"Sure," he said. "Keep your engines warm, and make your peace with God." He slammed the door behind him.

Yeah, too late for that, Rory reflected grimly. What in hell is down there?

Rory had an active imagination. Overactive, a psychiatrist had once told him. An inveterate insomniac, he had suffered from night terrors that started around the same time he was assigned Outlaw as part of the 18th Test Squadron, 492nd Special Operations Wing.

Not because of the aircraft and its many idiosyncrasies but because of the missions he'd had to fly in it. Or to be more specific, those missions which had cost innocent lives. Rory O'Donoghue wasn't that person who could accidentally drop a bomb on a grade school, or take out the family of a terrorist, then go back to his quarters at the end of the mission, order pizza and watch a movie—if anyone *was* that person.

Rory O'Donoghue was the guy whose dreams were filled with the faces of the civilians he *knew* he had killed. That was the problem with living in the age of information saturation. Collateral damage wasn't just numbered; it was named, if not in the official reports, then by human rights groups, open-source intelligence analysts, local media outlets.

They hadn't died because of anything he'd done with wanton carelessness, but that didn't matter to Rory. Children died in war, or they were orphaned, or maimed, despite the best intentions of warriors, because war was a messy, imprecise and unholy thing. Invented by Satan, and visited on the innocent by the unintentional. Rory was surrounded by their faces in his sleep, but he also heard their voices, and he *saw* them … standing in dark corners, hiding in closets, staring at him with dead, accusing eyes.

He drank a cup of vodka every night before bed, throwing down a handful of zolpidem with it. That combination got him through to about 2 or 3 a.m., when his ghosts would come to visit. It wasn't dedication to duty that got him up at 5 a.m. every morning … It was the fact he'd already been lying awake for at least two hours by then, tossing, turning, moaning into his pillow.

So why didn't he quit flying? Quit military flying at least?

And do *what*? Play golf?

If he quit the life, he'd have too much time on his hands: time trying not to look in the dark corners, not to walk in the shadows, not to look over his shoulder. Not to speculate about what could be hidden inside a subterranean base that could kill everything for *50 miles* around it.

***

The US Navy wasn't in Antarctica. Not officially. So neither was its deep-submergence recon vehicle—a drone sub sentimentally nicknamed *'Charlene'*—currently patrolling the waters under Antarctica's Ross Ice Shelf.

That's because military operations weren't permitted on Antarctica.

So *Charlene*'s crew wasn't US Navy either. It was led by Julie 'Trigger' Brown, submersible systems lead with private security contractor Aggressor Inc. Because having a civilian entity like Aggressor Inc. run your operations didn't, superficially, break any treaties.

And Trigger Brown's systems operator, Elvis 'Ears' Bell, had just identified an object under the glacier that also couldn't, or shouldn't, be there. Which meant Trigger and Ears were having a robust disagreement.

"Yes, that's a close match with the acoustic signature of a *Kilo* class submarine," Trigger said, pointing at a screen, "which it can't be, because Russia retired all its *Kilos*."

"Retired doesn't mean decommissioned," Ears insisted. Trigger was sitting beside him inside a two-person trailer attached to Concordia Station's research core by a flimsy and none-too-weatherproof fiberglass tube, prone to cracks that let the subzero air in. The trailer itself was warm enough, especially when Trigger got fired up about something. Like now. "And the AI is saying there's a Russian *Kilo* 500 yards off *Charlene*'s nose," he added.

"Screw the AI. It has to be something else …" Trigger said, reviewing the data on the contact again. "Yeah. Six-bladed screw. All the latest *Kilos* had seven-bladed screws. Except …" She paged through some data. "I knew it. It's the *Sarov*. Modified *Kilo*."

"*Kilo*, modified *Kilo*—I was close," Ears grumbled. But "close" wasn't right. He hated losing an argument to Trigger, especially on a technicality.

"Stay with it."

"*Kilo* is diesel-electric, right?" Bell asked. He had a steering yoke between his knees that controlled yaw and dive angle, and he adjusted it to keep *Charlene* behind the contact. He was following it using his drone's passive sensor array, not actively pinging it with sonar, which was why there was a level of uncertainty to their ID. "So how does a diesel-electric boat with

31

a submerged range of about 400 miles get from Vladi-bloody-vostok, 8,000 miles north, to Antarctica, undetected?"

"*Sarov* has a supplementary nuclear power plant is how. I'll take us down to 420," Trigger said tightly. "See if you can clean up the signal. Ice shelf is creating all kinds of noise."

Bell gritted his teeth. He'd been about to do that. This wasn't his first rodeo. He'd been hunting Russian, Iranian and Chinese boats for years as sonar operator on the USS *Canberra*, and in the recent global conflict, *Canberra* had painted five sub kills on its superstructure, including one of China's newest *Taifun* class boats.

Their DSRV, *Charlene,* had been on a "survey mission," with Bell ostensibly using an ice-penetrating radar to map the thickness of the Ross Ice Shelf, a plateau of solid ice off the coast of the US McMurdo base. "Ostensibly" because though *Charlene* could be used to map the thickness of the ice, that wasn't its primary mission. *Charlene* was a sentry, patrolling the waters between McMurdo Sound and an offshore US NOAA weather monitoring platform, to identify and, if required, deter underwater interlopers.

So Bell kept a wary eye, or ear, on passive sonar and logged every contact, natural or synthetic. It was, after all, less than two years since the US, Russia and China had waged a bloody war across the Pacific, and the occasional drone or missile was still being exchanged between Russia and NATO across tense border regions in Europe.

"Fifty bucks says the AI is right—it's just a plain vanilla *Kilo*, with an old screw," Bell said.

"You already owe me 200 from our last bet," Trigger pointed out.

"I still say that was a blue whale. Frequency was too low to be a humpback, but you were giving me your pouty look, so I paid out. Alright, double or nothing."

"Done. It will be a pleasure taking your money from you again, Lieutenant," Trigger said with a grin. She pointed at a screen in front of him that showed the Russian sub's acoustic signature as a set of lines, like those on a lie detector test. "I'm seeing a whole lot of rattle and shake from that boat. *Sarov* is a Cold War relic. It's totally the *Sarov*."

The submarine 500 yards ahead of *Charlene* was not a *Kilo* class submarine, but neither was it the *Sarov* Trigger Brown thought she knew.

Unique in Russia's navy, the *Sarov* had been a diesel-electric submarine with a small supplementary nuclear-powered reactor, which allowed it to stay submerged for nearly a month at a time. Russia had used it solely to test one of its prototype "wonder weapons," the intercontinental nuclear-powered, nuclear-armed autonomous *Poseidon* torpedo. The *Poseidon* project was intended to be the ultimate stealth weapon, able to navigate itself undetected to its target across hundreds, even thousands, of miles of sea. It was assessed by US defense analysts to be an utter failure as it was never seen to be deployed, except in fake-news press releases. *Sarov* was taken out of service and dry-docked in 2025 because the launch mechanism for the *Poseidon* occupied the entire front section of the submarine and left no room for torpedo tubes or vertical launch cells for missiles.

Russia never fully abandoned its *Poseidon* project. By 2030, it had a viable design, but since *Sarov* was quietly rusting in dry-dock, it had no platform to launch it from.

Refitting the *Sarov* to modern standards was cheaper than building an entirely new submarine for the *Poseidon* torpedo, but it was a herculean task beyond the Russian economy and its crippled ship-building industry at the time, so the refit—involving a new modular payload bay and a sonar system repurposed from a decommissioned *Kilo* class submarine—staggered from delay to delay. When war broke out between US allies and Russia in 2038, the *Sarov* refit was only 86 percent complete—it had just received a new, quieter, six-bladed screw. Resources were belatedly poured into the project, but too late for *Sarov* and its *Poseidon* torpedo to join the war before a ceasefire was signed between the US Coalition and Russia.

With the ceasefire, some sanctions were lifted, international finance began flowing again, and *Sarov*'s refit was finally completed, nearly 15 years after it started. His crew, since Russian ships and submarines were gendered male, had either been transferred to other ships or sent to war in Ukraine in the intervening years, but his captain had been brought back from retirement for the old vessel's re-commissioning.

Captain Yury Komarov hated the *Sarov*.

He'd hated it during the first phase of testing of the troubled *Poseidon* torpedo, and he hated it even more now, since *Sarov*'s "upgrade." Because *Sarov* was cursed. The list of things Komarov hated about *Sarov* changed with every deployment, since it was guaranteed that at least one, and often several, of the boat's critical systems would fail, usually at a critical moment.

The kludges that had been necessary to retrofit salvaged sonar systems from an old *Kilo* class boat and add a new bow section to the *Sarov* had introduced an unwelcome element of both unpredictability and unreliability. Unpredictability because the electrical system supporting their new weapons system was prone to random inexplicable outages that could affect other systems, and unreliability because the *Sarov*'s refurbished nose section included watertight doors that were so poorly fitted, the *Sarov*'s maximum safe operating depth was reduced from 300 meters to just 200.

At the moment Trigger's DSRV drone fell in behind the *Sarov*, leaking doors weren't Komarov's biggest problem though.

"Three hours?!" Komarov demanded of his chief engineer. "Lieutenant Akopian, if we don't get your reactor back online within an hour, we will need to rise to snorkeling depth to engage our diesel generators, and in case you hadn't noticed, we are currently under about *6 meters* of ice."

The man had the good sense to look uncomfortable, instead of argumentative. "Yes, Captain. But the control rod monitoring system is down, and without it, we can't be sure that …"

"Wait," Komarov said tiredly. "I was told there was a problem with the control rods. You're saying it's just a problem with the system that *monitors* the rods?"

"Yes, Captain," he said. "The monitoring system failed. I ordered a reactor shutdown because according to protocol we can only repair …"

Komarov grabbed the back of his chair and squeezed, counting down to five, slowly. "Akopian, I grew up in Murmansk. In Murmansk, we don't shut down our central heating just because we discover a smoke alarm isn't working. Because if we did, we would freeze to death." He watched the man's brain working through the analogy and saw he wasn't getting there. "We leave the heat on *while* we fix the smoke alarm."

"Ah. Yes, Captain."

"Screw your protocol, Lieutenant. This is the *Sarov*. We write our own procedures. Bring the reactor back online and fix the—"

"Contact on passive sonar, bearing one seven five degrees!" his sonar operator interrupted. He cupped his hands around the earphones over his ears. *Sarov* had no quantum-computer-powered AI to read the acoustic signatures of objects in the surrounding water. It had Sonar Operator Mikael Alekseev's bio-organic experience-based database. "Mechanical. I want to say … water over dive planes. A submarine."

Komarov straightened and turned to his executive officer, Lieutenant Commander Fedorov. "All sections to general quarters, XO," he said. "Load countermeasures. Helm, maintain your speed and depth, but make your rudder port one five degrees."

A red light started flashing inside *Sarov*'s control room, as it did silently in every compartment in the boat, signaling its crew to rush to their alert stations. Komarov's officers began repeating his orders throughout the boat, and he felt the 4,000-ton *Sarov* begin a slow turn to port.

"Give me a range, Alekseev," he said to the sonarman. "Comms, were there any reports of friendly undersea vessels in our patrol area at last check-in?"

"No, Captain. None," his comms watch officer reported.

"Estimate contact is 500 to 700 meters distant, bearing one nine zero now," Alekseev said.

"XO, arm countermeasures. Helm, center your rudder. Sonar, let me know if the contact turns with us."

Sarov might have been a mixed-race mongrel of a sea dog, but it had been given a set of sharp new teeth. As Komarov barked out his order, in dispensers either side of its hull, aft of the conning tower, *Piranya* homing anti-submarine mines were loaded and armed. *Sarov* could spit the swarming mines into the water behind it in clusters of four, and as soon as they detected an acoustic signal that wasn't *Sarov*'s, they would start guiding themselves toward it.

Komarov's orders were clear. *Sarov*'s mission was of critical importance, and he was authorized to do whatever was necessary to ensure his submarine successfully executed that mission.

Whatever was necessary.

***

"Contact is turning," Ears Bell told Trigger. "Now at three five two degrees. AI is still saying it's an unidentified *Kilo*."

"AIs don't know shit," Trigger said.

"Alright, we could go to active sonar, get a read on its displacement. *Sarov* is a thousand tons heavier than a standard *Kilo*."

"Good thinking. Light it up, Lieutenant. Let 'em know we're here," Trigger agreed. "I'll close separation." She squinted at the plot on her screen and moved *Charlene*'s engines to "ahead full." The two undersea vessels were under the Ross Ice Shelf. To the northwest was the Antarctic Peninsula and South America. To the northwest was … well, the US McMurdo base, just 100 miles distant. A couple of small dots 400 miles farther out in the Southern Ocean north of McMurdo caught her eye but only because she was looking for them … The label underneath one dot said "*Minerva 2*." An uncrewed weather monitoring platform. The other said "USCGC *Polar Warden*"— the newest of three *Polar* class US Coast Guard icebreakers and McMurdo base's nautical lifeline to the wider world. "I know we aren't at war right now, but having a Russian submarine sneaking around under the ice anywhere near a US base makes me edgy."

"Going to active sonar," Bell said, tapping icons on his master screen. Their extreme low-frequency commands were relayed from their trailer, up to a satellite and down to an ELF transceiver on the seabed off McMurdo before being pushed through the water to *Charlene.* Although *Charlene* carried no weapons, it had deployed with a payload module containing the same sonar suite as a Japanese *Soryu* class attack submarine, and Bell's screen filled with data as it got a return from the Russian boat. "This should get a reaction."

***

"Contact is pinging us," Komarov's sonar operator said, unnecessarily, since the hull of the *Sarov* was ringing. "Active sonar detected. Propulsion noises bearing two ten degrees. Range closing. Analyzing signal."

"Deploy countermeasures," Komarov said. "Helm, 20 degrees right rudder. Take us down to 200."

"Launching countermeasures," his XO confirmed.

"What is shadowing us, Alekseev?" Komarov asked.

"Still analyzing, Captain," the sonar operator said, manually running a database search on a recording of the adversary's sonar signal. "Here ... the sonar is a Hughes/Oki Type 3b, so it's a Japanese *Soryu*, or ... could be an American DSRV autonomous drone, *LD* class."

A Japanese submarine? Japan had an Antarctic research station, but it was on the other side of the continent. Unlikely then, but not impossible. More likely an American sentry drone. He felt relief at the thought.

Not because he had been troubled by the idea he could be about to kill a crewed submarine and send 60 submariners to their deaths. No. His relief came from the certainty that if he did kill a crewed submarine, whatever nation it belonged to would hunt old *Sarov* mercilessly, until it and its reluctant captain and crew lay rotting on the bottom of an ocean somewhere.

An uncrewed drone? Not so much.

***

"Incoming!" Bell said, voice suddenly high pitched. "Contacts bearing three five five, 200 yards, closing! Initiating sonar jamming."

"Evading," Trigger said, turning her yoke and pushing the control column forward. They were already descending, and she steepened the dive. "Ahead flank. Right full rudder; diving to maximum safe depth." *Charlene* had no countermeasures of her own. No decoys she could fire. Bell was blasting sonar energy down the bearing to the threats, trying to confuse their onboard sonar, but that only worked if they were sonar guided.

"Drone swarm," Bell said. "It's a damn *swarm*. One minute to impact."

A screen mounted head-high in their trailer simulated a 3D view of their boat relative to the ice above and the seafloor below. They watched, transfixed, as *Charlene* spiraled through the water like a leaf falling from a gingko tree, pursued by the small dots that were the Russian weapons.

Bell looked down at his tactical screen again. "Got a propulsion match. *Piranya* mines—multi-mode homing." He pushed his chair back from his console. "We're *screwed*. Twenty seconds."

Trigger wasn't about to give up. "Kill the sonar; I'm blowing ballast," she said through gritted teeth. "Emergency ascent. Dumping the payload module."

"Aye, sonar to passive, dumping … *what?*" Bell looked at her as though she were mad.

***

Sarov's four *Piranya* homing mines were untroubled by the sonar energy Bell had directed toward them; in fact, they welcomed it. Each was the size of a lightweight torpedo, with a 100 lb. warhead, behind which was a multimode sensor that either homed on the noise being made by their target or the sonar energy being emitted by it. At the moment Trigger blew her ballast tanks, the *Piranya* swarm was homing on *Charlene*'s sonar energy, but when Bell killed the sonar, they switched to acoustic homing. They had advanced signal processing algorithms that could sort the sound of a submarine moving through the water from the sound of US noisemaking decoys.

What they saw ahead of them in the last few seconds of their pursuit was a *wall* of noise. The sea in front of them was boiling, and their target could be anywhere in inside it. Or nowhere.

So they switched targeting mode again ... to magnetic anomaly detection. Somewhere inside that wall of noise, a huge metal object should be lurking. And sure enough ... with just seconds left to run, the Russian mines made a last course correction and powered forward.

Two of the *Piranyas* blasted through the cloud of roiling water and found nothing but empty sea on the other side. But two had locked onto the massive object inside the cloud, and struck it at 30 knots, warheads slicing through the hull until, milliseconds later, they detonated inside.

***

"Explosions ... That's a kill," Alekseev said with understated satisfaction. "Sounds like hull rupture. Got crush noises too."

"What was it?" Komarov asked. "Can you tell?"

"*Piranyas* went to MAD mode for the run in. Let me check the data …" the sonar operator said. "Here … estimated displacement: 1 ton. A small drone. Operators will probably have no idea what hit them."

Komarov wiped away sweat he hadn't noticed was lining his brow. "Good. Navigation, plot us a course that will get us back on mission. Helm, take us back up to cruising depth." He turned to see his chief engineer, still standing where he'd left him. "Lieutenant Akopian. You have one hour to bring your reactor back online, or you'll be joining that drone at the bottom of the Southern Ocean."

***

"That sound you are listening to is the noise a DSRV submersible makes …" Bell said, playing a noise over loudspeakers in his console, "when it slams into the underside of an ice shelf after an uncontrolled ascent."

"*Emergency* ascent, under full control," Trigger said. "More or less."

"Without its million-dollar payload module," Bell continued. "Containing *my* sonar suite."

"Stop whining," she countered. "Our boat is still alive. It wouldn't be if I had given up, like your pussy ass did."

Bell bit down a retort. "Whatever. You were right; we suckered the swarm into going for the payload," Bell told her. He had earphones jammed over his head and turned back to his console, manipulating controls. "And we're good. Contact is moving away. Suggest you keep us inert until we lose it entirely."

"Good idea," Trigger said. "Shutting down everything that might make a noise."

Trigger sent an engagement report to US Coast Guard McMurdo, with a copy to both Aggressor Inc. in Arizona and the USCGC *Polar Warden.*

A short while later, Bell pulled his headphones from his head. "I think we're clear now."

Trigger checked a status screen. "All critical systems nominal. Restarting propulsion," Trigger said. "Taking her down and laying in a course for McMurdo." She realized Bell was staring at her. "What are you looking at?"

"I'll admit, I wrote us off too soon," he said, looking away. "But for future reference, do you solve *every* problem so violently?"

Trigger reached over, grabbed him by the scruff of his neck and shook him. "Lieutenant, in my experience, the most violent response to a life-or-death threat is always the most effective."

***

Elvis Bell *had* been staring, yes. It was hard not to stare at Trigger Brown. She looked like one of those space marines you see in movies. Biceps like a power lifter, thighs like tree trunks. Born in Missouri, she wore custom-made Nicks tactical boots and Navy camo on duty, and rocked jeans and a leather jacket with a guitar patch on the back when she wasn't. Her face looked about 30, but he'd heard she was older, and you could bet he didn't ask.

He'd been warned about Julie Brown when he'd signed on with Aggressor Inc., and before he'd taken the Antarctica contract. He knew Aggressor Inc. by name. Of course, who didn't? It was the largest private military contractor in the Western hemisphere, supplier of training, personnel and supplementary hardware to nearly every nation in NATO at some point or other. But it was mostly known for air combat training and support—not naval and certainly not subsurface warfare.

"Combat tours in the Middle East and Pacific," the Aggressor Inc. operations planner who was his recruitment contact noted, looking through his application. He was former USAF and introduced himself as Captain Fibak. The name tag on his shirt said simply "Flatline." Ears assumed it was his USAF call sign. "Sonar operator, then Sysop on USS *Canberra*'s *Manta Ray* platform?"

"Yes sir," Bell said. "I'm also qualified on the *Sea Hunter* and *Orca*."

"Experience with the DSRV multi-mission platform?"

"No one does," he'd replied. "It's still a prototype."

The captain smiled, looking down at the tablet screen in front of him. "Hmm. I'm told it's a lot like the *Orca*."

"Then it shouldn't be a problem," Ears said, trying to sound more confident than he felt.

"Hopefully not. You'd be part of a two-person crew: pilot and sysop. You'd be the sysop."

"Like the *Manta Ray* station on *Canberra*," he said. "But it requires teamwork. What can you tell me about my driver?"

The pilot looked up again, a different smile on his face now. "She's our naval systems training lead," Flatline said. "If it can swim or sail, she can pilot it. She helped write the autonomous engagement code for the *Manta*, then did the combat testing. She was the first US Navy *Manta* pilot to get a Chinese *Type 95* sub kill."

Bell raised an eyebrow. "OK, that's a pretty cool resume."

Flatline shook his head. "I wouldn't try flattery on her." He looked at his tablet again. "Your psych profile says you are the kind of guy who can get along with just about anyone."

"I like to think so," Bell said.

Flatline pushed the tablet away. "*Trigger* Brown is going to test that out."

"Ah."

"Her call sign?" He pointed at the tag on his own chest. "Is short for 'Trigger Warning.' She'll say the things other people are thinking. Out loud. To you, and about you."

"Sounds awesome," Ears said sarcastically. "This *is* a recruitment interview, right?"

"She's had complaints made against her in the Navy, and in our employ, for everything from racism and coarse language to sexism, if you can believe that."

Bell stared at him blankly.

"How to handle her," Flatline explained, "is roll with it. She says something you don't like? Don't bite. But in a clinch, you should listen to her. She has great instincts and is a first-class operator."

He heard a lot of stories about Trigger Brown as he completed his onboarding. Everyone he met had one. Not everyone shared Flatline's opinion that her professional skills outweighed her personality deficits. In fact, a lot didn't. Nearly everyone sympathized with him when he told them his first deployment with Aggressor Inc. was going to be six months at Concordia Station, Antarctica, with Julie Brown.

As he'd walked out to the parking lot at Luke AFB the day before he flew out, one of Aggressor's pilots, a lieutenant he'd got to know called Keysha 'Heat'n'Eat' Cole, had walked out with him. It had been a typical Arizona winter day: blue sky, low 50s, cold air running off the slopes of the White Tank Mountains into Glendale. He'd been half-hoping for a warm goodbye from Cole, thought maybe they'd made a connection.

"So good luck at the South Pole," she'd said, lounging in the open door of the Aggressor Inc. admin building. "If you're deploying with Brown, you'll need it."

He'd grimaced. "People keep saying that."

"Yeah. No offense, but you're going to need thicker skin, Ears. She *loves* pushing people's buttons, and you have so many." Cole had looked out over the parking lot. "Hey, you drive that new Mustang Mach-E3, right?"

He'd frowned. "Yeah, why?"

She'd grinned at him. "You want to leave your spare key with me, maybe? In case you don't make it back from Concordia Station?"

The conversation came back to him now as an alarm started sounding in their trailer—one Elvis hadn't heard since his first-day induction. Brown, who had been at Concordia longer than him, wasn't reacting though. "Uh, isn't that the emergency evacuation alarm?" he asked. He was beginning to rue the day he'd said yes to this contract. He'd asked why they couldn't be based at McMurdo, or even Christchurch, since technically you could pilot their submersible from anywhere that had a satellite link. "Pentagon wants all Project Minerva activities run out of Concordia," he was told. "And what the customer wants …"

Trigger cocked an ear, listening. "Red evacuation," she said, reaching forward to flip a switch and turn the alarm off. She didn't look worried. "There's three levels: amber, red and black."

"And red doesn't worry us?" Bell asked, pulling the plug on his headphones and standing. "Aren't we supposed to move to an emergency muster station or something? Or is it an exercise?"

"No, they usually announce exercises, so it's probably real enough."

"But we aren't moving," Bell pointed out.

"No. Red is for nonessential personnel," Trigger told him. She spun her chair to face him. "Which you and I aren't. It's probably just a storm. They move nonessentials underground and clear the habitats if there's a bad one on the way."

"But not us." Elvis sat again.

Trigger smiled. "That's right."

"But a *black* alert …"

"Lieutenant, if you hear a black-alert alarm, don't bother looking for me. By the time your dopey ass reacts, I'll already be halfway to New Zealand."

***

The elevator from the newest of Concordia's three habitats went a half mile down into the Dome C ice cap—the thickest and coldest dome of ice on the continent, and one of its highest points.

Because of the danger of the ice moving over time—and even movement measured in inches could be dangerous—everything under the ice, from the elevator itself to the containment module they were descending toward, was built so that it would move *with* the ice if necessary, using the same engineering principles that were used to earthquake-proof high-rise skyscrapers.

"Stop jabbering!" Lau said, to the gaggle of engineers and scientists who had met him and Cohen out on the runway, and who were all trying to talk at the same time. He focused on the woman in front of him, his deputy director science, Doctor Henrietta Jansen. "Henry," he said, using her nickname in an attempt to project calm. "I know what the situation is. I want you to tell me what we're doing about it."

Henrietta Jansen wasn't a career bureaucrat. She was a particle physicist who also held an electronics engineering degree.

Her laser-straight fringe framed large glasses that were designed to ensure she missed not a single detail in the environment around her, and her clipped way of talking showed she didn't like wasting time, or breath, on anything irrelevant.

"We passed the subzero safety threshold six minutes ago," she said. "We're looking at containment failure in ..."

"Twenty-four minutes. Not what I asked," Lau said. "We worked that out for ourselves on the plane. The containment system is designed to use environmental cooling and has been operating nominally for months. What has gone wrong?"

"Two of six ice meltwater circulation pumps have ... failed," Jansen said. Their elevator bumped to a stop, and the doors opened to a brightly lit tube made of flexible tubing, which connected the elevator to workspaces left and right and to the aircraft-hangar-sized containment module itself ahead of them. Lau was quietly pleased to see people walking quickly back and forth with a sense of urgency but not running in panic. They began moving toward the station's control center.

"Backup pumps?" Cohen asked. "The system has multiple redundancies to protect against pump failure."

The deputy security chief, Cath Delaney, was walking behind Cohen and spoke quickly. "Out of commission. Logs say someone removed the impellers 'for maintenance,' but there was no maintenance scheduled and no record of where the parts were removed to."

Cohen frowned. "What are you doing here? Where is Chief Raleigh?"

"The chief was out on the ice when the alert sounded, checking on an instrument station," Delaney said. "We can't raise him." Cath Delaney was a former Kentucky National Guard sergeant from its 617th Military Police Company and knew never to share too much information about your boss with their

47

boss. What Raleigh had actually said before leaving was, "I'm headed out, and if Lau or Cohen or any of the other panic merchants try to reach me, I won't be picking up. You deal with it."

Cohen looked unimpressed. "And who was this *someone* who disabled our backup pumps?" Cohen growled.

"ID in the log was for a staffer who shipped off the ice last year," the security deputy said.

"Sabotage," Cohen said, speaking over his shoulder. "When this is over, pull the access logs and CCTV on every level. I want every single staff member and their movements accounted for."

The control room looked like the control room at any power plant: a sterile room with instrument stations and technicians peering intently at blinking lights and monitors. In the middle of the room was a man in his early 30s with a tablet PC in hand, his long greasy hair swept back from his forehead and tied in a very unattractive rattail at the back of his neck. He had a lump under his bottom lip, which Lau knew was a nicotine plug, and he pulled it out and flicked it into a trash can as they approached. *Disgusting habit*, Lau observed. *But a brilliant vacuum engineer.* "Doctor Bellings," Lau said, stepping up onto the central platform with Cohen as the rest of his entourage moved to check in with staff at different stations. "Tell me you can stop this runaway train."

The problem they were facing was both simple and complex. The scientists of Project Minerva had created the world's first antimatter "forge"—a small reactor that produced industrial quantities of antimatter. But for now, the prototype forge required continuous below-freezing temperatures to operate, and the US administration was loath to house it inside the continental USA—for example, in Alaska—in case the unproven technology resulted in an accident.

The agreed solution was to locate the forge under the ice at a US base in Antarctica. Lau and his team had been granted the use of the former French-Italian Concordia Station, closed down by the cash-strapped EU nations in 2032 and since purchased and expanded by the US government. The location would also provide operational security, as access could be strictly controlled.

There was a second challenge. Once collected, the fuel was bottled inside a magnetized vacuum chamber, which held the raw material and also had to be maintained under 0°C, or 32°F. From there, it could be transferred to a smaller "Bellings Trap" for onward transport. A Bellings Trap could be anything from the size of a coffee thermos to an air conditioner. The bigger the device, the larger the batteries that powered its cooling system, and the longer it could be disconnected from power.

The ability to transport antimatter using a magnetic "trap" was nothing new: it had first been demonstrated in the mid-2020s by scientists at CERN in Switzerland. The breakthrough had been the application by Bellings and his team from Argonne National Laboratory of near-room-temperature superconducting materials to miniaturize the traps and make them less power hungry.

Sitting atop the miles-deep ice cap of Antarctica, Concordia was one of the coldest places on earth, allowing not just the stable operation of the forge beneath the ice cap but also below-zero storage for Project Minerva's antimatter reserves. But both the forge and the storage systems generated heat, which had to be dissipated, so a constant flow of Antarctic ice meltwater circulated around the containment module.

Unless it didn't. In which case, the forge and traps would overheat and become unstable.

Like the legendary Manhattan Project, no one working on Project Minerva beyond Lau, Cohen, Jansen and Bellings, plus the director of the CIA and the US president, knew exactly what Project Minerva was. A cover story, national security classified, had been created when the different teams were brought together at Concordia. Known as the Energy Independence Initiative, its focus was on "the potential for novel sources of energy generation." The part of that initiative based in Antarctica, titled Project Minerva, was supposedly researching kinetic energy generation utilizing the movement of the inland ice across the underlying bedrock.

It was nonsense intended to obscure the next layer of truth: that Project Minerva was an effort to create the world's first antimatter energy reactor. Lau had established subproject sites distributed across the country, from Argonne and Fermilab in Illinois to Los Alamos, from California's SLAC National Accelerator Laboratory to the Oak Ridge National Laboratory (ORNL) in Tennessee. Each subproject was compartmentalized, separate teams of researchers and engineers working in isolation, until Lau had gathered all the core scientists, engineers and support staff at Concordia Station.

One of his teams, modeling the impact if a Bellings Trap containing antimatter catastrophically failed—had approached Lau for clarification. "Calculating the energy release is easy," he said. "You already know it, I'm guessing. Zero point one grams creates a 5-kiloton explosion, about a third of a Hiroshima. Two *kilos*? You're talking nearly twice the bang of the biggest hydrogen bomb ever detonated—call it 80-plus megatons. So what are you looking for?"

50

"I know the math," Lau told him. "But we might be transporting this fuel across the sea and sky, through rural and urban areas, to reactors across the country. It's a safety question, and we're going to have to have solid answers. Exactly what will happen if a Bellings Trap fails and our fuel goes boom? What is the optimal quantity for transportation purposes, in case of an accident? What is the best method of transportation? What would happen if there was an accident in different scenarios? I need you and your people to model every damn thing."

That conversation came to Lau's mind as he stood in Concordia's operations room. He was about to get an answer to his safety question, if the antimatter forge underneath them went critical in—he looked at his watch—*19 minutes*. At last count, there was more than 2.5 kilos of antimatter stored under Concordia. If it annihilated …

Bellings tapped his tablet, then turned it so Lau could see. "We flooded the containment shell with liquid nitrogen to buy us time as soon as we saw the risk the reactor would go critical. We're implementing a software kludge to boost revolutions on the four working pumps. That should theoretically start moving enough meltwater to return the forge to subzero stability." He took a deep breath, his forced casual demeanor fading. "And we're cannibalizing some air-conditioning heat pumps for impellers to replace the ones missing from the backup pumps, but that work will take at least another 40 minutes."

Lau took the tablet and studied the chart there. "The pumps aren't designed to be pushed to these RPM levels," he pointed out. "They'll likely burn out."

"We just need them to keep working until we get the backup pumps back online," Bellings said.

Lau looked at his watch and did some calculations. "Say 15 minutes to containment failure. Forty minutes until the backup pumps are online. The existing pumps have to sustain over-speed revolutions for 25 minutes."

"Don't do your administrator thing and tell me we need the crews working on the backup pumps to work faster," Bellings told him. "They know that. It's their lives on the line too."

"I'll get onto McMurdo," their military liaison, Colonel Sandilands, said. "Have them ready an emergency response, in case." He walked briskly to their comms station.

Cohen was tapping a ringed finger on a railing and stopped, turning to Jansen. "Why haven't you already evacuated all nonessential staff? You've had six hours since the pumps failed, three since you declared a critical event."

Concordia's security was managed by a private security contractor, with nearly sixty personnel working in three shifts to support the base's three hundred staff. Their role was mainly internal security—policing disputes, minor crimes, and drug and alcohol abuse. They were also responsible for evacuating staff in an emergency, but the decision to evacuate lay with Project Minerva leadership.

"I issued an amber alert as soon as we confirmed the backup pumps were down and sent ground vehicles out with about 50 personnel," Jansen said. "They're already 20 miles out. But we have 300 personnel on base now. There aren't enough lifeboats on this Titanic, Mr. Cohen. We can get another 150 on the airplane you just came in on, but that still leaves a hundred souls at risk. Do you want to be the one deciding who lives and who dies?" She looked into his eyes and saw that he very much didn't. "I've made a list. You just need to sign it, and we'll get as many as we can on that plane."

Lau winced. If the forge and their antimatter fuel store exploded … well, it didn't bear thinking of. Especially when he was standing *right on top of it.*

***

Rory was also thinking about what was going on under his feet and reviewing his options in case Outlaw had to get off the ground in a hurry. Two-Tone Hamilton had also grumbled about the modifications Rory O'Donoghue had requested to the AC-130X, but he had to agree they were necessary, to harden it against the ultra-cold weather of Antarctica and allow it to stow weapons like autocannons and lasers out of sight.

Of course, if she actually mounted those weapons, Outlaw would be in breach of the multiple treaties covering activities on Antarctica. But O'Donoghue had never been the kind of guy who turned up at a party empty handed.

O'Donoghue had a flexible relationship to things like rules of engagement, international law and multinational treaties. It was the reason he had found a home flying for a private military contractor. It was also the reason Uncle had mustered out as one of the oldest-serving lieutenants still on active duty … with he and Rory busted in rank for a mission gone wrong in Syria. Wrong in the eyes of USAF, not in the eyes of the men who he'd rescued by ignoring orders. Rory had taken a hit from major to captain, Uncle from captain to lieutenant.

With the date for renegotiation of the umbrella Antarctic Treaty approaching in 2048, every nation with a base on the continent was pushing the limits of what had traditionally been allowed, and several—including Russia, China, Belarus, North Korea and Ecuador—had "paused" international inspections. The USA had also blocked international inspections of

Concordia Station with the excuse that it was "under reconstruction."

The reason Rory was doing a mental inventory of his contingency options was that what he was seeing outside his cockpit—as base personnel bustled around tracked vehicles and ground crew hurried to refuel his aircraft—said the situation at Concordia was anything but business as usual.

Uncle reappeared in Outlaw's cockpit, checking the instrument panel by habit as he settled into his seat. "Engine preheater, battery heater and wing de-icing engaged," he noted. "You planning a quick getaway?"

"Chief Bellows just asked how many passengers we can squeeze in back if we have to help evacuate personnel," Rory said, and filled him in on their conversation.

"A *nuke*?!" Uncle asked.

"Worse than a nuke, is what he said," Rory told him.

"What's *worse* than a nuke?"

"Let's hope we don't find out, Uncle."

***

"We have to find out, Artur."

At the exact moment the two Aggressor pilots were preparing for a hurried departure, the Russian officer in charge of security for its own antimatter research program, Major General Tomas Arsharvin of the Main Intelligence Directorate of the Russian Armed Forces, the GRU, was meeting with his counterpart in the Sluzhba Vneshney Razvedki (or SVR, the Foreign Intelligence Service). The Russian research program was innocuously named Operation Chay, or "Tea"—a word that was similar in both Chinese and Russian—a name it had been given before the Chinese regime had capitulated to the West and the majority of its nuclear physicists had defected.

They were meeting at a former army base on the Argut River at the foot of the Ahai Mountains, 900 kilometers from the nearest Russian city, Barnaul, and 500 kilometers from any sizeable Chinese town. Its isolation on the border of two of Russia and China's least populous regions gave it anonymity and security. But it lay at the junction of highways that came east from Kazakhstan, south from Russia and north from China, so vital equipment, labor and supplies could be transported by road rather than a stream of air traffic that would attract unwanted attention.

The base was set on a small plateau. To the north, across a river tributary, were rolling hills covered in brown grass. To the south, a small lake and the Argut River itself. Beyond it, grassy plains as far as the eye could see. The Chay Complex, as it was known, had been Arsharvin's home for more than a year. If there was a more desolate part of either Russia or China, Arsharvin had trouble imagining it, and he had been stationed at some absolute shitholes. Luckily, he spent most of his time underground, in the complex of bunkers and tunnels that Russian engineers had constructed under the old army base.

Tea was something they had in abundance at the complex, and Arsharvin poured a large mug for Artur Eizen, Deputy Director (Science) at the SVR. It was not his first visit to the Chay Complex, and Arsharvin and the bespectacled former academic had formed a solid, if not companionable, working relationship based on the mutual understanding that neither of them wanted the shared task they had been given by the Russian premier.

"The operation to derail the Americans' 'Project Minerva' has been approved by my director as well," Eizen said to Arsharvin once he'd sipped his tea. He'd become quite a fan of the smoky, sweet Krasnodar tea, which Arsharvin brewed. "The proposal to assassinate researchers in the USA was refused, but the Antarctica plan was 'lighted green.'"

Arsharvin smiled at the man's misuse of English slang. "Green-lighted," he corrected him. He couldn't help himself, though he knew it annoyed Eizen.

"Thank you, my tutor," Eizen said sarcastically. "I am not a fan of this plan. It has too many moving pieces."

"The Americans are at least six months, maybe a year, ahead of us. They have a working antimatter reactor, their stockpile is 10 times the size of ours, their containment devices one-hundredth the size of ours ..."

"We don't need miniaturized containment systems if we are putting our weapon on a Sarmat super-heavy intercontinental ballistic missile," Eizen interrupted him.

"No, but we don't have the quantity of antimatter needed to make such a weapon, just as we don't have a containment system that would survive the violence of launch, let alone orbital reentry," Arsharvin reminded him. "So we need a plan for disrupting the Americans, with redundancy built in. We cannot afford for it to fail, so yes, there are multiple moving parts that will escalate from small and deniable to dramatic and impossible for us to hide."

"Well, I have delivered on my commitment," Eizen said. "It is now up to you to deliver on yours."

Arsharvin grimaced. "Ah, but have you?" In addition to throwing cyber and signals intelligence resources at the problem, Eizen had committed more than a year earlier to recruit a human source inside the American program. Yes, he had delivered on that promise, but Arsharvin had not been impressed by the quality of the intelligence Eizen's source was delivering ... yet.

"You have been given details of personnel and leadership, budget and resource estimates. You even have the results of an internal security review …" Eizen insisted.

"A review that reveals the American station is virtually unguarded. Do you believe that? Your source seems either overly optimistic or poorly informed."

Eizen sighed, letting his frustration show. "Their program is like our own. Highly compartmentalized. The left hand cannot see the right. No one sees the whole."

"Someone does. But you have apparently not recruited *them*," Arsharvin said. "Or you are hiding their best intelligence from me to protect their identity?" He searched Eizen's face. "No? I need to know one thing above all, Artur. Why are they stockpiling antimatter?"

"Our source says they are stockpiling fuel for more reactors. Larger," Eizen said. As he spoke, the automatic storm shutters outside Arsharvin's office began grinding loudly shut. It made no difference to the light in the office—winter light at Chay Complex never got more than a dull gray at best. A metaphor for the light Eizen's vaunted "source" was able to shine on the American research program? Perhaps.

Arsharvin shook his head. "Your source is either uninformed or misleading you, Arturka. This Energy Independence Program, Project Minerva, is a thin veil covering American weapons research in Antarctica. Your source may not have seen through it, but we cannot allow that veil to cover *our* eyes, can we?"

Eizen poured himself some more tea, then motioned to Arsharvin with a gesture that couldn't be mistaken. Arsharvin sighed and reached down to a drawer beside his knee, pulling out a small flask of brandy, which he handed across to Eizen, who dosed his tea liberally before handing it back. "We all want to know what the Americans are doing under the ice, Tomochka. But you said your most urgent needs were a personnel list and a security assessment, and I have delivered those."

Arsharvin grunted. "The GRU contingency plan has also been 'green-lighted.'" He looked at his watch. "Enjoy your tea. I need to go to our operations room. One of our moving parts is now on the move."

***

The blip on Rory O'Donoghue's radar warning receiver had been a Chinese Harbin Z-20 high-altitude helicopter, and Chinese Antarctic Research Center specialist Liu Zhen ruefully watched it disappear back over the horizon toward China's Kunlun Station.

There was little about the coming operation that he was entirely comfortable with, and the departure of their only way off the ice cap just reinforced that. The operation itself was simple enough on paper: set up a temporary weather monitoring station atop Dome C to give them wind, temperature and barometric readings at one of the most desolate, coldest points on planet Earth.

But the reality was that the weather data they got on Dome C would be little different from the data they could capture on Dome A, where Kunlun Station was located, which made the operation essentially pointless, scientifically. The crates strewn around them contained a pop-up bubble habitat to get them through the 48 hours they had been given to set up their equipment, ensure it was working … and then camouflage it from the eyes of prying satellites or drones. Because it wasn't just weather monitoring equipment. It was also signals interception equipment, which would allow China better chances to eavesdrop on the Americans at Concordia Station.

Just because China's Shanghai Pact alliance had lost one war to the Americans, and there were still US Coalition "Transition Government" troops on Chinese soil, did not mean China or Russia intended to lose the next war too. Not everything the defeated nations did was done with the approval of their conquerors.

Which was another element of the day's operation that Liu had reservations about. Some of the equipment they were setting up was Russian-made—a man-portable version of the *Khibiny* electronic eavesdropping and countermeasures system used by Russian fighter aircraft. And it required Russian technicians to assist with setting it up and optimizing it to intercept and, if necessary, interrupt radio signals coming from the American Concordia base.

Russia and China might have been close allies under the Shanghai Pact, but those days were over; it was every nation for themselves in the post Pact world. And Russia had made its contempt for the speed with which China had eventually capitulated more than apparent. It had made Liu wonder why the Russians at Vostok base, north of Kunlun, had agreed to help set up the Chinese listening station. He supposed they had been promised a share of any intelligence generated to entice them to send a detachment of technicians to meet with Liu and his team out on the ice.

Liu Zhen wasn't military. He wasn't even a spy. He was a simple electronics engineer, a polar specialist with the CARC who had more than three years' experience on the ice, both Arctic and Antarctic. So this operation ... this "mission" ... took him way outside his comfort zone—not least because, according to the weather report he'd seen before they left Kunlun, there was a storm front expected to hit Dome C in the next 48 hours, which could mean a protracted stay, since helos were unable to fly in the strong winds and blinding snows of an Antarctic storm. But he couldn't show his misgivings in front of his crew.

"Set up the camo!" he called out to his patrol second-in-command, Hao. CARC wasn't a military organization, but in many ways, it operated like one. The same disciplines were needed to survive out on the ice. "We need to be invisible inside 15, people." He checked his watch. They needed to get themselves and their equipment under cover before the next known American surveillance satellite passed overhead, which would be in … 20 minutes. The Russians were due to fly in 30 minutes after that.

"You heard the man," Hao bellowed. "Dig it in."

Each of his men swung the backpack from his back, and six of them pulled out camouflage tarpaulins and poles while the other five started hacking with picks and shovels to pile up snow and ice. They were already nearly invisible in their off-white Mylar and Kevlar survival suits, but he was taking no chances. Their suits were a streamlined version of the extra vehicular activity, or EVA, suits worn by China's space taikonauts, though taikonaut suits were designed to withstand the absolute zero of space while the commandos' polar survival suits had an adaptive heating system instead of the heavy, consistent heating systems used in space, enhanced ventilation and moisture-wicking liners, plus thermoregulatory vents to prevent moisture buildup. One thing they shared, though, was a rebreather system. Dome C's location at 10,000 feet altitude meant personnel could experience chronic hypobaric hypoxia—lack of oxygen in the brain—if they didn't use supplemental oxygen.

After 12 minutes, Hao reported back. "Equipment squared away. Detachment in cover."

Zhen nodded in approval and started moving into cover himself. "Once the satellite is past, we can get the survival dome up and dig it in, then start setting up the transceiver and relay station," Zhen said.

They waited five minutes longer than strictly necessary, Zhen enjoying the moment of respite, both from his duties and from Dome C's contrary weather. He checked the thermometer in his watch. Right now it was perfectly still, a mild -20°C, or -4°F. The flat white plain of snow around them merged almost seamlessly into the light gray sky, horizon unbroken except for a small row of snowy humps that … were *moving*?

He grabbed for the ice pick at his belt, as 50 feet ahead of him, 12 ghosts rose from the snow in a cloud of white powder. They were carrying weapons, and they were pointed straight at Zhen and Hao.

"What the *hell*?" Hao exclaimed, reaching for the carbine lying on a packing case that he took everywhere in case he saw something worth shooting.

One of the ghosts lifted a hand in greeting and called out to him in jovial Russian, "Privet, Kitay!" *Hello, China.*

***

An illegal military research program of some sort—that's what Zhen and the Russian agreed the Americans were working on at Concordia Station. They were sitting under a camo tarpaulin as their men set up the listening station. The Russians had been landed by their own helo, a half hour *before* Zhen, carrying only their tools in duffel bags and survival suits. They weren't planning an overnight stay.

They'd thought it hilariously funny to "ambush" their Chinese compatriots. Liu and his men, not so much.

"Maybe biological research?" the Russian said. Both were speaking English, which grated on Zhen's pride, but the Russian had offered to speak French, and Zhen was even less proficient in French than he was in English. Russian? Forget that. "Viruses can't survive in the cold, right? So if the virus escapes, there's no risk. Why else would you put your research in the middle of freaking subzero nowhere?"

"It could be a nuclear test program," Zhen offered, though he didn't believe it himself.

"Test some kind of new nuclear weapon under the Antarctic?" Kutuzov asked. "Even the Yankees wouldn't be so crazy. Not like the world wouldn't find out as soon as it went 'boom.'"

"No, but I'm thinking a nuclear-powered weapon," Zhen said. "Like your nuclear-powered cruise missile. What is it called?"

"Skyfall?" Kutuzov laughed. "A fantasy of Putin's imagination. It blew up on the launchpad, like most of his ambitions."

Zhen smiled. It was hard not to like the brusque Russian, who apparently wasn't afraid to speak his politically incorrect mind. Successfully ambushing his Chinese collaborators had been a potentially humiliating moment for Zhen, which the Russians had turned into a party, by standing together in the snow and singing a full-throated and completely mangled version of the Chinese national anthem, "March of the Volunteers," at the surprised Chinese personnel. He'd relaxed and laughed, a signal to his men to enjoy the moment too.

On the spot, Zhen had decided he could be honest around this man.

"Our security officer is former People's Liberation Army. He says the Americans have been excavating under Concordia. They say they are researching thermal energy potential. He thinks they are building a missile silo, to improve their ability to intercept hypersonic weapons in space."

"Hmm. Yes, we know about this excavation too," Kutuzov said. "Our GRU says the American base goes several levels under the ice. What else do you know about their installation?"

"Not much more than you, I suppose. We have some dated information on the layout of the three above-ground buildings," Kutuzov said, "because with all credit to our glorious intelligence services, the French and Italian Antarctic researchers posted it all online before the Americans bought the base from them, in 4K resolution." He shrugged. "Since they bought it two years ago, we only have what we can observe from a distance, and we shared that with you. Building three appears to be a satellite and radio installation. It draws the most power and emits the most signals. That is our target."

"*Da.* It was the one the Americans added after they took over the station. Outside, it looks just like the other two, but we have no intelligence on how it is inside either. Or what is under it. But the Americans, unless they work for Marvel Comics, have no imagination. If they dug a silo under Concordia Station, they put it under building three," Kutuzov decided. "What do you know about security at the American station?"

Liu thought about it. He didn't know anything specific, but he wanted to be helpful. "Well, it's big. Second only to their McMurdo base. We estimate maybe 200 personnel, so there are bound to be internal security of some kind, if just to settle disputes. If you're worried about them being able to find us here, we've got images of drones patrolling their perimeter, but never this far out."

Hao approached. "Equipment set up and tested. Everything seems to be working." He addressed Kutuzov directly and jerked his thumb at the Russian special operators, who had mostly just been lounging around until now. "Time for your people to go to work."

Kutuzov stood, sighing. "Yes, I suppose it is." He waved to his men, who reached for the duffel bags containing their tools. Liu smiled. The man sounded almost comically sad. Then Liu heard a shout and spun around. The Russians all had machine pistols in their hands, and a volley of suppressed automatic fire cut down Liu's men. Hao cried out too, staggering backward with his hands to his bloodied chest, falling just behind Liu. Liu turned back to Kutuzov to see a pistol in his hand, the gun still smoking in the cold air. He aimed it at Liu.

"I am sorry, *tongzhi*," Kutuzov said, mispronouncing the Chinese word for comrade. "You lost your war. Ours has just begun."

They were the last words an incredulous Liu heard. His head was punched backward as he took Kutuzov's bullet in the face, and he crumpled to the ground.

***

GRU Captain Anatoliy Kutuzov, 22nd Separate Guards Special Purpose Brigade, 411th Spetsnaz Detachment, looked down sadly at the body of the Chinese team leader.

Two years earlier, and they might have been brothers in arms. But China's war, as Kutuzov had been taught to think of it, had foundered on the rocks of Western unity. It had put too much faith in "superweapons"—autonomous robots, biological warfare, expensive and ultimately useless aircraft carriers—and too little into the branch of the armed forces that won or lost every single war in history: its ground troops. China's navy had been sunk, its air force shot from the sky and its inexperienced "million-man army" crushed like terracotta soldiers under the tracks of American tanks and the weight of American orbital bombardment.

Russia had screwed up too. Kutuzov and his fellow officers recognized that. It had gone in half-assed against Japan and been kicked off Japanese Kunashiri Island as soon as it landed. It sent the best part of its Pacific Fleet against the Americans on Hawaii, and only a few ships returned, some of them never to sail again. It had tested NATO resolve in the Baltics with a cross-border armored thrust into Latvia that had ultimately cost it its naval base at Kaliningrad when a united European NATO had unleashed itself against the invaders.

But Kutuzov knew his military history. And he knew that every Russian victory was preceded by humiliating defeat. Napoleon's armies had invaded in 1812 and reached the center of Moscow before being thrown back. In World War I, Russia had lost 120,000 soldiers in the Battle of Tannenberg, signaling the start of a collapse that ultimately ended in the leap forward that was the Russian revolution. Hitler's armies fought Stalin's armies all the way to Moscow before Russia turned the tide and rode victorious into Berlin. In Ukraine, a three-day war had turned into a five-year war, but one that ultimately restored Russian rule to the Russian-speaking populations of southern Ukraine and regime change in Kyiv.

The Russian national psyche was to blame. Resilient, skeptical, distrustful, the Russian people were also proud, emotional and optimistic. Resigned to humiliating defeat, confident in ultimate victory, they attacked before they were ready, defended with bloody-minded desperation, and then counterattacked with overwhelming force and conviction.

Russia had given up its Pacific ambitions, for now; Kutuzov could sense that. But he had spoken what he thought was the truth to the Chinese team leader. Russia was not done with the Americans, who thought Russia was beaten and broken. Kutuzov knew they had only succeeded in lighting the touch paper of Russia's superpower ego.

He called over to his second-in-command. "Lieutenant Spivak, gather the bodies, and take them at least 1 kilometer south. Bury them under the ice, not just snow. We want the Chinese to think they were lost in the coming storm."

Spivak was a dour man with a face as leathery as an old potato. "Yes sir. I double-checked the Chinese equipment. It's all there. We'll have it set up inside an hour."

He nodded. Had he and his men just fired the first shots in Russia's victorious counterattack against the West? For the sake of the Chinese personnel who had just given their lives in that cause, he hoped so.

He checked the data screen sewn into the sleeve of his survival suit. Nearly midnight now, good light. Storm front coming in at their backs, hitting in six to eight hours. Their weapons could function in conditions down to -20°C for up to six hours, but not longer. It would take his detachment five hours to cover the 20 miles to Concordia in current conditions, but he couldn't assume the calm weather would continue for the entire traverse. "Have Corporal Voeykov set the *Khibiny* unit to begin operation at 0400," he told Spivak. "We move out in 30 mikes."

***

"Starting countdown to annihilation," Ops DDG Solomon Cohen said, looking at a readout on the console in front of him. "Ten minutes and … counting."

"Just got the last backup pump online," Henrietta Jansen said, her voice preternaturally calm. She had the demeanor of a school principal who had just been informed a bus full of students had crashed and responded straightaway with "How many injured, how many dead?" "The curve is flattening …"

"Backup pumps have exceeded their rated full-load current but are within margin," Bellings said, eyes glued to digital dials on a screen in front of him. "Fluctuations on number three; the rest are holding. You should see temps stabilizing anytime now."

"Nine minutes," Cohen announced.

David Lau was impressed. His deputy directors had each taken charge of one aspect of the emergency response without debate, without needing to consult or argue with one another, and the operators in the control room knew exactly who to look to for direction. They'd rehearsed this eventuality, of course. Trained their teams to handle it. But the project had moved so quickly, there was always the risk they'd down-prioritized critical incident training time too dramatically. All it would take now was for one thing to go wrong, one step to be overlooked …

Deputy Security Chief Cath Delaney stepped up beside him. "The Aggressor AC-130 is airborne—150 souls aboard." Lau couldn't help but notice the disquiet in the voice of the stolid former chief petty officer and US Navy master-at-arms. It was good to see this was not just another day on the ice for her.

"Good, very good," Lau said. He turned to their military liaison. "The Australian C-17 diverted from McMurdo, Colonel?"

"Holding 50 miles out," Sandilands said. "In case we …"

"Need to evacuate survivors, I know," Lau said. But he knew full well, as they all did, that if the forge went critical, there would be no survivors.

"Eight minutes, 30 …" Cohen said, voice strained.

"Temperature stabilizing!" Jansen said, almost yelling. "No. Dropping! It's dropping again!"

A telephone rang, causing Lau to jump, and Bellings grabbed it, gripping the handset hard. "It's a start. Keep me updated," he said and slammed the handset back into its cradle. "Two of six primary meltwater circulation pumps online again. The rest will all be online inside 20 minutes."

"Can we …? Is that …?" The variables were too many for David Lau to process.

Henrietta Jansen came to his aid. "If the backup pumps hold, we only need two primary pumps online. Three, and it won't matter if the backup pumps fail; we'll be back in control."

Lau felt his legs go, and he slumped into a chair behind him. "Oh, thank our heavenly ancestors."

Solomon Cohen checked the counter. "Stopping countdown at zero zero seven minutes," he said with a wry expression. "Would you believe that? Like something out of a Bond movie."

Another 10 tense minutes passed, with Jansen updating them on core temperatures as more primary meltwater pumps came online. Three backup pumps burned out in that time too … but after 15 minutes, Bellings declared the crisis over. "Saved the world, with seven minutes to spare, people!" he said, pushing his long hair back from his face. His expression was one of unadulterated relief.

A ragged cheer broke out across the control room as a dozen personnel got to their feet and then started thumping each other on their backs. Lau grinned, looking across the room, then noticed the man next to him wasn't joining in. He was typing on the keyboard in front of him and ran his finger across a line of data on his screen. Lau recognized the man … Meteorologist, wasn't he? What was his name? Grant, right? Donovan Grant?

"Grant, isn't it? Not enough excitement for you, Grant?" Lau asked him.

"What? Oh, right." He looked around as though realizing for the first time what was going on. "Great, I guess. It's just …"

Lau could see worry in the man's face, where there should have been blessed relief. "What is it?"

Donovan pointed at his screen. "Storm front is intensifying. We're looking at wind speeds from 50 knots gusting to 70. Maybe 30 inches of snow."

"We're two stories underground, Donovan. We just survived an antimatter apocalypse. We'll probably survive a snowstorm," Lau said dismissively.

"Sure, Mr. Director," the meteorologist said. "But I heard someone say an aircraft took off with nearly 200 people aboard? You're going to want to get that aircraft on the ground again fast, or send it to McMurdo. Front won't hit McMurdo for another … I want to say, 48 hours."

"What about here?"

"Wind is gusting to 20 knots already. Going to hit 30 in the next half hour and ramp up during the next 12 to 20 hours. We're looking at whiteout conditions in six to 10 hours."

Lau called the deputy security chief, Delaney, over. "You can wave off that C-17. But I need that AC-130 back on the ground here, stat. It's two days until our field test. We can't afford to have our dedicated transport aircraft stranded at McMurdo."

Delaney conferred with the meteorologist, Donovan. "An AC-130 is good for 30-knot crosswinds. Anything more than that, they'll have to find somewhere else to land," she told him.

"Then get it down now!" Lau said. Delaney ran to the comms desk. Air Traffic Control for all aircraft over Antarctica was run out of McMurdo Station. "And get Chief Raleigh back here!"

Dammit, if it isn't one thing, it's another, Lau thought. Like the gods know we are just two days from proof of concept.

Except a simultaneous failure in two critical cooling systems? That wasn't the work of God; it was the work of Man. Lau's people—Cohen, Jansen and Bellings—were in a huddle, looking pleased. He should probably join them and get them back on task. Lau looked over at Raleigh, to find he was deep in conversation ... not on a line to McMurdo Station, but with a very solidly built Aggressor Inc. employee who looked ... *pissed?* What now?!

Delaney came quickly over. "Something you need to—"

"Is that AC-130 headed back down?" Lau asked him.

"McMurdo wanted them to divert to their runway, just to be safe. I told them as long as they were within safety guidelines, we want them down here. They say it will have to be up to the pilot."

"Dammit, Delaney ..."

Delaney looked impatient. "Leave it with me, sir. I'll talk to the pilot myself. You've got something else to worry about." He looked around the room. "We need Colonel Sandilands on this one too."

"Spit it out, woman," Lau told her. "What's wrong now?"

The Aggressor Inc. employee who Delaney had been talking with had followed her over to Lau and was standing behind her shoulder, listening. "What's wrong, *Mr. Director,*" she said, with exaggerated politeness, "is that your project is under attack."

"What? What the hell are you talking about?" Lau said, letting the stress and irritation show. "And who the hell even are you?"

"This is Julie Brown," Delaney said, stepping away from her as though she were a fire risk. "Aggressor Inc. submersible lead."

"*Lieutenant* Brown, Director. You just evacuated half the base. I don't know why, and don't need to. What I do know: a Russian submarine just tried to sink *Charlene* …"

"Who?"

"Our subsurface patrol picket," Sandilands told him.

"Is the submersible alright?" Lau looked worried at last.

"It was damaged, but not …"

"This is highly irregular," Lau said, shaking his head. He was a scientist, not a strategist. He drew conclusions based on evidence. Yes, there had been a containment emergency. Cause unknown. It had been successfully mitigated. A subsurface drone had also been lost? Coincidence, until proven otherwise. "You have proof a Russian submarine attacked your drone?"

"Yes," the woman said. "Since it was attacked by *Piranya* homing sea mines, and only Russia fields them."

Lau looked for loopholes. "So you got too close to a Russian submarine, and it tried to scare you off. An attack on your drone is not necessarily an attack on …"

The woman stepped right up into his personal space. Lau was Hong Kong Chinese, so his personal space was hard to crowd. But being a good six inches taller than him, she was succeeding. He took a step back.

"Director, this is not my first rodeo. Ivan doesn't start a shooting war unless he has orders to do so. That Russian thinks he killed my boat. He thinks we don't know what the hell happened out there, but we do. So you have a chance, right now, to act like the rocket scientist you are and respond to it." Her expression said she doubted seriously he would.

"The captain has a point, Director," Sandilands said.

71

Delaney intervened. "Director, it may be nothing, or it may be something. Given what just went down, I suggest we assume it's 'something.' I'll put base security on alert, double the watch. Put up an extra perimeter drone as long as the weather holds."

"Alright, yes. What about those robot dogs you people made me buy?"

Delaney paused, then realized Lau had actually made a valid suggestion. "The Legged Squad Sentinel units? They're still crated up, but yes, they're made for all-weather patrols."

"Well, get them patrolling ..." Lau suggested. The Aggressor Inc. woman was still standing there, glaring at him. "Yes, Captain? Was there more?"

"A *lot* more," Julie Brown said. "This is just the tip of a Doomsday Glacier-sized iceberg, Director. You need to get on the line to McMurdo. You need to call in extra security, extra personnel. You need air patrols overhead, you need Space Force with eyes on, you need US Navy looking for ..."

Lau waved her off. He'd had enough of her hysteria. "Yes, thank you, Captain. You can share your concerns with Colonel Sandilands. He is military liaison." Lau stepped around her and called out to his people in the middle of the control room, "Cohen, Bellings, Jansen ... find us a conference room. We need to get this show back on the road."

***

Trigger stood fuming. Sandilands put a hand on her shoulder, and she shrugged it off. She'd had several interactions with him since arriving on station and knew he was a former Army highflier who was pulled out of DARPA to be the Pentagon's eyes and ears inside Project Minerva. That meant nothing to Trigger. She needed to know what *kind* of colonel

Sandilands was: a talker or a doer. "Colonel, I had to drop my payload module to decoy that Russian attack. My boat is coming back gutted, but it's coming back. And no one—here, McMurdo, or Ari-damna-zona—has asked me the right question yet."

He nodded. "You mean, 'Where is that Russian boat headed next?' Right?"

"Correct. We picked it up moving northeast along the ice shelf, so I'd say its last port of call was Russia's Mirny Station, where it could have picked up food, water or ordnance. And the last heading we got was northwest. You know who's out there." It wasn't a question.

"*Polar Warden*," Sandilands said. "Docked at the NOAA platform."

Trigger checked there was no one else standing near them. "Look, I know I'm not the brightest bulb in the room, but I also know this program of yours isn't about thermal energy generation. You've had our aircraft flying delivery runs out to that NOAA platform, and I know it is not just monitoring the wind and the waves. I know you have a field test coming up, and that platform is central to it. I heard *Polar Warden* is taking the personnel off that platform, which tells me it is a part of your test, and it would be pretty damn inconvenient for us, but convenient for Russia, if *Polar Warden* or that platform experienced a spontaneous explosive disaggregation before we could conduct the test."

He frowned. "Look, I agree. We need to find that Russian boat. What is the status of your submersible?"

"It will take several hours for my DSRV to dock, get checked for damage, reconfigured and underway again, so we're out of play. But I'm guessing Navy has other assets in the Southern Ocean for this test of yours."

Sandilands didn't acknowledge her assumption, but he didn't deny it either.

"They need to be brought into play. Navy has sub-hunting P-8 Poseidons five hours away in Christchurch. They know this ocean better than anyone else. They can get ahead of the Russian boat and have the sea blanketed with sonobuoys as it comes out from under the ice."

Sandilands nodded. "I'll get onto it." He looked harried. "Right now, I need to talk to the pilot of that AC-130 about bringing it back before the storm front hits."

"That AC-130 is ours," Trigger pointed out. "I'll do that for you."

"Alright. Look, you heard right. We do have a field test of our transportation system, planned for two days' time. That aircraft is a key cog in the machine, and we can't have it grounded at McMurdo waiting for the storm to break."

***

Rory had taken off with, literally, his ass on fire. Outlaw had been fully refueled, and his loadmaster had drawn the line at 189 bodies in the cargo hold, sitting on the deck with knees around their ears, packed in like the proverbial peas in a pod. So they'd had to engage Outlaw's JATO solid-fuel rocket boosters and had lifted into the air with the end of Concordia's ice runway way too close for comfort.

McMurdo ATC gave him a holding position up at 15,000 feet, well outside the 10-mile safety perimeter the crew chief had mentioned.

"Funny kind of an evacuation if all you do is fly around the evacuation site," Uncle observed. "At least we'll get a nice view of the mushroom cloud."

74

"No nukes allowed on Antarctica; you know that, Uncle." Rory unbuckled his harness and unplugged his helmet. "You take the stick. I'm going aft to check on our passengers. Do my captain thing."

"Copilot has the stick," Uncle said. "And how come I never get to do the schmoozing?"

"The point of schmoozing," Rory pointed out, "is to reassure the passengers that we have everything under control, despite the fact we took off like a bat out of hell. Which you and your talk of mushroom clouds would not do."

"Fair point," Uncle allowed. Then he tilted his head, listening to a voice in his helmet, and reached out to the seat next to him to hand Rory's helmet back to him. "Brown on the radio for you."

Rory sat himself down, strapped in and plugged in. Outlaw was equipped with Scorpion VR helmet display configured just the way he liked it, which was best described as minimal. Rory flew Outlaw by feel and touch, relying on audio cues to alert him to new data, leaving his visual field largely free for tactical and navigational inputs or, as now, a nice profile picture of the person on the sat phone line for him: Trigger Brown.

"Hey, Brown, nice to see you haven't been vaporized yet," Rory said.

"Not yet, but thanks for offering me and Ears a seat on your bus. Oh, wait. You didn't."

"Gripe, gripe. What's up?" Rory asked.

Brown filled him in on both the averted emergency and the "request" they put down at Concordia again. "McMurdo ATC has left it up to you. Their opinion is you should divert."

Rory thought it over. "What's the wind over the field now?"

75

"Fifteen gusting to 20, out of the northwest. A regular bastard of a crosswind. But there's a blizzard a couple hours behind it, so it's now or never."

Brown was Aggressor Inc. first and foremost and Project Minerva second. "So what do you think?" Rory asked her. "How important is it we try to get down?"

"If it were just you, I'd say forget it. And with 200 people aboard? On an ice runway? I'd think twice," Brown said, with uncommon caution. "I heard McMurdo has a Dunkin' Donuts concession now. But I told management here I'd brief you on the situation. They badly want Outlaw down on the ice for some reason they haven't shared yet."

Rory turned to Uncle, who was listening in. "What do you say?"

"You know me," Uncle shrugged. "I'm a pleaser. I say we take her down, and if she isn't stable, we scrub the landing and go for donuts."

"I'm good with that," Rory said, tightening his harness. "Pilot has the stick. Let the crew and passengers know. Thanks, Brown."

"Alright, see you soon," she said. "Or not. Concordia out."

"Pilot has the aircraft," Uncle repeated, lifting his hands from the yoke, reaching for the radio to switch his mic to the internal aircraft intercom.

"And Uncle, sugarcoat it, please," Rory said.

"Aww, you're no fun," Uncle said. He undid his harness and climbed down the ladder to the cargo compartment. The evacuees were standing shoulder-to-shoulder, closer than Siamese twins, two airmen from Concordia pushing between them, handing out bottled water. Uncle grabbed a bullhorn so he could be heard over the engines. "Crew and passengers, this is the copilot speaking. We have received clearance to return to

Concordia. But there's a strong crosswind, and it may be a bumpy landing, so make sure you brace and, if you can, get a good grip on a cargo strap." He couldn't help himself. "You might also like to start a singalong back there. I recommend 'Don't Worry, Be Happy.'"

Rory shot him a disgusted look as Uncle came back up and buckled in. He rolled Outlaw onto one wing and began a sliding turn to put them on the glide slope for Concordia. "Seriously? 'Don't Worry, Be Happy'?"

Uncle shrugged. "It was either that or 'Livin' on a Prayer.'"

"Yeah. Hardy-har. Arm the drogue."

***

Meteorologist Donovan Grant was a polar surface and upper air observations specialist. And as far as he was concerned, one of the only true USAP (US Antarctic Program) researchers still working at Concordia. Sure, there were support technicians, IT staff, a few mechanics and riggers, but polar specialists like him? Guys who had really been out on the ice? Few and far between.

They'd been slowly supplanted—no, overwhelmed—by the geeks and engineers of Project Minerva, who did nothing but bitch about the cold, the crude conditions at Concordia and the lack of creature comforts and family interaction.

They had no freaking idea. Grant had spent more than 900 days on the ice, at McMurdo, Amundsen-Scott and now Concordia. Concordia had been three rundown cylindrical habitats when he'd first overwintered here a year earlier. Now it was three levels of below-ice habitats, labs and engineering spaces. Filled with people he regarded as *tourists*.

Grant resented their presence. He resented their air of secret squirrel superiority. When they'd first started flooding in, filling the small cafeteria with their noise, complaining about having to eat in shifts instead of when it suited them, he'd tried casually asking them about their work. Just making conversation. Every question was stonewalled. Even the most innocent inquiry was met with a look of suspicion. Or outright rudeness—people sitting next to him, elbow to elbow, not even acknowledging he was there as they moaned and gossiped about things he wasn't a part of.

He had been on Concordia for more than a year, but it was only two weeks ago he was finally indoctrinated into Project Minerva and told they were researching antimatter, for energy production. Not how, or why they were doing it in Antarctica. He was told just enough that he could do the job they needed him to do for the upcoming field test, nothing more.

He'd like to see how far their precious project would get without his weather forecasting helping them with everything from ground traverses to air and sea supply runs. No AI could do what Donovan could. Sure, quantum computers could compile the data and model weather patterns, but they were all based on history, on what had happened in the past. Their models were 80 percent "what happened last time" and only 20 percent prediction. Donovan had the spooky ability to see into the future and feel what was coming—like the ants running up a tree before a flood, or birds taking to the air before a quake. Take this storm rolling in from the northwest, for example. The models said it might make Cat 3, "heavy snow." But he'd looked at the data and gone out to stand in the wind and sniff the thin air himself. This one was going to be at least a Cat 4, "severe snow." They'd have to dig themselves out once it blew past, and anything not tied down was going to end up in the Ross Ice Shelf. But hey, why should anyone talk to him? He was just the meteorologist.

78

The arrogance came right from the top, from Project Minerva's fly-in, fly-out "leadership team," who barely even bothered to learn his name, even though his role was one of the most critical at the station, and no one knew conditions at Dome C like Donovan Grant.

He had a nickname for each of them. Professor David Lau, the Minerva Project director, was *Lema*, short for *leave me alone*, which was the attitude he gave Grant anytime the meteorologist tried to speak with him. Nothing Grant could say was so important it should disturb whatever else Lau was doing at the time, including filling a tray with lunch in the mess, apparently. The station security chief, Logan Raleigh, he called *The Decoy*. Whenever there was a problem and it looked like one of the other section heads was in the firing line, they called in Raleigh to take the heat. Any success was theirs to claim, but any problem, delay or failure was a "security issue" or Chief Raleigh's fault because he was being an inflexible hard-ass. Right now, in classic style, he was taking heat for being out on the ice during the incident and leaving his deputy in charge, as though she hadn't handled things just as well as he would have. The DD Ops, Cohen, Donovan called *Coma* because anytime Donovan told him something he didn't want to hear, he pulled that classic "cover my ass" maneuver of telling Donovan to put it in writing. The chief science geek, Dr. Jansen, he called *Harpy*. She was the kind who would shower you with praise one moment and then screech at you if you got a fourth decimal place wrong the next. He mostly avoided human interaction with her, because she seemed really bad at it, like it was a sport she'd never learned the rules of but had to play anyway.

Dr. Jake Bellings, a quantum engineer and former head of applied materials at Argonne, was the least annoying. Donovan called him *Mr. Fixit* because whenever there was a technical issue of any kind, everyone turned to him for the answer. Grant came up with the name because one of Lau's oft-shouted refrains was, *I don't need the details, Jake, just fix it.*

The military officer, Sandilands—Grant called him *Hollywood.* Not just because of his chiseled jaw, trimmed hair or stunt-double looks but because he did his best to try to make out he *wasn't* a serving military officer. "Call me Vic," he told civilian staff who referred to him as colonel. He dressed in civvies, trying to blend in with the scientists, engineers and tradespeople of Concordia, but he wasn't fooling anyone. He was the Pentagon's man in Concordia, and everyone knew it.

Of course, Donovan only used the nicknames in his own head, or with his girlfriend, Saara. He never spoke them aloud. Or at least not in the presence of other staff.

So why did he stick around? Why did he put up with them and their secret squirrel bullshit? That was simple. Donovan Grant had a secret too.

***

Rory O'Donoghue had plenty of bad memories. He'd served three combat tours and accumulated a therapist's filing cabinet full of those. He sincerely hoped the crosswind landing at Concordia Station wasn't about to become another one.

Flying a combat mission, they'd have a crew of as many as nine: two pilots, one combat systems officer, one weapon systems operator, one sensor operator and up to four special mission aviators. But when they were just ferrying human cargo, it was just himself and Uncle up front and two aviators in back: a loadmaster and his assistant.

Uncle looked out his cockpit side window. "Diamond dust. I think that weather is moving in."

Rory turned his head, looking where Uncle was facing. A wave of tiny ice crystals danced in the sunlight, blown by the wind of the approaching storm. Rory got on the radio again. "Concordia, Outlaw. We're … uh, 20 miles out, on approach. Wind over the ice, Brown?"

"Outlaw, winds are two eight zero, 17 gusting to 23 knots now," Brown said. "I'd say your window is closing."

"Roger that," Rory said, looking at Uncle, who gave him a tight nod. "Concordia, we're going to try to put down, but if we have to abort the landing, we won't go around; we'll bug out for McMurdo."

Rory had the course to the radio beacon lined up in his helmet TAC landing display, and after a tight turn, the strobing lights under the ice of the runway of Concordia were flashing off his nose. He was crabbing toward the runway with his nose pointed off-center, into the surging wind.

"Copilot to crew, buckle up for landing," Uncle said over the interplane intercom.

Rory and Uncle had a routine for the hairy landings. They kept it verbal, so there was no doubt about who was doing what, when.

"Fifty percent flaps, 155 knots approach speed," Rory said.

"Getting wonky now. You're losing heading to the beacon," Uncle said, though his tone wasn't worried. "Flaps 50 percent, speed 155."

"Coming back on heading. One thousand, gear down, skis locked."

"Gear down indicators, ski indicators, check."

"Pushing head, pulling tail."

"You are 100 above your altitude. There's your beacon."

"Roger."

"Drive it in."

"Standby flaps."

"Threshold, hack."

"On the noodle."

"Skating."

Rory could feel the big machine being shoved sideways and was yawing as much as he was comfortable with to keep them flying in a straight line down the glideslope.

"Speed's coming down, set 133. Flaps 100."

"Roger. Speed checks, flaps 100."

Outlaw began shuddering, balanced on the high side of a stall, buffeted by the wind.

"Copilot landing checklist."

"Copilot checklist complete. Flying check is complete."

"Wind feels like its coming from our 11 o'clock," Rory said.

"That's nice. Right where we want it."

With a bump, they dropped 100 feet and then lurched up 50.

"Yeehaw," Uncle said, through gritted teeth.

"150 feet, stable."

"You call *that* stable?" Uncle asked.

"Landing."

It was Uncle's last chance to disagree. "Roger, landing."

They were still diving at the ground, nose below their skids, and pointed off-center.

"Fifty, 40, 30 … 10. Bit of a balloon," Rory said as the aircraft rose and dropped, the threshold of the ice runway disappearing under their nose. As they settled, Rory flared nose up, and the skids hit the ice and bit into the powdery snow covering it as Rory yawed his nose savagely to put it on the runway centerline.

"Flaps 50, set trim takeoff."

"Roger. Flaps 50, trim set for takeoff. Power set."

They were slowing, but not as quickly as Rory would like. Uncle had his left hand on the throttles and ski release, ready for Rory to order full power and abort the landing. His right hand was on the release lever for their drogue chute.

The end of the runway was approaching *fast*. They'd already eaten up half its distance.

"Deploy drogue," Rory said.

"Drogue release, roger," Uncle said, hauling back on the lever beside him.

The drogue parachute mounted under Outlaw's big rudder was another of Rory's modifications for operations on the ice. The jet booster helped them take off fast, but they needed to be able to slow down fast too, since airspeed plus thin air plus ice plus gusting winds plus up to 45,000 lbs. of cargo could easily send her skidding off the end of the runway, even in good conditions.

"Drogue-deployed indicator," Uncle said. "Speed 120, 90, 70 …"

A ripple of applause broke over them from the passengers in the cargo hold.

Rory smiled, pulled in a big lungful of air and blew it out again through his nose. If he hadn't liked the conditions, he would have had no compunction about aborting the landing and heading for McMurdo base, but even so … that landing had pushed the envelope.

Uncle clearly felt it too. "Sweet, boss. Personally I would have saved the drogue in case we ended up vertical down that crevasse out there, headed for the center of the earth, but then you always were the cautious type."

Rory ignored him. "Concordia, Outlaw taxiing to the terminal …" "Terminal" was a grand word for the survival blister at the side of the runway that passengers sheltered in while awaiting transport, but Concordia had its own language.

"Nice job, Outlaw," Brown said. "Boss will be happy you didn't bend his airframe or de-life any paying customers. First round is on me."

***

Julie 'Trigger' Brown didn't feel she deserved her call sign, but then, who does? Was it her fault the world was full of asshats, snowflakes, deadbeats and losers? And what was better, lying about reality or confronting it? Should it be her fault people were so easily offended?

Bell was OK, for a city boy. He had backbone. Liked a good argument, stood his ground. She'd tried him out over a couple of beers on stools in the commissary, arguing over the one no one knew the answer to yet: what was Project Minerva, really?

"No way it's a weapons program," he'd said. "That's illegal. US government would never do that."

She'd looked at him like she'd just stepped off a UFO. "They what? This is the same government that tested LSD on soldiers, invented renditioning, invaded a country because of chemical weapons that didn't exist, and launched a preemptive invasion of North Korea."

"I'm just saying we aren't at war anymore. We don't need a treaty-breaking superweapon to win."

"We didn't beat the Russians, did we? Those sunnabitches are still making trouble." She took a swig of her beer. "Can't trust a Russian as far as you can throw one, and I could throw a Russian pretty damn far."

He'd smiled, not meeting her eyes. "What were your ancestors then? Not Russian."

"Pureblood Viking," she said. "Uncle did a family history thing, showed we came from Sweden. Name used to be 'Brun,' which is 'brown' in Viking."

"So marauders, pirates and thieves then," Bell said.

"And proud of it. What's Bell? You from a long line of fairies?"

"What?"

"*Tinker* Bell?" she asked. "Peter Pan's girlfriend?"

"Scottish," he said. "My ancestors kicked your ancestors' asses at the Battle of Clontarf. Look it up."

"Could be your new call sign," she'd said, making out she hadn't heard him. "Tinker. Got a nice ring to it."

"Funny. I saw what you did there," he said without a smile. "Someone called 'Brown' should be careful throwing around nicknames, considering all the gross shit that's brown, including, you know, actual shit," he said.

She'd laughed at that. He was alright. Gave as good as he got.

But she'd meant what she'd said. The Russians weren't beat, and you couldn't trust them.

***

Bunny had said a prayer of thanks for positioning satellites on the way back to Macquarie Island. During the war with China, there had been two fateful weeks where they'd lost just about all satellite and undersea cable comms, and the war had hung in the balance, messages being sent across the Pacific by old-school short-wave or relayed from ship to ship to ship. They'd lost their positioning satellites too, sending them back to inertial and celestial navigation—not much better than dead reckoning.

As she'd begun her nighttime approach, she'd found the entire area shrouded in thick fog. The Nemesis was a big, heavy machine that needed all the available runway. Miscalculate in the fog at Macquarie Island, and they'd be scraping you off Mount Jeffryes.

But the landing, like the escort mission, had been uneventful. After seeing to her aircraft, Bunny didn't head straight for the mess to check in with Grinspoon. The runway was an artificially constructed strip of concrete running east-west across a narrow neck of land on what the station's seasonal inhabitants called "the Green Sponge." And not affectionately. It was 21 miles long, 3 miles wide, cold, muddy, and isolated. But it was Australia's southernmost sovereign territory, and Australia had beefed up its military presence there in response to the growing Chinese footprint on Antarctica.

By 2040, it featured not just the airfield but a deepwater jetty that ran out into Buckles Bay, where Australia's sole icebreaker RSV *Nuyina* was currently docked. The RAAF personnel had their own workshops beside the airfield but shared accommodation and facilities with the rest of the station's inhabitants. A hut next to the geodesic satellite dome held computer workstations and video conferencing facilities, and Bunny used flagstones in the mud to navigate her way from the airfield to the comms center, waving to a couple of the other personnel before settling into a booth.

She was calling her unofficially adopted niece, 'Fi' Feng-yun Tsui, who was just about to graduate from Republic of China Taiwan Advanced Flight Training. Unlike the USAF, where anyone wanting to be a pilot first had to graduate from college or the Air Force Academy before they could complete basic and advanced flight training, Taiwan was a nation still reeling from the loss of hundreds of pilots in its war with China and didn't have the luxury of five to six *years* to put butts in cockpits. She could have joined the USAF, but Fi chose to return to her homeland because if she succeeded, she could be flying fast jets inside two years, and could be assigned to a squadron in three, while completing her degree on the side.

It wasn't going smoothly. She was a bright kid, who US forces had talent-spotted on Taiwan for her cyber skills after she delivered them a fully functioning Chinese autonomous slaughterbot, which she'd hacked and commandeered. She was 19 years old now but with an impatient and rebellious streak that Bunny didn't discourage. 'Fi' Feng-yun was an orphan like Bunny O'Hare had been, a slaughterbot having taken her family from her, and Bunny knew she'd have to be a junkyard dog to make her way in life with the start she'd had.

Fi started the video call in tears. "Uncrewed systems pilot!" she'd sobbed. "They want to put me in a trailer flying Fantom drones. I want to fly! Really fly! I kicked ass in the Boromae, my instructors recommended me for fighters, but the freaking psych assessment …"

"Demand a redo," Bunny told her. "A different psych, different test, something. Complain about whoever tested you. Play whatever card you've got to get it canceled."

"And what will that do?"

"You know what not to do and say this time. *Fake it*, Fi," she said. "You're smart enough to game any psych test. Give them what they want, not what you really think and feel."

"Forget it; they're probably right. I don't have the temperament," she sniffed. "I'll take Fantoms."

"The hell you will," Bunny said. "You don't fight for this, it'll set itself in you. You let them tell you you're a loser, you tell yourself you're a loser, and you'll become a loser."

"Is this your idea of a pep talk?" Fi asked. "Because it's just making me angry."

"Good. You got to learn to pack that negative shit up inside, don't listen to it, and then do what you need to do to get what you want."

She wiped her nose. "Right, because that works so well for you."

Bunny smiled. "Still here, still flying, aren't I?"

"And where even are you?" Fi asked. "You can't say what continent you're on?"

"No, but something weird happened today. I'll tell you, but just don't say I'm paranoid."

"You *are* paranoid." Fi sighed. "But I'm listening."

"Fair enough. Alright, so I'm flying over the middle of nowhere, no habitation, no roads, people, nothing, and I get a radiation spike on RWR," Bunny said. "I can check the data log, see exactly when, but it only lasted a second."

"How many times?" Fi asked.

"Just the once. And I was up at about 20,000 feet. If there was some kind of ground source, I shouldn't have picked it up flying that high, but I went lower and got nothing too."

Fi looked thoughtful. "Could just be a hardware glitch. Our KF-21s have radiation detectors installed too. They aren't always reliable," she said. "Random shit can set them off, like strong magnetic fields."

Bunny thought about that. She'd been told they were experimenting with electromagnetics at Concordia, but the spike had occurred while she was still *50 miles* out from the station. "OK, maybe."

"Can some kind of jamming or radar cause a spike on a radiation detector?" Fi asked her. "I mean, I've never heard of anything like that, but it's a thought."

"Not that I know of, but that doesn't mean it isn't possible," Bunny said. "I'm going to take a dive into the code base for the RWR tonight and see if there are any clues there."

"With *your* mad cyber skills?" Fi asked sarcastically. "You'll break it, Aunty."

"Well, I know who to call if I do," Bunny said. "And don't call me Aunty."

They ran through Fi's options for getting a psych test redo, and then Bunny cut the call. Problem was, yes, the first thing she did when converting to any new aircraft was to dive into its millions of lines of code to understand what made it tick. She'd crack open the diagnostic subroutines, then make tweaks to the code: make her combat AI more aggressive, comment out routines or functions that put limits on her that she didn't agree with. But she wasn't half the coder that Fi was.

That girl had hacked and taken control of a Chinese slaughterbot, for effing sake. A US Marine Bunny knew had found her on a Taipei street, walking the bot around like it was a pet on a leash. She could really use her help pulling apart the Nemesis RWR code, but though she'd been given US citizenship, Fi was a pilot in a foreign air force now. Bunny made a call to Two-Tone straightaway, rousing him from his bed. He was, strangely, unsympathetic.

"You will not be rooting around inside the code of your RWR," he said, disbelievingly. "And absolutely not with the help of a pilot from the ROC Taiwan Air Force."

"She was a cyber consultant to US Marine Corps Infantry Weapons Research Division on slaughterbot tech," Bunny told him. "At, like, the age of 17. She had clearances even I didn't have. Just ask someone at DoD, will you?"

"No. I'm not wasting my time on this nonsense," Two-Tone said. "And neither should you. Just have your RWR checked or replaced and get back on task. Now, I'm going back to bed. Get some damn sack time, O'Hare."

She rose from her chair and walked to the door of the comms hut. The sun didn't actually rise and set on Macquarie Island at this time of year; it just dipped toward the horizon, dimmed a little, then began climbing up again. Birds did go quiet, though, using the dusk to nap before starting their chattering cacophony again after an hour or so. The snow and ice around the station had melted, leaving only mud, rocks, moss and grass, and the island's unique peaty smell. It was a time of day that lent itself to contemplation about the day's events.

A Russian sub aggressively defending itself, an emergency evacuation for some unknown reason, and a radioactive tingle from nowhere? One of the reasons Karen 'Bunny' O'Hare had survived multiple combat encounters was that if bad things were happening, she just *assumed* they were connected until proven wrong. And Bunny O'Hare was a firm believer in the old adage, "Act first, apologize later." She was pretty sure that when Two-Tone said "Absolutely not," what he meant was "Do it. Just don't tell me you did it."

A little unauthorized coding, a solid sleep, ablutions and breakfast, and she'd be back in the cockpit, headed for Concordia again to pick up Outlaw for its return trip to Christchurch or wherever it was tasked next. To date, she'd been flying just with a minimal ordnance loadout and extra fuel, just for comfort.

She had a feeling that, tomorrow, she might be sacrificing a little of that comfort for some extra weaponry.

Wind Chill Warning

December 28, 2041
J-Day minus 3 days

"Welcome, and to those who had to leave us in a hurry yesterday, *welcome back*," David Lau, director of the US Office of Energy Research and Development, aka Project Minerva, told the assembled group of section heads and science program leaders. He waited for someone to chuckle at his little acknowledgement of the morning's near miss, but no one did.

But then, reading the room had never been one of David Lau's strengths. If it had been, he may never have written the letter to President Bendheim that kicked the whole hornet's nest.

Sir,

In recent years it has been made possible—through the work of Sjoberg at CERN, as well as Bellings and Holtz at Argonne Lab in America—for large-scale production and storage of antimatter to be achieved and, through this, for vast amounts of power theoretically to be generated, for purposes such as clean domestic energy generation, powering naval vessels or even space exploration.

You should also by now be aware that in China, a research project headed by myself identified a viable means to contain and transport antimatter in miniature, making the construction of antimatter bombs inevitable.

Imagine, if you can, the destructive power of a 1,000 lb. bomb, in a casing the size and weight of a hand grenade. Or a strategic battlefield weapon with the power of an 80-megaton hydrogen bomb, weighing just 4 lbs., able to be fitted on the warhead of man-portable missiles. And which, on detonation, release their destructive power with all the lethality, but without the long-lasting radioactivity, of nuclear weapons.

I regret to advise it was my team's estimate, before our work was interrupted by the surrender of the former Chinese government, that we would have a viable test weapon within two years. I know that our research was shared with the government of Russia at the highest levels and in great detail, and I have learned that many of my former colleagues on the Chinese weapons program fled to Russia after the war.

I shudder at the thought of that unstable regime possessing this capability before my newly adopted home, the USA. At risk would be not just our families, our economy and the military balance of power but our very existence as a species.

Yours very truly, David Lau.

He knew his letter bore a strong resemblance to the letter Albert Einstein wrote to US President Franklin D Roosevelt during World War II, because he'd used that letter as a template. Einstein's letter had led to the Manhattan Project and was the spark that lit a fire under the Roosevelt administration, allowing it to beat Germany, Japan and Russia to the nuclear bomb. Lau hoped for a similar outcome.

David Lau was no Einstein, though. In fact, he was more of a Werner von Braun, the Nazi rocket scientist who fled Germany to the US after World War II and became the linchpin of the US effort in the space race. David Lau, along with 1,600 other Chinese scientists, engineers and technicians, had been lured to the USA with the offer of citizenship and employment for him, education at Ivy League colleges for his family, and a lifetime pension from age 60 if he so chose. But he was no pop culture celebrity.

He'd been fully prepared for his letter to disappear without a trace into the labyrinthine corridors of a White House still reeling from its recent war with the former Shanghai Pact nations of China and Russia. Instead he'd been invited to a meeting that officially had never happened. At an anonymous farmhouse in Virginia, he found himself in a room with President Mark Bendheim and CIA Director Boniface Antonio.

"My God, more powerful than nuclear weapons?" Bendheim had gasped.

"More correctly, Mr. President, infinitely more powerful, in a fraction of the size, without the attendant long-term radiation effect," Lau had told Bendheim. "By the end of the Pacific War, my team in China had shown that 0.06 *micrograms* of antimatter would create an explosion equivalent to an 82 mm. mortar round. Our goal was to develop a device that could unleash the power of the biggest atomic bomb ever built, using just 2 kilograms of antimatter."

Antonio leaned forward over an ironically simple table made from local pine. "If they beat us to deploy antimatter weapons, the temptation to use them would be almost irresistible for our adversaries, since they leave no lasting radiation and there are no treaties covering their use." Th CIA director was a former ambassador to both China and Russia, who had headed up the NSA during wartime, leading its successful effort to decrypt Chinese battlenet communications. His Italian roots had bestowed on him the looks and dress sense of a Mafia godfather, which hadn't hurt his career at all.

"I always wondered why China's generals didn't reach for the nuclear button the moment the US Coalition crossed the border from North Korea. They were betting on an antimatter weapon breakthrough that never came."

"Or they were afraid of the hell they might unleash since the US could only retaliate with nuclear weapons, Mr. President," Lau said.

Antonio waved at Lau the briefing folder he was holding. "Your report says strategic antimatter weapons, the size you describe, could still create a nuclear winter if there was an all-out missile exchange."

"Exactly why we must be the first to show the world their terrible power, and bring Russia to the treaty table at a strategic disadvantage, sir," Lau said. "We may be only six months ahead of Russia, worst case. I know they've produced enough antimatter to begin small-scale weaponization experiments already. They could be ready to test a strategic-level weapon within a year."

Antonio nodded, turning back to Bendheim. "You've seen our reporting, Mr. President. Russia is building up its forces again. Imagine Russian forces going into Poland with a tactical antimatter weapon advantage. A single, well-placed missile could wipe out an entire NATO Army Corps, and there is no treaty or precedent to stop them."

"You're suggesting this 'worst case' has to be our base case," Bendheim said. He stood and walked to window that looked out over an incongruously bucolic scene: an apple orchard in full blossom. "This threat is more perilous than the one our forebears faced in the Second World War, gentlemen. In the race to develop atomic weapons, we were competing only against an isolated and nearly defeated Germany. Japan was on its knees too, and Russia didn't start taking atomic weapons seriously until after Hiroshima." He flipped through a few more pages of the brief. "Can we slow Russia down?" he asked. "In the Second World War, as I recall, the Allies delayed Germany's atomic research program by blowing up their heavy water production facilities. Is there something like that we—"

"Not without reigniting a world war," Antonio said. "German heavy water production was concentrated in Norway in the Second World War, which made it easier to disrupt. Russian antimatter production is spread across Russia at several sites in remote locations. You'd have to hit them all, and to do it discreetly, with special operations troops or sabotage, which would take months to set up and execute. Most of their central research facility in the Altai Mountains is underground. Nothing less than an orbital bombardment would be able to take that out, and we'd have no hope of hiding a strike like that."

Bendheim had dropped the briefing folder on his desk. "Then we simply have to move faster. Professor Lau, you said your China team was on the verge of producing viable weapons. What if I give you whatever and whoever you need in order to be ready to test a weapon inside a year?"

"A year?" Lau had gulped. "Sir, I … yes. We could do it. I have already picked out a site, isolated from any population centers, with the conditions we would need to be able to—"

"Let me guess." Bendheim smiled. "In the middle of the desert in New Mexico?"

"Quite the opposite, Mr. President," Lau said, missing the joke about Los Alamos. "Antarctica."

Antonio frowned. "Aren't there a half dozen treaties banning military activity in Antarctica in general, and nuclear research in particular?"

"Mr. Director, those treaties were not signed by an America facing extinction if antimatter weapons are deployed by Russia first," Lau said.

"We'll create a multilayered cover story," Antonio assured Bendheim. "Peaceful research into new energy generation technologies."

That conversation had been less than a year ago, and Lau was about to reveal the true scope of Project Minerva to its functional leaders for the first time. He knew that many suspected, but some were going to have the dots in the puzzle connected for them.

***

Among those who definitely hadn't connected all the dots were the personnel of Aggressor Inc., represented at Lau's briefing by Trigger Brown, as uncrewed systems lead, and Rory O'Donoghue, its chief Antarctica pilot.

Both of whom were flagged in planning as crucial to the success of Project Minerva, though neither of whom yet knew it.

"That was our glorious leader thanking you for the marvelous bit of piloting that returned his precious aircraft and 200 of his scientists to him in one piece," Trigger said, nudging Rory as the scientist's little quip about "hurrying back" hit the floor with a thud. "Don't tear up."

"I'm blushing," Rory told her.

"What I'm about to tell you is national security classified," Lau continued, with a nod to his deputy director operations, Solomon Cohen. "Which means you may not discuss it with anyone outside Concordia. But you may discuss it freely with your people after this briefing." He was standing on a raised platform at the front of the room in Concordia's above-ground habitat module movie theater, aka The Meat Locker, since no matter what efforts were made to improve the habitat's insulation, its ambient temperature never rose above 60 degrees.

Movie nights were not a big draw card at Concordia, with most personnel preferring the warmth of the under-ice rec spaces.

Lau had recently had laser surgery to correct nearsightedness, which gave him a tendency to look down his nose when trying to focus at the back of a room. It wasn't a charming look, and Trigger was already predisposed not to like the bureaucratic head of Project Minerva because he was—as he had proved the day before—a head-up-his-own-ass bureaucrat. Had he reacted to her warning about Russian submarine activity under the Ross Ice Shelf? Hell, he'd palmed her off on the Pentagon liaison, Sandilands, who at least had the smarts later to look chagrined when he gave Trigger an update that wasn't. All she registered was that the Russian sub had disappeared.

Trigger Brown didn't do thumb-twiddling. She'd gotten online immediately with Two-Tone in Auckland, and he hadn't needed convincing about the threat. Pre-warned by Rory earlier, he'd already begun banging on doors at the Pentagon, and Trigger's report just filled out the picture he was already building.

"Project Minerva is reaching critical mass," Two-Tone said. "My US Navy contacts tell me they've moved a task force into the Southern Ocean off McMurdo, which includes the USCG cutter *Polar Warden*, two *Constellation* class frigates paired with *Sea Hunters* and *Mantas*, and they've got at least one P-8 Poseidon out of Christchurch overhead 24/7. I've passed on your report, but they're confident they've got the assets in place to take care of your Russian boat if it tries to cause problems."

That hadn't reassured Trigger. "We're confident" was usually the last thing Trigger heard before a military fiasco.

"Wake up. Here it comes." Rory elbowed her, noticing her eyes had glazed over.

"People, you have been—you are—a part of the most significant research program the USA has conducted since the

Manhattan Project. You have designed, tested and built a functioning antimatter forge, capable of producing enough power to supply not just this facility but every single research base on Antarctica, if they were hooked up to it. That forge is now also producing industrial-scale amounts of antimatter. You have developed and miniaturized methods to safely transport that antimatter in Bellings Traps. And today, you proved that the system is fail-safe!" He held a clipboard under his arm and gave a short-lived round of applause, with Cohen, Jansen and Bellings following suit, equally briefly.

"But Project Minerva has a greater purpose," Lau continued, "one that some of you may have suspected, and which I can now confirm." Trigger noticed for the first time that Lau had notecards attached to his clipboard, and he looked down at one now, reading from it. "We are in a race against the clock, a race which, if we lose, could lead to nothing less than a new world order, with the USA in ruins." He pointed at the ice above their heads. "On the other side of the hemisphere, Russia is researching antimatter weapons. I know from my role in the former Chinese antimatter program that, until a few months ago, Russia was *ahead* of the USA in its research. Imagine what it would mean for the world if Russia obtained antimatter weapons before the US or its allies." He paused, and even Trigger could feel the mood in the room change. "If it gets them, it *will* use them," Lau said. "We cannot allow that to happen." He stepped to one side and nodded to Jansen. "Doctor Jansen …"

The deputy director science, Henrietta Jansen, stepped forward. Trigger knew her less well but probably liked her more, since she seemed a "just do it" kind of person who could get just as frustrated about bureaucracy as Trigger did.

Jansen cleared her throat. "Thank you, Director. Some of you are familiar with our work on Minerva-J, or 'Juliet,' as we call her: the largest of our Bellings Traps, currently holding nearly 2 kilograms of antimatter. If you look around you, the 'J team' are the ones who shed a couple of kilos in sweat during the incident this morning …" This time the joke did get a chuckle. Jansen smiled and continued. "From this point on, all teams, D through M, will either support or be reallocated to work directly on Juliet. We are *all* on the J team now. And in case you haven't already guessed, Juliet is the Project Minerva equivalent to the Manhattan Project's 'Trinity' effort, which delivered the first atomic bomb."

Trigger pricked up her ears. Did she just imply they were building an antimatter *bomb*? Suddenly a lot of things made a lot more sense. Why all the compartmentalization and secrecy. Why the almost unlimited resources. What the panic had been that morning. And why Russian spy submarines were poking around Antarctica.

But the news shook a few people. Trigger guessed there were more than a few head-in-the-sand personnel on Project Minerva, who had spent the last year with their heads wrapped in equations without thinking about the bigger picture, without realizing the whole "civilian energy production" cover story was just that—a cover story. The idea they were all working on a weapons program was not going down well with everyone.

"Boom. That shattered some illusions," Rory whispered.

"It has been a not-so-closely-held secret that J team was preparing a transportation test of the Juliet Bellings Trap, from Concordia to a NOAA platform out in the Southern Ocean, off the Ross Ice Shelf," Jansen continued. Trigger looked over at Rory. Jansen was finally getting to the part of their announcement that touched on the support Aggressor Inc. had been providing. Trigger and Bell, with their undersea patrols of the waters between McMurdo and the NOAA "weather-monitoring" platform, and Rory, with his return trips to the NOAA platform, delivering small payloads by tiltrotor Vigilant drones. "This workstream is now moving to its active phase. Director Cohen," Jansen said and stepped aside as Cohen stepped forward.

"Everyone wants their names in the history books today," Rory muttered.

Trigger pointed at the ever-discreet Colonel Sandilands, standing well off to the side, against a wall. "Not *everyone*."

"Thank you, Doctor Jansen," Deputy Director Operations Solomon Cohen said. "The Juliet test will in fact be a test both of our ability to transport the large Bellings Trap device safely from Concordia to the platform and … to collapse it."

Any pretense of polite attentiveness among the audience disappeared immediately, as exclamations of surprise and consternation broke out, some of them shouted at Cohen.

Trigger was sitting next to Chief Logan Raleigh, the base security head—who did not appear surprised by the news—and she leaned over to him. "You missed all the fun yesterday."

He grimaced. "Tell me about it," he said. "There's never a good time to head out onto the ice. Something *always* happens."

"No rest for the wicked. So what are they all worked up about?" she asked, gesturing at the people around them.

"Well, DD Cohen said 'collapse,'" Raleigh told her. "In your and my language, he means 'explode.'"

"Oh, right, thanks," Trigger said, and sat back in her chair again.

Raleigh looked at her and shook his head. "No. You don't get it. Juliet holds 2 *kilos* of antimatter. You collapse the magnetic bottle around it, which is essentially what a Bellings Trap is, and it goes boom."

"No, I get it," Trigger said.

"As in *mother-effing* boom, with a bang nearly twice that of the biggest hydrogen bomb ever detonated."

Trigger blinked. "OK, cool. Thanks, Chief." She leaned over to Rory. "You hear that?"

"I heard."

"Now we know why they needed Outlaw on the ground here, not McMurdo," Trigger said. "Guess who is flying the big bomb to the little platform in the middle of the huge ocean?"

Rory had seen Cohen looking right at him as he explained what the field test of Juliet was going to entail. "Well, I assumed we're part of this test, or we wouldn't be at this briefing. But how, exactly?"

Bell was sitting beside Trigger and folded his arms. "Glad we're going to be sitting warm and safe back here under about a mile of ice while you and Uncle do your 'delivery run.'"

It took several minutes for Lau and his deputies to get control of the room again. Cohen still had the mic, and he waited as one of his people started pasting large posters to the walls by the doors. "Thank you, we'll be moving into functional teams now for briefings. Your room assignments are being posted." He pointed at a clock on the wall. "As we went into this briefing, this base moved into full lockdown. There will be no new personnel coming in, none going out and no communication with the outside world without section head approval, and all communications *will* be monitored. Your loved ones back home will be proactively told a storm has interrupted communications, and they should not worry." He took a deep breath. "At 1500 hours, it will be J-Day minus three. Three days until the first test of an antimatter weapon by humankind. Good luck and godspeed, everyone."

Everyone stood, but not everyone moved. Military personnel got it; they were filing out of the room to their briefings. The rest could best be described as a civil-scientific rabble. Some made a beeline for coffee and snacks; others milled around, still arguing with each other. Chief Raleigh looked over the room with undisguised frustration. Trigger tugged at his sleeve. "Chief, he may not have verbalized it yet, but I'm guessing we're getting new orders, am I right?"

"Safe assumption, Brown," Raleigh told her. "But even I don't know what they are. After all, I'm just base security," he said, dryly.

Trigger frowned. "You aren't read in on everything?"

"No ma'am," Raleigh said, surveying the room. "DD Cohen is playing a lot of things close to the chest." He sighed, as a half dozen scientists concerned about the implications of the lockdown began bearing down on him.

Trigger left him to it. She joined Rory, Uncle and Bell among the crowd at the wall looking at room assignments for their briefings. "You're with us," Rory said, reading from the poster. "Aviation and Subsea (Aggressor Inc.), room 2.42." He tapped a finger on the wall and turned to her.

"Cool. Let's find that room," Trigger said.

Rory held her sleeve. "Nah. I got a better idea."

***

Meteorologist Donovan Grant button-holed Professor 'Lema' Lau the minute he stepped off the stage.

"Director, can I have a word?" he said, as Lau finished speaking with Cohen.

"Yes. Meteorology, isn't it?" Lau said. "I think you are needed in the base facilities briefing."

"Sir, yes, thank you," Grant said. "I just want to be sure you are aware we are probably looking at whiteout conditions around your 'J-Day.'"

Lau gave him a patronizing look. "We are 100 meters under the ice. And we have contingency plans for different weather scenarios. Your concern?"

"If you are planning to fly Juliet onto that platform, you don't have three days to get it out of Concordia. Visibility here will be zero and winds gusting to 50 knots inside two days. No aircraft will be able to take off or land."

"Be more precise," Lau snapped, suddenly paying attention. "When will the bad weather hit?"

"We'll have blowing snow and gusts to 40 knots by midday tomorrow. An aircraft might get out, but no one will be able to land. By midday the following day, the blizzard will hit, and shortly after, we'll be looking at whiteout conditions, gusts to 50 knots."

"Weather over McMurdo and the NOAA platform?" Lau asked.

Grant didn't have to check. "Strong winds at both sites, blowing snow at McMurdo by J-Day. Heavy seas and winds gusting to 30 knots at the NOAA platform, but clear skies."

Lau relaxed, though Grant couldn't see why. "Good. Be sure to send that information to the Aggressor people. They are handling the aviation side." Lau smiled, looking past Grant. "Anything else?"

"This bomb, Director—it's more powerful than a thermonuclear weapon?" Grant asked.

"Several orders of magnitude, yes," Lau said, getting impatient.

"Has anyone modeled the possible impact on coastal ice shelves?" Grant asked. "Ross, or Thwaites? You break up one of those, and you're talking an extinction-level climate catastrophe …"

Lau took a step to go around Grant. "That has been modeled down to the kilojoule level. The explosion will be 400 miles out and won't accelerate the breakup of either the Ross or Thwaites ice shelves. Now please, update your forecasts for the test." He walked briskly to the exit before anyone else could intercept him, but only got as far as Sandilands.

Thank you, Director, Grant thought. I now know not just the date and time but also the place for the test, and that it's going to be an underwater test, if it won't impact the ice shelves at that range. Probably lowered from the deck of the NOAA platform.

Grant made for the door too. He had to update his forecasts, as Lau had said. But first he had an errand to run. Concordia might be in a comms lockdown, but that didn't mean Donovan Grant couldn't get a message out.

***

Chief Raleigh wasn't particularly worried about policing the comms lockdown. He had appointed Byron 'Brick' Wilson as "personnel liaison officer" for the duration of the lockdown, and not for his client-facing skills. The former Navy ensign, Wilson, had been a maritime security specialist aboard the USNS *Montford Point*, and he'd seen it all, from drunken ratings to apoplectic admirals. He met all protests, complaints and unreasonable appeals with the same stone face, and tried and tested refrain. *I can see your concern there, sir or madam. I'll take that up with the chief.*

Brick passed very, very few things on to Chief Raleigh.

What Raleigh was worried about was that pain-in-the-ass Aggressor sub operator, who was making noise about the station's physical security.

Director Lau had wanted every staff member who had arrived in the last three months re-vetted and the possibility of sabotage of the cooling pumps investigated. Raleigh had told him he didn't have the people, or the time, to do the kind of investigation Lau and Cohen had demanded before J-Day. So he'd further restricted access to critical operational spaces, reset locks and keypads, and removed all older or expired credentials.

The abrasive Aggressor submersible driver had also spooked Lau regarding perimeter security and forced Raleigh to revisit that too. He had two-person teams on the three entrances and exits to the above-ground base facilities, mostly to ensure that anyone going out on the ice had a valid reason, and to be sure they were checked back in again. There was a six-person team on metal and explosives detectors inside the central accommodation silo at the entrance to the underground facility, and a two-person drone team that managed the optical-infrared surveillance drone that lapped their perimeter. That team was also the only one that could run the new LS3 Legged Squad Support systems Lau had inconveniently reminded him about.

The cold-hardened LS3 "sentry dogs" were a new addition to Raleigh's inventory, and he'd kept them in their factory wrap because they gave him a capability he didn't want. They looked like metal Rottweilers with snowshoes for feet and smelled of ozone and machine oil. So what if they could navigate snow and ice, and could stay outside in temperatures down to -20°F for up to an hour—well beyond what his people in their best gear could sustain? His aerial drone team could make 20 laps of the perimeter in the time an LS3 could make *one*, so though he'd told Lau he'd deploy them, he was in no hurry.

His 60-person security complement was scaled to the challenge of managing 300 base personnel, with all their minor grievances, drunken bar fights, petty theft and drug abuse issues.

He only had 20 on duty at any one time, 40 if he laid on a double shift, which he hadn't deemed necessary, despite the Aggressor pilot's hysteria. His people had access to weapons if he approved it, but they didn't need them for the kind of low-level policing they were called on to do, so they didn't carry. The scientists and staff of Project Minerva could usually be kept in line with a frown and a growl.

Raleigh however, had just taken a little detour to check a sidearm out of the Concordia armory. *Forewarned, forearmed*, right?

He checked his watch. Most of the base personnel were in J-Day briefings. He should go topside and check no one was out on the ice who shouldn't be.

***

Rory had taken Brown and Bell out onto the ice. He wanted to dial in Two-Tone back in Christchurch, and Rice and O'Hare on Macquarie Island, so Rory had insisted they hold the briefing in Outlaw's command and control center since it meant he could set up a link that didn't have to go through Concordia base security.

The Project Minerva engineer leading the briefing, one of Bellings's team leaders called Anna Venice, had tried to object, but she was too badly outnumbered by Aggressor Inc. personnel.

Outlaw's remote vehicle control and command center was a cramped cubicle jammed up in the front of the AC-130 behind the cockpit, barely able to accommodate the five people who were sitting on chairs and leaning on walls.

Bellings's team leader, Venice, waited for Rory to dial the remote Aggressor personnel in. The Pentagon liaison, Sandilands, was already on the video feed from inside the facility.

"What do you do for coffee back here?" Brown asked, looking around at the array of instrument panels, aircraft controls and sensor systems.

Uncle pointed outside the module. "Espresso machine is down back at the loadmaster station."

"I'll go," Bell said, unsticking himself from a wall. "Who wants what?"

"Uncle was joking, Tinkerbell," Brown said. "But seriously. All this high-tech stuff and not even a brew maker?"

Uncle thumped Rory on the shoulder. "See, boss, I told you we should have gone for the comfort upgrade instead of the JATO pods."

"Alright, everyone is here now," Rory said, ignoring him as Two-Tone and O'Hare appeared on a wall screen. "Hey, boss, you hear us?"

"Loud and clear," Hamilton said. Their images were nearly double life-size, which made the two-tone colors of Hamilton's eyes stand out even more. "So I take it you people are about to join the J-Day inner circle," Hamilton said with a smile.

"Meaning you already have?" Trigger asked.

"This morning," Hamilton said. "I got a call from Aaronson, who told me he was brought into the loop by the president himself."

Mark Aaronson was Aggressor Inc.'s billionaire owner, and given how deeply embedded Aggressor Inc. was with the US military, President Bendheim's administration had him on speed dial.

"Aaronson assured the president that the success of his trillion-dollar program is safe in the hands of Aggressor Inc.'s finest," Hamilton continued, "which should mean all your boots are filling up about now."

"And me without my piddle pack," Trigger said.

107

"Ms. Venice, the floor is yours," Rory told the Project Minerva engineering team leader, who was standing at the back of the control center, looking a little pale as she glanced at her cell phone.

"Uh, I just got a message that Director Lau wants to join this briefing, but he's delayed. Maybe we should …"

"Start the briefing, and he can join in when he works out where we are, since he already knows what's in it …" Trigger said helpfully. "We need to get back on top of our submersible's refit."

"Fine by me too," Sandilands said.

"Ah, sure, yes," Venice said. She didn't fit the mold of science geek very well, Trigger reflected. She was wearing Army green cargo pants and a black crewneck under her survival suit overalls, had red hair squared away behind her ears with a green scrunchy and, if Trigger wasn't mistaken, mascara applied so well you couldn't be sure it was there. She put away her cell phone and pulled a tablet out from under her arm. She began reading, "Um, pursuant to the Antarctic Treaty of 1961, which prohibits military activities on …" She looked up and registered the looks on the faces of the Aggressor Inc. officers, then put the tablet back under her arm. "Forget it. Since the director isn't here, why don't I just give you the short version up front, and you can ask questions?"

Trigger turned to Rory. "I like her."

"Me too." Rory nodded. "Go right ahead, ma'am."

"Since military activities are banned on Antarctica, and Aggressor Inc. is technically a civilian commercial entity, you've been given the task of transporting the Juliet device to the test site," she said.

"Well, shoot," Trigger said.

"I knew it," Rory said. "All those delivery runs with Outlaw out to the NOAA platform with those Vigilants."

"Yes," Venice said. "And no." She glanced at the screen showing Sandilands. "Due to the likelihood of bad weather at the test site, and the risks involved with air transport, Juliet will be transported to the test area by submersible, from McMurdo."

Brown whistled. "Lucky we didn't lose *Charlene* to that Russian sub, I guess," she said.

"Navy could have filled the gap," Sandilands said. "But for the integrity of the narrative, it's better that it's Aggressor Inc."

"Ah, the old 'integrity of the narrative' determinant." Uncle nodded sagely.

Rory shook his head. "Wait, so all you people need Outlaw to do is fly the big scary bomb, under escort, 700 miles from here to McMurdo?" Rory asked. "And once it's on the submersible, we won't be needed?"

"Yes, and again, no. While the bomb travels by submersible, you'll still be flying a payload out to the platform," Venice said. "The test will take place 50 miles north of the NOAA weather station, 1,000 feet underwater, 400 miles from McMurdo. At J-Day minus one hour, you'll land a remote-sensing package on the platform to record the event."

"Which could have been installed any time in the last few months," Uncle pointed out. "So why do it at the last minute?"

"*Decoy*, Uncle," Rory said, not sounding too happy. "They're using Outlaw as a decoy while Brown and Bell sneak their bomb into position by submarine."

"Yes, I won't lie. Because of concerns about operational security, all personnel not directly involved with transportation of the bomb are being told it is being transported by air," Venice said. "But your own people have assessed the risk of adversary action as minimal."

"Hooray," Uncle said.

"Minimal, but *not* zero," Trigger corrected her.

"Come on, people," Two-Tone said. "Did Paul Tibbets in the *Enola Gay* complain he might run into a Japanese fighter on his way to Hiroshima?"

"Bad analogy, sir, but you're forgiven because you're British," Rory told him. "B-29s flew above 30,000 feet, and Japan had nothing that could touch them. Outlaw is a fat-assed missile magnet."

"You'd be sending that Vigilant in from about a hundred miles out, under US Navy frigate cover, with your Nemesis on overwatch, so I've signed off on the risk," Sandilands said. "And based on a careful assessment coordinated with the Pentagon, so has your boss, Mr. Aaronson."

Rory scowled at Venice. "There's a snow front moving in. You tell your people we need that device aboard this aircraft as soon as possible, if you want us to move it anywhere."

"Noted," Venice said, looking at her tablet. "It should be ready to load by 0400."

Venice's telephone rang. She turned away, spoke quickly and turned back again with a frown. "It's Director Lau. He wants to know, quote, 'How the hell do I get into the plane, and what the hell are those soldiers doing out on the ice?'"

Rory turned to Uncle. "Get the crew access door, will you, Uncle, and—" Rory froze. "Wait. *What soldiers?*"

Blowing Snow Advisory

December 28, 2041
J-Day minus 3 days

GRU Spetsnaz Captain Anatoliy Kutuzov was sick of being out on the ice. Their cold weather survival suits had been designed for use by cosmonauts in space, not soldiers on the surface, and unlike the suits their Chinese counterparts had been wearing, they sucked at wicking sweat away from the body and venting it. So after his visor fogged so badly he couldn't see out, he'd had to flip it up and use goggles under his helmet, which let sub-zero air in around his face. Every 20 minutes, they had to drop their visors again and warm their faces so their eyeballs wouldn't turn to gel in their sockets, and brush the diamond dust buildup off each other's suits, which put them behind schedule.

They'd been warned about the Americans' optical infrared aerial drone sentry, but it was a civilian, not military type, and one of his men had just dropped it with a jamming rifle.

They were crouched around him as he surveyed the base through binos from about a mile out. Three cylindrical habitats, shaped like low, squat water towers, painted white with orange windows and roofs. The newer one was on the right, festooned with antennae and satellite dishes. It had some satellite domes radiating from it, which he'd seen on recon images, though they didn't know what was inside. The entrance to the underground facility should be there, though. And their "inside man" should be waiting for them.

He swung his binos right.

Well, hello. When did you *arrive?* Kutuzov wondered, as his binos settled on the huge aircraft parked out on the ice about 100 yards from his target. There was a single person standing underneath it, but the propellors were still, and there was no other activity around it. *We'll have to deal with you, too*, he decided. *But before or after we hit the base?*

Before. Deal with the person under the machine, and a single grenade in the landing gear would probably be enough to disable the aircraft. He didn't want anyone making an emergency getaway while he and his men were occupied below ground.

He got on his tactical radio. "Spivak, take three men. Deal with the tango by the aircraft, and prepare to disable it with a grenade between the tires. We'll move into position at the habitat and get ready to breach. Don't blow it until my order."

"Understood," Spivak said, pointing at three of his men and rising from his crouch. They began shuffling across the ice on their snowshoes as they unslung the weapons from their backs.

***

Chief Raleigh arrived at the security gate inside Habitat C with his radio crackling in his earpiece.

"Chief from UAV unit."

He stopped behind the security gate in the middle of the habitat. It was ringed with armored plate glass and had two metal detector gates that could also pick up chemical compounds … like drugs or explosives. It was the main entrance to the complex below, though there were of course emergency exits and entrances.

112

"Chief, go ahead," he said, one hand on his ear.

"Uh, we just lost contact with our drone. Link is down, and we lost vision," his drone pilot said. "Leroi has gone down to get the reserve. Can you send someone out to pick it up? We know where it went down, can give you a GPS position."

Raleigh hesitated. It wasn't unknown for a drone to drop. Battery issues, usually. The hairs on his neck began to rise though. "Roger that. Send coordinates to the gate; I'm here now."

He lifted his sidearm out of its holster.

***

Uncle was at the sensor console in the middle of the command center. On Outlaw's port side, just above the wheel well, was the camera pod for its 'Gunslinger' weapons system. Their 25 mm. Gatling had been removed for operations on Antarctica since it was an obvious treaty breaker. The cameras used to survey the ground and aim it were still operational though. He panned them around the aircraft.

They saw Director Lau, bundled up in cold weather gear, hands on hips and looking impatiently at the aircraft as though waiting for someone to teleport him inside. He turned and waved, uncertainly, to someone off-camera.

Then he ran. Puffs of snow chased his heels as he disappeared behind the landing gear.

Uncle panned the camera. A half mile away, he saw two men in white camo, kneeling, assault rifles aimed toward Outlaw. Two more, pushing through the snow just ahead of them, rifles across their chests.

Uncle had seen combat in Syria, the Pacific and China; he took no time to understand what he was looking at. He stood. "Hostile troops assaulting the aircraft," he said, looking at

Trigger and Bell. "Weapons locker, now! Use the crew access door for egress."

Rory was already moving, out the command module door and across the deck of the AC-130 toward a locker on the bulkhead behind the cockpit. He thumbed a DNA lock and pulled the locker door open, throwing a rifle each to Brown and Bell and pulling out two for himself and Uncle. Then he bent and opened a drawer, throwing Trigger and Bell loaded magazines, which they slapped into receivers before charging their carbines.

Trigger heard Uncle yelling into the mic at Sandilands. "Colonel, we're looking at an armed assault on Concordia. Maybe platoon-strength. You need to alert Chief Raleigh!"

Venice watched them load their weapons, nonplussed. Uncle looked over at her. "Don't suppose you're ex-military—National Guard maybe?" She shook her head. He pointed forward. "Then go up that ladder and into the cockpit. Try to raise someone inside the base on radio or SATCOM, and let them know what is happening."

Trigger dropped her rifle, grabbed the door handles beside the locker and pulled them down, shoving the crew door open. She didn't climb down; she picked up her rifle in one hand, and with the other, swung down, using the access door's vertical support like a fire pole. She landed like a gymnast. Bell hit the ground right behind her and fell on his ass.

***

The cold air hit Trigger like a hammer blow. She was still wearing her survival suit overalls but had taken off two layers of overclothes, gloves and her headgear. She skidded as she landed, but kept her feet and saw Lau sheltering behind Outlaw's big

114

portside gear stanchion, saw bullets smacking into the tires and ground beside him.

Two white-clad figures were powering through the snow toward them, 100 yards out. Two more were half a mile out, kneeling, firing.

"I'll take left; you take right," she told Bell. He nodded wordlessly.

Trigger crouched, leaning against a tire, showing him three fingers, then two, then one, and then rotated out onto one knee, raising her rifle.

She fired twice, bullets smacking into the chest of the man closest to Outlaw. Re-sighted. Fired twice more, missing the man beside him as he threw himself into the snow. Bell's fire followed him down.

Trigger pivoted back into cover as Uncle and Rory stumbled to the ground behind her and took cover behind the other set of tires.

"What is happening?!" Lau yelled.

"Stay where you are," Rory barked, raising his rifle.

"Two attackers, 11 o'clock, suppressed," Brown told Rory. "Two more a half mile out …" She ducked as a bullet smacked into the tire above her head. "Correction. *Not* suppressed." Trigger replayed in her head what she'd seen during her five-second engagement. "Maybe more, farther out, moving toward the base."

"We'll suppress; you knock 'em down," Rory yelled at Brown, and she nodded tightly, checking Bell was with her. He and Uncle swung out on one side of the tires, firing, and Brown took the other. Trigger let Rory and Uncle pour fire downrange before leaning out to see the man she had shot struggling to rise, as Bell put a couple of rounds into his chest and threw him backward. She saw two shooters farther out, one lying, another crouched. Trigger took the one on the ground first, a quick burst sending him rolling across the snow to avoid her fire. Then she put two more shots into the man crouching. He toppled over and lay still.

Uncle and Rory swung back into cover as a volley of fire smacked into the tires and snow around them.

"One more down, I think," Trigger said. "But they've got body armor. Can't be sure."

"Suppressed weapons. Could be special forces, whoever they are," Rory said. He looked at Uncle. "Squad weapon?"

"Squad weapon." Uncle nodded.

Rory grabbed Trigger's shoulder. "We've got an XM250 in the weapons locker, but we have to get it out and loaded. You'll have to keep them busy. Can you do that?"

Trigger's hands were shaking from the biting cold. "If I don't turn to ice first."

Rory rose into a crouch and grabbed Lau by one strap of his overalls, then stood, hauling him to his feet. He had his hands around his head for some reason. "Mr. Director, we're going up those steps and inside our aircraft. You follow us, alright?"

"Alright," the man said, clearly teetering on the edge of paralytic terror.

Rory yelled at Trigger. "Covering fire, Brown! Keep 'em busy!"

Trigger had moved back about 5 feet, flipped her carbine to auto and swung out on the right side of the tires this time. Rifle fire thudded into the ice where Uncle and Rory had been, right ahead of her. She saw the shooter—the man lying splay-footed in the snow 100 yards out—and sent a burst of automatic fire toward him that made him duck his head, but that was all.

Rory and Uncle, with Lau between them, scrambled up the steps. *Hopeless shooting, Brown*, she thought as she swung back into cover. *Not even close. Ammunition?*

She looked at her carbine properly for the first time. *Old Army surplus M4. Of course.* She jacked out the magazine. It held, what, 30 rounds? Four into one target, four into the other, then another half dozen … She slapped it back into the receiver. Call it 15 shots left. She switched the carbine back to semi-auto as bullets thudded into tires, ice and snow around her.

If these guys knew their stuff, the incoming fire was just for show. Someone would be working left and right of them, looking to flank. She signaled to Bell, lay herself down on the frozen earth, grimacing at the biting cold, and watched the arc of ground to her left. Bell covered their right.

Keep them busy? Sure, we'll keep them busy. Like clay pigeons keep a skeet shooter busy.

***

Bunny O'Hare's boots pounded across the tarmac as she ran for the flight line on Macquarie Island. RAAF ground crew and armorers had been getting her Nemesis ready, but the urgency in her voice when she'd called them after the line to Concordia was cut had them scrambling.

She'd already told them to load her Nemesis for bear— that meant that in addition to air-to-air and air-to-ground ordnance in her payload bay, she was taking off with two GAMBIT drones hanging off hardpoints under her wings. Her stealth profile would be shot to shit, but she wasn't headed into a stealth-on-stealth confrontation. Hostile ground forces were attacking Concordia Station. She might be called on to run some close air support, take out attackers on the ground … or knock down drones, if they had any in the air supporting them.

Her flight helmet was in the cockpit but she had tactical comms built into her suit and touched her throat mic. "Grinspoon, you see anything strange on RWR, you get real low real fast, got me?"

"Roger that, ma'am," Brad 'Grinspoon' Rice said. He had a Stingray refueling drone circling out over the Southern Ocean waiting to top her up so that she arrived over Concordia with fuel for a fight. The FB-22 had the range to make it to Concordia without refueling, but only on fumes. They couldn't afford to lose that Stingray.

She was looking at six lonely, fretful hours in the cockpit between now and Concordia, and the fight could be won, or lost, by the time she got down there.

Not for the first time, Bunny O'Hare cursed whatever shortsighted fool had signed a treaty banning military activities on Antarctica, or at least the fools who hadn't renegotiated it for nearly 100 years.

***

Chief Raleigh's cell phone rang again. He checked and saw an internal number, tagged with the name "Colonel." He thumbed the button to take the call. "Raleigh."

Sandilands spoke with rapid-fire urgency. "Chief Raleigh, listen up. I was on a call with the Aggressor team when it was interrupted with gunfire. They report armed troops approaching your base, platoon-strength …"

Raleigh nodded. "Understood. You have anything more than force strength? What about location?"

"Airfield side of the base, visible from the aircraft," Sandilands said quickly.

Raleigh cursed. What in hell were Aggressor personnel doing out on the ice when they were supposed to be two levels below in briefings?

"Understood. I'll trigger the base alarm. I need you to—" Raleigh said. Then he realized he was talking to dead air. He frowned and looked at his sat phone. It was showing "no signal."

Jamming? It's started.

He entered the security area at a fast walk. One of the people at the gate saw him coming and gave him a lazy salute. "Hey, Chief," he said. "How's it—"

Raleigh raised his pistol and shot the man in the face. There were five other personnel on the gate, and he emptied the pistol into them in quick succession, only the last of them making any attempt to find cover. His bullet caught her in the shoulder, spun her around, and he finished her standing over her as she held a hand in front of her face, too shocked even to plead for her life.

He swapped out the used magazine and looked around. No base personnel in the lobby, as he'd hoped. They were all in briefings, two or three levels below. He pushed a body out of a chair and sat down at a console. There were six subterranean levels, and he tapped the keyboard, paging through cameras on each level, watching the scientists and specialists of Project Minerva going blithely about their work.

It was probably a kindness they were oblivious, he reflected, given that he was sure now a team of Russian special operators had just arrived. The dropping of the perimeter drone and loss of comms had been his signal to move.

"UAV team for Chief. Leroi is back. We're heading to the roof to launch the reserve bird."

Raleigh put his sidearm on the console. His drone team was in Habitat A, a different building. "Uh, belay that, Reynolds.

Winds are picking up. I've sent someone down for those LS3 units. They can fill the gap while we retrieve the drone that went down."

"Uh … OK, boss."

Raleigh checked that the main doors out to the ice were unlocked, then sat himself down in plain view with his hands up and fingers laced behind his head, as he'd been advised to do.

Chief Raleigh had been easy pickings for the Russian agents who'd come knocking at his door two years earlier. He'd lost everything he had in a California wildfire the year before. His wife had left with his kid two years earlier, so at least they weren't home. He'd been on the other side of the globe when it happened, and Navy had denied him leave to go back and try to salvage what he could from his home before scavengers picked it clean. When he finally got back there a month later, there was only rubble and debt.

He didn't have fire insurance. Hell, who could afford that? But he still owed a million two on his mortgage, and his land was basically worthless since the city had announced it wouldn't be restoring services to "fire-prone areas."

He'd separated from the Navy, gotten a job with the US Antarctic Program so that he could service his loan, and ended up at Concordia. The nice man from the shady real estate company had contacted him shortly afterward and offered Raleigh a million five for his worthless land. "We're buying up abandoned properties all across California," he'd explained. It had seemed too good to be true, and of course, it had been. He'd discovered how good when he flew stateside to sign the papers for the property deal and the nice man revealed his real ask.

Well, he'd done worse things in his life, before joining the Navy. Yeah, he'd had that fantasy a lot of bad men had—that military service would make an honest man out of him—but that was BS. He'd been a small-time street thug before the Navy and made a nice career as a corrupt master-at-arms. So he hadn't blinked at the shady corporation's "request" in return for bailing him out of debt. Provide information on Project Minerva, on Concordia, and then, in a message a month ago, find a way to sabotage the project.

They'd been very unsatisfied with the little information he could give them about Project Minerva, but it was so damn compartmentalized. His plan for sabotaging it, though, they'd loved. They'd even agreed to pay him an extra half million for the risk he was running to his own life, if he succeeded. "I could get vaporized if I don't get away in time," he'd told them. "I want something for my kid if that happens."

Concordia's backup systems had worked too well. The pumps he'd disabled had been brought back online, the Juliet containment module stabilized. So his benefactors had gone to plan B, and his only job now was to facilitate their entry.

He looked at the bodies around him, without satisfaction but also without guilt.

Mission accomplished. He checked the lock controls for the double entry doors and the vestibule beyond that led to the external doors. *Entry facilitated. So what are you waiting for?*

Then he jerked upright in his seat, as outside, he heard the unmistakable ripsaw sound of a 25 mm. Gatling opening up.

***

Trigger heard thumping in the fuselage above her that sounded like someone kicking out a door or panel, but tried to ignore it. Her shaking hands had her rifle aimed into the space just ahead of the tire she was sheltered behind, waiting for movement, waiting too for a line of bullets to chew up her spine and end her, coming from the guy who was probably circling around behind her and Bell. She had to trust that the Aggressor sonarman had her back.

Before she even registered the movement out on the ice ahead of her, her rifle bucked reflexively, and the man who had been trying to get an angle on her was thrown backward. Without waiting, she rolled onto her back, looking for a target between her feet. *Just Bell.* No one else beyond. She rolled again, sighting out onto the ice as her target out there lifted himself up onto his side, and she put a single bullet into him again.

Up! Get up! she told her frozen body. The starboard side of the plane should be clear now. She rose, numb legs refusing to cooperate as she staggered, stumbled over to the starboard wheel stanchion and threw herself into the snow behind it.

About a half mile ahead of Outlaw, she saw a line of white-clad troops shuffling across the snow and ice toward the new habitat building. Then there was a solid metallic *thunk* from the other side of the fuselage, a panel fell to the ground, and a light machine gun over her head opened up on the column of Russian troops.

The first volley went high, tracer flashing over their heads, sending some of them to the ground while the others bent low and tried to move faster.

It also flushed out the operator who had been moving to flank Trigger from behind. Surprised by the chatter of the squad weapon, he forgot all about Trigger and rose out of the snow, aiming his rifle at the aircraft, trying quickly to decide where to shoot to punch through the fuselage to the gun crew inside.

Bell was ready. He aimed for his midsection, but numb hands betrayed him. His carbine jumped, his grip weak, and the bullets he'd aimed at the attacker's thorax struck the man in the head.

Alright, that works too, Trigger decided as the attacker fell.

She tapped Bell's shoulder and ran for Outlaw's crew access stairs.

***

In the cockpit, Venice was on the aircraft's radio and getting nothing but static.

"You know how to work it?" Lau asked, hovering behind her after joining her in the cockpit.

She frowned. "I know how to work a radio." She pointed at a knob. "We've got power. I've tried VHF, UHF, HF, SATCOM ... there's just static on them all."

"Maybe it's the lockdown?" Lau asked. "Security is blocking all signals?"

"No, it shouldn't be that," Venice decided. "We were able to get a satellite video link to New Zealand. This is something else."

She reached forward to try again, then heard the metallic whine of the 25 mm starting up behind them.

***

Anatoliy Kutuzov had been an officer in the GRU for 13 years. He'd served three combat tours: two in Syria, one in Latvia.

All had been shit shows.

Here we go again, he'd thought grimly, as the squad he'd sent toward the American plane was suddenly prone on the snow, exchanging fire with someone under the damn machine! *Expect minimal resistance*, he'd been told. *Base security will be unarmed.*

He stopped his column, grabbed his binos and panned them around. There, behind the tires—a single shooter.

"Spivak, one armed tango, right side undercarriage. You see them?"

"Got them," Spivak replied. "Will fix and flank."

123

Suddenly one armed tango became four, and he saw his men throw themselves to the ground.

Gavno!

He collected himself. Spivak could handle a couple of USAF maintenance techs who had probably never fired a rifle outside a range. He had to get inside that facility.

He raised an arm and got his column moving again, feet zigzagging as they paddled across the ice. The firefight to his right, about a half mile away now, intensified with outgoing and incoming fire. None coming his way. Yet.

A couple of tense minutes passed. *There.* The two big doors in the habitat that were his ingress point. He pulled off his googles and dropped his tactical visor. "Visors down," he ordered. "Marking ingress point." His left hand pressed a button in the palm of his glove, creating a cursor on his visor, which tracked his eyes. As it settled on the doors, he pushed the button in his right palm twice, locking it in place. "Ingress point marked," he grunted. "Team A will—"

He heard the staccato thud of a heavy weapon coming from the direction of the aircraft. He spun around and saw tracer fire from a hatch on the portside fuselage of the gunship under its cockpit, flashing over their heads. The men behind him stopped and crouched to make themselves smaller targets.

"No!" he yelled, grabbing the man behind him and hauling him to his feet. "That gun can't traverse past its nose. Get up, keep moving!!"

He put his head down and made best speed for the beckoning door. The operator in the gunship had steadied his aim now, and Kutuzov felt, as much as saw and heard, a line of cannon fire chewing along his stumbling, shambolic column, from the rearmost man and forward.

"Move!" he yelled again, trying to ignore the cries of dying men and grunts of the desperate. He shot a glance over his right shoulder. The barrel of the airship's autocannon was disappearing behind its fuselage now. A last volley of tracer fire chewed into the snow and blood behind him, and then he was on solid ice, covered in gravel, swept clean of snow by regular foot and vehicle traffic. He stopped, gathering his breath, clicked himself out of his snowshoes and ran for the double doors, slamming into the wall of the habitat beside them.

The machine gun had fallen silent, but not his wounded. Back out on the ice, under the sights of the American gun, he heard a man moaning. Hugging the wall beside him, he counted the men who had made it off the ice.

Six. Including himself. *Six out of 12!*

He shot the American aircraft a baleful glare. Saw the name emblazoned across its nose: OUTLAW. *If you are still here when I reemerge, my friend, it will not end well for you*, he promised the squat black machine. *Or those you carry.*

***

"I still have movement," Uncle said, peering over the barrel of the XM250. "One tango on the ground. Wounded, I'd say. Trying to signal his buddies by the wall. Can't see a weapon."

Rory was looking at the tactical monitor that covered Uncle's view. "Doesn't look like anyone's coming to rescue him," Rory said. He looked at the open crew access door, then at Brown.

"What? Let him bleed out," Brown said. "Bastards tried to kill us."

"No, we need eyes on the troops at the base," Rory said. "See what they're doing. They could be doubling back on us."

125

Trigger ran to the open crew door. She saw a half dozen white-clad troops lined up beside the habitat entrance. None were looking toward Outlaw. Or their fallen comrades, their blood leaking into the snow.

Wow, that's some tough love, Trigger thought. As she watched, the soldier at the front of the group heaved a door open, and the others filed inside.

Trigger ran back to Rory and Uncle, collecting her rifle before hitting the weapons locker and fishing another couple of magazines out of a drawer. "They've gone into the facility," she yelled. "Mount up!"

Rory and Uncle were still staring at each other as she flung herself out of the crew access door and swung down onto the ice hanging from the vertical support by one arm.

***

Chief Raleigh stayed stock still as the entry door was flung open and six very intense men filed inside and spread out, two with their rifles trained on him.

When they were satisfied the lobby was clear, five men watched the entries and exits while the sixth approached. He raised his reflective visor, and Rory saw frost-covered lashes, burned cheekbones and ice-blue eyes. The man's mouth was covered by his Balaklava, and his rifle was pointed at Raleigh's chest.

"*Wisdom,*" the Russian said.

"*Sedan,*" Raleigh replied to the challenge.

The man relaxed his stance, but his eyes didn't soften, and he didn't lower his rifle either. "Your intelligence was deficient. There was nothing about troops and weapons in that transport."

"And I didn't know they were armed," Raleigh said. "It's a damn transport."

"They were armed," the Russian said. Raleigh could feel his life hanging in the balance, until at last, the man lowered his rifle. "Time is short. I need to know what is below, and no more mistakes."

Raleigh had printed a map of the underground complex and pulled it from his back pocket, unfolding it on the counter in front of the Russian. "Living and recreational spaces are in the other two habitats. Above us is water and power, equipment storage. Below us, levels one through four are labs and offices. Level five is the control center. The forge, the reactor, is on six. What exactly is your objective?"

"Destroy the reactor," Kutuzov said simply. "With timed charges."

"Uh, sure, but …" Raleigh said patiently. "You'd have to be *50 miles* away when it blows, because of gamma radiation or some crap. I hope you have a fast helicopter right outside."

"Fifty miles?" The Russian furrowed his brow.

Ah, they didn't tell you that, did they, Ivan? "Think of it like setting off an atomic bomb," Raleigh said. "You need to be a long way out when it blows."

"Alright. We bring forward our extraction," the Russian decided. "We did not want a Russian helicopter to be seen near your base, but we can meet it 1 mile out, instead of 10. It is not a problem." The Russian studied the map. "How do we get to level six? These stairs?"

"No, they're blocked by a nuclear-bomb-rated blast-proof door between five and six. You'd never get through that way." Raleigh pointed across the lobby. "There's a freight elevator across the lobby that will take you to five, the control center level. If the staff there get suspicious, they can completely lock down the reactor level and lock you in. So you need to take them out first, if you want to live."

"Take them out ..." The Russian officer was nodding, then looked up from the screen and around the lobby, as though noticing the bodies on the floor for the first time. He took in the pistol on the table and then looked at Raleigh again. "You killed them?"

"Yes."

"How many security people on floors five and six?"

"Two on each floor. They're unarmed—only carry tasers and batons."

"You thought that transport was unarmed."

Raleigh held up his thumb. "This is the key to our armory. No one but me can access it."

Two weeks before, Raleigh had taken a pistol and ammunition from the armory, then used the excuse of a weapons audit to flag them as stolen and issue a recall of all firearms. He had locked them away in the armory, with only himself and his deputy able to access them, but he'd disabled his deputy's access that morning. He hadn't known about the weapons aboard Outlaw. He'd tried to ensure *he* was the only one carrying a weapon in the entire facility.

The Russian picked up the map, and Raleigh's pistol, stuck the pistol in his belt in the small of his back. "Lead the way."

Raleigh shook his head. "No, no, no. I've done what I was asked to do. I set everything up and got you inside." He pointed to the exit doors. "That's me. I'm taking a snowmobile 5 miles out, and a Russian helo is going to pick me up and take me to your base at Vostok. Right?"

"Not right. You will come in helo with us, *after* we set charges," the Russian said, then slapped the map back down on the table. "Take us to level five."

***

Brown didn't run to the double doors since the main lobby would now be full of very pissed commandos. She and Bell ran to the dome they'd occupied when they were piloting *Charlene,* with Rory and Uncle puffing in their wake. The connecting tube still ran into the main lobby—there was no way around that— but it wasn't the most direct, obvious route, and they could always retreat again if they came under fire.

They didn't. At the entrance to the main lobby, Trigger put her eye to the corner.

"What do you see?" Rory asked, still panting.

"I see your breath fogging up the air," Brown said. "Back up."

"Sorry."

Trigger looked again. "Bodies. Three, maybe four. Lobby is empty."

"I didn't hear shooting?" Uncle said.

Trigger shrugged, taking a better look. "Suppressed weapons. The lobby is empty."

They moved out, Trigger out front, Bell behind, Rory covering left, Uncle right. Trigger moved to the security gate and had to choke down rising bile. It was a slaughter. Uncle looked down at a woman who had been shot multiple times. She still had a bloodied hand up in front of her face. "Those are small-caliber wounds," he said dispassionately. "They were executed, not killed in combat."

Trigger wasn't looking at the bodies. She was looking at the view from the security cameras. She saw movement in one of the small windows and tapped it just in time to enlarge it as the assailants stepped into an elevator.

With Chief Raleigh in the middle of them, looking very unhappy.

"They're going down, and they've taken the chief hostage," she said. "But going where?"

"You don't come in hot like they did without a plan," Rory said. "They must be going for the reactor, or worse ... Juliet."

"To blow it up?" Bell asked. 'Is it like a nuke—you can destroy it without setting it off?"

"If you can't, they're on a suicide mission."

"Whatever they want with it, we need to get to it before they do," Trigger said. "The reactor and fuel isn't stored on levels one through five, or I'd have noticed. So how deep does this damn base go?"

Uncle picked up a piece of paper from the desk in front of him, looked at it and held it up. "Six levels," he said, thumb on a map of the base that showed a silo six levels deep, with the sixth level marked *Restricted: Authorized Personnel Only*. "Pretty good guess the reactor and fuel are somewhere on six."

"Restricted. That's why they needed Raleigh," Rory guessed. He squatted down, looking under the desks.

"What are you doing?" Bell asked.

"Panic button, there must be ... somewhere ..." He crabbed a couple of feet left. "Found it." Every security station had a panic button in case a situation got out of hand. He slammed his palm upward on it. Nothing happened. No blaring siren, no flashing lights. He hit it again.

"Disconnected, or just silent?" Bell asked.

"Silent, I hope," Rory said. He saw Brown pick up her carbine. "Oh, hell no, I just realized. They took the only elevator. You're going to have us running down six levels of stairs, aren't you?"

"My freaking knees," Uncle moaned.

"You think *I'm* loving the idea?" Trigger said, checking her magazine, then staring at them with ruination in her eyes. "I was

130

shaking like a leaf out there, and it *wasn't* just the cold. But there are 300 people on this station who probably don't want to be vaporized today. So are we doing this?"

"You're right," Rory said, picking up his carbine too.

Trigger sighed and moved toward the stairs. "I was kind of hoping you'd say no, we should wait here," Trigger said.

Rory pushed ahead of the others and hit the stairs first. "Try to keep up, then."

"Forget those commandos; you wannabe heroes are going to kill me," Uncle grumbled, following them down.

***

Leroi Fontaine had been a US Army tactical drone recon specialist before joining the US Antarctica Program. First Infantry Division, the Big Red One, he'd been a corporal in the 18th Infantry 'Vanguards' when they'd driven into Beijing to take the Chinese surrender.

USAP paid a *lot* better, if you didn't mind the cold. And he'd told his mama there was a lot less chance of something bad happening to him down at the South Pole. Except now he wasn't so sure. There was the evacuation the day before, some people saying it was just a drill, but rumor was it was the real deal, a runaway cooling system failure. Now a full-base lockdown, a drone down and the silent alarm from the security gate flashing right in his damn face!

Their UAV station was just under the roof of Habitat B, so they didn't have to go too far to get to the roof to launch their drones. But their equipment room was off a corridor around the other side of the silo. He'd come jogging back into their station from fetching a backup drone to find his shift partner, Sully, sitting and gawping up at the red flashing light on the wall.

131

Leroi Fontaine didn't make it all the way through brutal campaigns in North Korea and China by sitting on his ass when shit was going down. He dumped the drone on the floor. "Sully, wake up! Get the chief on the radio."

The VHF radio handset was sitting on their control console, and Sully grabbed for it.

"UAV station for Chief Raleigh, come back?" Sully let the button go, then winced as a high-pitched whine came out of the speaker. He turned down the volume and tried again.

"Switch channel," Leroi said.

Sully clicked to their alternate channel and tried again. "Nothing."

Leroi's battlefield-honed spider senses were tingling. Protocol in case of personnel at the gate triggering the alarm was for on-duty personnel to send at least one person to the lobby. "You keep trying," he told Sully. "I'll go to the gate."

Leroi jogged out of their station toward the stairs. *Go to the gate via my locker,* he was thinking. When the recruitment officer at USAP had told Leroi Fontaine personal firearms weren't allowed on Antarctica, he'd nodded and said, "That's fine with me, ma'am." And back home, when he'd packed the shipping trunk he'd been allocated, he'd very carefully sequestered his disassembled Glock in among his electronics, then helped himself to some 9 mm. on each of the few occasions they'd had firearms drills.

Leroi Fontaine was a great believer in the 18th Infantry's rallying cry: *to the last round.*

***

Trigger Brown and Elvis Bell overhauled Rory O'Donoghue on the first flight of stairs, and by three levels down, they could only hear puffing and panting from he and Uncle somewhere above.

The attackers had to be headed for the device containment level on six, either to destroy the reactor or to compromise the Juliet device. Of course, they could just be terrorists, looking to inflict mass casualties, in which case they'd start at level two and work their way down, but there was nothing the Aggressor officers could do about that. Securing Juliet was their priority, given that if it was damaged, and its cooling system failed, the entire station and everyone in it would be lost.

Finally, she reached the fire door to level six and stopped, leaning on her carbine to get her breath. Rory pounded down the stairs a minute later, and they could hear Uncle still a level above, bringing up the rear.

"Plan?" Rory asked, only able to get a word out at a time between gasps of air.

Trigger had more time to recover. "They would have beaten us down here if they came straight down in the elevator," she whispered. "If this level is like the others, there's a corridor on the other side of this fire door, and a second door in to the facility. They'll have this first door either locked, or covered, so we have to expect to take fire going in."

"No sense committing suicide," Rory told her. "I'll try the door first."

Trigger stood to one side as Uncle arrived at the bottom of the stairs at last, and she pulled him against the wall with her. He leaned on his carbine, sucking air. Rory took his place beside them, reached out and turned the handle on the fire door.

It moved. Not locked. He nodded to Trigger, who slipped the safety off her carbine again. Uncle did the same. Taking a step back to get some leverage, Rory pulled the door hard and jumped back.

Trigger swung her barrel around the doorframe and sighted into the corridor beyond. All levels above had a similar layout: offices, labs and engineering spaces or living quarters around the outside of the silo, big open plan spaces like lounges, cafeterias, and control centers in the center. She'd never been on six but suspected if the devices were here, they'd be stored in the central core.

No one fired on them. No white-clad troops, but there was a new problem. She pulled back from the door frame. "Clear. Ten feet of corridor, then a solid metal door saying 'No Entry.'"

"My kind of invitation," Rory said, stepping around her into the corridor. Trigger and Uncle followed. The short section of corridor ended at a sliding metal door with an inset handle. Halfway up the wall, about chest high, was an intercom with a single button. In a corner of the ceiling above, the dome of a security camera. Rory motioned the others back, grabbed the handle and pulled, but the door wouldn't budge.

"End of the line," Rory said. "Unless we can get someone to buzz us in."

"And if the attackers are on the other side of that door?" Uncle asked.

"I guess they won't let us in," Trigger said. She shrugged and handed Rory her carbine. "Get back to the stairwell and cover me? I'll do my best to look harmless for the camera," she said, pointing at the CCTV dome.

When Rory, Bell and Uncle were back behind the fire door, Trigger pressed the button on the intercom. It buzzed. She counted to 10 and waited, then pressed again.

"There is no entry to this level for unauthorized personnel," a voice said through the speaker. A human voice, not AI generated, which gave Trigger hope. And one she vaguely recognized, but couldn't place.

"Listen!" she said, thumbing the intercom button again and looking up at the camera. "You have armed intruders on the way down. Six or more. If they aren't there already, they must have taken a detour but they're on the way. You need to prepare to …"

"Is that you, Lieutenant Brown?" the voice said.

Now she had him! Security specialist, and pool shark, Franco Venturi. Who had taken an easy $50 off her in a game of eight ball just two nights earlier. "Franco, that you, you loser?"

"Yes ma'am. I'm sorry, but I can't buzz you in. We're in lockdown, and the base alarm was just tripped … You aren't cleared."

"That was us! We tripped the alarm!" Trigger told him. "Franco, are you armed?"

"No ma'am …" he said.

"Well, the men headed your way are. They killed a half dozen of your colleagues at the security gate, and they'll be headed down in the freight elevator …"

There was a muffled discussion at the other end of the line, and Franco came back on. "Freight elevator has stopped on five," he said. "They'll need special access to take it another level down to here."

"Then we have time," Trigger said. "You need to let us in, Franco, if you want to live to play another game of pool."

He said nothing, but the door began grinding back into the wall. On the other side stood Venturi, in blue security uniform, radio in his hand. "I can't … I can't raise anyone," he said, as Trigger waved at Bell, Rory and Uncle to join them. Rory ran up and handed her carbine back to her.

"Don't you have hard-wired comms between every level?" Trigger asked.

"Yes. When the alarm was tripped, we all checked in, except the lobby level, and the chief ..."

"Where is your armory?" Trigger asked him. Over his shoulder, she saw several heads poking out of offices along the corridor. "Everyone back in your rooms, and get under your desks!" she yelled, and the heads disappeared as quickly as they appeared.

"Level three," Venturi said. "But only the chief can open it."

"What dumbass came up with that regulation?" Trigger growled.

"Uh, Chief Raleigh?" Venturi said.

"Elevator?" Bell asked. "Where does it let out?"

"This way," Venturi said. He hit a button to close the sliding metal door, and headed down the corridor at a jog.

***

The elevators on level five let out into the round corridor that circled the underground facility, and the Russian captain had pushed Chief Raleigh to the front of their small group, white-clad soldiers at his back with their weapons out of sight behind their legs or their comrade's backs.

Raleigh saw no one outside and stepped into the corridor, the Russians moving out behind him and taking up positions either side. Raleigh pointed to a small LED light on the opposite wall, strobing red. "Someone hit the panic button. Security will be on alert." He nodded back inside, at a thumb reader at the elevator wall. "And the elevators will be locked down. You'll need me to authorize them."

Right on cue, a tall woman and a short man in blue uniform came jogging around the bend in the corridor ahead of them. The man held a radio in one hand, the woman a baton.

Both of them stopped, frowning at the strange procession of white-clad troops behind Raleigh. "Chief? Someone triggered the silent alarm …" the man said, his voice on the edge of panic. The woman beside him didn't look much more composed.

Raleigh kept walking toward them. "Warren, Everton, stay calm. We are—"

From behind Raleigh's shoulder a suppressed weapon coughed, the two officers fell to the floor, and a hand shoved Raleigh in the back. "Keep moving."

Raleigh got a couple of steps ahead of the Russians and heard a weapon cough again, delivering a coup de grâce. He was thinking furiously. He'd contrived to be out on the ice for the reactor cooling system failure he'd rigged earlier, only to come back and find it had been averted. He was supposed to be waiting for a Russian chopper to fly him out, not headed *deeper* into the station. On the way down in the elevator, he'd revised his chances of coming through this alive from a hopeful high 90s when he'd woken this morning to the low 50s. As he stepped over his subordinates' bleeding, twitching bodies, he revised that estimate again, down near zero.

They passed empty offices and glass-walled meeting rooms. Most of the Minerva personnel, not needed to keep station ops running, were on the levels above in briefings. Before another bend in the corridor, Raleigh held up a closed fist, and Kutuzov joined him. "Control center is 'round this bend," Raleigh said quietly. He pictured the control center in his mind. "Opening on your right, no doors, 12 workstations on a lowered floor."

The Russian captain had signaled to his troops before Raleigh even finished talking. They filed past him with weapons raised and deadly intent in their eyes.

They stepped into the doorway to the control center, and a second later, Raleigh heard the sound of automatic weapons firing.

But the sound was receding, because as soon as the last Russian soldier passed him, Raleigh had backed up, and he was now running at a sprint, back toward the elevator. A new plan was forming in his mind. Take a Beowulf tracked vehicle, get as far out as he could before the Russians blew the reactor and hope distance and the thick ice cap would be enough to protect him. There should be nothing left of Concordia except a lake of meltwater where the base was, and no evidence of his treachery. He could use the excuse again that he was out on patrol, return to the base to "look for survivors" and wait for rescuers from McMurdo to arrive.

Hell, he might even get a damn medal.

***

Trigger and Rory surveyed the corridor outside the elevator door. It helpfully showed which floor the elevator was on. Level five, like Venturi had predicted.

"Elevators can only be used by security once the alarm has been tripped," Venturi said, holding up his thumb. "They're DNA coded to security personnel."

"Must be why they took Raleigh with them," Rory told him. "These guys had insider intelligence."

"We've got a few minutes," Venturi said, looking up at the elevator floor indicator. "They're still on five."

Trigger stood against the wall opposite the elevator doors. The distance was about 5 yards. "No cover for a direct line of fire into the elevator." She looked up and down the curved corridor. "We could pile furniture up outside these doors, though, so stuff falls forward when the doors open. Give ourselves a couple of seconds' mayhem while they work free."

Rory nodded. "You and Bell down the left corridor. I'll take right, with Uncle."

"The Juliet device—it's here too, right?" Trigger asked Venturi.

"Farther around," he said, nodding to the right. "There's a room looks like an industrial refrigeration plant. The reactor is inside it. There's an output trap underneath that takes the antimatter feed from the reactor. Juliet has her own room next door, dedicated power supply and cooling system."

"Could that be why the attackers are on five?" Rory wondered. "They're just going to cut the power to the cooling systems from the control center? Collapse the trap on Juliet?"

"It has a hydrogen fuel cell backup, so they'd need to get down here to really destroy it," Venturi said.

"Kind of weird to *hope* they're coming here," Bell pointed out.

"Whoever they are, these guys are heavy hitters," Trigger said. "They'll have frags, try to push on us straightaway."

Rory shrugged. "The corridor is a circle. So we back up, until we got nowhere to back up to." A few heads were sticking out of offices again. Rory sighed and turned to Venturi. "How do we get personnel out of the crossfire?"

Venturi bit his lip. "The containment doors are hydraulic. There's a machine room on the other side of the silo that powers the mechanism. Plenty of room in there."

"Uncle, you and Franco here start clearing the offices out?"

"You got it."

Rory put his rifle strap over his shoulder. "Alright you two, let's start moving furniture."

As they turned, the elevator on five started moving.

Up.

***

"Find him," Kutuzov snarled.

They'd dispatched the personnel in the control center with merciless efficiency, and Kutuzov had turned back to find their American collaborator … gone. Very inconvenient, if what he said was true and the elevators could only be operated by the thumb reader, and the fire stairs on level six were blocked by a heavy blast-proof door.

The men he sent after Raleigh came jogging back. "He's taken the elevator back up."

Kutuzov cursed. *Coward.* Kutuzov might even have let him live if he'd proved himself a true ally. He should have known the man thought only of his own skin—the way he had executed his own comrades in the lobby could have told him that. It saddened Kutuzov that his nation had to rely on lowlifes like Raleigh to advance its cause. The association was not flattering.

Kutuzov had a thought. He spun on his heels and marched angrily out into the corridor, to where they had encountered the two security officers on arrival. With a sigh of disgust, he pulled a knife from his boot, lifted up the man's hand and sawed off his thumb. *Seriously, you make me do this humiliating thing, traitor?* Kutuzov thought. *This man might have family.*

It occurred to him that if they completed their mission, and incinerated this unholy experiment, then there would be no bodies for the Americans to recover. That thought calmed his conscience. The man's wife would never know.

He straightened and threw the thumb to one of his men. "Try this on that thumb reader, and get that elevator back here."

***

Trigger, Bell and Rory finished piling all the furniture they could find against the sliding elevator doors. Because it was a freight elevator, the doors were at least 20 feet wide and opened in the middle. Their furniture barricade reached all the way across, but only about 4 feet high.

"Where is Franco?" Trigger asked, as Uncle returned.

"Trying to corral 20 panicking civilians into a small room, who just want to get to ground level and run," Uncle said, "anywhere, except here."

"I don't hear any shooting from above," Rory said, cocking an ear to the elevator shaft, then shaking his head. "This is insane. I've seen better protected grade schools."

"It's *Antarctica*," Bell said. "Next stop: South Pole. You can't get a more isolated place. The event yesterday, and now this? These attackers have someone on the inside."

The elevator wasn't moving yet. "They have to be coming here," Trigger said. "Nothing else makes sense." She surveyed the pile of furniture they'd stacked against the elevator doors with an unconvinced glare. Desks, cabinets, chairs piled on top of them … they might surprise the attackers for a second or two, but not much longer than that. *Just give us some clear shots as they try to break out*, Trigger thought. *Even up the odds a little.*

Rory pointed down the corridor back the way Uncle had come. "You take that side; I'll take the near wall. If they push you, pull back to that machine room and try to defend the civilians," Rory said. They'd also lain metal filing cabinets down across the corridor behind them, stacked on each other two deep and two high, to serve as cover. Most were filled with paper, and would probably stop a standard Russian 5.45 mm. round. They wouldn't be any use against grenades. They took up positions behind them, carbines aimed at the doors.

Trigger had line of sight to the elevator display. "It's on the way. Get into cover."

***

Leroi Fontaine emerged into a scene of carnage. He wasn't the first of the security personnel to respond to the silent alarm, but he *was* the only one who arrived armed.

Unfortunately for him, Leroi knew the difference between people who'd been shot in combat and people who'd been executed at close quarters, caught unawares. Only one of his dead workmates looked like she'd realized what was happening, and she'd been shot twice, once in the torso, once in the face.

Cold-blooded murder.

All the personnel in the lobby were contractors, working for the US Antarctic Program, most with private security experience, only one other with a military background. Cath Delaney.

The other contractors were standing in small huddles, talking in muted tones, waiting for Chief Raleigh to appear and take charge. Delaney, his deputy, wasn't waiting. Leroi found her crouched beside the dead woman, lifting the hand away and then putting it back again. She pointed at the body. "Shot here. Fell on her back, put up her hand to protect herself, shot through the hand, into the head," Delaney said. "Small-caliber weapon." She stood and saw the pistol in his hand. "Like that. Hand it over," she said, using her "don't argue" sergeant voice.

But he understood her worry, and handed her his Glock without hesitation, falling straight back into military mode. She smelled it, jacked out the magazine and inspected it. Then handed it back. "Alright, not fired." She frowned. "You smuggled a personal sidearm in."

142

"And glad I did," Leroi said, working the action. "Can you open the armory so we can get at the weapons Chief Raleigh locked away after the audit?"

"I tried on the way here. My access is blocked. Some kind of glitch," she said.

"And no word from the chief?"

"Nothing but static, which is also suspicious, don't you think?" Delaney asked.

"I do." Leroi nodded. "Chief Raleigh said he was here just before we lost comms, before the alarm went off. You think he triggered it? Went after whoever did this?"

"Most likely," Delaney agreed. She looked around the lobby at the half dozen security personnel standing around uselessly.

"Alright, people!" she said, taking charge. "We got to get our shit together, right now. This facility is full of civilian personnel, and there are one or more killers inside. I'll sound the critical incident alarm and make the announcement. Fergus, Belgre, you get to the CCTV servers; review footage of this lobby for the last hour. Call me here when you get it. Boots, Granger, you take levels two to four. Vance, Fellows, five and six. This person or people are armed, and we are not, so do not engage— just report any sightings via fixed line to this position."

"What about the armory?" one of the officers asked. "We need weapons."

"I checked the armory on the way up," Delaney said. "It's locked. Chief Raleigh is the only one who can open it, and he's missing."

"Tasers against firearms?" someone else said. "We need to take shelter ourselves."

"That's not how it works, Boots." She looked at Leroi. "Leroi is armed. He'll stay here, wait for you to report a sighting, and respond. I'll check the other two habitats when I'm done here."

No one moved. "Get going!" Delaney said. "Stay in your pairs. Find this shooter and call it in!"

The lobby started clearing. Delaney ran to the security gate main desk and pulled up a menu on the screen there. "Fire, medical ... come on ... here!" She jammed her finger down on a key. A high-pitched alarm started sounding in bursts of three beats, letting staff know a critical incident was underway. The same sound they'd heard just the day before during the containment emergency. On the desk next to the screen was a handset and dial that directed voice between different floors, habitats or the entire facility. Delaney switched it to "ALL" and grabbed the handset, jamming her thumb down on "SEND" as her voice overrode the alarm. "Attention, attention, this is a security announcement. This is not a drill. We have an active shooter situation in the facility. Please remain calm and shelter in place. Find a secure location, lock or barricade the doors, and turn off any lights. Stay quiet, and do not attempt to leave your location if safe. Follow all instructions from security personnel. Further information will follow." She pulled up the security menu again and set the announcement to repeat every 30 seconds.

"I'll stay here, wait for a call," Leroi said. He looked at the bodies again, bile rising in his throat. They'd trained for just about everything, from petty crime and suicides to drunken or drug-crazed personnel running amok with ice picks. But it was just about the literal middle of *Antarctica*, dammit. A mass shooting just wasn't something you planned for, especially inside a top-secret quasi-military facility.

Delaney grabbed his arm. "You OK? I can take the weapon and respond if we get a sighting."

144

"No. Yeah, I'm good," he told her. "Just find these sick bastards."

A minute later, Leroi Fontaine was alone with the sound of the alarm, and the smell of the dead. He hadn't smelled that particular smell since China, but it came flooding back with overwhelming power again. Warm blood, and the stink of bladders and bowels that had let go.

He couldn't hold the disgust down any longer. Tucking his pistol into the small of his back, he ran to the entry doors, flung one open, staggered through the vestibule, pushed open an outer door and heaved his guts out onto the ice. The frigid air was like a slap in the face, and brought him back to himself, as he stood in the vestibule panting and wiping his mouth.

When he got back inside the lobby, over the sound of the alarm and Delaney's recorded warning, he heard a telephone ringing. He ran to the security desk. The fixed line was buzzing, and he snatched it up. "Fontaine."

"It's some kind of special forces! It's—they—" the voice said. He recognized Fergus, one of the two Delaney had sent to look at the CCTV footage. The man was yelling, the telephone squelching.

"Fergus, slow down, speak normal. I can't understand you." He heard panting, an argument in the background, then Fergus came back on.

"OK, alright. We're looking at the CCTV recording from the lobby. Five or six guys, snow camo, automatic weapons. They disarm the chief and take him away."

Leroi gripped the telephone harder. "You're sure?"

"Watched it twice, man," Fergus said. "He's at the desk, they come in hot, they talk, take his sidearm, and then they … Wait. What did you …?" Leroi heard muffled voices, Ferg and

145

Belgre talking. Then Ferg came back on. "Gets worse. You still there?"

"Yeah." What was that noise? Muffled by the alarm, but around the corner from the lobby? Was that the sound of an elevator bell? His hand crept to the weapon behind his back, but Ferg was still yelling into the phone.

"Belgre says the bodies were already there when the storm troopers arrived. We rolled the video further back. It was the *chief* killed them. Before the others came in." Leroi heard Ferg sucking in air. "The chief, man! He's with them. He killed them all!"

"Okay, I understand, no problem," Leroi said calmly. "Just keep me updated."

"What? You listening? I just said, *Chief Raleigh is the killer.* We got to let the others—"

"All good. You tell the colonel; I'll just wait here," Leroi said, and put the telephone back in its cradle. He stood and waved through the armored glass to the figure walking quickly across the lobby toward him. "Hey, Chief."

***

Anatoliy Kutuzov was standing at the back of the elevator, three men in front of him, and one on each side. The elevator carriages were a decent size, doubling for both personnel and equipment transport, he guessed.

Before they'd stepped into the elevator on five, an alarm had started ringing throughout the facility. "Attention, attention, this is a security announcement …"

Their short-lived element of surprise was lost, it seemed. But what could a small force of unarmed guards do to stop him? Unless that bastard traitor had changed sides again and run up to unlock their armory? Kutuzov could take no chances.

146

"When the doors open, cover left and right," he said tightly. "Shoot anything that moves."

Raleigh had told them the reactor was in the center of the silo-like installation. The elevator jerked to a halt, the doors slid aside, and he lifted his weapon up to his chest.

What the …?

He grabbed the shoulder of the man in front of him and pulled him back. Blocking the exit from the elevator was a chest-high pile of desks, chairs and tables. "Hold!" he barked. The elevator doors chimed and began closing. If the corridor outside the elevators had been wider, if the defenders were armed and had a clear line of fire into the elevator carriage, Kutuzov and his men might all be dead already. Kutuzov leaned forward and jabbed a finger on a button to hold the doors open. Furniture tumbled into the elevator.

He couldn't assume whoever was out there *wasn't* armed— not anymore.

"Roman, Andre, Igor, on my mark, push that top layer of furniture out into the corridor. Dmitri, Ari, frags out. As soon as there is space, you frag left and right. Then we push out. Roman, Andre Igor, left; Dmitri, Ari and me right, understood?"

His men grunted their assent and checked their weapons, two of them pulling fragmentation grenades from belt pouches.

"On three," Kutuzov said, finger still hard down on the elevator door button. "One, two …"

***

Russians. Of course it's Russians, Trigger thought, hearing the voice inside the elevator. Trigger Brown had done a Russian language course in the Navy, and she knew a few phrases. Her favorite was *Ruki vverkh, svin'ya!* (Hands up, swine!) But she also knew how to count to 10, just like she knew that when you heard

147

a Russian voice change from giving orders to counting—*odin, sva*—something bad was going to happen on *tri*.

She started firing short bursts into the elevator door frame even before the first chair toppled from the pile they'd made. She saw a hand, an arm, saw it disappear with a cry of pain. From beside her, Bell did the same, and from the other side, Uncle and Rory sprayed the elevator area with bullets too, a little more wildly.

A table toppled down the pile, another arm emerged, and something flew through the air toward them.

"Grenade!" Trigger yelled, ducking behind the filing cabinets.

It fell short, hitting a wall opposite, bouncing sideways, and exploding low, with a deafening crack. Another crack followed hard on its heels, farther away, nearer to Uncle and Rory. A rain of metal shards hammered into the filing cabinets, but not through them, and ears ringing, Trigger raised her head again to see smoke and white-clad bodies shoving through furniture, trying to bring weapons to bear.

One stumbled as the pile gave way, emerging into the corridor in a tangle of arms and legs, throwing himself to the floor.

Too late. A burst from Rory caught him in the chest and neck, turning him into a ragdoll.

A second attacker rolled out, arm back, ready to fling another grenade. Uncle's next spray of bullets punched him in the back, shoving him forward, his grenade dropping behind him.

Before it exploded, just *outside* the elevator doors.

The last thing Trigger saw as she dropped was Uncle, screaming at the top of his lungs, running straight for the elevators as he sprayed the corridor with automatic fire.

***

Leroi thought fast. Chief Raleigh had given him a small wave and a tight smile. He was still on the other side of the security glass, but headed for the security personnel entrance. Leroi had to let him inside the glass, but not close enough the chief could tackle him.

"Fontaine," Raleigh said, as he pushed the waist-high security barrier aside. "Where is everyone else?"

Another yard, Leroi thought. "Looking for the shooters," Leroi said, hand sliding behind his back as casually as he could move it. He gripped the butt of his Glock.

Chief Raleigh launched himself at Leroi the moment he was through the gate. Leroi saw a glint of metal in his hand, stepped aside and clubbed him on the back of the head with his pistol as he stumbled past, sending him crashing to the ground. A small push dagger clattered to floor.

When Chief Raleigh rolled onto his back and tried to grab the knife, he was looking up into the unmoving barrel of Leroi Fontaine's Glock from 4 feet away.

"Please give me an excuse to end you," Leroi spat. "Just one."

***

Anatoliy Kutuzov was thrown against the back of the elevator carriage not by the grenade blast but by the man in front of him.

He landed heavily, the body on top of him, his rifle jammed under one leg as he tried to free it. He heard screaming outside, someone firing a rifle on full automatic, and as he pushed the bloodied body of his man off him and struggled to free his rifle, a large man in a flight suit with a shock of wild gray hair, blood flowing down his forehead and a crazed look in his

149

eyes, was standing in the buckled doorway to the elevator. Panting. His carbine pointed down at Kutuzov through a tangle of furniture.

He was joined moments later by another pilot, this one taller and broader, also waving a carbine.

"Ruki vverkh, *svin'ya!*" she said, in terrible but unmistakable Russian.

Kutuzov stopped struggling and raised his hands.

Severe Blizzard Warning

December 29, 2041
J-Day minus 2 days

"The test goes ahead," David Lau said, putting down a SATCOM handset.

Six hours had passed since Chief Raleigh and the Russian attackers had been subdued. Two hours since communications with McMurdo and the outside world had been re-established, the mysterious energies jamming their radio and satellite communications stopping as abruptly as they had started.

"You are joking, right?" Solomon Cohen asked. He'd been listening in on Lau's side of the conversation with the US president and director of the CIA. He, Lau, Jansen and Bellings were in an executive meeting room on Concordia's fifth level, having just delivered a report on the Russian attack and reassured the president there had been no material damage. "We have 14 dead. Fourteen! Not counting the dozen Russian bodies in storage in the ice tunnel."

"Maybe it escaped you," Lau said. "That was the *US president* on the line. Not some Pentagon flunky. The president. He's about to convene an emergency session of the National Security Council and raise our alert status to DEFCON 2, the highest it's been since hostilities with the Shanghai Pact ceased. But the test goes ahead."

"I agree with Solomon," Jansen said. "In the last 48 hours, we've faced sabotage, an attack by a Russian submarine on our submersible and now an assault by Russian commandos that cost 14 innocent people their lives." She shook her head sadly. "To expect us to continue is not only unreasonable; it is *madness.*"

"We thought we mitigated the risk of a hostile intervention by moving here for the final phase," Sandilands said. "Espionage, cyberattack, covert operatives, even a full-scale military assault—all were supposed to be negated by this location. The security assessment said a security force of 30 would be sufficient, and we went with 60! Yes, in hindsight we underestimated the security threat. We didn't allow for our attackers having inside help from the head of our security team. There should have been more oversight of Chief Raleigh, and alarm bells should have been raised when he ordered all weapons to be returned to the armory for an audit." He tapped the table to make it clear he felt strongly. "But the enemy has failed. What matters now is the integrity of the weapon and the test timeline. Neither of those has been compromised."

"The crisis is over," Bellings said. "Raleigh and the surviving Russian are locked up. There is no reason to delay."

"We don't know if Raleigh was the only one the Russians got inside Project Minerva," Solomon said. "He hasn't said a word since he was taken into custody. There could be others."

"If we delay the test, the Russians win," Lau said.

"This isn't a win-lose thing," Jansen protested, fixing Lau with a pleading look. "People are in shock. They lost friends, work colleagues. They aren't battle-hardened Marines. You can't just call them together, give them a rousing speech and put them back to work. They need psychological support, counseling. They need to know they're safe …"

For the first time since arriving at Concordia, Lau's executives saw the normally unflappable colonel lose his cool. "Dammit, this isn't a research lab on a university campus full of snowflake undergrads playing around with theoretical physics!" Sandilands said. "This is the most important weapons research program the US has ever attempted, and *every day* matters. We could have lost the war with China if it had just dragged on another few months and Dr. Lau's team there was able to finish its work. Now, half of his people are in Russia, working day and night to beat us to a viable weapon." Sandilands glared at Jansen and Cohen, with pinpoint pupils. "What do you think will happen if Russia gets antimatter weapons before us? You think they'll just do a test in the middle of an ocean just to show us how clever they are?"

"No, they'll obliterate a naval port in the Baltics, or an air base in Poland." Cohen sighed. "And demand NATO pulls out of Eastern Europe."

Lau raised a hand gently, to quiet Sandilands. "That is more or less word for word what President Bendheim said to me," Lau noted. "We have a task force of Navy ships and aircraft out in the Southern Ocean waiting for this test. And a nation's security riding on it." He pinched the bridge of his nose, closing his eyes. "Which … What do we do about the Aggressor personnel?"

***

The Aggressor personnel had a bizarre few hours after resolving the attack on the station. First, they'd been sent to the medical clinic, where they were checked over for injuries. Not just those from Aggressor Inc., but the engineer, Venice, too. Then they'd been put in an interview room together, and a base security specialist called Delaney had appeared. "So the doctor tells me you're all fit for duty," she said. "Which is amazing, considering."

"You got Raleigh and that Russian locked up tight, I hope," Rory said. "They would kill their guards in a heartbeat if they saw a chance to escape."

"I know it." She nodded. "They killed 14 personnel, outright. No wounded; they were all just executed. Chief Raleigh killed six."

"The Russian will probably get renditioned and then traded for American prisoners in Russia, but Raleigh ... I hope he fries, or hangs, or whatever Antarctic law allows," Uncle said.

Delaney gave him a bleak look. "There is no Antarctic law," she said.

"What?" Trigger asked.

"There's been at least a half dozen murders in Antarctica since the first base was established here. People gone crazy with pickaxes, a couple jealous lovers, drugs, a poisoning ... not a single one properly investigated, no one ever charged. Raleigh would have known that."

"You are joking." Rory shook his head.

"Wish I was. Antarctic treaties cover a lot of things, but investigating murders isn't one. It's always left to the country whose base it is, and none of them are interested in publicizing murders at their bases, so they all get swept under a rug."

"You can't sweep 14 bodies under a rug," Bell pointed out. "Even, like, figuratively."

"No, but you can call it a terrorist attack at a national security facility and throw a big black official secrets blanket over it," Delaney said, then made a hand gesture taking in the Aggressor personnel. "Which leads me to you five."

Venice looked severely pained. "Us? I was locked in the cockpit with Director Lau through the whole thing." She looked to Rory. "Right?"

Before Rory could answer, Delaney interrupted. "There were 10 Russian bodies out on the ice, and all five of you were in the aircraft that killed them."

"Luckily for you," Uncle growled.

Delaney growled back at him. "*And* five dead Russians down at level six. You know what the Russian captain you captured is saying?"

"Some kind of total BS, I'm guessing."

"He's saying he and his men were sent here to conduct an unannounced inspection of Concordia Station, as allowed under Antarctic Treaty protocols. He says Russia received intelligence we were conducting weapons research here, in breach of those protocols."

"A heavily *armed* inspection?" Trigger asked sarcastically. "Under cover of an electronic warfare attack? Accompanied by a coincidental mass shooting event?"

"He says his people were armed for self-defense only, and you opened fire on them without warning, as they approached the base."

"They shot at Director Lau!" Venice said.

"Was that before or after you people opened up on them with a 25 mm. cannon?" Delaney asked. "Then, according to the Russian captain, chased them down through the facility and tried to slaughter them on level six?"

"That is crazy," Rory said, shaking his head. "No one believes him, I hope."

Delaney gave him a tight smile. "Not for a New York minute."

"Good."

155

"But you all have to give statements," Delaney said. "In writing, separately. We already have Director Lau's. Who sends his profound thanks for saving all our asses, by the way, or would do, if he wasn't a self-obsessed, ungrateful robot."

"Alright, girl," Trigger said, holding out a hand to high-five Delaney. "But next time, tell us what you really think."

"Wait, so, we're *not* all going to be investigated over what happened?" Venice asked, frowning.

"I'm sure you will," Delaney said. "In the way of things. Your statements will be read into the record. A report will be written, filed and forgotten. Ten years from now, one of you might be tempted to write a book about today, and you'll get a polite knock on the door from some agents in black suits, and your manuscript will be filed and forgotten too."

"Way I like it," Rory said. "I have looked upon the world for seven times seven years; and I have seen that the world is full of secrets."

Uncle frowned. "Was that Mark Twain or something?"

Rory shook his head. "Shakespeare. Othello. I got more if you want to hear 'em."

"No, thank you."

Delaney continued. "So the ungrateful Director Lau has asked me to ask you if you still consider yourselves mission capable," Delaney asked. "Considering he still needs you to get his device out into the middle of the Southern Ocean, so it can do whatever it is that it is supposed to do."

They'd written up their statements and gone back to mission planning with Venice—Trigger and Bell to decide how to rig *Charlene* for the trip under the ice and out to sea with the Juliet device, Rory and Uncle to plan the flight out to McMurdo, and then to the NOAA observation platform, with whatever

156

payload it was decided they would be carrying for their decoy mission.

That was when Trigger announced she wanted herself and Bell to hitch a ride on Outlaw when they moved the bomb to McMurdo so it could be loaded aboard *Charlene*.

"With us?" Rory asked. "Makes sense. Concordia is going to be socked in by the storm. And the Russians showed how easily they can shut down Concordia's comms. You can run the submersible out of McMurdo."

"Makes sense," Bell agreed. "Not that I'm crazy about sharing a ride with an 80-megaton bomb."

"Not just to McMurdo," Trigger said. "If they could compromise Concordia's comms, they could shut down McMurdo too. It isn't some hardened military facility. They just need to get a drone or long-range electronic warfare aircraft overhead at the right time, and we'd be screwed too. That submarine we evaded could be carrying cruise missiles zeroed in on Concordia or McMurdo. We're safer in the air than we are anywhere else."

"What are you thinking?" Bell asked.

"We can pilot *Charlene* from aboard Outlaw," Trigger said. She turned to Rory. "Outlaw is hardened against EW attack, and O'Hare will be flying shotgun for us."

Venice didn't look convinced. "We'd be putting all our eggs in a 40-year-old basket," she said. Then looked at Rory a little sheepishly. "No offense."

"None taken. I assume you're referring to Outlaw, not Uncle," Rory said. "And Outlaw *is* an old dog—but with the best bag of new tricks that a billionaire can buy, and she's tooled up with the newest hardware the USAF has in its inventory, protected by our best pilot, in a flying *tank*, thanks to your Director Lau and his White House benefactors."

Uncle was also looking a little perturbed too. "She's right though. If something happens to us …"

"*Charlene* would already be on autopilot and sailing herself to the ops area. Two-Tone and the Aggressor relief crew in Auckland could take over for the final run in," Trigger said. "You might lose your decoy, but you wouldn't lose your boat."

Venice opened her mouth to object again, but Trigger interrupted. "It's not just jamming that could screw up our comms," she said. "If the blizzard hits McMurdo while our boat is in transit, ice crystals in the atmosphere could cause signal scattering. Our safest bet is an airborne control platform, right overhead, which can avoid the storm and cut the distance our signals have to travel."

They played around with the variables until Anna Venice was happy. Rory didn't mind her asking the tough questions; their plan was the better for it. And she asked good questions.

"You know, I'm thinking, we could use a weaponeer on this mission," Rory said to Trigger before they broke up. "To keep an eye on Juliet."

Brown saw where he was going before Venice did. "Right. Definitely. But who the hell can we bring into the mission at this late stage that knows the device inside and out?"

"Gee, I don't know," Rory said, as they both turned to stare at Venice.

"What? Me? No … I …" she stuttered. "It's designed to be initialized remotely. You don't need a 'weaponeer.' And besides, I'm a particle engineer; I'm not military."

Uncle feigned disapproval. "Neither are we. Military operations are not permitted on Antarctica."

To Trigger's surprise, Venice didn't kill the idea dead. "Uh, what exactly could you use me for?" she asked.

"You saw how easily things go sideways if our comms get jammed," Rory told her. "So imagine we're 30 minutes out from the test, and they can't get that signal out of Concordia to initialize the device. Now, instead, imagine you were circling in an aircraft overhead of the submersible carrying Juliet."

"I don't know," Venice said. "We've been working toward this moment for two years. You've all been rehearsing for it, though you didn't know it at the time. I haven't. Last-minute changes like this …"

Rory held up a hand to quiet her. "*Enola Gay*. You know the name?"

"Of course, the bomber that dropped the first atom bomb." Venice frowned. "Your boss mentioned it the other day. Why?"

"Not many people know that Colonel Tibbets, the pilot who flew *Enola Gay* over Hiroshima, wasn't *Enola Gay*'s normal pilot. That man was Robert A. Lewis. He was swapped out for the mission and flew as copilot instead. They also trained two weaponeers to arm the bomb and only decided which one would fly the mission just before takeoff. Any mission like this, you take the best person for the job when it's go time, and as mission commander, that's what I'm doing."

Venice bit her lip and nodded. "Alright, I think I can sell it to DD Cohen and the colonel."

Uncle gave her a fist bump. "Welcome aboard the good ship Outlaw."

***

Bunny O'Hare had arrived in VHF range of Concordia as the crew of Outlaw was doing their preflight planning.

Her radio call was patched through to Rory.

"Thank you for your concern, Captain, but we muddled through without you," Rory said. He filled her in on the outcome

159

of melee of the day before and looked at his watch. "We're getting the bullet holes in Outlaw patched and changing the tires. You have enough fuel to hang around until we take off 0400 and fly overwatch to McMurdo?"

"Not unless you want me to walk half the way," Bunny told him. "I'm loaded for bear. I'll declare an emergency—for the record—and put down at Concordia to refuel."

"Typical Air Force," Trigger said, loud enough O'Hare could easily hear her. "Miss all the work, just fly in for the beer and hot dogs."

"Oh, well, when we get to McMurdo, maybe I can help you fill the hole in your submersible you left when you shat your payload and ran from that Russian sub, Trigger?" Bunny replied. "Always happy to help."

"Fill it with your tattooed ass," Trigger muttered.

"Ladies, heads back in the game, please," Rory said with a smile. "See you down here, O'Hare. Concordia out."

***

"So you're saying one of our moving parts has stopped moving?" Major General Tomas Arsharvin, of the Main Intelligence Directorate of the GRU, said with a sigh. The view out the window of his office toward the gray Argut River was as uninspiring as his mood.

His SVR foreign intelligence counterpart, Deputy Director (Science) Artur Eizen, was looking worried. He nodded. "Our source inside Concordia missed a scheduled report-in. His last communications said the base was going into a communications lockdown, but he would still be able to get a message out. That was six hours ago."

Arsharvin looked at his watch. It was seven hours since his Spetsnaz team had been due to hit the American base, with the

160

help of Eizen's "human source." They had not turned up for their extraction rendezvous, and like Eizen's source, there had been no communication from them, either.

"The assault on the American base failed," Arsharvin said, stating the obvious. "Your source said it was a science facility and only lightly defended. Your intelligence was wrong."

Eizen reddened. "You are already trying to allocate blame? Do you want me to point out your GRU has an *outstanding* record of incompetence, from the Skripal poisonings to your failed Montenegro coup, and more recently your clumsy attempts to bug foreign diplomatic offices, which resulted in the arrest of 15 of your people across Europe? And yet you talk to me about failure?"

Arsharvin ignored the outburst. "Luckily for Mother Russia, we have not been entirely reliant on the SVR for our intelligence on the American project," Arsharvin said. "And we planned for multiple contingencies."

Eizen laughed. "You are referring to the *Sarov*? That leaky old bucket and its semi-retired captain are your contingency plan?"

Arsharvin turned back from the window and sat at his desk, opposite the spymaster. "Only one of them, my dear Eizen, only one. Your *Sluzhba Vneshney Razvedki* has been suffering from funding starvation for the last decade whereas our military branches—which the GRU is pleased to serve—have been slowly and surely building back, despite recent setbacks. Where you make excuses, we have been making preparations."

Eizen scowled. "What is that supposed to mean?"

"It means what I said," Arsharvin said. "You have seen but a fraction of the force we have put in place for this action."

Eizen was clearly annoyed, and not just at having failure thrown in his face. "Your grand plan must be informed by intelligence beyond that which our human source was able to provide," Eizen said. "And you, of all people, must know how dangerous it is to depend only on signals and cyber-intelligence."

Arsharvin steepled his fingers, raising his eyebrows. "Ah, but I agree. That is why we developed our own *human* source inside the American project. And I can assure you, our source did not miss their last communication window."

"And yet you shared none of this with me. Such trust," Eizen said. "Why is it we must always be our own worst enemies?"

"I think Uncle Joe Stalin said it best: *Trust is good, but control is better.*"

***

USAP Meteorologist, Donovan Grant knew all about war. Not the petty wars that man fought against man. In fact, if you'd asked, Grant would have called himself a pacifist, as far as military matters were concerned.

No, Grant was a resistance fighter in the only war that he felt really mattered—the fight for Mother Earth, against the brutal insouciance of Man. He'd done everything he could to make an individual contribution ... sacrificed part of his salary to the Sea Shepherd organization to fund its fights against whaling and overfishing, added his name to petitions, joined marches, written to members of Congress, worked in the Arctic and Antarctic as part of projects documenting the melting of the ice at the poles and its catastrophic consequences.

None of it had mattered. The ice kept melting. Too little, too late, the small contributions of a million climate activists had been dwarfed by the greed of the big corporations, the blind politicians, the billionaires with their spaceships and undersea biodomes, prepping to desert the sinking ship and leave the unwashed billions behind. He had even begun considering suicide—until the day, that one fateful day, when Saara had messaged him.

The contact had been so unremarkable he had almost ignored it. She was a PhD student at Helsinki University, fascinated by his research. More than fascinated, it transpired after he finally got back to her. She was *outraged*. How could the world ignore his warnings? How could his superiors in the US Antarctic Program be so apathetic? How could *she* help?

She'd invited him to speak at a student gathering at her university, and her wealthy father had paid for his airfare. That gathering had turned into a sit-in at the Finnish Fisheries Authority, which the Helsinki police had broken up, ending with Saara and Donovan running hand in hand through back alleys to avoid arrest. Ending at the bottom of a bottle of vodka. Ending with Donovan in Saara's bed, in her tiny flat high above the Bohemian streets of Kallio.

He'd nearly missed his latest deployment, reluctant to leave her, but she'd insisted because his work was too important. From their very first interactions, they'd communicated only through encrypted apps, which Saara insisted on, since she had ambitions to work in the USA one day, and a discoverable record of climate activism would not look good on her visa application.

He'd kept Saara updated on his work at Concordia, and shared with her his shock and disgust as the base transitioned from Antarctic climate research to … to what? He hadn't been sure at first. Energy research? His work evolved from providing weather advice to researchers pulling ice cores from the million-year-old ice around Concordia to advice on flying conditions for the nearly daily flights suddenly ferrying personnel and materiel into Concordia for the mysterious Project Minerva.

He'd considered quitting, but Saara convinced him to hang in. They couldn't communicate on video link; that wasn't safe.

But he had a photo of her face against her profile in their messaging app, and he gazed at it longingly whenever they connected and he unburdened about the asshats he was increasingly surrounded by.

"Maybe this energy project is really something?" she'd said. "Imagine. Clean energy that could power entire cities without pollution or radioactive waste? That's *amazing*, Donovan!" She wanted to know everything. Suddenly his contribution wasn't meaningless. Not to Saara, at least.

Then Project Minerva had turned dark. Donovan had been security cleared and briefed on what he thought was its true purpose—an antimatter forge, buried in the ice. Nuclear research on Antarctica was *banned*. They could try to argue an antimatter forge wasn't a fission or fusion reactor, but it was still nuclear, right? And it was producing antimatter at industrial scale. Beyond the amount needed for basic scientific research. What for? More reactors?

"I have to blow the whistle on this," he'd messaged Saara. "The world has to know what is happening down here."

She'd agreed. She'd offered to be his conduit, to help disguise his identity. "Send me everything you have. Anything you can get—anything at all. I will put it all together, and when the time is right, I will help you expose them."

He'd sent her weekly summaries of what he saw and heard, but she wasn't happy with that. "We can't decide what's important and what's not," she'd said. "Everything about this project is wrong. Everything is important. Just send me every detail—emails, reports, digital records—and I will compile it. Index and reference it. The world can decide what is important and what is not."

She was streetwise beyond her years. Wiser than him. He sent her *everything* he could lay his hands on. Details large and small. Thousands of files pulled from Concordia servers. His access was limited but still substantial. He gave her everything, from the telephone list that held contact details for every person on the base to the meteorological data requests he got from the various research and logistics teams and the "motivational" progress reports helpfully sent to staff by its egomaniacal director.

After a year on Project Minerva, he'd decided he wanted out. His conscience was plaguing him. Every day he worked at Concordia was a day he would have to atone for in hell; he was sure of that. He'd joined USAP to save the planet, not to help the US government develop some kind of new superweapon that could destroy it. And, of course, there was the constant fear of being discovered.

"You *can't* leave now," Saara told him, whenever his courage flagged. She threw the name of the greatest whistleblower in modern history at him. "Snowden left too early. If he'd stayed in longer, his impact could have been 10 times greater. A hundred times!"

"Snowden got out before he was arrested," Grant had pointed out.

"And you are not the kind of guy who puts your own well-being before the fate of this planet," Saara had chastised him. "They can put you in jail, but your information will still be free, and the world will hear your voice. I will make sure of it," she said. "Even if it puts me behind bars too."

Grant was coming up on the end of his contract. He and Saara had a plan. He would gather the data, he would serve out his contract, and then they would both get off the grid. They had irrefutable proof that the US was conducting banned activities on Antarctica.

And now, 'Lema' Lau had confirmed his worst fear. Grant's soul had been crushed. He had been, indirectly, helping develop a *weapon* all this time. And they were about to test it.

You couldn't hide an 80-megaton explosion. The world would be in a state of uproar. Mass panic even. The world media would be desperate for information, and Grant and Saara could provide it. Saara had spoken with her father, and he supported their work, 100 percent. Grant had googled him. The guy was huge in tech and finance. Saara said he would get them the best lawyers, fly them both to a country that didn't have an extradition treaty with the US. So they could be safe. So they could be together.

Three months earlier, Saara had sent him a "care package" containing an encrypted satellite phone he could reach her on, even if his official access to the outside world was cut. "Find technical details of these 'Bellings Traps.' We need as much scientific documentation as we can get, to convince people our material is authentic."

"How did you get this kind of technology?" he'd messaged to her in wonder at the encrypted phone.

"My father has deep pockets," she'd replied. "He is one of the few 'good' rich guys. I can't wait for him to meet you. He wants the same thing as us—a safe world, a healthy planet. When I told him what the Americans are doing in the Antarctic, his fury was incandescent."

Incandescent.

That was how Donovan Grant felt, now the J-Day test was confirmed. At that moment, he imagined the fury that burned in his guts could melt through to Antarctica's bedrock.

But he had to keep the information flowing to Saara, and his eyes fully on the prize. Even as the scientists and soldiers of Minerva took the world to the edge of oblivion, he and Saara were holding the safety line that would pull it back again. The world would soon know *everything*, and America would not be able to obscure the truth behind whatever fiction it was planning to create.

The Russian attack on Concordia? That had been wild. Terrifying, but he hadn't been surprised. America's enemies would have to be blind and deaf not to be worried about what was happening at Concordia, even if they didn't know exactly what was going on. And he couldn't blame Russia for trying to stop it. *The enemy of my enemy is my ally*—wasn't that what the old adage said? Russia wanted to destroy the forge and stop this insane weapons program? Well, so did Donovan Grant.

***

There were no beers or hot dogs for Bunny O'Hare. Apart from her brief refueling stop, most of her flight down from Macquarie Island had been on autopilot, and she had catnapped. So she caught up with the Aggressor team, grabbed a bacon and egg roll, got unofficially "indoctrinated" into Project Minerva and was giving herself a "field wash" with a wet wipe when Trigger walked into the ladies'.

"Holy shit," Trigger said, closing the door behind her. "That is an insane amount of ink."

Bunny O'Hare had a tattoo on her body for every comrade lost, every battle won, and every lover who'd betrayed her. It had been a short but traumatic life, and she didn't have much real estate left for new tattoos, so she wasn't surprised by Trigger's comment. She reached for her T-shirt and pulled it on again, slipping one arm into the flight suit hanging around her waist. "Yeah, well, you show me yours, I'll show you mine."

Trigger stood beside her at the washbasin and pulled up the left sleeve of her uniform. The tattoo there showed a Panda in a conical hat, with its eyes screwed up in pain, a very large torpedo sticking out of its backside. Bunny whistled. "OK, that's not subtle."

Trigger rolled her sleeve down again. "I know. But would you believe some snowflake in my own crew reported me to my CO for racism?"

"Would this snowflake have been Chinese American?" Bunny asked.

"Goddamn Chinese American snowflake, yeah," Trigger said. "I had to do a written apology. Got an AI to write it."

Bunny started zipping her suit up. "You know, I am so glad you joined the Aggressor team, Brown."

Trigger looked at her with suspicion. "Oh, yeah?"

Bunny slapped her on the shoulder, heading for the door. "Yeah. Until you arrived, everyone thought *I* was the mad bastard."

***

Minerva-J, nicknamed 'Juliet,' was loaded aboard the AC-130X Outlaw at 0310 on December 29, 2041. A severe blizzard warning was in effect, with visibility low and winds at the US Concordia base gusting to 28 knots as Outlaw and its escort taxied out to takeoff. Bunny was playing a mind game with herself, writing her epitaph as she sat in her Nemesis on the flight line at Concordia beside Outlaw.

She looked across at him. It was funny how she thought of most airplanes as "her," but not Outlaw. Outlaw was definitely a "he." An ass-whomping, take-a-punch-to-the-jaw-and-keep-fighting bar brawler.

As she strapped in, Bunny was wondering what the official history would say, if the J-Day test was successful. Would Aggressor Inc. personnel even get a mention in it? Of course, if

Outlaw's coming transit flight somehow failed, there would be no official history, only a classified after-action report in which the names of the crew of Outlaw might well be redacted.

She ran through her preflight checklist and stopped at the radar warning receiver. Grinspoon and the RAAF ground crew at Macquarie Island had checked it and found nothing wrong. And she hadn't seen a radiation spike on the way in to Concordia this time. Which only made her more suspicious. A Russian sub. Russian Spetsnaz. A radiation spike where there should not be one, and then *not* there where it should be?

She pulled up her ordnance menu. Internal: 10 AIM-260 missiles, range 10 to 150 nautical miles. Two CUDA short-range missiles. External hardpoints: two parachute-retarded Very Light Torpedoes in case that smartass Russian submarine tried to bother anyone, anywhere, and two GAMBIT air-combat drones, one in air-to-air and one in electronic warfare configuration.

Next, she checked her takeoff weight. She'd only loaded enough fuel for McMurdo plus 20 minutes at military power in case of … contingencies. But, *oh baby,* she was heavy.

She was going to need as much runway as Concordia could give her.

***

Trigger had eyed the device in their payload bay with undisguised distrust before she strapped herself into a seat inside Outlaw's command module, beside Bell and their newly appointed "weaponeer," Anna Venice.

It had seemed innocuous enough: a matte-black cube 4 feet by 4 feet, with a few blinking lights and an LCD panel on it, which a team of engineers had checked way too often for Trigger's liking until Rory booted them off his aircraft.

169

Trigger had watched it being loaded and secured by the Concordia ground crew, standing beside Venice. She didn't look much more relaxed than Brown felt. "What actually is inside that box? Layman's explanation," Trigger asked her.

Venice swallowed visibly. "A year's production of invisible antimatter, which is 2 kilos, held in a vacuum by an incredibly strong magnetic field, generated by power cells that can keep it stable for about 24 hours." She smiled. "But right now it is plugged into the aircraft's power, so that's, um, good."

"OK, but if the magnetic field fails …"

"The magnetic field is *designed* to fail, on command," Venice said unhelpfully. "A signal will be sent to activate the trap-failure once your submersible reaches the test area, 20 hours from McMurdo."

"And when the trap fails … boom?"

"Big *bada* boom," Venice said, without a trace of humor. "All of which is why taking it overland to McMurdo isn't an option. That's a two-week traverse. Too long and too many ways for something to go wrong."

Trigger had turned to Rory. "You still want to bitch about how you don't get to fly that thing out into the Southern Ocean?"

He didn't have to answer. His face told the story.

Trigger was going to use the trip to McMurdo to run remote system checks on *Charlene*, after the new cargo module was installed in her payload bay. She would be carrying Juliet, and the module was designed so the bomb could be plugged in and pull power from her fuel cells. Venice was going to spend the flight being trained by Bell in how to use the comms equipment in case Outlaw was needed to send the trigger signal to arm Juliet.

Trigger couldn't help but notice that Elvis Bell was already being *particularly* patient and helpful in instructing the petite scientist how to strap herself in. It was quite sickening.

"Uh, you two probably want to hurry up and buckle the hell up," Trigger said to them, as Rory turned Outlaw at the end of Concordia's runway and faced it into the near-gale-force wind.

To be honest, their banter disturbed Trigger's normally Zen-like focus. Rory and Uncle were about to light a booster rocket under Outlaw's ass, and Trigger was trying to calm a bad case of preflight heebie-jeebies that she was not going to admit to anyone. Rory had assured her they'd tested the jet-assisted takeoff (JATO) system with heavier payloads than today, but Trigger had never seen an AC-130 perform a JATO takeoff in a damn gale, from an ice runway. And more to the point, not with *her* inside, sitting next to a freaking doomsday bomb.

Once we get off the ground, we'll be fine, she told herself. She replayed the comforting words of Colonel Sandilands, who had dropped into their mission planning session. "Anyone who might try to interfere with your flight, like Russia or China, would have to already be based at Chinese or Russian airfields on Antarctica, which Space Force assures us they aren't, or fly some crazy-ass mission from South Africa or South America without us knowing, which they can't, *and* get past your FB-22 escort, which they won't."

Trigger wished O'Hare had looked happier at that vote of confidence.

The engines spooled up, and Trigger leaned her head back against the seat's headrest. It was hard to know if the AC-130X was shaking so badly because of the raw horsepower Rory and Uncle were urging from the engines or the winds buffeting the fuselage from three directions. After three combat deployments with the Navy, and a year with Aggressor Inc., there weren't many aviation firsts left for Trigger Brown to notch on her bedpost, but this was about to be her first JATO roll. The module they were in had no external view, but she could feel Outlaw straining against its brakes, whining to be released like a racehorse in the starter's stalls, and then they jerked forward. Trigger started counting with her eyes closed … *one Mississippi, two Mississippi* … until at *18 Mississippi*, just before she figured they had to be about to run out of runway, with a teeth-rattling roar, the four jets either side of the fuselage ignited, their nose rotated to about 45 degrees, and Outlaw screamed into the sky like an F-35C on full afterburner blasting off the deck of a carrier.

Trigger screwed her eyes tight and waited for something on the 40-year-old machine to fall off, like a wing.

At *30 Mississippi*, the roar died as suddenly as it had started, the nose bunted down, Trigger went weightless and floated up against her harness, and Venice let out a small scream. From outside the module, Trigger heard equipment come loose and clatter around the cargo hold.

Trigger swung her seat back around. Bell looked as surprised as she felt, to still be alive.

"I *never* want to do that again," Bell said through gritted teeth. "I'm a damn submariner. Man was not meant to fly, and certainly never like that."

"Oh, but man was made to dive 500 feet deep in the ocean in a nuclear-powered drainpipe?" Trigger asked.

"We evolved from sea animals, not birds, so yeah, we are."

"That was *insane*," Venice said with a big grin. "Will we be doing that again tomorrow?"

Trigger brought up her comms menu and dialed up a link to their operations base at McMurdo. "McMurdo's runway is longer and conditions should be better. So, maybe not," she told Venice.

"Aw."

Rory's voice came over speakers in the bulkhead. "Captain speaking. Hope no one lost any fillings. We are outbound Concordia and have just contacted McMurdo ATC. We have a nice tailwind and flying time today will be two hours 30. Conditions expected at McMurdo are for light winds, good visibility and a balmy 30 degrees. Ladies and gentleman, please sit back, and enjoy your flight."

Venice looked too relaxed, which just pissed Trigger off.

She raised her voice to be heard above the roar of the engines. "Hey, science geek. I heard tools bouncing around the cargo hold. You maybe want to check one of them didn't put a hole in your bomb?"

***

"Signal energy at zero nine four degrees. USAF VHF frequency."

"That's our target. Show me the escort."

Colonel Roman Gusev's heads-up visor display blinked, and two boxed crosses appeared in glowing green on the bronze background, showing him the position of their target and the US stealth fighter.

"Same one as yesterday. AI is still coming up blank," Adamov said. "But I checked the webpage for this Aggressor Inc. Very helpful. They run F-22 Raptors and P-99 Black Widows, and they just bought six FB-22 'Nemeses'—a strike fighter, based on the Raptor, that never went into service."

"So if it isn't in our database, it's a Nemesis," Gusev guessed. "We'll treat it with the respect we'd give a Raptor, until it shows us otherwise."

"That's one *big* return though," Adamov said. "Like it wants us to see it."

173

"Maybe it does," Gusev mused. "You feeling scared, Captain? Maybe we should abort ..."

"Your sarcasm is hurtful, Colonel Gusev. Targets are locked; AA-13s armed. Su-71s armed."

"You are clear to engage. Send Monochromes."

"Sending Su-71 Monochromes, copy," Adamov replied, tapping icons on the flat panel in front of him.

What made the Tu-190 *Envoy* Russia's most formidable airborne weapons platform was not just its stealth and advanced radar. The threat could be boiled down to four words: 20 *tons* of ordnance. Among its loadout options was the system Adamov was about to unleash: the twin diagonally stacked air-to-air missile magazines, each carrying either 20 AA-13 Axehead long-range hypersonic missiles or 20 AA-12 Adder near-hypersonic medium-range missiles. But the missile magazines were not all the *Envoy* was packing.

"Targets 10 degrees off our nose, altitude 25,000, range to targets 190 and 180. Monochromes set to semi-autonomous, flanking attack. Launching."

Thanks to their QE radar, they had perfect missile solutions on their adversaries, who were completely unaware they were about to die. Inside the *Envoy*'s payload bay, mounted along its centerline, were four Su-71 Monochrome air-launched autonomous combat drones. Adamov was about to send one north of their first target and another south of the second. At his command, they would go "active" and launch missiles at the two targets.

The payload bay doors flipped open, the two drones were kicked out inside a second, and the doors snapped shut again. Delta-shaped wings snapped out from small dolphin-like bodies, and the two drones lit their turbofan engines and accelerated to 600 knots as they flew downrange, on headings that would put the targets in a pincer grip. Gusev yawed his aircraft, keeping its knife-edged wing oriented toward the American fighter as he swung around to increase separation with the Americans again.

He didn't expect the air-launched combat aircraft to bring down the American fighter, if its pilot was half-awake. But they were disposable and only needed to distract the enemy long enough for Gusev to sneak through his killer punch.

***

It was quiet. Too damned quiet.

O'Hare's Nemesis was cruising through snowy skies at 20,000 feet, sprinting and drifting so that she put herself 10 miles ahead of Outlaw before she swung around to let it overtake her as she checked its six, then got ahead of it again. Optical sensors were near useless in this weather, but her infrared and radar worked fine … and showed her nothing.

Bunny had put herself in the Russians' shoes. They'd tried sabotage. They'd tried armed infiltration. Neither had worked, but clearly, they had someone on the inside in Project Minerva, feeding them intel.

It was the only explanation.

Which meant they would know the bomb was being moved, and that made it vulnerable.

That little devil on her shoulder called "insecurity" was chirping at her, though. *You're being paranoid, O'Hare. Again. Russia has nothing in its air force that can reach this far south. Submarines, sure. Ships, maybe. But not aircraft. That's why you are up here in a plane that lost an Air Force competition to something 20 years older. Alone.*

No. That wasn't fair. She liked the FB-22 Nemesis. Didn't love it … yet. Love had to be earned. But it was a little like her

175

soulmate, the Black Widow. Not as much punch, but if it ever got into a knife fight she—

Spike.

There it was again. The damn radiation spike on her radar warning receiver—a quick flash, then gone. Over the ice 100 klicks out of Concordia now? No, no, no … this was not something down on the ground; this was something in the bloody air. The signal—if that's what it was—was no coincidence.

"Aggressor Two, Aggressor One, we might have company," she said. "Recommend you get down with the penguins. I'm launching GAMBITs."

Rory knew better than to fire questions at her, even though he must have had dozens. "Good copy, One. Two going low."

Bunny kept her radar in search mode and hit the button that would release her two GAMBIT drones. Her Nemesis bumped higher as the weight disappeared from her wings, and she shoved the nose down again, then banked hard left to take herself on an oblique angle to the possible contact. The two GAMBITs fell into formation, one off her port wing, the other off her starboard wing, waiting for orders.

No, a radiation spike wasn't a *contact*. But then what the hell was it?

She brought up a tactical map, trying to work out where an attack might come from. The most likely vector was behind them, to the west. Russia had two research stations back there, both with ice runways. Even farther back were Russian bases at friendly nations like South Africa and Chile. She tapped a sector directly behind them and sent one GAMBIT toward it in search mode. Tapped another sector, a little north of it, and sent her second GAMBIT there, also in search mode. *RoE, Bunny*, she reminded herself as she armed the missiles on one drone and the

176

electronic warfare suite on the other. *Don't shoot until shot at.* Even after the Spetsnaz assault on Concordia, Two-Tone had reinforced that their RoE hadn't changed. She was flying a nominally civilian aircraft, and civilian aircraft did not shoot first.

Yup. And if a Russian falls in Antarctica, will anybody hear?

She soon had three radars sweeping the sky around them, but still nothing. She had her GAMBITs sweep wider, sending them high and low.

She was scanning the sky, eyes flicking to instruments as she yawed her aircraft left and right to give its passive infrared sensors a chance at picking up any movement in the sky. Rory's voice in her ears nearly made her jump.

"One, Two is down at 500 feet," Rory said. "We're skiing the moguls here. I don't like the air this low, so you let me know as soon as it's safe to take us higher."

Bunny had her focus on both her tactical monitor and the data streaming to her from her two drone wingmen. Was she overreacting? She was burning precious fuel, her separation to Outlaw increasing uncomfortably. No. Something felt wrong. "Just assume we're *not* safe until you put down at McMurdo," Bunny suggested. "And even then. One out."

She opened windows on her tactical display showing the 360° picture of the airspace around Outlaw, generated by her radars and the data being fed to her thanks to saturation coverage by low earth orbit micro-comms satellites, which in turn was relaying data from the air traffic control radar at McMurdo, the Australian AWACS aircraft to their northeast and even the *Constellation* class frigate USS *Congress* out in the Southern Ocean.

She also flicked through their USAP, USAF and USN radio cooperation channels like a nervous card player shuffling a deck, listening for anything out of the ordinary.

And she heard it.

A chime in her ears, and an icon appeared on her helmet visor, tagged by her electronic warfare, or EW, GAMBIT. She got straight on the radio. "Rory, GAMBIT Two has picked up an unidentified fast mover west-northwest. I am moving to intercept and identify." She pushed the data from the GAMBIT to Outlaw's tactical display, so Rory could see it in his cockpit too. "Recommend you turn port 20."

"Uh, you sure, One?" Rory asked. "That contact is nearly 100 klicks out. Probably a recon bird or commercial flight. Should we worry?"

"I'm not worried about the aircraft we can see, Two," Bunny said, bringing her missile-armed drone around to bracket the contact. "I'm worried about the ones we can't."

***

Rory had given Uncle the stick so that he could monitor the action.

"Take us down to skate the glacier," Rory told him. "I don't like this."

"There is no *down* from this altitude," Uncle told him, pointing at hills of snow and outcrops of ice flashing past their wings. "Unless you want to drop the skis and turn us into a 70-ton bobsled."

In the command module, Trigger and Ears were watching the tactical plot that Bunny was pushing to Outlaw. "Where did that contact come from?" Ears wondered. "Something like that can't have a range over a few hundred miles, right?"

"Launched from a ship, I'm guessing," Trigger said, the sailor in her seeing a naval answer to most problems. "Russia has a ghost fleet of hundreds of commercial vessels. Any one of them could hide something like that in a container and shoot it into the air."

"Yeah, but Space Force is supposed to have blanket coverage of this whole area. You've got to hope they'd notice a Russian container ship where it shouldn't be."

"Can it attack us?" Venice asked.

Trigger looked at her with undisguised pity. "Well, it isn't here as a gesture of international solidarity, woman."

Outlaw nudged lower, and their ride got decidedly bumpier as they hit pockets of warmer air rising from the glacier.

***

A minute later, as Bunny flipped her EW drone from search-and-track to jamming mode, she also armed the missiles on her wing hardpoints. Firstly, the contact she was investigating was flying toward her GAMBIT at 600 knots—too fast to be a commercial jet, and anyway, too far from any known airfield to be anything but military.

Her combat AI finished analyzing the data being sent to Bunny by her GAMBIT and presented her with a contact ID that confirmed her suspicions: *Su-71 Monochrome*. Russian drone. Could be a combat variant, could just be a recon bird, but it was military. She ordered her EW GAMBIT to start jamming the drone anyway. If she could cut its link to whoever was controlling it, she might be able to drop it without firing a shot.

But how the hell did you even get all the way down here? Bunny asked the drone in her head, looking at the plot showing the unidentified aircraft, just north of the Antarctic coast. The Monochrome didn't have the range to be this far from home, all alone. Sure, it could have taken off from the Russian airstrip at Vostok, or the Chinese ice landing strip at Kunlun, but Space Force had satellites providing overlapping coverage of the South Pole with both infrared and optical motion detection capability, and they should have notified them if an aircraft were taking off from either the Russian or Chinese bases.

The idea the unidentified contact could have been launched from a Tu-190 *Envoy* never crossed her mind because the *Envoy* was just a rumor. And Bunny had a tendency to take rumors about Russian wonder-weapons with a grain of salt.

She was about to learn the price of that kind of arrogance.

***

"I have the target on QE radar," Adamov said. "C-130 type, right?"

"Correct."

"It's still outside high kill probability range. You'll have to take us south."

Gusev didn't like that. His *Envoy* was not designed for bare-knuckle, close-range combat with American fighters. It was more of a longbow archer, built to pierce shields and drop targets from great distances.

"Enemy drone is trying to jam our Monochrome," Adamov said. "Hasn't achieved burn-through yet, but it will at any moment."

"We'll take out the escort first," he decided. "Set the Monochromes loose on it. Prepare to launch Axeheads."

"Good copy, engaging. Axeheads armed and ready to launch on your mark."

***

As Bunny's EW GAMBIT closed on the bogey, the benign interception turned lethal in a heartbeat.

An alarm screamed in her helmet. Missiles started converging on her EW GAMBIT both from the contact that had been identified and another, farther south, that had not. Her EW

GAMBIT switched automatically from trying to jam the radar of the Russian drone to jamming the missiles coming toward it.

It was a classic sucker punch, but Bunny was ready for it. She tapped a button combination on her flight stick, and her second GAMBIT snap-shot two AIM-260 missiles down the bearings to the attackers and dived for the sea. She ordered her EW GAMBIT to break off and make speed for Outlaw's wing, to act as a close escort. At the same time, she uncaged her own weapons and went "claws out." Somewhere behind those drones was the mothership controlling them. With her radar up, she lit her tail and powered toward the sky between the two Russian drones where instinct told her it had to be hiding.

The fact she and the AWACS circling over the Southern Ocean couldn't already see it bewildered her. It was either a very long way away or stealthier than any Russian she'd flown against before. Or both …

"Aggressor Two, Aggressor One. I am engaged with contacts northwest. Moving to support my drones. Alert the Navy, and watch your six," she said over the radio.

***

"Watch our six?" Uncle said with dismay. "That furball is 100 miles back, and that's still too close. Can you get any more power out of the engines?"

Rory grunted. "Not unless you want me to get out and push," he replied.

They were listening to the cockpit conversation in the command module. "What's a furball?" Venice asked in a quiet voice.

"Air-to-air engagement," Bell told her, before Trigger could say something sarcastic. "Russians coming at us again, by the look of it."

181

"Pilot," Trigger asked on internal comms. "You got Trophy on this bird, right?"

The Trophy air-defense system had become standard on larger USAF aircraft from the C-130 and up, since it had been adapted from a projectile defense system for tanks to a missile defense system for aircraft. Using millimeter-wavelength radar to identify and track threats, when a missile closed, it spat a hail of lead slugs into the missile's path to blow it up at what was hopefully a safe distance.

"Turrets top and bottom," Rory replied. "But Trophy is …"

"Near useless against the newest hypersonics. I know," Trigger finished the sentence. "So we better hope whoever is out there isn't carrying Axeheads."

***

"Launch Axeheads, two per target, stagger."

"Launching Axeheads, two per target, 15-second stagger, copy."

The American drones had parried the Russian Su-71 Monochrome attacks in copybook fashion, picking them up as soon as they began their attack, launching a counterattack before maneuvering to avoid the drone's slower AA-12 Adder missiles. They took down one Su-71 Monochrome, dodged the incoming missiles and closed on the second before it could fire again, getting a second volley of missiles away at the remaining drone from two angles. Two clean kills to the Americans.

That didn't worry Gusev. What worried him was the American heavy stealth fighter barreling straight toward them, the ghostly fingers of its radar reaching out in front of it, desperately trying to get a return from their *Envoy*.

But launched at the escort by Adamov minutes earlier, two of the *Envoy*'s Axehead missiles went from supersonic to Mach

5 hypersonic, closing on one of the GAMBIT drone escorts at 97 miles a minute. Adamov had ripple-launched them, 15 seconds apart, two missiles at the drone attacking their Monochromes, two at the American stealth fighter, guiding them in invisibly with their QE radar.

The first two missiles homed on their targets as the GAMBIT circled in the sky, trying to find new targets, and the icon in Gusev's helmet visor bloomed to indicate a kill. Their next two missiles were less than a minute from the enemy fighter.

"Scratch one," Adamov said with satisfaction. "The enemy EW drone is bugging out. Missiles closing on the American fighter. Ah … we just got painted by a low-frequency radar to the east. AI says Improved E7-Wedgetail. No lock, but they could have gotten a return." He worked his sensor suite.

Gusev frowned. A low-frequency radar hit could give the enemy AWACS a bearing to their *Envoy*, which the American stealth fighter could use if they didn't kill it straightaway. The airspace between his *Envoy* and the target was starting to glow red hot.

His GRU tasking mandated the destruction of the enemy heavy aircraft, but the orders from his superior officers in the Aerospace Force were also clear: destroy the American AC-130X, but *do not* risk losing our multibillion-ruble *Envoy*. With the gunship's escorts out of play, even with the added complication of the two new contacts, the slow-moving target had become easy prey, and Gusev saw no point in tempting fate further by staying in contested airspace a moment longer than needed.

"Give me a four-missile salvo at the target heavy. Ripple-fire two AA-12s; stagger launch two Axeheads."

"*Four* missiles? All at the target? What about the stealth fighter?"

183

"It has problems of its own, and I don't plan to get any closer," Gusev said. "We shoot and bug out. Execute."

***

"Aggressor One," the AWACS with the callsign 'Turtle' out over the Southern Ocean said, alerting Bunny to the danger to her northwest. "Large fast mover south-southwest, 30,000 feet. No data on heading, probable stealth. No type ID."

"Good copy, Turtle."

Russia had experimented with launching combat drones from everything from Antonov cargo planes to Tu-160 Cold War–era bombers. Bunny had been hoping the Russian drone mothership was something old and slow. But stealth?

Seconds later, one of her two GAMBITs, now just 50 miles ahead of her, disappeared from radar.

She didn't need another warning. She killed her radar, broke off her search, rolled her Nemesis onto one wing and hauled it into a screaming 500-knot turn that would put her perpendicular to the contact spotted by the AWACS. Because that's where its missiles were probably coming from, and she had no doubt, they *were* coming.

She pointed her nose at the sea, trying to force the Russian missiles to follow her around and down. She was making them burn precious fuel, hoping they would overshoot. At 500 feet, she flattened out, head screwed over her shoulder, looking at the suddenly hostile gray sky, not trusting her optical targeting system to spot the—

A chime on her RWR, and two boxes in her helmet visor. *There!*

The Nemesis, like the F-22 Raptor it was based on, had thrust-vectoring engines that enabled it to perform maneuvers that no other aircraft its size had a right to be able to execute.

But Bunny knew her own limits. With the incoming missiles locked, seconds from impact, and her visor showing her they were *hypersonic*, she thumbed the button that gave her combat AI control of her fighter.

Without regard for the health or welfare of its human occupant, the AI threw the fighter into a 9-G skidding turn. Bunny's flight suit inflated to try to keep blood from pooling in her legs and abdomen, forcing it back up to her brain, but the maneuver was too violent.

Her vision went gray, and her head rolled to her shoulder.

The two Axehead missiles were moving so fast, there was too little time for them to adjust to the Nemesis's radical maneuver. They made a last correction and tried to aim themselves at the point in the sky ahead of the American fighter where their radars told them it would be within milliseconds, but it wasn't headed there anymore. They slammed into the sea ahead of Bunny's port wing, and the Nemesis quickly rolled onto its port wing, swung around in another 9-G turn and put its nose on a heading to its attacker.

When Bunny's vision cleared and she was able to lift her head from her chest, icons in her helmet visor were blinking for her attention. Bunny had tweaked her AI to always choose an aggressive posture over a passive one, and it was already back in pursuit of the Russian mothership, trying to get a radar lock on it now that it had multiple data points to triangulate it with.

Bunny took back control, looking for Outlaw. There *must* also be missiles headed for the big transport. But her escape had taken her off its tail, and she was in no position to directly help it. Or maybe …

She swung her aircraft around, radar pointing at Outlaw now, a narrow pulse of powerful energy that filled the sky directly behind the big machine. Contacts! The Russian missiles. Her heart fell.

"Aggressor Two, you have incoming," Bunny warned. "Two supersonic, two hypersonic ..."

"Nothing on RWR, One," Rory replied.

"Trust me, Rory," Bunny said. "Go defensive *now!*"

She sent the data from her radar to her EW drone, which had rejoined with Outlaw. It peeled off Outlaw's wing to jam the threats. *It might defeat one or two missiles*, she thought, despair flooding her mind. *But four?*

***

Rory gripped his flight yoke tighter. He was already swinging Outlaw around, putting it broadside on to the missile threats, forcing them to maneuver laterally as they curved down from height, like raptors falling on a mouse. He kicked in right full rudder, causing Outlaw to slide across the landscape like a charging hippo in mud.

In the command module, Trigger pulled her harness even tighter.

"Shouldn't we be maneuvering?" Bell asked. "Like, *harder?*"

"This *is* maneuvering." Trigger stared straight ahead at her screen. "I'm not sure this old girl has any more in her."

"Arm Trophy!" Rory ordered Uncle.

"Trophy armed."

"Give me a fuel state on the JATO," he asked.

"The *what* now?"

"JATO!" Rory roared. He had one eye on the tactical monitor and saw the incoming missiles converge on Bunny's EW drone. The two hypersonics reached the GAMBIT first, then flew wide, losing their track, the GAMBIT blinding them. The two supersonic missiles trailing them were outside the

GAMBIT's effect area; they blasted past and continued toward Outlaw. The readout in Rory's visor told him they had 20 seconds to do something completely insane. Or die.

"Twenty percent fuel on that JATO," Uncle told him. "You got a two-, maybe three-second burn left."

Rory watched the incoming missiles, hands tight on Outlaw's flight yoke, its four 4,700-shaft-horsepower engines screaming, white snowy ground merging with gray sky so he could barely see a horizon. "Prepare to activate JATO," he said through gritted teeth, rolling level.

"I'm ready on JATO," Uncle said tightly. "And I ain't gonna ask."

Nine … eight … seven … now! "Hit it!" he cried, hauling back on the yoke at the same time as he twisted it hard right and stomped on his rudder pedal. Like a water buffalo rearing out of a mudhole, Outlaw's nose reached for the sky as the jet boosters on its fuselage ignited, and Rory felt a mighty kick in the spine as the AC-130X reared up and began twisting through the sky.

JATO wasn't some kind of miraculous thrust-vectoring system that would enable Outlaw to maneuver like a jet fighter. But it could help bring *both* Trophy turrets to bear on the incoming missiles as the aircraft rotated.

"Firing decoys!" Uncle yelled.

Rory had his eyes closed as he panted to keep breathing through forces trying to pull him apart at the seams. In his mind's eye, he saw the matte-black Outlaw, rearing up from the ice on a pillar of fire, twisting slowly as it rose, infrared decoy flares and clouds of chaff pumping into its wake.

If you gotta go, he told himself, go in style, O'Donoghue.

***

Bunny's EW GAMBIT had spooked both hypersonic Axeheads. The Russian AA-12s were 1,000 miles an hour slower, which meant Outlaw's Trophy system was able to get a lock on the incoming supersonic missiles.

A half second from impact, the two Trophy turrets began spitting walls of explosively formed penetrators—lead slugs—into the path of the incoming missiles. One was pulled off target by the incandescent fury of the decoys trailing behind Outlaw, and detonated harmlessly 100 yards behind them. The other continued directly into Outlaw's path, meeting the hail of lead from their underside Trophy turret as Outlaw rolled onto its belly. Its JATO pack sputtered and died, and the big machine began falling from the sky, just 5,000 feet above the ice.

***

Rory heard a crack that could have been a wing breaking, or their tail, or a missile exploding. He had bigger problems.

They had rolled inverted and were headed for the ice. He didn't have the altitude to roll level. Correcting their spin so that they were crabbing diagonally through the sky, hanging from his seat harness with his head just above the cockpit ceiling, he shoved the yoke forward and their nose began to inch up toward the horizon. Their JATO was still sputtering, which wasn't helping him regain control. "JATO!" he yelled. "Kill the damn—"

"I'm killing the damn JATO," Uncle said, and Rory saw him flipping switches on the instrument panel. "Don't let her pitch over any more, or we'll auger in."

"Rolling left," Rory told him, and turned the yoke in the same direction their big broad rudder was trying to take them—namely, upright. Rory saw their right wing coming up, snowy ground a blur beneath it, then as he watched it with shoulders hunched, he saw it swing toward the gray sky and applied opposite rudder to stop their roll as the ailerons began to bite again.

"Nearly got it back again, Uncle," Rory said between panting breaths.

"Death would be kinder than this," Uncle groaned, staring out his cockpit window at the ground rushing past just a few hundred feet below.

Wings level. Rory breathed out, looking across at his red-faced copilot. "Yeah, maybe we need someone younger in that seat," he said. "How about I ask Brown if she'd like to try out for flight duties? Can't be that much different to piloting a sub."

"Oh, yeah, great idea," Uncle said. "The dumb leading the dumber."

"I heard that," Brown's voice said from the rear. "You're still on comms, which you should be able to tell from the sound of puking back here."

Rory smiled. "If you're puking, you aren't dead. Embrace the puke, woman."

***

'Uncle' Bob E. Lee stayed with Rory O'Donoghue not because he was a rodeo-riding cowboy of a pilot, though he had just reaffirmed that. Rory could make Outlaw do things its makers said should never be attempted, yet somehow, they came out the other side with souls, minds and airframe intact.

No, Uncle stayed with Rory because he knew if wasn't riding shotgun for him, the man would be dead. And Uncle was already living with one of those on his conscience: Uncle's best buddy from flight school, the guy who did the grind with him, Fred 'Doc' Doolittle. Doc had been a gambler, not a drinker like Rory, but addiction is addiction. Doc was the kind of guy who would bet against his heart beating, then hold his breath until it stopped. So, of course, it was just a matter of time until he came to Uncle in deep shit.

But not the usual, "Can I loan a couple hundred bucks?" kind of shit.

"I need 20 grand, Bob, and I need it this weekend, or I'm a dead man," he'd told Uncle.

"Twenty grand?" Uncle had nearly spat beer through his nose. "You think I got 20 grand lying around?"

"No, I know you don't," Doc said. "I actually owe these guys 50. I found 30, but I'm still 20 short. And I know you got approved for that car loan …"

"That's a bank loan, Doc," Uncle had said. "That's not money I have; it's money I owe."

"You bought the car yet?"

"No."

"That money sitting in your account?"

"Yeah, but …"

"Then it's money you have," Doc said, with the simple, desperate logic of an addict. "I'm good for it. Give you the 20 plus vig inside the month. Get yourself that car. Get yourself all the options. I'm in deep, Uncle."

"The *vig*?"

"Interest," he said. "These guys are bad news. Colombians. I should never have gone to them, but I did. I'm already late paying back; they said next time they see me, I'll be paying with my kneecaps."

"I can't afford to owe a bank 20 grand for a car I don't have, man. I'd be underwater for years."

"And I'll be in a wheelchair, my disability check going straight to the Colombians, so what's worse? Dammit, Uncle, I'm begging here."

Except it wasn't the first time Doc had come begging. Sure, it was the biggest loan he'd ever asked for, but the story was always the same. It was always the money or his life. And no, he'd never actually managed to pay it all back before he was asking again.

Uncle didn't just say no. He persuaded Doc to hide out on base where the Colombians couldn't touch him, and he made an anonymous call on the Air Force Office of Special Investigations hotline. Because hell, the guy needed help. Something had to happen to stop the spiral he was in. He told himself that was the best thing. But the reality was it was the easiest thing. He made a call and turned his back on Doc Doolittle. Told himself it was tough love, when it was no kind of love at all.

The AFOSI doesn't move fast on anonymous calls, even about gambling-addicted Air Force officers racking up huge debts. Sure enough, the dumbass left base one night, looking for some action, and the Colombians caught up with Doc Doolittle. They didn't kneecap him. They must have wanted to make an example of, someone, because Doc Doolittle was found shot in the back of the head in an alley behind a bar in his USAF uniform, so of course it was headline news for a couple weeks, and everyone on the base who knew Doc was interviewed. Inexpensive advertising really, if all it cost them was $50,000 and a bullet. "You can't pay? You read about that hotshot pilot they found in an alley a few weeks back? He told us *he* couldn't pay."

Yeah, Uncle blamed himself. Plenty of people told him he shouldn't, and he wanted to believe them, but he could have saved his buddy's life for a lousy $20,000. And no, he would never have seen the money again. And yeah, Doc would probably have died in another alley, some other day. But that wouldn't have been Uncle's fault. Uncle could have given him the money and said, "If I do this, it's no more, man. Last time.

Ever." And stuck to that. Or given him the money and contacted AFOSI, right? Force the guy into gambling rehab. Put a little love into the "tough love."

So many different ways he should have done it.

So when one day he realized how damaged Rory O'Donoghue was, in that moment, when maybe any other copilot would have asked for a transfer, or just reported Rory to his CO, or just plain ignored the depression, the delusional ranting and the drinking, Uncle hung in. He never let the man fly if he was going to be a risk to himself or to others, and he became an expert at making sure Rory never broke the USAF's unwritten six-hour "bottle-to-throttle" rule. He found Rory a chaplain he could talk to about his delusions and nightmares without it going on his record. Helped him pay for it, so there was no record on his health insurance.

Rory didn't want his help at first. The addicted never do. But when he realized he was going to get Uncle's help whether he wanted it or not, he gave in, an inch at a time. And as they staggered from combat tour to combat tour together, it began to seem more like a mutual dependence than a one-way thing. Uncle needed to think he could save Rory O'Donoghue from himself, and Rory had saved Uncle's life more than once in situations they had no right to have come out of alive.

Embrace the puke? Wasn't that how you balanced the ledger of life?

***

For Bunny O'Hare, watching Outlaw survive the onslaught of missiles was like watching a blindfolded toddler cross a busy freeway. She knew there was little chance they'd make it, but she couldn't look away.

With fury like a fever setting her alight, she spun her FB-22 Nemesis on its axis and tried to find their attacker, but was afraid to stray too far from Outlaw again. After several minutes, she gave up with a disgusted groan. The Russian had appeared from nowhere and disappeared back into the ether.

"Aggressor Two, One," Bunny said. "Whatever drugs you are taking, O'Donoghue, I want some."

"Not drugs, One. Luck of the Irish," Rory said.

"A streak of insanity helps too," Uncle added.

***

Rory said to "embrace the puke," but Trigger Brown didn't need to embrace it; she was wearing it. During their rocket-powered spiraling ascent, Bell had lost his breakfast. As soon as they leveled out, he unbuckled, staggered from his seat and out into the cargo bay, looking for the heads.

Venice unbuckled too, wrinkling her nose. She looked remarkably well for someone who had just survived what was probably the world's first alligator death roll in an AC-130. "I'll just … I have to check on the device," she said, giving Trigger an apologetic look as she disappeared out of the suddenly very claustrophobic command module.

Trigger tried to unbuckle her harness without smearing Bell's breakfast all over her flight suit. Uncle appeared in the doorway, with some rags. "Concierge service, ma'am?" he asked, approaching reluctantly. He held out a rag. "Do you want to, or shall I …?"

"Let me do me," Trigger said. "Bell can swab his own deck."

Anna Venice came running back into the module, neatly jumped over the mess on the deck and stopped herself against the bulkhead between stations. "We've got a big problem," she said.

Trigger paused her cleaning. "How big?"

"About 80 megatons big," Venice said. "Something has triggered a cooling system shutdown on Juliet. We're looking at temperature escape and trap failure inside three hours, and I don't know how to stop it."

"This is the same thing that happened on Concordia?!" Trigger asked, exasperated.

"Yes. No. That was a failure of the entire cooling system for the containment level. This is a failure of the transport system for a single device."

"Dammit, am I the only one seeing a fatal design flaw here?"

"We haven't had a single trap failure in thousands of transport hours," she said, helplessly. "I don't understand ..."

"So you get it under control, or in three hours ...?"

Venice swallowed. "J-Day arrives early."

***

Rory left Uncle to fly Outlaw and went aft, to where Brown, Bell and Venice were gathered. The latter was on her knees in front of an open panel in front of the bomb, with some kind of diagnostic device plugged into a port.

An incongruously small LCD display at the top of the panel showed a simple timer, counting down: 2:47:20 ... 2:47:19 ... 2:47:18.

"I declared an emergency, told them we are carrying a live nuke, like the cover story we were briefed to use, and McMurdo ATC freaked. They've told us to hold 20 miles north of the base, over the Southern Ocean, while they get direction from someone authorized to tell them what the hell is going on," Rory said. He sent Trigger a look somewhere between shock and resignation. "We lost a GAMBIT in that attack, and even the AWACS barely got a return from the attacker. What the hell does Russia have in its inventory that could pull off an attack like that?"

Venice sat back on her haunches and blew her fringe out of her eyes. "I need to get onto Professor Bellings at Concordia. Now."

Bell ran back to the module and returned a few minutes later with a small relay radio and headset, which he handed to Venice. "Concordia command center on the line. They're trying to find Bellings."

Another frustrating couple of minutes ticked past.

"How far away from McMurdo are we?" Venice asked.

"About two hours," Trigger told her. "But if they won't let us land …"

"They … we might *have* to land," Venice said. "We might need to crack Juliet open physically, and we can only do that at Concordia …"

"Which is now snowed in," Rory said.

"… or McMurdo," Venice finished.

"They're going to send us out to sea and wait for the fireball, I know it," Bell said.

"Way to cheer us all up, Navy," Rory said.

"Actually, it's not a fireball, like you get from a nuke," Venice said, fitting the radio headset over her ears. "It'll be more like a huge white ball of electricity inside a glowing blue sphere."

"How do you know, if no one has ever seen an antimatter bomb go off?" Trigger asked her.

"Oh, I've seen antimatter annihilations," she said. "But, like, less than 10 nanograms." She looked balefully at Juliet. "Nothing like this."

"Ten *nanograms*?" Bell asked. "A nanogram is, what, a billionth of a gram? How do you even see something like that?"

"You can see it," Venice said. "When it annihilates. A billionth of a gram of antimatter cooks off with the power of a hand grenade. We've got a team working on a trap small enough to put into the warhead of an air-to-ground missile or even a mortar shell or rocket launcher. Even something that small would still go off like a 1,000 lb. bomb."

Rory looked horrified. "Am I the only one thinks the human race isn't ready for this kind of power?"

"I think our position on that is that it is better we have it first, before the Russians or Chinese," Trigger said.

"I know, and my question still stands."

Venice turned her attention to her headset again. "Professor, yes! No, the countdown started at *three* hours ..." she said, explaining their situation, what had happened, and what she had done about it so far. She grabbed at her headset and handed it to Rory. "He wants to speak with you."

"O'Donoghue," Rory said.

"Jake Bellings, Captain," the engineering director's voice said. "I need to know, was there anything unusual about the engagement you just fought?"

"Unusual?" Rory motioned for Bell to hand him the radio relay device, which had a speaker function loud enough it could be heard over the drone of the engines. "Say again, sir—what do mean by unusual?"

"Juliet is hardened against electronic interference, like radio energies, radar, even EMP. But before we start working on internal causes, we need to rule out external interference as a cause."

"Well, sir, as engagements go, it was pretty standard ... The enemy aircraft launched combat drones, so we figure it for a missile-carrying stealth bomber of some type, given how far it would have had to fly, and the fact we haven't seen any aerial refueling aircraft north of here. Chinese, maybe, since Russia doesn't have—"

Trigger grabbed his arm. "Russia *does* have. I just remembered reading a report that their first Tu-190 rolled off the line a few months ago. Too late for the Pacific War, but it's just the first of about 20 they're building."

"Alright, so keep going … say it was a Russian stealth bomber. What kind of radar does it use? Some kind of multi-band pulsed Doppler?" Bellings asked.

Bell disappeared for the command module. "I'll look it up."

"Pulsed Doppler shouldn't affect the trap's electronics," Venice said. "We tested it against every kind of radio signal …"

"What range was this attacker?" Bellings asked.

"About 100 miles away," Rory said. "So it must have had a pretty powerful radar to pick us up at that range."

"We tested our traps against high-powered naval and air-to-air radars at ranges from 100 down to 1 mile," Bellings said. "Their shielding showed no leakage."

Bell came running back with a tablet PC. "QE … that's, ah, a quantum entanglement radar."

"That's not a thing," Rory said.

Bell showed him the tablet. "It is now."

Venice grabbed it. "Show me that. Oh, shit …" She leaned into the radio relay. "A radar that uses entangled *photon* streams, Jake."

"Damn. Quantum interference?"

"That's what I'm thinking."

"If that's true, it's a miracle that …"

"Don't even say it."

"But it gives us a possible kludge."

197

"Zero-point energy stabilizer reset?"

"It might be the only way," Bellings said. "But I can't ask you ..."

"You didn't; it was my idea. Venice out." She straightened and tapped the transmission key.

Rory looked from Venice to the others to see they hadn't understood any more than him. "You want to tell us what just went down?" he asked Venice.

The woman was already lost deep in thought. "What? Sorry," she said, blinking.

"What do you need from us, Anna?" Trigger asked.

"Right. Alright. Photons from the Russian's quantum radar have introduced energy anomalies into Juliet's Bellings Trap, causing unpredictable effects. So what we're going to do is, basically, we're going to shut down, then restart, the trap's energy stabilization system, without shutting down the trap itself. Like, uh, closing and restarting an app without rebooting the whole computer. It's called a 'trap burn.'"

"Sounds simple enough," Rory said.

"Sure, if the computer was an 80-megaton bomb, and restarting the app *could* cause it to explode," Venice added.

Rory took the mic. "You listening to this, Uncle?" he asked his copilot.

"I'm listening," Uncle confirmed.

"Tell O'Hare to pull herself and her GAMBIT off our wing, just in case," he said. He turned to Venice. "What kind of distance should be safe?"

Venice thought about it. "Fifty miles? Seventy would be better."

"Fifty *miles*?" Rory repeated disbelievingly.

She shrugged. "I'd want 70."

198

***

Captain Yury Komarov of the Russian diesel-nuclear electric submarine *Sarov* had a potential uncontrolled explosion of his own to worry about. He had just received a burst transmission over Russia's globe-spanning extra-low-frequency transmission system, which confirmed orders that would almost certainly mean death for the *Sarov* and everyone aboard her.

Orders he had been expecting but which his officers had not.

So the explosion was a human one. He had been reading in his tiny cabin aft of the vessel's sail when his chief engineer, Akopian, and XO, Fedorov, burst in and thrust the ELF message under his nose. There was suddenly very little air in the cabin, since what was there was being consumed by an irate Akopian. Komarov found himself longing for the old days, when an ELF message could say little more than 'STOP' or 'GO'. Data compression technology allowed longer messages, and created more problems.

"It's insane is what it is," the engineer was saying.

"Suicidal," Fedorov added.

Komarov sighed, rubbing his eyes, then looked at the two men looming over him as he sat at his small foldout table. "I recall you both said the same when I told you our patrol would take *Sarov* from Vladivostok to the Antarctic," he reminded them. "Why does anything come as a surprise to you now?"

"The idea we could get this rust bucket from Vladivostok to Antarctica with an unreliable reactor, leaking torpedo tube doors, a crew not given enough time to be trained on this type … that was insane," Akopian said.

"But we did it," Komarov pointed out.

"Yes, but we assumed we would stay under the ice. Not be sent out in the middle of the Southern bloody Ocean, into the middle of a bloody American naval task force."

Komarov scanned their faces, reading between the lines on their brows. These officers were cowards. Under the ice, they could be hunted by submarines but not by destroyers, drones and aircraft. Under the open ocean, there were more predators, and they saw themselves as prey.

"You already killed one of their submarines," Komarov tried pointing out. "And you will have near-real-time satellite data on the positions of their surface vessels."

"Submarine? Pah, a drone," Akopian said, dismissively. "Probably unarmed."

"I am not so worried about American ships," Fedorov said, "as I am about submarines and aircraft. This is not some peacetime cat-and-mouse game in the Atlantic or Mediterranean. A simple covert insertion on an African coast. We already fired the first shots. If the Americans find us, they *will* kill us."

Komarov read the orders again, looking between the lines. "Our original orders called for us to deploy the special weapon from 200 miles out. Now, we are to launch from 100 miles. Clearly our superiors want a shorter running time, and I am not going to second-guess their reasons since the change matters little."

"Little?!" Akopian said, nearly choking. "At 200 miles, we would be *outside* the American anti-submarine picket, and close to the ice shelf. At 100 miles, we are in the open sea, *inside* the American naval patrol area!"

"And we would need to escape again to hit our secondary objective," Fedorov pointed out.

Komarov's patience frayed. He waved the new orders. "Gentlemen, we will execute these orders. We will evade detection, execute our missions, and then we will get the hell out of the Southern Ocean, and if by some miracle our reactor does not melt down underway, we will return to Vladivostok bloody heroes. Issue the necessary orders. You are dismissed."

Akopian scowled at Komarov, but they both retreated.

Komarov tossed his book aside in disgust. What had they expected him to say? That he would question his orders? Even refuse them?

Komarov was no fool. He knew he had been pulled out of retirement—out of a drunken, cancer-ridden nonexistence as a veteran in a squalid state apartment in the crime-plagued Moscow suburb of Krasnaya Presnya—not just because he was *Sarov*'s last captain, but also because he no longer had anything to live for, and would gladly follow any order to his death.

What Fedorov and Akopian could not see, and what he was unable to tell them because of the secrecy of his orders, was that it could be a glorious death. A worthy death. A death that could buy Mother Russia the time it needed to be ready for the war to come.

Because a new war was coming, and you didn't need to be an old sea dog like Komarov to see that.

Perhaps Fedorov and Akopian were not happy about being sent to an almost certain death because they had families. Komarov had not bothered to ask them. In that case, their new orders were doing them a favor. If this mission ended as Komarov expected, they would likely not be around to watch their families burn in the fire Russia was about to ignite.

***

"Test burn in five," Venice said. "Four … three … two …"

The Ross Ice Shelf extended 70 miles out into the sea from McMurdo Station. Rory had piloted Outlaw to a position 50 miles farther northeast of the ice shelf's seaward edge. It was far enough out that—Minerva's specialists assured him—if Juliet detonated in the air, it might break up some of the sea-facing ice floes, but it wouldn't have a catastrophic impact on the larger shelf. Or McMurdo.

Which was a great relief to Rory and Uncle, since at that moment they were very worried about the health of the ice shelf.

Not.

Even though he knew the Minerva engineer, Venice, was running a simulation, Rory couldn't help but wince as she counted down. Back at Concordia, dozens of quantum engineers were watching the in-silica simulation of the zero-point energy stabilizer reset, and deciding whether it was worth trying.

"*One,*" Venice said, her disembodied voice over the radio sounding like something from a Cold War documentary about an atom bomb test in the Pacific. Which, Rory had to admit, was kind of fitting. The next few words, however, didn't really fit that image. "Holy crap, it worked!" Venice said. Rory could only hear her side of the conversation with her colleagues back at Concordia, but it was enough.

He'd been measuring his lifespan in hours because it was still more than an hour until the timer on Juliet—which was counting down to cooling system failure—reached zero and Outlaw was turned into a miles-wide blue-white ball of lightning. Now, Rory had to measure his lifespan in minutes because, with the successful simulation of the stabilizer reset, Venice was already moving to execute the real thing.

"Uh, pilot, Concordia has said we are good to conduct the reset," Venice's voice said from the payload bay a few minutes later. "So do you want to …?"

"Say my prayers?" Rory asked.

"Bail out?" Uncle quipped.

"Uh, no, do you want to try and keep it straight and level for me?" Venice finished her sentence.

Rory had been flying Outlaw in a gentle clockwise racetrack pattern in the sky, and leveled his wings.

"Systems?" he asked Uncle. Outlaw had been given a thorough shakeup during the Russian attack, and Rory had Uncle regularly checking every critical system for signs of trouble.

"All green," Uncle replied. "If we die, we're gonna die pretty."

"Ain't nothing pretty about this bird," Rory said through gritted teeth. "But green is good." He tapped his throat mic. "Pilot to weaponeer. You are clear to run your reset."

***

Trigger and Ears had been hovering behind Venice as she worked, trying not to crowd in over her shoulder, not that they would have understood what she was doing anyway.

She had a laptop plugged into a port on the front of the bomb and was watching lines of code flow down her screen, stopping it occasionally to lean closer and read. Trigger Brown was no technological slouch, but without context, she was as lost as Bell.

After what felt like an eon since the simulated reset, Venice put the laptop down and looked back over her shoulder at them as Outlaw leveled out and Trigger felt it settle into straight-line flight.

The countdown timer was showing 01:20:23.

"Alright," Venice said. Her elfin face showed no fear, only a kind of intense curiosity, as though she was objectively interested in what the next few minutes would bring, without being subjectively engaged in whether she would survive them.

Nice work if you can get it, Trigger thought.

203

"Should we get into the module and buckle up?" Bell asked her, weight moving from one foot to the other.

"Uh, well," Venice said, standing and brushing her hands as though dusting flour from them. "Since if this fails, you'll be at the epicenter of an explosion hotter than the core of the sun, I don't think ..."

"Right, good, I'll just stand here, then," Bell said, putting his hands in his pockets and spreading his feet wide.

"I feel like someone should say something," Trigger said, "since these could be our last moments on earth."

"That's kind of dark," Venice said. "The simulations say this should work."

"*Should*, meaning there's a chance it won't?"

"I guess."

"Let me misquote my favorite Missouri philosopher then," Trigger said. She gestured to Venice and Bell to join her, and threw her arms over their shoulders. "Alright. *'If you don't like what you got, make it into what it's not.'*"

Bell looked at her, a little surprised. "Poetry?"

"Sheryl Crow. Singer. Famously argued we could save the planet by only using one square of toilet paper per wipe," Trigger said, raising a finger.

"Inspiring," Venice said unconvincingly, and lifted Trigger's arm from her shoulder. "Shall we get this over with?"

Trigger stepped back and gestured at Juliet. "She's all yours."

Venice squatted, lifted the laptop onto her knees and peered at its small screen. "Pilot, I am initiating burn countdown. Hold her steady."

"Good copy, and godspeed," Rory replied.

Venice took a deep breath, typing slowly, checking and double-checking the text on the screen until she was satisfied.

"Alright, here goes …" She tapped her keyboard and sat back on her haunches, reading the screen. "Reset in 10 … nine … eight …"

Trigger looked around herself. Deafened by the barrage of noise from engines and airframe. In darkness, except for the floods lighting Juliet. Alone, except for Bell, Venice, Rory and Uncle up front. So not alone, really. She heard Venice count "three" and used the last few moments of the countdown to review her life on fast forward.

It had been hard, lonely, strange. But full. Always full. Not the best life she could have led, but not the worst. It just didn't feel anywhere near long enough.

"One," Venice said.

Juliet gave an audible *snap*, and Trigger recoiled. The air filled with the acrid smell of ozone. Trigger saw Venice's red hair lift from her shoulders with static discharge, floating around her head like she was in zero gravity. Venice fell onto her backside, and as she touched the deck, there was another *snap*, and she lifted her hands from the deck in shock. "Ow!" she yelled.

***

Donovan Grant was shocked to learn Russia apparently had tried to shoot down the aircraft transporting Juliet. He'd told Saara about the transfer flight, about them moving Juliet to McMurdo before the severe weather hit, about the test, how he'd been copied on a communication between Concordia and Aggressor Inc. that asked for an updated forecast for the location of the NOAA platform out in the Southern Ocean. He and Saara weren't so naive that they thought they could stop the test by exposing it, but they could steal the narrative, establish their bona fides if they released their information just before the test.

Establish their bona fides. That was Saara talking. She thought of everything.

But Russia had tried to attack the transfer flight? Who else could it have been? The damn thing might have exploded right on top of Concordia! *That* made him nervous. Now he was worried that the telephone and app she'd given him might be compromised. Russia listening in, maybe?

He'd started freaking out, sent a brief, panicked message, but Saara, as usual, had brought him back to what mattered. "We have to stick to our plan, make sure your friends at Concordia didn't die for nothing. Stay strong," she'd told him. "Find out exactly where and when this test is happening. Every detail. If it fails, they'll try to cover it up. We can ensure they cannot keep it secret."

Saara. Body as lithe and flexible as a sea lion. Hair as white as Antarctic snow. Mind like a bear trap. Eyes as blue as the Southern Ocean, seeing right into his soul.

He looked down at the latest message he had queued to send to her. "Test will proceed. Date is locked in despite Russian interventions. Delivery vector via aircraft to the NOAA platform, but I am being asked to prepare two weather prognoses—one for the location of the platform, and another 50 miles north. Coordinates follow. Might be able to say more when Juliet aircraft is airborne out of McMurdo. Test will be within two hours of the plane taking off." His thumb hovered over the "Send" icon, but he tapped on the screen and brought the keyboard up again. "This will be over soon. Already thinking of waking up beside you in Kallio again."

***

Major General Tomas Arsharvin of the Main Intelligence Directorate of the Russian Armed Forces, the GRU, pushed himself back from his desk. He looked out his window, across the Argut River at the desolate plains of the Altai governate and sighed.

Arsharvin was, despite all his years in Russian military intelligence, an optimist. But perhaps that was the curse of being Russian. No matter how desperate, how impossible the world around them seemed, the average Russian could delude themselves into thinking that tomorrow would be better.

Without misfortune, there would be no happiness, Tomka. Wasn't that what his old friend, the fighter ace Major General Yevgeny Bondarev, used to say over a shot glass when things looked bad? Bondarev, who'd died on some windblown rock off the coast of Japan, in a war Russia and China had no chance of winning. Had he died happy? Tomas doubted it.

And yet there was always the hope that for Tomas Arsharvin, things would be different. The GRU source inside Project Minerva was still delivering, so that was something. Arsharvin had no idea who the source was, any more than he knew the name of the source's handler. All he knew was that the operation was being managed out of the GRU's Helsinki Station, which was about as far from the Antarctic as it was humanly possible to get before reaching the North Pole.

And they'd learned things were much, much worse than they had feared. The Americans had not only successfully built an antimatter forge; it had generated enough fuel in the past year that they were ready to test a strategic weapon. A test that was imminent. The attack on the weapon had been authorized in desperation. Arsharvin's physicists had warned him that destroying the aircraft would trigger the weapon. He'd recommended to his superiors they proceed anyway. The Americans would still get their "proof of concept," but not on their terms. If they could shoot the transport aircraft down over continental Antarctica and detonate its special weapon, they could tell the world it was an irresponsible nuclear accident and proof the Americans were treaty breakers.

But now this. He turned to his screen again, and to the latest message there.

Interdiction of transport aircraft failed. Test will proceed, date is confirmed, delivery vector is by aircraft. Two possible test locations within 50 miles identified. Coordinates follow. Will confirm final location and timing earliest opportunity.

It was bad news, but it was also good news. Yes, their efforts to disrupt the American program had been frustrated, but they had literally and figuratively been long shots. His overcautious superiors had made him scale his plan so that it started small and deniable (a simple act of sabotage), escalating through a minor conventional military intervention (infiltration by special operators) to a risky interdiction by their *Envoy*, and finally the most effective of all responses, as a last resort.

Arsharvin stood and walked to the window. Gray water flowed slowly past, and gray sheep grazed the gray grass. He could still disrupt the American test, still had tasking authority for that Tu-190, even though it had failed him once already. And the *Sarov*'s captain had confirmed his stealthy vessel had left the ice shelf, and was passing through the American naval picket. He could still sabotage the American test, and they could deal with the reactor later.

As long as the remaining GRU source at Concordia was still alive and reporting, there was hope.

He needed it. He'd just seen a report on the progress of Russia's own antimatter weapons program, though it was only confirmation of what he'd already seen and heard. Their latest attempts to create a practical, stable antimatter transport system had failed again, catastrophically. Their engineers had tried to move just 0.00007 grams of antimatter—1 percent of Russia's current stockpile—in an electromagnetic bottle a distance of 1 kilometer. From one side of the Argut River base to the other. On vibration-dampened rails, over flat terrain.

After just 200 meters, the device had detonated with the power of a 3,000 lb. bomb. Arsharvin had been watching the transportation test on a screen, inside a concrete bunker on a hillside a mile away, and he had still heard and *felt* the explosion. Russia's best physicists and engineers couldn't move a small mass of antimatter more than a few hundred meters, yet the Americans were able to produce kilograms of antimatter in Antarctica—and not just that, *fly it* safely from base to base!

The report Arsharvin had read with disgust estimated that it would be at least six months until they had solved the problem of safe antimatter transport, and a year to reach the levels of miniaturization the Americans had achieved. By that time, America could already be replacing the warheads of its long-range nuclear land attack and intercontinental ballistic missiles with antimatter warheads.

No, that is outdated, conventional thinking, Tomas, he told himself. Antimatter weapons would not just be more powerful, less radioactive missile warheads. Once perfected, an antimatter containment system would be the same size whether it held a milligram or a kilogram of antimatter. A suitcase-sized device such as the Americans were reported to be developing could be smuggled almost anywhere, including right into the Kremlin, and less than 0.01 grams of antimatter would level entire buildings. Nowhere in Russia would be safe anymore when just 0.7 grams of explosive could flatten a city center.

Arsharvin slammed his fist against the double-paned window, cracking it.

Russia would not be the first to deploy antimatter weapons; he had to look that reality in the eye. It may not even be the second, if the latest reports about China's progress were accurate. Russia had abandoned its goal of being a major power in the Asia-Pacific, but it still had ambitions in other spheres: dreams of recreating the kind of influence it had enjoyed in Soviet times. Governments under its sway, economies dependent on Russian energy, Russian trade, Russian diplomatic and military protection.

Dreams that might be made impossible in a world where only its rivals possessed uncontestable military power.

He may not be able to stop that day arriving altogether, but he might be able to delay it—to buy Russia a window in which it could throw everything it had against the West in one fateful gamble, before it was too late.

If their source could just give them absolute certainty on the test coordinates.

***

Bunny had set herself up to the west of Outlaw, on what she now thought of as the "threat" side. Not 70 miles distant. Not even 50. But she was closer to McMurdo than she was to Outlaw.

She was running her own post-mission analysis as she waited for Outlaw's crew to either turn back for McMurdo or (very) briefly set the world record for first humans to witness an antimatter bomb explosion.

Their attacker wasn't invincible, or invisible. Bell had updated her on the attacker's likely type, and its curious radar— a new kid on the block, with a powerful new capability, able to see even stealth aircraft across previously unimaginable distances. But it had a tell the Russians probably weren't aware of.

It triggered the radiation sensor now built into every American radar warning receiver. Not enough to give a bearing to the threat, but enough to let you know it was out there, looking for you. Looking *at* you.

If Outlaw survived—*when* Outlaw survived—she'd put down at McMurdo to refuel and rearm her GAMBIT. She was fairly sure all treaty niceties would be waived now that Russia had openly declared its intentions.

Which … She opened a satellite link to Two-Tone in New Zealand, risking a signals energy leak, but pretty confident Russia was done for the day.

"O'Hare, good job up there," Hamilton said. "O'Donoghue has filled me in. You're still in a blocking position?"

"Yes sir," Bunny replied. "Fuel enough to hold here another hour, assuming I get permission to put down at McMurdo, since, you know, that would probably break a few treaties."

"You will," he said. "I'll make sure of it."

"Sir, we burned a missile-armed GAMBIT, but our EW drone did a great job spoofing the Russian Axehead hypersonics. Looking at the threat environment, I've concluded I need more jamming and fewer missiles."

"Tell me what you want, Captain," Hamilton said. "If it's here in Christchurch, I can get it on a C-17 inside the hour. It can be at McMurdo in six."

"I need a replacement GAMBIT airframe, with EW module. Next time I go up, I'll go ninja, with internal missiles for my Nemesis and two EW GAMBITs stuck to Outlaw like flies on blue mutton." She tried not to sound overconfident. "I figure Russia only has one of these beasts in theater, and we've already seen what it can do."

211

"Which was not unimpressive," Hamilton warned. "From what Rory told me, it's a miracle Outlaw survived."

Bunny rankled. "We didn't know what we were up against then. We do now."

Hamilton went off air, then came back. "Just checked what kind of support you'll have tomorrow. Two *Constellation* class destroyers, one of which can cover Outlaw from the moment it leaves McMurdo, all the way out to the test zone. You can position yourself farther west, patrol the most likely threat axis. You'll have AWACS again. And Navy has an electronic warfare ship up that it can bring west, so it can do more than just watch the fireworks."

"What I'd like," Bunny admitted, "is a couple of Black Widows north and west in case I get caught out of position."

"Can't give you what Air Force doesn't have in theater," Hamilton said. "The threat environment is much more intense than anyone foresaw. Russia is better prepared ..."

"Better informed ..." Bunny said. "There's a leak at Concordia. Has to be."

"You might be right. But the fact they've got that nuclear attack sub and their only strategic stealth bomber in play ... They're not playing around."

No shit, Sherlock, Bunny thought. "Wouldn't we?" she asked. "If Russia was on the verge of creating some new doomsday weapon, wouldn't we do everything in our power to derail it?"

"I want to hope so," Hamilton said. "Uh, I've got Rory on the line, got to go. Will see if there is anything else Air Force can give us."

Bunny had been flicking her eyes between sky and instruments as she spoke, and she put her Nemesis into a slow banking turn to take it closer to Outlaw again. If Rory was contacting Two-Tone, they were still alive, and she could probably rejoin. There might have been good reasons for locating Project Minerva at the literal ass end of the planet, but right now, she wasn't feeling sympathetic to them.

There wasn't enough vacant skin on her body to put the names of Outlaw's entire crew.

***

Everyone in Outlaw's payload bay froze in place until the lightning flashes of static stopped their mad dance.

As she levered herself off the deck, Anna Venice at least had the decency to look surprised she was still alive. "That was not the outcome I expected," she said, bending to look at the LCD display on Juliet's status panel.

It was frozen at 1:19:09.

Trigger was looking over her shoulder. "Does that mean it's back to normal, or just frozen in a state of 'might explode any moment'?" she asked.

"I don't know," Venice said, reaching for her keyboard again as she smoothed down her hair. She plugged the keyboard into the access port, settled her radio headset on her head again, and as she did, the LCD panel wiped itself completely, showing only a slowly rolling cascade of binary code. Venice bit her lip, then looked up at Trigger and Bell. "We're deep in uncharted territory here. But maybe you could give me a bit of space? Shouldn't you be watching out for Russians or something?"

Trigger was fairly sure Bunny, Rory and Uncle would shout at the first sign of new trouble, but she got the hint and tapped Bell on the shoulder. "Alright, you can clean up your mess, then run another systems integrity check. I'm going forward."

She threaded her way through and over the clamps, belts and harnesses holding Juliet in place on the deck, then pulled open the door into the AC-130X's cockpit. She put a hand on Rory's and Uncle's shoulders.

"Since I haven't heard from our weaponeer and we aren't dead, I have just told Two-Tone that all is back to normal, and we'll soon be headed for McMurdo," Rory said without turning his head.

"Totally," Trigger said. "The spooky voodoo lights have stopped flashing around the cargo hold. And the countdown has stopped."

Uncle turned. "Spooky voodoo lights?"

Trigger nodded. "Some kind of static release, I'm guessing. Cargo bay stinks of singed hair." She rubbed her scalp and looked at her hand. "Not mine, I'm glad to say."

"But the countdown timer stopped. That's good, right?" Uncle asked.

"Unless it's just stopped because the display got fried," Trigger observed.

Venice appeared in the cockpit door. "No, we're good. Temperature has stabilized. You can put us down."

Rory put Outlaw into a slow banking turn as Uncle got on the radio with McMurdo air traffic control. Trigger saw relief in Venice's face, but something else too. "Russia could come at us again. How do we make sure this doesn't happen again if they do?" Trigger asked.

"They're already working on that at Concordia. A quantum radar should use a proton stream for detection, and protons are charged particles. They shouldn't have been able to penetrate Juliet's Bellings Trap, let alone introduce energy fluctuations."

"I understood none of that," Trigger told her.

"There's a lot we still don't understand about antimatter containment," Venice told her simply.

Trigger nodded and waited, then rolled her hand at Venice to encourage her to continue. "And now you say something reassuring …"

"Oh, right." Venice pushed herself back from the door. "But it's probably an easy fix." She paused. "Unless that Russian submarine out there also transmits some kind of energy we haven't tested for."

"You suck at reassurance, you know that?" Trigger told her, following her back out of the cockpit.

***

A short time later, Colonel Roman Gusev and Captain Andrey Adamov were feeling the suck too.

They were standing at attention in front of a video wall at Chile's King George Island air base as a GRU general paced back and forth, every ounce of his frustration focused on the two pilots on the screen in front of him.

"You broke off your engagement before the target was destroyed?!" Major General Arsharvin repeated Gusev's words in disbelief.

"Sir, our orders …"

"Your orders were to destroy that cargo aircraft, Colonel. You had it locked and boxed. But you aborted your mission without destroying it!"

"Sir, our orders were to abort the mission if we believed our aircraft to be at risk," Gusev said, realizing it sounded like an excuse, not a reason. "The adversary AWACS had picked us up on radar, we had already repelled an attack by two adversary uncrewed aircraft, an unidentified stealth aircraft was inbound our position … Even if we had stayed in the area and observed the survival of the target, a follow-up attack was not tenable."

"Not *tenable?*" Arsharvin was clenching and unclenching a gloved fist. He looked down and pulled a folder off his desk. "Listen to me, Gusev. Both of you. You seem to be under the misapprehension that orders from your superiors in the Aerospace Forces supersede mine. That the protection of your precious aircraft comes before the fate of the Rodina. Am I right?"

Gusev felt like an insect being fried under a magnifying glass. "General, please …"

"You think perhaps that your superiors have your backs, that *they* can protect you from the consequences of failure?"

Before Gusev could answer, Arsharvin pulled something from the folder he was holding and turned it to the camera. It was a photograph. The general's image on the video wall was life-sized, and Gusev had no trouble seeing who was in the photograph.

His wife. The photo appeared to have been taken in their local supermarket in Artem, Vladivostok.

Arsharvin turned it and read the name off the back. "Anzhelika. Nice name. Looks like an angel too." He put the photograph down and pulled another out of the folder, but he didn't show it to the screen. "Captain Adamov, *you* are not married?"

Adamov flinched but didn't reply.

"The question was rhetorical," Arsharvin said. He turned the photograph he was holding to show a man in his 30s, dressed in a heavy winter coat, shoulders hunched, hurrying down a street. "This is your life partner, Sergei, yes?" Arsharvin held the two photographs up beside each other. "Gentlemen, right now, there is a GRU agent parked in a car outside each of the

216

apartments of your nearest and dearest. My agents will execute your wife, Gusev, and your partner, Adamov, if you fail me again. They will also execute Anzhelika and Sergei if you report this conversation to your superiors. Is any of this unclear to you?"

Gusev felt a mix of terror and fury rise in his throat, but he choked it down. "No. General."

"Adamov?" Arsharvin asked.

"No, General Arsharvin," Adamov replied.

"Your machine will be needed again. Make sure it is ready for immediate deployment. And do not fail me again."

The GRU general reached forward and cut the link. The wall screen turned to static, then went black.

Adamov staggered, taking a step back as though he were about to collapse. He gripped his waist, sucking air into his lungs in deep breaths. "He's serious. You think he's serious?"

It was not Gusev's first brush with the GRU, but it was his first direct conversation with Major General Tomas Arsharvin. There was no mistaking the cold menace in the man's voice. "He was serious."

"I have to call Sergei," Adamov said, looking around the room. "We have to warn—"

Gusev stepped toward him and slapped him across the jaw, hard. "You will do nothing, Captain. If you want your Sergei to survive this, you will do nothing, say nothing—you will not even bloody *think* anything. You heard the man. That conversation did not take place."

Adamov reddened, holding his face and glaring at Gusev. "Then what do we …?"

"We go out to the flight line and make sure our *Envoy* is 100 percent combat ready; that's what we do," Gusev said, pushing him toward the door. "And when new mission orders come, we will execute them without consideration for our safety

217

or the safety of our aircraft." Gusev grabbed Adamov by the shoulder of his flight suit and spun him around. "We will kill whatever bloody Americans that GRU maniac asks us to kill, or we will die, so that Anzhelika and Sergei stay safe, right?"

Adamov nodded tightly, and Gusev shoved him, stumbling, out into the corridor.

Extreme Cold Alert

December 30, 2041
J-Day minus 1 day

The combined forces of Task Force Minerva had been designed to counter undersea interference from attack submarines or to scare off nosy surface vessels and aircraft. Its few ships, a single submarine and the Aggressor aircraft were considered more than adequate for the task of securing the Minerva test site at the bottom of the world.

After Russia's attempts to sabotage the forge, infiltrate Concordia, and bring down Outlaw, Colonel Sandilands had recommended the US Navy boost the task force with the addition of the air warfare coordination capabilities of the USNS *Lorenzen*, which had been sailing south from Christchurch in New Zealand in any case, to monitor the test from afar. Space Force tasked additional satellites. USAF had no fighter aircraft close by on New Zealand that it could easily add to the task force but, given the heightened threat, was sending a flight of F-35s and a Stingray refueling drone from Darwin in Australia to New Zealand. It would be 20 hours before they were able to be on station over the Antarctic; until then, Bunny and Outlaw were on their own.

Concordia's reluctant acting head of security, Cath Delaney, knew all this. None of it made her feel safer or more confident. And certainly not when she was looking into the heavily lidded eyes of the Russian commando whose troops had killed 14 of her colleagues. She sat across a metal table from him in an interview room, careful not to get within reach. He had been dazed when he was brought up, but was handcuffed now to the leg of the table, which was bolted to the concrete floor, with one hand free so he could scratch himself.

"What else is Russia planning?" she asked him. She'd asked the same question of her former boss, Chief Raleigh, and he had refused to respond, not even reacting to her offer to provide him with a lawyer by video link if he was worried about incriminating himself.

Not entirely true. He had said one thing. "Why would I need a lawyer, when there is no law?"

The Russian seemed amused at her question. He'd asked for water, so she'd brought it. He'd asked for coffee, so she'd gotten that. He'd asked to go to the toilet, so she'd had a bucket and paper towels brought to him. He wouldn't tell her his name, military affiliation, rank, anything, but he'd given her the clearly rehearsed story that he and his men were conducting a "legally sanctioned unannounced inspection of the US facility" when they were attacked by US military personnel from a US military plane and then hunted throughout the base. "What Russia will do? Russia will make *very* strong protest at United Nations." He smiled. "Illegal US military action in Antarctica." He clicked his tongue and shook his head. "There may even be shouting."

"Very funny," Delaney told him. "Let me tell you what the US is going to do. When the storm lifts, some men in black are going to fly in here, put your head in a bag and take you to Guantanamo. Have you heard about Guantanamo?"

She could see he had. He tried to sneer, but it wasn't convincing.

"You probably think your government will make some sort of deal to get you back, but that only happens in movies," she said. "People like you who get renditioned to Guantanamo never leave. They get interrogated." She said the last word while making air quotes with her fingers. "Then they go crazy, and then they die. In Guantanamo."

He shrugged. Again, unconvincingly.

"But maybe you and me can make a deal," Delaney said, leaning forward. "You tell me what you know, and I let you go. You can take a snowmobile, a sat phone, contact your people at Vostok. And you can fly out of here on the chopper you rode in on."

He looked away in disgust at the suggestion, but she could see it had gone home. He looked back again. "Why you would do that?" he asked.

"All I care about is getting through the next 48 hours alive," she told him. "If Russia has a Plan B for destroying this base because you don't report back, that doesn't help me, *or* you."

He was thinking about it. "You do not have the authority," he scoffed. "You are just security guard."

"Since my boss, your informant, was killed trying to escape, I do," she said. They had kept both prisoners separate since they were captured, Raleigh and the Russian, so neither knew the fate of the other. "But you need to decide right now, while the storm prevents those men in black uniforms from flying in." She mimed putting a bag over his head.

He looked at her, weighing her up, trying to decide if she was serious. "You lie. You would not do this," he decided, leaning back in his seat.

"I will. And you have nothing to lose anyway. You can tell *me* what you know, while the information you have can save your life, or, you can tell them on Guantanamo, sooner or later, when it can't."

He was silent a moment, fighting some kind of inner demon, but the chance of escape won out. "Alright." He sighed. "Our mission was to destroy your reactor. Your boss would help us get in, help us get away. I know nothing about any 'plan B.'"

He tried to speak with finality, but she could see he was trying to read her face, see if she believed him. He was holding something back. Of course he was. She stood.

"You are not helping yourself here. Tell me something I don't know, or you will not see me again, and your one chance to get out of here, to avoid rendition, is gone." She took a step toward the door.

He weighed the odds again. Something flickered behind his eyes, and then it was gone. "*Sarov*," he said. "I heard them say *Sarov*. Just the word, not more, but I think I know what it means."

Delaney frowned. "*Sarov*? Is that some kind of code word?"

"No. In our briefing, there were officers from the GRU general staff. One of them said, 'What happens if this special operation fails?' Another one said, 'In that case, we have the *Sarov*.' This was all they said."

"What is 'the *Sarov*'?"

"I only know one thing called *Sarov*," he told her. "It is a submarine. Long-range. Stealth. Cruise missiles. I think my country will nuke your base." He smiled. "We can say it was your mistake, an accident with *your* reactor. Now, maybe you want to come with me when I escape?"

Delaney stood. He doesn't know about the weapons test, she thought as she walked quickly to the door. But that doesn't mean Russia doesn't know.

***

'The chartered civilian AC-130X aircraft, call sign 'Outlaw,' took off from McMurdo field at 1000 hours on December 30, 2041. At the controls were Captain Rory O'Donoghue and copilot Robert E. Lee. An extreme cold warning was in effect, with visibility moderate and winds at the US McMurdo base steady at 18 knots as Outlaw taxied out to take off.'

Bunny was playing a game of writing her epitaph in her head again from the cockpit of her Nemesis. She had been circling over McMurdo at 30,000 feet for the last hour, scanning for intruders, watching her new, "field-upgraded" RWR for a radiation spike.

During their downtime at McMurdo, O'Hare had gone over her engagement with their "weaponeer," the quantum engineer Anna Venice.

"I got this spike on the radiation detector," Bunny told her. "I think it's the Russian QE radar. But that just tells me the Russian aircraft is painting me with its radar. It doesn't give me any idea where the hell it is, so I can look for it."

"I'd have to look at your RWR, but you say it has a radiation detector built into it?"

"Yeah, since the Chinese rebels cooked off a nuke in space, it's been standard in US fighter cockpits," Bunny said.

"To pick up the photon stream from a QE radar, your radiation detector must include silicon avalanche photodiodes …"

Bunny gave her a blank look. "And?"

"And so, if it does, we could build a diode array and mount it, say, in a circle, plugged into the RWR's radiation detection software. The software detects the spike, and the array lights up to show you what direction the signal is coming from. I mean, very rough, points-of-the-compass kind of direction, but …"

Bunny looked skeptical. "Because you just happen to have brought a whole bunch of 'silicon avalanche' doohickeys with you?"

Venice smiled. "No. But they're used for low-light atmospheric, astronomical and environmental observation, like auroras, that kind of thing. McMurdo's engineers would have a supply."

Venice had built the array—a fan-like system of detectors and tiny LEDs they'd bolted to the Nemesis instrument panel—but Bunny couldn't get it to play with the Nemesis RWR software.

There was no way around it; she'd have to go off-reservation and bring Fi in on the problem. Which Two-Tone would lose his shit over, if—when—he found out. But what was the alternative—fly into an Antarctic storm blind, deaf *and* dumb? Two-Tone had never been up against anything like the Russian *Envoy*. If he were the one in the cockpit, would he just say, "Yes sir," "no sir," "I'll just drop the idea, sir"? Well, yeah, he probably would.

But Bunny O'Hare wasn't Two-Tone Hamilton.

Working together on opposite sides of the globe, Fi and Bunny massaged the Nemesis RWR's computer code to recognize the jerry-rigged array. But they had no way of testing it until that damn spike showed itself again.

Bunny's eyes flicked from her new RWR array to the sky around her, to her instruments and to the ground below, where Outlaw was taxiing out for takeoff. She initialized her two underwing EW GAMBITs and ran through their prelaunch flight checks. As soon at Outlaw was airborne, they would be glued to its wingtips.

Flight checks complete, she returned to writing her epitaph. Escorted by the Nemesis, the crew of Outlaw were flying into the unknown. US intelligence agencies had analyzed the Russian attacks and determined they were based on leaks that could only have come from within the Minerva Project. It was therefore decided that replica devices would be loaded aboard the civilian contractor's submarine and its aircraft. The only persons who knew which vehicle was carrying the real device were the director of the Minerva Project, David Lau; US President Mark Bendheim; and CIA Director Boniface Antonio.

And the personnel of Aggressor Inc.'

***

The four-engined beast that was Outlaw trundled down McMurdo's ice runway, slowly picking up speed. JATO wasn't needed for McMurdo's long runway, so Venice, Brown and Bell were only strapped loosely into their seats.

Several hours earlier, the chartered deep-submergence recon vehicle, nicknamed '*Charlene*,' had departed McMurdo Station, bound for a position 50 miles north of the NOAA weather monitoring platform, 400 miles north-northeast of McMurdo Station.

Trigger checked the weather report just updated by Donovan Grant. Surface water temperature 28.8°F, with extensive pack ice and drifting floes south of 74°, with new ice forming rapidly due to the extreme cold. Swell low but persistent, 1.5 to 3 feet. Open-water leads narrow and unstable. Not great if you were on the surface, not bad if you were riding under it, like Charlene. Trigger looked over at Bell, who was busy calibrating Charlene's sonar. The fact that he was about to make history seemed completely lost on him. He acted like it was just another Monday. She knew he'd seen action in the Red Sea and Mediterranean, and of course the Pacific too, though he didn't seem to want to talk about that, and she didn't really care enough to ask twice.

Trigger swung her chair back and forth. *Charlene* was steering herself to her next waypoint, hundreds of miles off. That was the thing with piloting submarines ... they were so damn *slow*. Bell at least had something to keep him occupied, monitoring the subsea acoustic environment, on the lookout for that Russian submarine ... even the occasional whale.

In her Navy role—weapons development—there was always some new milestone to hit, something going wrong that had to be fixed. She'd taken the contract with Aggressor Inc. to give herself a break from the mental and physical wear and tear of two years of Pacific war, but she was pretty sure the boredom of routine operations wasn't good for her mental health—Russian submarine, commando and hypersonic missile attacks aside, of course.

Trigger and Ears had a bet going about whether the bomb really was on *Charlene* as they'd been told it was, or whether it had been covertly loaded into the Vigilant drone tucked under Outlaw's wing for delivery to the NOAA platform after all—a double bluff, if you will.

Juliet's unlikely godmother, Anna Venice, had to know whether her bomb was going to be sailing or flying toward obliteration. She'd supervised the loading of both black boxes—one aboard the submersible, *Charlene*, the other aboard Outlaw's Vigilant, poker-faced throughout. Now they were airborne though. As Outlaw settled into a slow climb, making for her destination out in the Southern Ocean north of the NOAA platform, Trigger unbuckled and walked to Venice's station on the other side of Bell.

"Alright, Ms. Venice, we're airborne now."

Venice looked up from the laptop she'd been working on and frowned. "Yes?"

"So this is where you lift the walnut shell and show us the pea …" Trigger prompted.

"What?"

Trigger sighed. "Is Juliet on *Charlene*, or did you pull a switch on us and put it on Outlaw's *Vigilant*?" Bell's head snapped up, suddenly showing interest in the world outside his own screens. "Because, we know you people love your secrets."

"Oh, on *Charlene*," Venice said. "Just like we said. The box inside your *Vigilant* is externally identical, but it is just a …"

"Decoy?" Bell asked.

"No, actually, a sensor suite for monitoring the above-water effects of the Juliet detonation, from 50 miles' range," Venice told him. "Air pressure changes, temperature, humidity, gamma and neutron radiation—there are similar sensors already mounted on the NOAA platform's underwater pylons, but we didn't want to give the game away early since it makes no sense to visibly mount sensors on a platform you're planning to pulverize."

"But the NOAA platform is going to be *50 miles* from the bomb, which you are setting off *1,000 feet* underwater," Bell pointed out. "It's going to be pulverized that far out?"

"Well, the models predict that …"

Trigger listened to the woman's matter-of-fact tone and, again, it didn't seem to fit the epoch-changing mood of the moment. "No, in *non*-scientific terms, when this bomb goes off, what's going to happen? In a sentence, since my brain tends to fuse when scientists talk for more than that."

"In a sentence?" Venice looked up at the ceiling for a moment, arms behind her neck. "OK, try this. First, everything within 50 miles dies, and then the sea catches fire."

"That's *first?*" Bell asked. "What's next?"

"Next, it gets worse."

Trigger wished she hadn't asked. She'd harbored the innocent notion after two years at war that she'd already seen the worst that man could do to man, and nothing could shock her anymore. She'd been wrong.

"We are inside the US Navy air defense zone," Rory's voice broke in over internal comms. "Two hours to Vigilant deployment, four hours to J-hour. All crew, action stations. Repeat: all crew to action stations."

***

"American *Sea Hunter* still moving astern," *Sarov*'s sonarman, Mikael Alekseev, advised in a hushed tone.

Sarov was creeping forward on battery power alone, reactor damped. They had threaded themselves between a line of sonobuoys that must have been dropped by an overhead aircraft, behind what their AI told them was a prowling *Virginia* class attack submarine, then glided past a US *Constellation* frigate that was making revolutions *away* from their objective ... a spot between the US weather monitoring platform and the other coordinates they had been given. But trailing it, well inside the 100-mile circle the US ships were making around the platform, was a *Sea Hunter* drone—a dedicated submarine killer with towed array sonar and the ability to drop two very lightweight torpedoes right on top of them if it got a return off *Sarov*'s anechoic hull.

"No sign it heard us," Alekseev said. "We're clear to increase revolutions."

"You see, Fedorov," Komarov said to his XO, with a cheer he didn't really feel, "this leaky old piece of junk can still tiptoe through the graveyard when it has to." The words had an irony that Fedorov probably wouldn't pick up on, since Komarov was still fully convinced the rusty old hulk that was *B-90 Sarov* would be the death of him yet.

Fedorov treated him with passive aggressive silence, studying a nav screen on a table in the center of *Sarov*'s control room. "We are coming up to the launch waypoint," he said, standing. "We need final target coordinates."

"Bring us to ELF radio depth," Komarov said. "How far to the waypoint?"

"Ten miles," Fedorov said. "Thirty minutes if we increase to 50 percent revolutions. We are clear now."

"Revolutions to 50 percent, XO," Komarov confirmed. "Maintain heading and depth. You have the conn."

"XO has the conn."

Komarov ducked through a hatchway and began moving forward to his cabin, where the small handheld device for coding or decoding fleet base messages was kept in a safe. *Sarov* was a big boat, nearly 90 feet longer than a conventional *Kilo* submarine, with a bulbous bow section originally designed to accommodate the launch mechanism for the *Poseidon* intercontinental torpedo and two conventional 25-inch torpedo tubes, one deck down, under his feet. There were no torpedoes in those tubes: they held two Kalibr-M land-attack cruise missiles with penetrating HE warheads, designed to punch through 50 feet of glacial ice before detonating.

Komarov entered his cabin and opened the safe. Some things had changed since he'd captained his first nuclear submarine, the ballistic missile "boomer," *K-84 Yekaterinburg*, but much had not. A "special weapon" launch on the *Yekaterinburg* had to be approved by both its captain and its executive officer, usually a GRU-approved appointee. Aboard *Sarov*, the special nature of their weapon meant he could launch it on his own authority, but it could only be armed or disarmed underway by a quantum encrypted ELF signal from the Kremlin.

That made his job, and his decision, much easier, though he still needed a damn target to launch it toward.

***

"Coming up on USAF air defense zone," Captain Andrey Adamov said. "Scanning for the target."

Colonel Roman Gusev looked at the data being generated by their quantum radar. The last time they had attacked the American cargo plane, they'd had the element of surprise and had easily overcome its air defenses. How the target itself had escaped was a mystery to Gusev … It simply should not have been possible, with four missiles locked onto it, drone escorts or not.

Gusev's *Envoy* had been airborne and circling north of Russia's Mirny Station when word came from the GRU that the American aircraft had taken off from McMurdo. He would have liked to have been closer, but 750 miles' separation from the intense focus of American surveillance around their McMurdo base ensured they could stay undetected until go time.

They'd lit the *Envoy*'s tail, Kuznetsov NK-32 engines pouring fire so that they could haul the target in before it reached safety.

But both sides had learned from the earlier encounter.

"Three naval air defense radar signatures," Gusev said, reading the data. "And there's our target. One fighter escort, two drones. No AWACS visible yet, but I'm seeing low-frequency energy, so it's back there somewhere. They've got a P-8 Poseidon sub hunter circling too. Scan for surface contacts."

The *Envoy*'s quantum entanglement radar was a huge advance over conventional scanned array radars, but it used a very tightly directed beam. It could scan sky or sea but not both simultaneously.

"Optimizing for surface scan," Adamov confirmed. Their smart tactical display kept the aircraft contacts on screen, AI predicting their paths, ready to correct the tracks when it got another return. Near 3D images of the ships on the sea out in front of them started filling the screen too. "*Constellation* class, two, where the last satellite pass said they'd be, a couple of *Sea Hunter* drones, that US Coast Guard cutter and … ah, *dammit*."

Gusev looked at the screen, which showed the AI-generated ID for each of the vessels based on its physical and electronic signature, but he couldn't see what had Adamov so exercised. "What?"

Adamov pointed at the screen in front of them. "Coming in from the north. USNS *Howard O. Lorenzen*. The Americans call it a missile range instrumentation ship, but it's built for electronic warfare. Optimized for stealth detection and hypersonic missile interception. S-band, X, ULF *and* passive sensors. Has its own 50-kilowatt laser for air defense. It will be networked with those *Constellation* frigates and fighters too, directing any surface-to-air engagement."

"Will it see us?"

"You get close enough, of course it will. But out to 50 miles, we'll be alright. Maybe."

"Do you have a heading yet? Is it going to that platform?"

"Need more data to get a track," Adamov said. "But the first couple of data points say … maybe not. Seems to be headed toward one of the frigates. For protection?" Adamov sounded surprised. "I'm assuming it's there because of us. But maybe it's just there to monitor what's happening."

Their intel said the Americans would be testing a weapon from their weather observation platform. They were still too far

231

out to see it, but all the activity told Gusev a test was imminent, as they'd expected.

Gusev wanted to believe that. "If the Americans are doing a weapons test from that platform, it makes sense they don't want such a valuable vessel anywhere near it. What about the other vessels? You said Coast Guard. That Coast Guard vessel was docked at the platform—where is it now, relative?"

Adamov ran a calculation. "Ninety miles out, give or take a mile," Adamov said. "And it's moving away too."

"*Koshmar*," Gusev swore. "Those *Constellation* frigates have 32 interceptor missile cells each. That spy ship will be feeding them long-range targeting data." A new icon came up on the radar screen. "Our missiles have to get past those, *and* the fighter escort, to have a chance."

"I think that's what our GRU general might call '*our* bloody problem,'" Adamov muttered.

Gusev frowned. The adversary had put a ring of steel around the test area, but it was a long way from the NOAA platform that Gusev and Adamov had been briefed was the likely location for the American weapons test. The two frigates were about 100 miles out. Now the Coast Guard icebreaker was headed out too. Had something gone wrong?

"Run an analysis of radio traffic for the last three hours up to now," Gusev said. "See if there is some kind of peak, something that would explain why they are putting so much distance between themselves and the test area. An accident. Radiation release. I don't know …"

Adamov had access to satellite signals intelligence monitoring data collected by passing Russian satellites, and had his AI analyze the volume and type of traffic for patterns. It took mere moments. "Nothing. High levels of traffic, like you'd expect. No major comms peaks in the last three hours. No radiation release detected by satellite."

Now Gusev swore. There could be only one explanation. Whatever the Americans were planning to test, it was dangerous—maybe lethal—out to a range of at least *100 miles.*

The GRU general had not shared that level of detail with the VVS pilots. A test, he'd said, of a new weapon. Gusev and Adamov had their theories, of course. A hypersonic glide vehicle was top of the list, since the Americans were still far behind Russia and China in hypersonics. But this … this could only be one thing.

"It's a nuke," Gusev said. "They're testing a damn nuke."

"And it isn't tactical," Adamov said. "Blast radius of 100 bloody nautical miles? It has to be the mother of all strategic weapons."

Adamov couldn't disagree, but he also couldn't help but point out the obvious. "Our target is headed inside that zone, probably to deploy the weapon …"

"And if we don't kill it, the people we love will die," Gusev said. "I know, Captain. So we have to be *sure* we kill that damned AC-130 this time." He had his AI run an analysis of their stealth profile against the identified enemy naval and air threats. It told him they could risk pushing in deeper. "Keep your eyes on adversary radar signal strength. Let's see if we can find a gap in their radar coverage and get ourselves closer before we shoot."

***

J-hour minus 90 minutes

"That damned AC-130" was 200 miles from the NOAA platform, and Uncle was preparing to launch their Vigilant tiltrotor drone toward the platform, with the sensor package snugged into its payload bay. The technical and engineering smarts needed to land a jet aircraft vertically on a helicopter landing pad had been perfected by private space contractors decades before, and the task was largely automated—from approach, to transition from horizontal to vertical flight, and to touchdown. The Vigilant was on a one-way trip. The sensor package in its payload bay didn't need to be unloaded to function since it would only be monitoring things like vibration, air pressure and radiation, not images.

The personnel who had been stationed at the NOAA platform had been taken off overnight and were aboard the US Coast Guard cutter *Polar Warden*. *Charlene* was still making her long, slow run toward her terminal waypoint. "Terminal" in more ways than one.

None of that concerned Bunny. She had only to focus on one thing: the threat environment around Outlaw. Two-Tone had tried to reassure Outlaw's crew that another Russian intervention was both unlikely and, *if* it happened, unlikely to succeed.

"Navy brought up a T-AGOS electronic warfare ship overnight to help spot stealth aircraft and swat hypersonics if needed. Air Force has a P-8 Poseidon out searching for your ghost submarine, together with Navy's *Sea Hunters* and a *Virginia* class submarine that is covering the sea between the test site and the ice shelf where you ran into the *Sarov*." Two-Tone had been reading off a screen and took a breath. "Never before have I seen so much protection put in place, so far from enemy borders, for so few people."

"Well, that's our problem right there, sir," Rory had said. "Those units aren't there to protect Outlaw; they're there to protect *Charlene*. All that matters is their damn test. We are the decoys."

234

"You are also the crew piloting *Charlene*, so don't overdramatize, Captain," Two-Tone had chided. "Outlaw is no sacrificial lamb—especially not with the mods I had to fight Aaronson for."

Bunny was with Rory on that one. There was an Aggressor crew standing by in Auckland to take over remote piloting of *Charlene* if anything happened to Outlaw. Assuming their satellite signals could get through—and they could be boosted by both the *Constellation* frigates and *Howard O. Lorenzen*—any interruption to control of the undersea drone would probably only be measured in seconds, which was near instantaneous for submarine operations.

Bunny's self-preservation instinct had never been particularly strong, but her protective gene was, and she had developed something akin to love for the ancient, lumbering near wreck that was Outlaw. It should have been assigned to a boneyard or stripped for parts years, even decades ago. It had taken ground fire in Syria, shrapnel from a near miss with a missile over the Baltics that had ripped an aileron from a wing, evaded Chinese missiles over the Pacific and narrowly dodged a Russian missile over the Antarctic the day before. Bunny knew its luck was due to run out, but she was determined it wouldn't be on her watch.

She'd jettisoned the GAMBIT hardpoints from her wings and restored her Nemesis to its sleek, stealthy self. Which might not help against the Russians' new QE radar, but Russian missiles were terminally guided by old-style, multi-band radars, which her Nemesis was designed to dupe.

She had a belly full of air-to-air missiles, a jerry-rigged QE radar detecting array and a burning desire to put it to lethal use. She was almost hoping that Russian Tu-190 *would* try to come against them again.

***

In big militaries, the paths of soldiers, marines, sailors and pilots cross in ways they often don't recognize until years later, if at all.

And standing on the bridge of the USNS *Lorenzen*, currently making steam away from the NOAA platform that Outlaw's Vigilant drone was headed toward, was a sailor whose life Trigger Brown had once saved, though neither would ever know it.

The Chinese *Type 095* submarine that Trigger Brown's *Manta Ray* submersible drone had stalked and killed had itself been hunting for prey. And the prey in its sights at the time it was sent to the bottom of the Pacific was none other than the expeditionary mobile base USNS *John L. Canley*, on its way to support US operations on Taiwan. It was under the command of Master Sincere Jones, formerly of the US Coast Guard. And Sincere Jones had already had one ship sunk from underneath him by a Chinese submarine. It would have been the end of his career, if not his life, to have suffered it twice.

Fast forward several years and two vessels, and Master Sincere Jones was now commanding officer aboard the cruise-ship-sized USNS *Howard O. Lorenzen.* And once again, a lynchpin in an endeavor that could mean the triumph, or humiliation, of his nation.

Not that he knew it, because no one had told the officers of the *Howard O. Lorenzen,* including Sincere Jones, one iota more than they absolutely needed to know to perform their duties.

With *Lorenzen's* first mate on a video link to the ships of the Minerva Task Force at that moment, Jones had the conn. And *Lorenzen* was, without doubt, the weirdest damn vessel Jones had ever served on—which was saying something, considering he'd started his military career in the US Coast Guard on cutters, served in the US Military Sea Lift Command on expeditionary bases and fleet oilers. Because now he was on a vessel being operated for the US Air Force.

Yes, *Lorenzen* was an Air Force ship.

Which introduced its own challenges. With H-hour, or "J-hour," as the Minerva Task Force was calling it for some unknown reason, about one hour away, the bridge was heavily populated. Besides Officer of the Deck Lieutenant Andrew Stiles, *Lorenzen*'s bridge accommodated a junior officer of the watch and enlisted ratings such as a helmsman, lee helmsman, quartermaster, two lookouts and that necessary anachronism, a messenger or runner. And that was just the Sea Lift Command crew. Taking up valuable real estate at the back of the bridge were three USAF personnel: the Combat Intelligence Center (CIC) communications officer, a captain; the tactical action officer, a lieutenant, and the USAF engineering officer of the watch, another lieutenant.

Luckily, Jones's relationship with the USAF CIC comms officer, Lieutenant Juan Perine, was pretty smooth. He knew the real test of that was about to come soon, but Perine had a decent sense of humor and the street smarts to realize he and his people needed to be on the good side of *Lorenzen*'s MSC crew if he was going to succeed in his role.

Jones stepped over to his station and waited until he got off the line with the USAF CIC two decks below and looked up. "Captain?" Perine asked.

"Unfair question for you, Perine," Jones started, "but one I have to ask since your people are the only ones aboard this ship who seem to know what the hell my vessel is really doing down here among the penguins and icebergs."

237

"Ah, the million-dollar question," Perine said, then raised his voice. "As you would know, Captain, for reasons of operational security, I cannot disclose information about Project Minerva, or on-water operations related to it."

Jones sighed. "I know. Forget I ..."

Perine stood, turning to his TAO. "Lieutenant Pile, you have CIC watch. I'm going for coffee before it's too late." He picked a mug up from his station and turned to leave, pausing by Jones. "Join me, sir?"

Jones didn't need a second invitation. "I think I will. OOD, you have the conn. I'll be back in five."

"Officer of the Deck has the conn!" Jones's next-in-command confirmed.

Jones followed Perine out to the afterbridge stairwells, but they didn't head for the wardroom.

"Well, sir," Perine said, checking they were alone. "Tell me what you know."

Jones spoke quickly. "It's a weapons test. I've been told to maintain a 100-mile separation from the test position and that there may be high winds, turbulent seas and 'atmospheric electrical discharges and disruption to electronic systems,'" he said. "So my guess is it is a nuke. A very, very big nuke."

"Sure. Or it's just something very secret we aren't supposed to see." Perine shrugged. "But it seems we don't know any more about the actual test than you."

Jones continued. "And I've been told to ensure all available power is routed to your Cobra Kaiser radar system for the duration of the operation, which means shutting down any nonessential electrical systems for one hour before, until one hour after, the test," Sincere added. "But I haven't been told why, and I do not like being in ignorance of matters that might affect the safety of my vessel. Which is why I'm asking."

Perine weighed his words. "You know Cobra Kaiser has the ability to analyze background radiation and look for holes in the sky that might be stealth aircraft."

"Of course."

"So we were ordered on alert 30 minutes ago, at the same time as a civilian AC-130X took off from McMurdo. We are data-linked with every ship in the task force, and with every aircraft overhead. Which gives us control of a crazy amount of firepower. Pile and his team are that AC-130's guardian angels."

"*Civilian* 130X?"

"Aggressor Inc." He stood and waited for Jones to catch up.

Jones let his wheels turn. "So this weapon, or system, or whatever it is being tested, is being flown out of Antarctica by Aggressor Inc., so it doesn't look like a military flight, but someone is still worried an adversary will try to spoil the party."

"Rumor is they already tried," Perine said. "Aggressor is flying overwatch on their own aircraft, and I heard they lost two drones in an air engagement yesterday, but neither our *Constellations,* nor our AWACS, got a solid on the attacker. Navy found the wreckage of a Su-71 Monochrome after the action."

"A *Russian* Monochrome drone? Over in the Southern Ocean? A drone like that wouldn't have the range for operations over the Southern Ocean. It would have to launch off a ship or …"

"We're thinking air-launched, which means someone has a heavy out there somewhere …"

"Stealth? Could it be Chinese? The old Shanghai Pact rises again?"

"Not likely. US Army in China has every Chinese strategic aircraft under lock and key. You ever heard of the Tu-190 *Envoy*?"

Jones made it his business to know something about every aircraft America's enemies could try to sink him with. "Only a couple ever built, still in flight-testing."

"Maybe not. And those things can carry *20 tons* of ordnance. Drones, air-to-air, anti-ship hypersonics. Out best guess is that *Envoy* is why you were told to go to max revolutions and get us here pronto. They're flying battleships."

Sincere Jones suddenly felt like a very small man, on a very big ship, in the middle of a very exposed sea. "We'd better get back on the bridge," he said.

***

Probing the American radar perimeter had revealed no gaping holes for Gusev and Adamov. The two frigates were each covering hundreds of square miles of sky, and sliding in behind them was the big spy ship with its huge radars, radiating energy like a second sun. Circling around their target like sheepdogs around a flock of sheep were the American stealth fighter and its drone wingmen.

With so many targets to track and a radar that used a narrow beam, they were constantly losing and then regaining their target AC-130. It was a game of radar tag in a circle of sky of about 1,000 square miles. But they'd closed to within 100 miles of the projected position of their target now—near-point-blank range for their *Envoy*—and were trying to reacquire the target, before the American AWACS, fighter escort or warships spotted them.

"Got a contact!" Adamov said with unsuppressed excitement. "Low and slow, right where we want it. Has to be our target!"

"Very low. Could be that maritime surveillance plane we got a return from earlier?" Gusev asked.

"QE return is too dense," Adamov said, working the contact. "Yes! AI says that's our bird."

"Arm all ordnance," Gusev ordered.

"Arming anti-air and anti-ship ordnance," Adamov confirmed.

Gusev thought fast. They'd reanalyzed their last mission failure and concluded their mistake was just sending a volley of missiles at the target without being certain they'd dealt with *all* the escorts, naval and air, which might intercept those missiles. "That damn spy ship changes the equation. We can't get closer without coming under attack. We have to knock out the defenders before we launch on it," Gusev said.

"The enemy will be on alert after yesterday," Adamov pointed out. "They'll react the moment we begin our attack."

Gusev reached forward and slapped the instrument panel between himself and Adamov, where their ground crew had glued a small toy ghost on a pedestal, painted black. NATO called his aircraft '*Envoy*'—a deliberately harmless, meaningless name. "Then it is time to show them what our *Envoy* is capable of," Gusev said.

Among the 20 tons of munitions they deployed out of Chile with were Monochrome drones and a mix of 20 AA-12 and AA-13 air-to-air missiles. But based on their post-mission analysis, Gusev included six smaller KH-32 supersonic and two large Tsirkon hypersonic anti-ship missiles, capable of speeds up to Mach 9, or 100 miles a minute. He'd had to reduce his air-to-air missile loadout to a single rotary launcher, but they suspected it was a naval vessel that had saved their target last time by intercepting their hypersonic missiles—one of America's new *Constellation* class frigates, in all probability.

"Monochromes in electronic warfare mode," Adamov said, tapping keys. "Target priority: enemy frigates, AWACS, anti-submarine aircraft, fighter aircraft ..."

"No," Gusev said. "Target that electronic warfare vessel first. If we can take it out, we might be able to stay invisible."

"If we don't, they'll track the missiles back to us and know where to look," Adamov warned.

"Program a dog-leg waypoint," Gusev said. "They won't be able to trace it back."

Adamov went to work. "Attack profile programmed. Do you approve?"

Gusev reviewed his proposal as he brought the *Envoy* around to a launch heading, took them down to 2,000 feet over the icy ocean and trimmed for a 10 percent nose-up attitude. "Profile approved. Prepare to launch Tsirkons."

***

The spike was back. When she wasn't watching her instruments to make sure she wasn't going to smack into the sea in the milky-white nothingness surrounding her, Bunny was watching the detector array she and Venice had mounted on the instrument panel to supplement the RWR. It had detectors at all the key points of a 360-degree compass-like display, but when the RWR flickered with ghostly radiation, the array began strobing. It wasn't showing her a clear direction.

Could it be the enemy wasn't directing its radar right at her? That she was only catching incidental signals? Outlaw had to be their real target, and she was circling it a good 5 to 10 miles out as it plowed through the sky.

"Aggressor Two, Aggressor One. I think we have company," she said tightly. "I'm going to have to piggyback your position to get confirmation."

"Good copy, One," Rory replied. "Try not to spook the horses."

Bunny banked her Nemesis to put it on an intercept heading for Outlaw and matched the big aircraft's altitude, adding several hundred feet for safety. She also had to avoid the GAMBIT drones that were flying off Outlaw's port and starboard wings. When she got within a mile, she slid in behind the three aircraft, easing herself into formation right above and slightly behind the AC-130 so that it didn't have to fly through her jet wake.

Her eyes flicked between Outlaw and the detector array in front of her.

Spike. Right behind her. *Gone. Back again. Gone.* It was flicking on and off, like the attacker was having trouble keeping it locked on. *Or using it to track more than one target,* Bunny thought.

Pushing the capabilities of her Nemesis to their maximum, she stayed in Outlaw's shadow, yawing her aircraft while still flying straight ahead—first left, then right, watching the lights on the detector array. It took precious minutes, but she got a bearing and hailed the task force below.

"*Lorenzen* from Aggressor One, possible contact bearing two eight four degrees my position, altitude and range unknown. Aggressor One prosecuting."

With that, she flipped the Nemesis onto a wing and hauled it around to the bearing she had just given the big ship, pointing her nose at the sea. Their last encounter had taught her that, stealth or no stealth, the Russian could see her at ridiculous distances.

Rory would have been monitoring her radio call, but she "tapped him on the shoulder" anyway. "Aggressor Two, One. I'm going low, try to hide in the wave clutter. Suggest you do the same."

"Two copies. Will do our best impression of a flying fish. Out," Rory told her.

***

"More like flying whale," Uncle said, looking nervously at the sky and sea ahead of them. "And for the record, I can't see where the sky ends and the sea starts."

"Eyes on the altimeter," Rory told him, getting a feeling for the air around Outlaw as he pushed his yoke forward and took them down. "Going to be some pretty ugly air pockets and shears as we get lower. I can't risk going under 500. If that's our friend with the hypersonics out there, it could already have launched on us," Rory said. "Get that Vigilant away, now."

"Roger that," Uncle said, pulling a flat screen on an articulated arm from the wall of the cockpit beside him and waking it to life. Releasing the short take-off vertical landing drone from its underwing pylon was a "fire-and-forget" process—it would pilot itself to the NOAA platform.

"Vigilant spooling up … systems green. AI is running preflight," Uncle said. He flicked his eyes to the altimeter. "Altitude: 10,002 feet. Vigilant preflight complete; ready to release."

"Go for release," Rory told him, momentarily leveling their dive.

Uncle tapped a couple of icons on his foldout screen. "Releasing at 8,000: eight four, eight three, eight two, releasing … now." He strained his neck, looking over his shoulder out the cockpit window. "That's … good separation. Wings deployed; accelerating to cruising airspeed."

Rory felt Outlaw bump a little higher as the heavy drone dropped off its pylon, held their aircraft level another 10 seconds, then pushed his yoke forward again, sending them toward the sea in a curving dive. They'd done half their job. Now they just had to get *Charlene* into position.

He got on the intercom to the command module. "Trigger, Vigilant is away, but we may have a hostile aircraft tracking us. I'm taking us low. Buckle up back there."

***

"*Dead air*, bearing two seven four, altitude two to five, range 209 klicks. No heading data ..." Perine's TAO, Pile, intoned. The Aggressor pilot had told them where to look, and that was all Perine's team needed. "*Constellation*'s moving to search and track down the bearing, interceptors up. AWACS alerted. Aggressor One is outbound."

Jones listened carefully as the USAF lieutenant set wheels in motion like a quarterback calling a play. Their Cobra Kaiser system had spotted "dead air"—a moving hole in the ambient background noise of the sky where there shouldn't have been one. A stealth aircraft, reflecting and blocking the radio waves around it.

"That's nearly *inside* our air defense zone, dammit. Helm, come to niner zero," Jones told his helmsman. The Cobra Kaiser radar array was mounted on the *Lorenzen*'s rear deck aft of the superstructure and could only cover a 180-degree arc of sky. Angling their stern toward the possible contact also minimized their own radar signature and brought the laser turret on their superstructure to bear.

"Niner zero, aye," his helmsman replied.

"Ensign Peters, get my XO out of that video call," he told his runner. "Officer of the deck, sound action stations."

North and south of them, the two *Constellation* class frigates, USS *Congress* and USS *Galvez*, would be scanning the sky down the bearing to the dead air with their long-wavelength L-band radars, their higher-frequency arrays and optical infrared systems looking for the telltale signatures of incoming missiles.

It was the moment in any air defense engagement that Jones hated most. A threat detected, unidentified, unquantified. If it was the Russians, and they had hostile intent, it could have, probably *had*, already launched long-range missiles at the task force or the aircraft it was protecting.

They were operating at the frozen bottom of the world, inside a military exercise exclusion zone. Under a cloud of absolute secrecy. Nothing and no one would ever know what was about to happen, until someone in the White House or Kremlin decided to tell them. And that version of reality could be completely different to the one *Lorenzen* was sailing into.

***

"*What the* …*?* Aborting Tsirkon launch," Adamov said. "Break contact!"

With so many adversary radars on the horizon, Gusev had been focusing on flying an attack profile that would allow them to optimize their stealth profile while still allowing their radar to sweep the sky and sea in the direction of their targets. "Why?" he barked. He banked away, breaking contact with their targets and increasing separation to the American task force. Then his radar warning receiver flashed, data started streaming across the bottom of his helmet visor, but it was too much to assimilate. "Talk to me, Adamov."

"They know we're here, somehow," Adamov said. "Big spike in radio traffic, and the target AC-130 launched a drone and broke off, diving for the sea. Its escort also broke off on a heading directly for our position. We got hit on multiple radar frequencies by the spy ship, and the AWACS L-band radar intensified. No lock, but if we opened payload bay doors, they'd have gotten a return for sure."

Gusev thought fast. So the element of surprise was lost. Their overwhelming advantage in firepower was not. And neither was the urgency and importance of their mission. He brought the *Envoy* around again and steadied it.

"Reacquire all targets, Captain," he said calmly.

Adamov stared at him with dread, but then started working his QE radar again.

"All targets reacquired except the American stealth fighter," Adamov said. "You want me to keep searching, or …?"

"We need to take out those naval vessels first," Gusev said. "Launch anti-ship ordnance."

"Arming Tsirkons. Targeting enemy EW vessel. Launching in home-on-radar mode. *One away. Two away,*" Adamov said. "Recycling. Arming KH-32s."

Gusev heard and felt their payload bay snap open, saw the ship-killer missiles light their booster rockets and shoot out ahead of them as they curved toward the sea below, where they would ignite their scramjet engines and accelerate to Mach 9.

Inside the payload bay, one of their two rotary missile launchers was rotating as their supersonic, wave-skimming KH-32 missiles powered up. Each weighed 10,000 lbs., and the launcher held two. "KH-32s armed, systems nominal. Target data transferred. Launching in optical recognition mode." The thump of payload bay doors flipping open. "One away. Two away."

Gusev felt the bay doors close and pushed his throttles forward, the enormous thrust of their Kuznetsov engines against their suddenly lighter airframe pushing him back into his seat. Their real target was out there, seeking the illusory safety of its

247

Navy friends. The attack would continue until it was dead, or until Gusev and Adamov were.

"Bring the air-to-air systems online and find that damned stealth fighter," Gusev said between gritted teeth.

Adamov began working his radar, then spoke uncertainly. "Uh, I have a lock on the drone that separated from the target aircraft. Altitude … climbing through 10,000, for 15,000. Airspeed 400. Heading … it looks like its headed for that NOAA platform."

"Delivery drone, must be. But delivering what?" Gusev bit his lip. Could the new contact be their real target? The GRU general wanted the AC-130X dead, but he was a spook, not an aviator. An AC-130X could not land on the helipad of an oil-rig-style platform to deliver a weapon system—but a drone could. And with the protection the Americans were putting around it, that drone had to be carrying one critical payload.

"Is the new contact in range of our Axeheads?" Gusev asked.

Adamov quickly ran an intercept calculation. Their Axeheads flew faster but had a shorter range. "No. AA-12s are in range, not AA-13s." He was still working his radar, but it was the radar warning receiver that got their attention, flashing to alert them to a new and intense radar signal almost directly ahead of them. Flooding the air around them, but without luck. Yet.

"F-22 type," Adamov said. "It's our friend, the stealth fighter."

"Lock him up, dammit!" Gusev said.

"No return," Adamov said. "If he's down low, I'll need to switch to surface scanning mode, to separate him from the sea clutter."

"Not yet. Target the drone our target launched. Two AA-12s."

"Another launch will …"

"Compromise our stealth, yes. Noted, Captain," Gusev said. "The enemy naval vessels might be taken off task trying to protect it. Execute."

***

Bunny was flying at Mach 1.2 into that terrifying milky nothingness, where the only things telling you that you were flying through the air, not the water, were your instruments, and the fact you weren't already dead. Her radar altimeter was constantly intoning softly in her ears … *Collision warning, 200 feet, pull up. Collision warning, 180 feet, pull up …*

She ignored it, eyes flicking from her instruments to the radar screen, where her AI was executing a search of the sky down the bearing to the dead air that *Lorenzen* had pushed to her, and to the RWR radiation detection array bolted to her instrument panel, which …

Lit up like a Christmas tree!

The three LED lights on the "compass rose" at 11, 12 and 1 o'clock glowed brightly, swinging back and forth as though the Russian were waving a torchlight across her nose. Then it settled.

One o'clock! She yawed right, and the LED at her 12 o'clock lit brightly. *Found you, bastard.*

***

"Vampires! Inbound our position! Hypersonic, bearing zero two two, altitude 1,000, range 40, time to impact … 20 seconds," *Lorenzen*'s TAO, Pile, called.

"Weapons free," USAF CIC Comms Officer Juan Perine ordered.

"Weapons free, aye," the TAO confirmed.

Sincere Jones blinked, a sudden feeling of helplessness nearly overwhelming him. A hypersonic missile engagement happened at quantum speeds, faster than any human chain of command could manage. Once Perine gave the order to release weapons, he slipped the leash on a multi-domain kill chain that went from the *Lorenzen* to overhead satellites and down again to detection and weapons systems aboard both *Constellation* class frigates, and to the Aggressor aircraft overhead.

On the two *Constellation* frigates, hypervelocity projectile railguns on their foredecks, sitting between twin banks of vertical missile launch tubes, trained themselves toward the incoming missiles. At the same time, interceptor missiles blasted from the frigates' vertical launchers.

The two frigates could each fire six railgun projectiles a minute from their double rails, and with under a half minute to run, they would only get one shot each at the incoming Tsirkons. But the Tsirkon could only sustain Mach 9 during its cruise phase, because its extreme speed pushed a wave of plasma out in front of it that both made it easier to detect and also blinded its own terminal guidance systems. To see its target, a moving warship, and to pick up the radar energies they needed to lock onto, they had to slow to a more modest Mach 4.5, or 3,500 miles an hour. And they did not have terminal evasion capability, meaning they were making a beeline for *Lorenzen*.

Which didn't mean they were flying straight and level. The cold Antarctic air, filled with flurries of snow, was a maelstrom of warm and cold air, and the two missiles blasted from air pocket to air pocket, jumping up and down as they closed on the big white warship.

Quantum computers aboard the *Lorenzen* made one last calculation and sent it to the two *Constellation* frigates at the speed of light, and they each spat four projectiles into the path of the Russian missiles.

One connected, the Tsirkon it hit dumping itself into the cold ocean, to skip once, twice, three times across the surface and explode a mile short of *Lorenzen*.

Three railgun projectiles missed. *Lorenzen*'s bow was facing the unidentified aircraft threat. The two Russian missiles had approached from its starboard side, and it was nearly broadside on to the threat.

The interceptor missiles fired by the *Constellation* frigates into the path of the hypersonic Russian missiles fell uselessly behind, unable to get a lock. *Lorenzen* had one last hope. The laser turret on its superstructure was also tracking the incoming missile and began pouring a 2,000°F beam of energy into the missile's path. It would have been enough to burn through to the warhead of a common supersonic missile, but the Tsirkon had a ceramic nose cone designed to withstand the extraordinary temperatures of Mach 9 flight.

Having warmed and expanded, and then suddenly cooled and contracted as the missile slowed, the nose cone was brittle, but still intact. As *Lorenzen*'s laser heated it again, it cracked. A hundred meters out from the *Lorenzen*, the laser burned through and touched off the Tsirkon's 800 lb. warhead.

Jones had run to the starboard bridge wing. The space around the ship was a disorienting, swirling milky white, gray sea merging into gray-white air. A mile out, he saw a flash, heard an explosion. *Interception!*

For a moment, he dared hope.

Then, from out of the air right in front of him, a flaming arrow appeared, faster than his eyes could follow. He didn't even have time to flinch. *Lorenzen*'s laser did its job, but too late. The missile detonated about 50 yards out from *Lorenzen*'s hull, and about 50 yards behind where Jones was standing. Fuel, metal and plasma slammed into *Lorenzen*'s superstructure. Jones was thrown off his feet. The big ship heeled over with a deep, metallic groan.

And the dying started.

***

For the second time in his career, Sincere Jones pulled himself, dazed, cut and bleeding, to his feet, as the supersonic KH-32 missiles Adamov had fired at the two *Constellation* frigates closed on their targets.

The *Constellation* class frigate was a formidable platform. With or without the support of the *Lorenzen*'s powerful radar and jamming suite, a single *Constellation* could track up to 200 targets simultaneously and engage 32 at a time with its vertically launched interceptor missiles. Its powerful radar could jam a missile's radar seeker. To cope with drone swarms, it had kinetic and laser-based close-in weapon systems. China had found, to its dismay, that it was almost impossible to overwhelm the defenses of a *Constellation* frigate.

Russia had already learned that lesson, and incorporated the learnings into the latest versions of its KH-32 anti-ship missile. Gusev had taken off with three upgraded KH-32s in his weapons bay. Each could fly at wavetop height, at Mach 1.4, using inertial guidance to reach their target area, and then use unjammable optical guidance with AI matching to locate enemy ships. As they closed on their targets, they maneuvered randomly up and down, left and right, to frustrate interception. What set them apart from the last generation of KH-32s was none of these things. As they made their terminal approach and started evasive maneuvering, each KH-32 suddenly rose in the air and *split* into

10 gliding submunitions. Six were decoys and started streaming chaff and flares to attract interceptor missiles to themselves.

Four submunitions in each KH-32 held live warheads.

The math was suddenly against the *Constellation* frigates. They'd used four missiles each against the hypersonic threats to the *Lorenzen*. Each frigate's radar saw 30 incoming missiles, but at such close range, they could only launch 16 interceptors at them as they brought their CIWS defenses to bear and fired hovering decoy drones into the air behind them to try to pull some of the Russian missiles away.

The sky down the bearing to the incoming vampires became a maelstrom of explosions, decoy flares and metal foil. From the chaos, seconds from impact, 14 missiles streaked toward the USS *Congress* and USS *Galvez*. Four held live warheads. AI-guided laser turrets took down six of the 14 submunitions. Six hit the *Congress*, and two the *Galvez*.

Several were jamming decoys, but *Congress* took all four of the *Envoy*'s live warheads, in a line amidships that started at its RIB boat station and ended at its twin torpedo launchers. Which, since the *Constellations* had been part of the hunt for the Russian *Sarov*, were loaded when the KH-32 warheads hit. *Congress*'s starboard torpedoes exploded, adding their 1,200 lbs. of high explosive to the fury of the Russian strike, opening a hole in her side the size of an entrance to the Lincoln Tunnel. She began taking water immediately.

Galvez was luckier, but only for a few seconds. The two warheads that hit it were jamming decoys, and had emptied their load of tinfoil and flares. But each weighed about 1,500 lbs., and they struck the *Galvez* beneath its helicopter deck at supersonic speed, filling its hangar bay with molten metal, touching off the avgas and oil stored there. Soon, fire and smoke poured from every opening and vent at the rear of the frigate, and a minute later, an explosion cut power to her twin shafts. *Galvez* was dead in the water.

***

The first time a ship under Jones's command had been struck by a missile had been off the coast of California in the opening days of the war with China, and that one had flattened their bridge, with him in it, putting him in the hospital for several months. This one had missed the bridge, and as soon as *Lorenzen* righted itself after the hammer blow and he regained his feet, Jones began barking orders—sending damage control crews aft, ordering a rating to find his XO, asking his watch officers for status reports on systems, propulsion and steerage …

"Lieutenant Perine, detection systems status!" he called out to the USAF officer.

"Cobra Kaiser still operational, though we've lost L-band," Perine said. "Still transmitting; pushing data to AWACS. Christ …" He had a cut on his forehead leaking blood onto the console in front of him, but that wasn't why he was looking white. "We've lost our links to *Congress* and *Galvez*."

"Did we lose our comms antennae?" Jones asked.

"No, or we wouldn't be able to link to the AWACS. I think …" He swallowed. "I think *Congress* and *Galvez* are down."

The situation was spiraling out of control, but Jones didn't do spiraling. He took a deep breath, ordered priorities in his head and motioned to his comms officer as he grabbed a headset off the floor and settled it over his cap. "Get the *Polar Warden* on VHF."

His comms specialist was still setting herself up again after tumbling to the deck and started tapping keys. A few moments later, Jones saw her lift her head. "XO on the *Warden* on the line."

"*Warden*, this is *Lorenzen*. What's your situation?" Jones asked.

Jones didn't know the XO of the *Warden* personally, but he sounded rattled. "*Lorenzen*, we are undamaged, making speed for *Congress*. Are you in a position to come to the aid of the *Galvez*?"

Are we? Too early to say. "We took a hit, *Warden*. Still assessing damage, but we have propulsion and steerage way. If we can make for *Galvez*'s position, we will. Do you have contact with either *Galvez* or *Congress*? We can't raise them."

"*Congress* is gone," the Coast Guard officer said, choking on the last word. "She's *gone*. Our helo is overhead—she's on fire. Crew are abandoning. She's … she's gone, *Lorenzen*."

"Alright, easy man. We'll get to them if we can," Jones said. "*Lorenzen* out."

Damage reports started coming in. And casualty reports. Among the first was an explanation of why *Lorenzen*'s first mate had not appeared on the bridge. The Russian missile had entered *Lorenzen*'s thin-skinned superstructure 2 yards below the vessel's video conferencing center and detonated right beneath the feet of the mate.

It might have been the second time Jones's vessel had been hit by a missile, but this time, he was still on his feet. And he was going to make that count.

He pushed that thought aside. "Lieutenant Perine, keep that link to the AWACS alive, and push them everything you have. That Aggressor fighter up there might be our only hope if the enemy comes at us again."

***

Trigger Brown could see everything on her tactical display that the Wedgetail AWACS could see. That is, whenever Outlaw was steady enough for her to focus. It was jumping and shuddering as it rode the mogul-like pockets of cold and colder air just above the Southern Ocean.

They had lost their "decoy" Vigilant to a long-range attack by the Russian aircraft as it approached the NOAA platform. What she couldn't see was the bastard Russian ghost that was out there somewhere, dealing killing blows to the Minerva Task Force. She could only hope O'Hare could find it.

"Brown!" said a very perturbed Rory O'Donoghue from the cockpit. He was online with the AWACS, but didn't have the big-picture view Trigger had. "Sitrep!"

"It's a shit show out there," Trigger said, trying to pool the data she was seeing on her tactical display. "Both *Constellation* frigates hit and badly damaged, maybe sunk … The *Lorenzen* was hit too."

"That takes the *Sea Hunters* out of action too," Bell said. "No motherships, no drone control. Unless *Galvez* can rope them in."

"We aren't at war," Venice said, eyes wide. "They … they can't do this!"

Trigger checked *Charlene* was at least still on track. She was less than 90 minutes out from her terminal waypoint.

'We are at the bottom of the world, with no one watching," Bell explained. "Whatever is happening right now, Russia will deny. It'll be our word against theirs, and when your bomb explodes, the water literally gets even muddier."

"*If* it explodes," Trigger said. "White House has to be shitting kittens about this. They'll call the test off."

"They can't," Venice said. "They wouldn't. Not when it is so close."

Trigger saw a mayday flash across her tactical screen from the stricken USS *Galvez*. An emergency locator beacon was also flashing where the USS *Congress* had been. "I guess we're about to see what kind of stuff the president is made of," Trigger said.

***

"How the hell did we allow this to happen a second time?!" President Mark Bendheim asked. He was being hurried down to the White House Situation Room in the company of CIA Director Boniface Antonio. The two of them had been sitting in the Oval Office, on the line with Project Minerva Director David Lau and his staff.

With the test just hours away, the full Joint Chiefs of Staff had been brought into the circle of secrecy. The heads of Navy, Space and Air Force knew about Project Minerva, of course, since they had contributed ships, aircraft and satellite capacity to the Minerva Task Force. But like so many other elements of the US military and political complex, they had been blind to exactly what Project Minerva was about to test.

Like every high-ranking officer not fully read into Project Minerva, they had been told it was hypersonic nuclear weapons research, concealed in the Antarctic under the flimsy cover of the Energy Independence Program. As Bendheim joined the call with the Joint Chiefs, Minerva's military liaison, Colonel Victor Sandilands, was still taking questions from the Joint Chiefs, who were also trying desperately to keep up to speed with events in the Southern Ocean as the attack on the Minerva Task Force unfolded. Was *still* unfolding.

"Mr. President," Sandilands said, halting himself mid-flow as the President's image came on screen. "The floor is yours."

"Thank you, Colonel," Bendheim said, sitting down at the polished mahogany table in the Situation Room and addressing the assembled officers on wall screen. "Let's get one thing out of the way. You will see my own Chief of Staff is not present on this call. I know you are all, with the exception of the colonel, pissed that you weren't fully briefed on Project Minerva before now. I have one thing to say to you. Get over it."

Bendheim let the order land, knowing that few, if any, of the officers on the call would ever have heard him speak to them that way. It didn't come naturally to him. At that moment, he was channeling the steely determination of his predecessor, a woman who seemed to have a preternatural belief in her own destiny, and that of her nation, which brooked no argument.

He got none. There was only silence from the other end of the line. "General Maxwell, please summarize the latest information from the Minerva Task Force."

Chair of the Joint Chiefs General Earl Maxwell had served Bendheim's predecessor, leading the prosecution of the war against the Shanghai Pact from start to finish. He had requested early retirement, but Bendheim had asked him to stay on, suspecting he would need his experienced counsel. It had been a wise decision. The man was not fazed by the moment. He calmly looked off-camera, muted his mic, conferred with an aide, then returned to the call, referring to a tablet PC in front of him.

"Mr. President, the task force securing the Project Minerva test site is under air attack. USS *Congress* has been severely damaged, possibly destroyed, casualties unknown. USS *Galvez* is on fire; they are attempting to restore propulsion and contain the fire. Casualties unknown. USS *Lorenzen* has sustained damage. Her critical systems are still operational; casualties are light. USCG *Polar Warden* is undamaged and going to the aid of *Congress*." He paused. "The, uh … the engagement is still ongoing."

"This is the Russians?" Bendheim asked.

"We assume so, Mr. President," Maxwell said. "They were behind the earlier attacks on Concordia and the attempt to destroy the Minerva device in flight, so yes, got to be Russia."

"Air Force?" Bendheim asked in shorthand.

His Chief of Air Force Staff, General Spencer Lock, was caught looking off-camera, and pulled a piece of paper from someone's hand. "Mr. President. We … we believe this is the same aircraft that attacked our transport aircraft and escorts yesterday. A new … a prototype Russian stealth bomber. We have a fix on the attacker, and are actively engaged. No air losses reported at this moment, nor kills."

Bendheim blinked. "Wait. One Russian aircraft shot down a drone yesterday, nearly took out our weapon transport, and today it hit *three* of our warships?" After the actions of the day before, Bendheim had wanted to expel Russian diplomats, reinstate sanctions, set up a heated call with the Russian president. But he had been talked down off that ledge by Antonio, who'd insisted it was better to keep Russia's leadership in the dark about whether their actions were disrupting Project Minerva at all.

Lock looked deeply uncomfortable. "Sir, yes. It's a stealth platform like our B-21 Raider, but carrying a bigger payload. It has advanced radar, and … well, we believe Russia only has one in operation."

"Which tells you they are playing for keeps down there," Antonio whispered to Bendheim.

"Mr. President, if I may, there is something requiring your immediate attention," Colonel Sandilands said, breaking into the discussion.

For a junior officer to do such a thing, at such a time, required balls; Bendheim knew that. "Colonel?"

"Sir, we have information from one of the Russian soldiers captured yesterday that the Russian nuclear submarine we briefly made contact with two days ago, the *Sarov*, has orders to deploy nuclear weapons to disrupt our test."

Bendheim frowned. "Deploy nuclear weapons against what?" he asked. "Concordia Station? The NOAA platform? Would a nuclear attack on either of those targets prevent our test?"

"No sir," Sandilands replied. "But it would confuse the narrative immensely."

"The *narrative*?" Bendheim said. "Speak English, Colonel."

"Sorry, sir," the man said. "Sir, if Russia detonates a strategic nuclear weapon proximate to our antimatter weapon test in either time or space, it will be almost impossible for us to convincingly claim that our weapon is not just a large nuclear bomb. Everything about our test will be open to dispute, to claim and counter-claim. I'm also told the data we would get from our test would be confused, almost useless."

"But Russia would know the truth, Colonel," Antonio pointed out.

"The world would not; our allies would not," Maxwell said. "We'd have doubters inside our own government."

"So where is this damned Russian submarine?" Bendheim asked.

"We ... we don't know, Mr. President," the Chief of Navy said. "And Russia just knocked out several key naval antisubmarine assets. We still have air assets and a *Virginia* class submarine searching ..."

Bendheim slapped his desk. "Gentlemen, you will get control of this shit show," he said, surprising even himself with the determined tone in his voice. "Russia may not have declared a new state of war with this nation, but it has declared war on

260

this program, which makes it all the more critical that it succeeds. You will deal with that Russian aircraft, and you will find and kill that Russian submarine. You will rescue our people. And the Project Minerva test *will* proceed. Even if we lose every ship, plane and submarine in that task force and Concordia Station is turned to meltwater, the test will proceed. We are racing our adversaries to be the first to deploy the most powerful weapon humankind has seen, and it is a race we cannot lose. Now get back to work," Bendheim said.

Boniface Antonio leaned forward and cut the call. An aide appeared in the doorway, and Antonio waved him away. "Holy hell, Mr. President," Antonio said. "This is a new side of you. Didn't know you had it in you."

Bendheim leaned back in his seat, arms spread in front of him, palms flat on the table, looking up at the ceiling. "No, Bony, but I knew I'd have to find it. You know what President Carliotti said to me the day I won the post-war election?"

"You never told me," Antonio said.

"She told me I would need to grow a pair," he said. "She said China was beaten, but not Russia. And that Russia was like a boxer in a ring who was going to keep fighting until you knocked them flat. We're seeing that right now. Project Minerva is supposed to persuade them to give up the damn fight, and I'll be damned if we don't deliver that message."

***

CIA Director Boniface Antonio could be forgiven for being surprised at the US president's robust address to the Joint Chiefs, because he didn't have perfect insight into the mind of Mark Bendheim. What he didn't know was that Bendheim felt like a man walking a wire over a pit. And inside the pit, the Russian bear was snarling.

261

The CIA wasn't the only agency with sources inside the Russian government, and the "POTUS Eyes Only" briefings Bendheim was seeing from agencies from Cyber Command and NSA to the DIA Human Intelligence Directorate and FBI told him one thing: Russia was preparing to go to war. Antonio and the other members of the National Security Council and Joint Chiefs of Staff knew it, of course, but only Bendheim was seeing and hearing it in the very voices of Russia's politicians and generals.

Just before getting on the line with the Joint Chiefs, Bendheim had been listening to a subtitled recorded conversation between the admiral of Russia's Black Sea Fleet and his Chief of Staff and vice admiral. Several months earlier, DIA Humint Directorate officers had managed to recruit the owner of the garage in Sevastopol, Crimea, where officers of the Black Sea Fleet had their vehicles serviced. Whenever a Russian Senat limousine was brought in for service, the vehicle's communication software was modified with Israeli-developed code that directed its telephone microphones to record and store in-vehicle conversations. Each time the vehicle was returned for service after that, the conversations were downloaded.

Vice Admiral: "Admiral, is there any more on my request for additional sealift capacity?"

Admiral: "I got you two *Lavina* class amphibious assault ships, despite the screaming from that bastard Velnikov. With your *Ropuchas* and *Alligators*, it will be enough."

Vice Admiral: "Not if I am to move 100,000 troops inside a month, Admiral. With current capacity, we can move a division, with armor and equipment, a week. In a month, 50,000 troops. Either I need more capacity or more time."

Admiral (grunts): "Time I might be able to get you. But capacity, no. We need to move while the Americans are still licking their wounds from their Pacific adventure, and before they elect someone with more backbone than that … what do they call the fluffy candy on a stick?"

Vice Admiral: "Cotton candy?"

Admiral: "That's it … Before they replace their 'cotton candy' president with someone tougher."

The petty insult didn't worry him. What worried him was that Russia was preparing for war, and neither DIA, CIA, NSA nor the State Department could agree on where it was planning to strike. State was convinced it had to be Ukraine again, or an attempt to retake Kaliningrad. DIA said it planned to expand its footprint in Africa while the US was focused elsewhere. The CIA said it was going to make a play to control the Bering Strait and choke off US arctic maritime traffic. The only thing they agreed on was that having mobilized in support of the Shanghai Pact war with the West, Russian industry, its economy and its population were geared for war.

Clearly none of the usual deterrents—economic, political or even nuclear—were working on the Russian president, Andrei Dyumin, who had not only refused to meet with Bendheim or other Western leaders in the aftermath of the collapse of the Shanghai Pact but also would not even agree to a telephone call. He seemed determined to turn Russia into a hermit kingdom that saw nothing but enemies outside its walls.

Bendheim needed Project Minerva to deliver that deterrent to him, and he needed it *yesterday*.

***

There was only one message Colonel Roman Gusev of the 121st Advanced Bomber Aviation Regiment cared about, and that was the one that had been delivered to him in no uncertain terms by GRU Major General Arsharvin. "My agents will execute your wife, Gusev, if you fail me again."

The American stealth fighter was frantically searching for them, radar energies approaching dangerous levels, but hadn't achieved a lock on his *Envoy* yet. Gusev kept the nose of their twin-engined machine in a 10-degree dive toward the sea as Adamov gave him a post-attack damage assessment. "*Constellation* picket radars are down; we must have got hits. That EW spy ship is still radiating, still a threat, but has no lock. AWACS is up, searching—no lock on us yet. In addition to hits on the vessels, we've killed one drone."

Gusev shot a glance at their tactical display. "Where is our target?"

"I took the QE radar off him to guide the KH-32s in," Adamov said. "Scanning low … Got him."

The AC-130, which had two drones welded to its wings as it changed course, was trying to increase separation to his *Envoy*, indicating it knew it was being hunted. Considering all the missiles he had sent at it in their last engagement, Gusev had to assume the cargo plane's crew were more than competent, and it was probably *more* than a conventional cargo plane.

An AC-130, a worthy adversary for his *Envoy*? Who would have expected that? They'd thinned out the naval surface-to-air defenses protecting their target, and sown confusion among its air defenders. It was time.

"The moment of truth is upon us, Captain," Gusev said. He set his throttles and stick for a gentle climb.

Adamov looked across the cockpit at him. "I know. We have only 10 missiles left, and that bastard stealth fighter is still between us and the target. It will get a lock any moment unless we—"

"He will be looking low, among the wave clutter. I am taking us up to 60,000," Gusev told him. "We'll take out that fighter, then knock down the cargo plane from point-blank range."

Gusev had been with the *Envoy* program since its inception, and was its most experienced test pilot. He'd invented a maneuver that made the big stealth bomber near invisible to radars below it, whether naval, surface or airborne. He watched the altimeter as they climbed from 30,000 through 40,000 and 50,000 feet, to 60,000 feet.

The very edge of the flyable atmosphere for a machine like the *Envoy*.

"Going oblique," he told Adamov.

Adamov pulled his harness tighter and pushed some papers back into place in the pocket on the cockpit wall beside him. "I'm ready."

Their *Envoy* had a trick no other stealth bomber could copy. Like the bat-winged American B-21 or Chinese H-20, it was a double-delta-winged aircraft with a flattened fuselage and insane thrust-to-weight ratio. Gusev rolled the big aircraft through 60 degrees, so it was sliding through the sky, starboard wing down, port wing up, without losing altitude. Up at 60,000 feet, it would normally be presenting its big flat underside at enemy radars. But AI-assisted fly-by-wire flight control surfaces combined with flexible wings and powerful thrust-vectoring engines meant it could tilt obliquely and fly straight and level with only a disc-like side profile exposed to radars underneath it.

To anything looking up at it, the huge aircraft suddenly had the radar cross section of a bumblebee.

Gusev couldn't help but feel proud. His *Envoy* was an amazing piece of aeronautical engineering. The most powerful airborne weapons platform Russia, perhaps the world, had ever seen. Configured like this, radar energies, even the low frequencies which were a danger to a stealth aircraft, slid right over it and into the upper atmosphere.

Gusev held his gloved hand out and grasped Adamov's forearm. "For Sergei," he said.

"For Anzhelika," Adamov said, gripping his hand. "Let's get this bastard."

***

"Contact lost," Pile said aboard the *Lorenzen*.

"Wasn't it moving closer?" Stiles asked, checking his display. Once they'd locked onto the hole in the sky that was a stealth aircraft, they rarely lost it until the aircraft either pulled out of range and disappeared into the radiation clutter again or went so low it could hide behind terrain.

"Moving closer and climbing higher," Pile said. "Then it disappeared. The Aggressor fighter is right in front of it, 30 miles out, and can't see it either."

Sincere Jones was too busy managing the constant flow of information from damage parties to follow the continuing air engagement closely, but he had one ear on the conversation between the USAF bridge officers, since their survival might depend on it.

They'd come out of the missile strike with a high number of casualties but relatively little damage. The Russian missile had exploded before reaching *Lorenzen*, molten metal burning through the thin skin of her superstructure below the bridge deck level, laying waste to the wardroom, CO's accommodation and officers' showers. Since they were at alert state, the officers who weren't on duty had gathered in the wardroom, and *Lorenzen*'s first mate had been in a small room between his accommodation and the wardroom that served as its video conferencing center, on a call with other officers of the task force, when the Russian attack hit like lightning from a clear sky.

Lorenzen's first mate, third mate and first assistant engineer were confirmed dead, along with her cargo officer, a steward and a cook. Six crew were injured, some burned so badly, Jones had been told it was unlikely they would survive unless they could get critical medical care, and fast. But *Lorenzen*'s medical officer and small team of paramedics were overwhelmed.

They were headed toward the USS *Galvez*, to assist with firefighting, put it under tow if it couldn't get power to its screws, or worst case, take the crew off. His second mate, Ira Clancy, had joined him on the bridge to navigate—no easy task since they also needed to keep their radars oriented toward the threat—while Jones focused on getting help for their wounded. Usually they'd draw on the medical resources of other ships in the task force, fly their wounded out to infirmaries aboard *Congress* or *Galvez*. That wasn't happening. The USCG *Polar Warden* was headed for the *Congress*, its helo already occupied trying to save any sailors who'd gotten off the frigate and into the freezing water. Despite its size, *Lorenzen* had no helicopter of its own, nor a helipad.

Because of the weapons test and the possibility there would be unexpected atmospheric effects or turbulent seas, McMurdo base had an additional two Polar Jayhawk helicopters on standby, but even in good weather, in non-contested skies, they'd take over an hour to reach *Lorenzen* or the other ships in the task force. Neither the weather nor the combat environment were in Jones's favor.

"I understand there's a storm, Lieutenant," Jones said to McMurdo's harried Coast Guard duty officer, who was triaging calls from the vessels of the devastated task force without being able to offer any practical help. "I'm asking *when* you expect to be able to effect rescue operations."

"Sir, we still don't have a full overview ... *Polar Warden*'s chopper is dropping life rafts ... They've got four hypothermia cases they lifted out of the water to deliver to the *Warden*, so they can't ... and our Jayhawks won't be flying until tomorrow morning, earliest, now the storm front is here. We're socked in, sir."

"We're on our own, you're saying," Jones said.

"I'm sorry, sir, there's nothing we can—"

"Understood. *Lorenzen* out." Jones cut the call. He passed the news on to his medical officer.

"Tomorrow morning? They'll prioritize *Congress*, then *Galvez*; we'll be last in line," he said. Jones heard a muffled conversation before the doc came back on. "We're looking at another 24 hours at least without help, and we'll do what we can, but I've got two burn cases here who probably won't make it through the night, and that's the bald truth, sir."

"I hear you, doc," Jones said. "I'm not giving up. I'll let you know if anything changes."

"*Dead air!*" Pile said suddenly. "Anomaly at two eight zero degrees, altitude 60,000, range 80 miles. Pushing data to AWACS ..."

"Light it up with active radar, Lieutenant," Stiles said. "Everything you've got. Get the Aggressor pilot a solid fix."

***

"Search radar," Adamov said tightly. "Eighty miles. Right off our nose. S- and X-band. Tight beam. And L-band from the AWACS. High probability of detection."

They had managed to stay hidden longer than Gusev could have hoped, with the US stealth fighters only 30 miles away. But their luck was about to run out. They were going to have to shoot through and around the fighter escort to get to their target, but he had one last card to play before they committed their last missiles.

"It's that damn spy ship. Launch Monochromes on full auto," Gusev said. He dropped his port wing, bringing their aircraft wings level for the coming attack.

"Monochromes spooling up," Adamov confirmed, throwing switches on a panel beside his right hand. "Setting to fully autonomous engagement mode. Failure on M2. Good boot on M1. Recycling … no, M2 is dead!"

"Drop it anyway; it'll give the enemy fighter a return to chase if nothing else."

"Good copy. Launching M1 … M1 away. Jettisoning M2. M2 away."

The *Envoy*'s payload bay doors snapped open, then shut again. A Monochrome drone was kicked into the sky below them, lit its tail and began searching for the American fighter. The payload bay snapping open a second time, the defunct Monochrome was also kicked into their wake. With no electrical power, its engine wouldn't fire; its wings couldn't open. It fell like a bomb toward the water 60,000 feet below.

***

If this is peacetime, give me war any day, Bunny O'Hare was thinking, gritting her teeth. At least you knew who and what you were up against.

She wasn't blind to the carnage behind her. It was laid out across her tactical display in all its devastation. But with the two air defense frigates offline and their USAF electronic warfare defender wounded, Bunny and her two GAMBITs were the only hope that remained for Outlaw and its submersible.

269

Bunny O'Hare had a compartment in her chest where she buried any fear that threatened to overwhelm her. It crawled out again when she was alone, in the dark, but until those moments, she kept it locked away, where it couldn't pull her off-task.

And that task right now was to kill a Russian ghost.

A ping from the *Lorenzen* behind her! New icons appeared on her helmet display, labels underneath them telling her what she was looking at: Su-71 Monochrome drones. One up at 60,000 feet was painting her with radar, and a second was doing … what? Dropping in a bomb-like parabolic curve toward the sea? Going low, for another ship strike maybe?

Then her own radar chimed. A solid return from the enemy above, as its payload bay doors opened and it launched its drones!

She tapped a key combination on her joystick and sent two AIM-260s in self-guiding mode at the Russian Monochromes that had just appeared. Hard-won combat experience told Bunny not to ignore the drones. They were short-range, lightly armed nuisances, but nuisances that could kill you if you underestimated them. Her missiles would keep them busy. She wanted the mothership that had launched them and lit her search radar, pointing it ahead of the area where the Russian drones had first been detected as she pulled her nose up and climbed out of the clutter of the sea, pushing her throttle forward to close the gap to the tiny arc of sky 30 miles ahead of her. Her optical infrared scanner was also looking for any sign of heat or movement in the dark sky above as she rocketed upward.

Come on, come on, she urged the AI running the search pattern. Give me something. A radio squeak. A radar lock. A reflection. Anything …

Infrared lock. Contact! She killed her radar immediately— it could only give her away now. A square appeared in her visor, high and to her right. Her Nemesis was already at max thrust, climbing at 25 degrees, but she pulled her nose even higher so she could follow the contact around as it went past her starboard wing, 20,000 feet above her.

"Center contact on tactical. Magnify," she ordered her Nemesis's AI. The target wasn't sending out an Identify Friend Foe code, but she couldn't afford to fire on a commercial airliner by mistake, so as her AI put it on screen and ran a visual identification algorithm over it, Bunny was already matching it with images in her own head. It looked like a Tu-160 Blackjack, but the wing shape was different, more delta shaped, and … no vertical stabilizer?

Tu-190 Envoy, the AI announced. Valid target.

Hell yeah, valid target, Bunny agreed. She had already cued two AIM-260 intermediate-range missiles and jabbed her thumb down on the button on her joystick that launched them. "Fox three by two," she intoned.

She barely had time to register the launch when her own missile proximity alert started screaming.

A Russian Monochrome had managed to evade her missile and launch at her.

***

"Missiles inbound!" Adamov called, Bunny's launch detected immediately by infrared sensors lining their fuselage. "Bearing 170 degrees, low. Impact in … *18 seconds*."

Gusev had been expecting the attack. The Monochrome drone they had launched had been unable to lock the American up straightaway, which meant its pilot was free to continue his search without distraction. And he'd found them. A brief flicker of radar came and went as the American got a return off their

271

Envoy, and then it was gone, as he tried to go dark, no doubt tracking them on optical infrared sensors.

Adamov lost the American as he passed below and behind them, but then picked him up on their own infrared sensors, 20,000 feet underneath them and climbing, trying for a lock to set up another missile shot.

Their *Envoy* was no longer invisible. They were not going to get any closer to the American cargo plane than they already were—but they had clear sky between themselves and their target, except for its own escort drones.

"Fifteen seconds to impact. Jamming," Adamov said tightly. "AC-130 is locked. All missiles allocated."

Gusev's helmet display was blinking at him insistently, showing him the bearing to the incoming American missiles at the lower edge of his display, and painting a suggested escape maneuver on his screen, as a warning in his ears began escalating in intensity.

"Launch now!" Gusev confirmed.

"Launching air-to-air," Adamov said.

It took precious seconds for the 10 missiles, six AA-12 and four Axehead hypersonics, to blast from their rotary launcher into the sky. After nine seconds, their payload doors snapped shut.

Their Monochrome drone was engaged now, forcing the American fighter to break off its pursuit.

"Five seconds to impact!" Adamov said. "Deploying decoys."

"AI has the aircraft," Gusev said, tapping a control and lifting his hands away from his joystick and rudder to brace himself. His pathetically slow human reflexes would be inadequate in the moments ahead.

The AI pilot immediately seized control of the behemoth that was the *Envoy*, rolled it inverted and pulled its nose toward the sea. From vents along its fuselage, traditional tinfoil radar-decoying chaff and infrared-decoying flares poured into its curving wake.

But from a port just under its tail, drag chutes trailing behind them, the *Envoy* spat a half dozen *dikobraz* "air mines" into the path of the American missiles. As the AIM-260s closed on the Russian bomber, they had to pass through the swarm of air mines, which detonated, spraying thousands of metal slugs into the sky.

The American missiles were shredded, exploding harmlessly behind and above the diving Russian bomber.

Gusev and Adamov didn't celebrate. They knew an American sixth-generation stealth fighter, if that was what was chasing them, could carry anywhere from 12 to 14 air-to-air missiles internally, and their radical maneuver, though it enabled them to keep some separation between themselves and the American, only gave him an easier shot at their fleeing tail.

They had little chance of living through the next few minutes. But with 10 Russian missiles closing on it, the American cargo plane had *zero* chance. Of that, they were sure.

***

The two electronic warfare GAMBITs on Outlaw's wingtips received their targets from the New Zealand AWACS and peeled out of formation, headed behind the fleeing Outlaw without a signal to its pilot.

They didn't need to look for the incoming Russian missiles. They had both the AWACS and *Lorenzen* telling them exactly where to look.

273

Both GAMBITs were unarmed but had powerful jamming suites, and the Russian missiles closing on them, hypersonic or not, relied on old-school, multi-band radar and optical-infrared seekers to find their targets.

The two GAMBITs conferred with each other at the speed of light over laser communication links, and divided the 10 incoming missiles between them. They recognized the hypersonic missiles as the greater threat, and blasted radar-jamming energy at them. Behind the hypersonic Axeheads were supersonic AA-12s, and the GAMBITs began spraying tinfoil chaff and infrared flares into the sky to distract them.

Outlaw was down low, and zigzagging across the water, Rory trying to confuse any incoming missiles with random changes in direction, trying to stay so low that that a Russian missile coming from down on high would need to aim at the water ahead of him to make an intercept.

He looked across at Uncle, who was glaring over his shoulder out the cockpit window as though pure disdain could scare Russian missiles away.

***

"*Lorenzen* is still up," Trigger said, shaking her head in disbelief as she was buffeted left and right by Rory's maneuvers. She'd been monitoring radio traffic between the task force ships, AWACS and shore and had just about written off the big electronic warfare ship. "Bunny's got a lock! Sixty miles back on our six, 60,000 feet high. Get some, Aggressor!"

"We're not out of the woods," Rory said. "We—"

Trigger, Bell and Venice heard the warning from the AWACS, call sign 'Turtle,' at the same time as Rory and Uncle in the cockpit. "Aggressor Heavy 158, Turtle—Aggressor One reports missiles fired down your bearing by the bogey. Contrails

274

spotted. Count is 10, repeat: one zero. Recommend immediate evasive action. *Lorenzen* will assist with tracking," the AWACS controller said. "Estimated time to missile merge … 60 to 70 seconds."

"Missile merge?" Venice asked. "What is 'missile merge'?"

"A polite way of saying rapid explosive decommissioning," Bell told her.

Rory acted immediately, putting Outlaw into a skidding turn. "Can we evade *10* missiles?" Venice asked, grabbing at her console for balance.

"If the USAF and Navy can jam a couple of them, our Vigilant might be able to intercept a couple too …" Bell said, trying to reassure her. "It's possible."

"No, it's not," Trigger said, contradicting him. "Not a chance. We got bloody lucky last time; we won't get that lucky again. But we aren't dead yet. Pull your straps as tight as you can. Stow anything not secured."

Venice grabbed for her harness and pulled her belts tighter.

"Trigger, we're seeing *10* incoming, you copy?" Rory asked.

Trigger Brown looked at the updated data on her tactical screen. "Copy that. At least two hypersonics?"

"The way they're separating, have to be," Rory agreed. "Forty seconds to first impact. I'm sending Uncle back and pulling us higher; I'll kick you out at 5,000. I'll punch out at 2,000. Understood?"

"Good copy. We're tying down here," Trigger said, unbuckling, running down to Venice's station and checking she was buckled in tight.

"What's happening?!" Venice asked, as Trigger checked Bell too.

"We're about to find out how many lives I've got left," Trigger said. "I think I'm on six, but I stopped counting a while back."

***

An argument broke out in the cockpit. "The hell you're sending me back!" Uncle said. "We both go, or no one goes."

"You stubborn old coot," Rory said. "Someone has to stay and fly her."

Uncle glared at him, and then fumbled in the bag he always kept beside his seat in the cockpit. He came up holding a pistol.

"What the hell, put that down!" Rory yelled.

"There's only one of us can swim," Uncle said. "And it ain't you. Move, Captain, now!" He racked the slide. "I ain't joking."

Rory knew when he could argue with Uncle and when he couldn't, and the look in the man's eyes, coupled with the loaded pistol pointed at his face, told him there was no point arguing. And no time for it.

With an angry growl, Rory unbuckled and headed for the ladder down to the cargo deck. He paused. "You better punch out before that missile hits!"

Uncle put his pistol in his lap and grabbed the yoke. "Go!" he yelled.

***

Trigger slammed herself down into her own seat and buckled up, pulling her harness so tight she could hardly breathe. A second later, Rory appeared in the door to the command module, then pulled and locked the hatch behind him. "Damned fool pulled a *gun* on me." He stood there, panting. "And I swim better than him."

276

"Swim? Who's swimming?" Venice asked, as Rory sat down in the jump seat at one end of the module and clicked himself in.

Outlaw's engines roared, and it leveled out, then pitched nose-up, sliding through the sky with its nose in the air and tail pointing downhill. Trigger checked that the hatch lock indicator was showing red, checked Rory was buckled into the jump seat, then slammed her hand on a nondescript mushroom-shaped yellow button on the console in front of her. "Uncle, deck bolt release charges are armed," Trigger said into her mic.

"Opening ramp," Uncle said. "Bon voyage."

Trigger saw Anna Venice open her mouth to ask another question, but then there was a sound like multiple shotgun blasts from beneath their feet. The command module shuddered, and then they were thrown left as the entire command module, explosively released from the bolts holding it to the cargo deck, began sliding backward on Rapid Dragon rails toward the open maw of the cargo ramp …

And tumbled *out* into the sky.

***

A green light on Uncle's instrument panel told him the crew module had been jettisoned. His RWR showed the Russian missiles passing the two GAMBIT EW jamming drones, and four veered off-course, distracted or blinded by the GAMBITS.

Six blasted past the GAMBITs and closed on Outlaw. Reaching forward, he flipped the switch arming their Trophy air defense system, though he knew it would be useless against so many missiles and at this low altitude.

Punch out? Now? And then what? He'd lied to Rory; Uncle couldn't swim. He'd nearly drowned in a wading pool as a kid and hadn't gone near water since. He looked out the glass window of the cockpit by his feet, at the water rushing by below, barely visible through blowing snow. He couldn't swim, but maybe Outlaw could *float*.

He hit the lever that raised their rear ramp and shoved the aircraft's nose down.

Reaching for the gear lever, a plan began to form. He couldn't out-fly the Russian missiles, but maybe he could get them to overshoot. Outlaw had skis, right? He'd just put the big old bird down on the water, glide it in, then pancake. Missiles would either lose him in the radar clutter of the sea or lose their track as their target suddenly went from 400 knots to zero.

Yeah, right. The skis would just bite and send the lumbering bird somersaulting across the waves. He took his hand away from the gear lever again. He was going to have to belly flop.

But it was still a plan.

Missile alert. Missile alert. Missile alert, an automated voice began screaming in his ears. He ignored it, one eye on his altimeter, one on the RWR showing the range to the closest incoming missile. He pulled the throttles for the four engines back to 20 percent, dropped flaps and deployed air brakes.

500 feet, 10 miles.

400, 8 miles.

300, 6 miles.

200 …

Airspeed 200. Closer up now, he could see the sea wasn't flat. There was a rolling swell. He kicked the rudder to yaw the nose and line up parallel to the swell.

100… 4 miles.

Outlaw hit an updraft coming off the crest of a wave and bobbed back up into the air.

200 feet, dammit! Two miles. He gritted his teeth, pulled the throttles all the way back, eased his yoke toward his belly. Airspeed 130.

100 feet and dropping fast.

He heard the *thunk thunk thunk* of his topside Trophy turret firing at a missile. Outlaw slammed into the sea, hard, but she didn't nose in. Props bent, wingtips digging into waves on either side, the flat-bellied aircraft skewed across the sea, hit a wave side on, bumped into the air and slammed down.

Uncle was thrown against his straps, air punched from his lungs, saw a missile spear into the sea out his port window, gout of white water rising high into the air. He felt a moment of elation …

Then an AA-12 missile, arriving late, homing on the heat of Outlaw's engines against the icy background of the sea, spearing down almost vertically at the nearly stationary aircraft, buried itself in the wing 5 feet from the cockpit and detonated.

***

Bunny had dodged the two short-range missiles fired at her by the Russian Monochrome, then watched in horror on her optical targeting screen as missile after missile screamed away from under the bomber and speared south, white contrails trailing, even as her own missiles closed on their target.

She warned the AWACS, counting as the Russian got away six, eight … *10* missiles!

Then, seconds before her own missiles hit it, the big Russian beast flipped onto its back like a killer whale basking in the sun, and dived vertically for the sea.

It wasn't a fighter jet. The inverted dive took lethal seconds to execute, and her missiles closed, following it down as it streamed chaff and flares. Then, they exploded.

279

Harmlessly, in its wake.

She thought she'd seen a cluster of small parachutes just before the explosions, but she was still 25 miles distant. She lit her afterburner to begin hauling ass, to stay with the Russian as it accelerated northwest, away from her. The Russian Monochrome dropped in behind her, trying for a second shot, its targeting radar sliding over her radar-reflective skin without getting a lock. It was slower, but close.

Goddammit! she thought. With a twitch of her stick, she inverted her Nemesis and hauled it through a 180-degree split-S to face the Monochrome. As soon as she rolled wings level, her targeting radar chimed to tell her she had a missile lock, and she snapped off a single CUDA short-range missile in optical-infrared mode.

It tracked true, smacking the Monochrome on the nose before it could get a lock on her Nemesis. She reversed her maneuver, pulling her nose high into a half loop before rolling wings level again and resuming her pursuit of the Russian. She got onto the AWACS again. "Turtle, Aggressor One, am engaged with the bogey. They're bugging out to the northwest."

"We copy, Aggressor One," the AWACS controller said. "Get some."

Bunny worked her radar. She'd fallen 30 miles behind the Russian again. It was pulling away from her at Mach 2, and her maximum speed was Mach 1.2—she was 600 knots slower. She was pushing the envelope in trying to get a lock on the stealthy bomber, but used the optical-infrared bearing to direct a narrow beam right at the target, and got a missile solid lock tone, even at 30 miles' distance.

She might have been falling behind, but her AIM-260s could reach Mach 4.5 and had the range to haul the Russian in. She cued up four missiles this time, launching two immediately, and two more with a couple of seconds' separation to reduce the chances the Russian could outmaneuver them. Her missiles would steer on her radar lock until they could "see" the target themselves.

"Fox three by four," she said with grim satisfaction. "Dodge *this*, Ivan."

Bunny watched her missiles disappear over the horizon, one eye on the sky, the other on her instruments, keeping her radar locked on until the absolute last moment. Then she twitched her stick, chopped her throttle and rolled off, heading southeast and looking for Outlaw.

It was gone.

She searched for it frantically on her tactical screen. She saw one GAMBIT, circling aimlessly. No Outlaw.

"Turtle, I'm not seeing Aggressor Two …" she reported. *Please, no. Please …*

The surface plot showed two crosses where the US Navy frigates had been, one red, indicating a probable loss, the other yellow, indicating severe damage. Dots with small labels under them marked the position of the sub-hunting *Sea Hunter* drones, but they were blinking, indicating they were "untethered"—not under human control. The *Lorenzen* and *Polar Warden* were the only two ships still underway, one headed for the USS *Congress*, the other for the USS *Galvez*.

No! Bunny thought, as she saw the other icon on the screen. An emergency locator beacon started strobing, where Outlaw had been minutes before.

***

"Target down!" Adamov cried, relief in his voice palpable.

Their QE radar was no longer tracking the American cargo plane, but they had received data from their missile radars, and the story they told was clear—the target had been destroyed.

Gusev leaned his helmet back on his headrest. They were down at wave-top height now, fleeing at more than twice the speed of sound, and had American missiles closing on them, but it no longer mattered. *Anzhelika was safe. Sergei too.*

Gusev twitched his stick, yawing the big aircraft to port. Their *Envoy* was snaking through the sky, forcing the four pursuing American missiles to burn precious fuel with constant changes of direction. Two of the American missiles were definitely flying wide. But the two that had been fired last were coming down toward his *Envoy* from high altitude, closing fast, and Gusev was trying to trick them into aiming at the sea ahead of him as they went for an intercept solution.

The air mines that had saved them last time were not an option when they were so low. But his *Envoy* was not a one-trick pony.

"Pulling up. Launch M3," he said. He executed a quick popup, pulling them from 100 feet above the sea to 500 as Adamov punched their last Monochrome drone out of their payload bay and sent it spinning on its axis into the sky behind them. Headed right for the incoming American missiles.

Their last drone was a dedicated missile defense platform. It blasted jamming energy into the sky toward the incoming missiles, trying to blind their radar. Clouds of tinfoil and laser-sparkling infrared decoys shot from ports along its fuselage. From its nose, a 10-kilowatt laser locked onto the two American missiles and began flicking between them, trying to burn out their optics.

***

Bunny had fired a salvo of two missiles first, followed by two more, one after the other. The first two lost their track, and one of the remaining two went for a cloud of foil, then detonated hopefully, nearly a half mile behind *Envoy*.

The *Envoy*'s last Monochrome ran out of decoys. The limited power cell for its laser ran dry, and the laser stuttered. It made one last desperate course change, putting itself right in the path of the incoming missile. The last of Bunny's missiles saw the small aircraft in front of it, recognized it as a decoy and bunted under it, then corrected again just before it hit the sea, and headed right for the big bomber's blazing engine ports.

As it disappeared behind them, Gusev let out a sigh of relief. "We're clear!" he said, turning to Adamov. "We bloody—"

Bunny's missile emerged from the haze over the ocean and rocketed into *Envoy*'s starboard engine nozzle before exploding.

The explosion ripped the engine from its mount, and the huge bomber was thrown into an unbalanced roll. With no room to maneuver and no time to correct its roll, the aircraft dug a wing into the sea and tumbled nose over tail across the waves, scattering pieces of wing and fuselage in its foaming wake.

Barely conscious in the crushed protective shell of their cockpit, Gusev and Adamov stayed aware just long enough to realize they were still alive, before they began to drown in the icy sea.

***

Aggressor Inc.'s finance chief had baulked at the list of modifications Rory O'Donoghue had demanded be made to Outlaw so that it could carry out the Antarctic mission.

"Ski undercarriage, jet assisted take-off, ejection seats, gimbal-mounted concealed 25 mm., *and* reconfiguration of the remote piloting module to a Rapid Dragon mount, so it can be jettisoned with crew *inside?*" he'd asked, in disbelief. "The leasing cost alone for that machine is already $10 million a year."

"Well, we can't have the pilot and copilot punching out and leaving the rest of the complement to fight over the parachutes, can we?" Rory had argued. "That wouldn't be right."

"I'll have to clear this through Mr. Aaronson," the man had said with a sigh. "And USAF has to approve."

"I'm pretty sure the Project Minerva budget will cover it," Rory had said, based on rumors he'd been hearing about the project having a big blank check.

"Aaronson still has to agree."

The warning hadn't cost Rory any lost sleep. He'd already cleared the upgrades with Aaronson. But then, Rory didn't have much sleep to lose.

Their command module slid down the Rapid Dragon rails and tipped out the back of Outlaw 20 seconds before *Envoy*'s hypersonic missiles caught the ditching AC-130X. They'd registered the module dropping from Outlaw, but their onboard targeting systems had rejected it as a decoy.

The occupants of the module were thrown on their sides, then pitched violently forward as the module's chute deployed. Rory hung from his straps, listening to the fading explosions and cursing. But not at the bruising he was getting as the module swung, one end toward the sea, under the chute. "Goddamned senile old lunatic," he muttered. "Bloody-minded fool."

"He could have bailed out, right?" Bell said. "You had ejection seats fitted?"

"We did, and he could have," Rory agreed. "But would he? Land in a frozen ocean, with no hope of rescue? Old dog would have gone down with the ship."

"Brace!" Trigger yelled. The module had its own emergency power supply and basic sensors, and she could see their altitude on her helmet visor display. "We're going to hit the water in about 10 seconds …"

Rory grabbed his shoulder straps in both hands and counted in his mind. *Five … four … three … two …*

Instead of slamming into the Southern Ocean in freefall at 74 feet per second, they hit the water at a parachute-retarded 21 feet per second. Airbags exploded from a ring around the waist of the module. It submerged, then bobbed up like a cork.

Splashdown.

Rory hit his harness release, trying to stand but falling to one knee as the module corkscrewed in the waves, finding its head. Their parachute was designed not to detach, so that it would fill with water and act like a sea anchor if they ditched in the sea and pull them perpendicular to the waves. It did its job, the module lining up behind it and riding into the swell head-on. Rory tried unsuccessfully to stand again, before finally finding his sea legs. He walked unsteadily from one end of the module to the other. "No leaks or cracks I can see. You got power?" he asked Trigger.

"Batteries at 99 percent, and pulling about 200 watts from the solar panels," she said. "Enough for heat and light, but we only have about 10 hours of systems power."

"Locator beacon lit," Bell said. "AWACS will see we're down. If there's anyone left to rescue us …"

"You take comms," Trigger told him. "Get us a satellite link, and tell Concordia we're still mission capable."

Venice had been quiet all through their plunge into the sea. Rory gave her credit for that. She wasn't panicking now, either. "We still have control over the submersible?" she said, struggling to keep the incredulity out of her voice.

"Oh yeah," Bell told her, tapping icons on their comms screen. He reached out a fist to Trigger, who bumped it automatically. "Aggressor Inc., baby ..."

"... *We Bring It,*" Trigger said in unison with him. Not the war cry of winners—not yet—but of survivors.

Rory tuned them out. It was way too early for "business as usual" for him, even though he knew they still had a mission to execute. He was feeling sick to his stomach, and it wasn't because of the pitching sea. "There's a reason we got this contract, ma'am," Rory told Venice. "Why that fool in the copilot seat probably gave his life to get us here. He knew the mission wasn't over just because he was kicking our asses out of his airplane."

"Link is up," Bell announced.

"Aaaaand ... steerage and propulsion control re-established with *Charlene,*" Trigger confirmed. "Our little girl is 60 nautical miles from target position."

"Turtle, this is Aggressor Heavy 158 ..." Bell began, calling in to the AWACS. Then he held up a hand to get their attention. "Message from the P-8. They just dropped a new line of buoys and got a sonar hit ..."

"Our friend the *Sarov?*" Trigger asked.

"Unknown, but who else could it be?" He punched some keys. "Updating the plot with data from the P-8 Poseidon."

"Where away?"

"Eighty miles southwest *Charlene,*" Bell said. He checked the intelligence being pushed to him by the AWACS. "*Virginia* class boat, USS *Brooklyn,* has been vectored to intercept, but it's closer to the ice shelf than it is to the contact. It will get here too late."

"Eighty miles," Rory said. "That's good, right? They'll never catch *Charlene.* She has about an hour to run."

Bell and Trigger exchanged looks. "The Russian boat doesn't have to get near ours. It probably has cruise missiles. All it needs is an approximate target position," Bell said.

Trigger turned to Venice. "Anna, you got your abacus with you?"

"You want me to run some kind of calculation?" Venice asked. "I can do that from this station if we have a satellite link."

"Good. Model this for me. Assume that Russian sub is going to launch a tactical nuclear cruise missile at *Charlene*. It will detonate at sea level. How deep would *Charlene* have to go to avoid the shockwave and EMP effects of a 10-megaton explosion?"

"A tactical nuclear ... Are you *serious*?" Venice asked.

"And while you're at it," Bell added, "I just got a read on our own relative position and heading. We are only 70 miles from Juliet ground zero, and drifting closer. You might want to model what affect your 80-megaton antimatter bomb is going to have on a floating reinforced-steel remote vehicle command module and the lucky people inside it."

***

Trigger Brown was not the only one concerned about the *Sarov*.

The new acting chief of security for Concordia, Cath Delaney, had passed the Russian commando's intel on to her boss, Operations Director Solomon Cohen. And it had sunk like lead.

"We know about the Russian submarine," he'd said. "The Navy is dealing with it." All the others in Lau's executive team were bunkered down in the command center on level five, monitoring communications from the Minerva Task Force and

Aggressor Inc., watching the countdown timer to J-hour, when they would send the signal to the submersible to trigger Juliet.

The control center had been cleaned up after the slaughter of the previous day—bodies removed, floors and surfaces scrubbed down, equipment replaced—but Delaney could still see bullet holes in doors and walls.

"Navy knows Russia is willing to launch *nuclear cruise missiles* at this base?" Delaney had asked.

"Here? Nonsense. Just because they have a nuclear-powered submarine in the area doesn't mean they are going to launch a missile at Concordia," Cohen said, pulling her out of earshot of the others in the center. "Keep your voice down. We don't want unnecessary panic."

"And what if the target *isn't* just Concordia?" Delaney had insisted. "What if it's our test site too? We deliver the bomb to the NOAA platform, and Russia nukes it? That's going to mess up your test, right?"

A couple of staff looked over at Delaney, and Cohen pulled her farther out into the circular corridor. She could see he hadn't considered that possibility. "We have, uh, contingencies against that kind of thing." He put his hands on her shoulders, and she felt like shaking them off, but resisted. "But it's more likely your Russian friend is just trying to spook you. Why do you think he chose to tell you this *now?*"

"I told him I would release him if he told us everything he knows," she told Cohen. "I think he's telling the truth."

Cohen looked back into the control center space, trying to listen as excited voices began speaking over one another. He stepped away, waving a hand at her. "So release him, or shoot him and throw him down a crevasse. I don't care."

"Seriously? Release him?" she asked.

But Cohen was already walking away. "I. Don't. Care."

"Where is Colonel Sandilands?" Delaney asked.

Cohen paused just long enough to look over his shoulder at her. "On a video link with the Pentagon, with bigger things to worry about than a grandstanding Russian commando."

Bigger things than a possible nuclear strike on the base he's sitting in? She left Cohen and tried to pull Sandilands out of his call, but he had waved her off, so she sent a written message in to him. He'd replied with a short note of his own. "Check that the prisoner said <u>nuclear</u>—conventional cruise missile strike not a major concern."

Delaney had walked away fuming. Sure, she'd check, but she'd looked in the Russian's eyes as he told her about the submarine nuking Concordia, and she could tell he believed what he was saying.

Whiteout Conditions

December 30, 2041
J-Day minus 1 hour

Donovan Grant was doing some modeling too. He'd just been asked by 'Lema' Lau to refine his forecast for conditions at the test site and report to the control center once he'd forwarded it, in case they had questions.

But they didn't want an update on weather at the NOAA platform, only for the second set of coordinates, which he had assumed was an alternate drop zone for the weapon. Fifty miles northwest of the NOAA platform. And they wanted as much data as he could provide on the sea state, not the atmosphere.

Sea state? Had the alternate now become the primary drop zone? And was it possible the bomb was aboard a naval vessel? *Not* the aircraft? He needed to let Saara know, be able to prove to her later that everything he told her was accurate … but he couldn't do that if he was stuck down on five, inside the control center. It would be impossible to get a satellite signal out from that deep down, and who knew how long they would keep him there? And he couldn't just *assume* the second set of coordinates was the final drop zone.

He had run his models. He had access to NOAA's high-performance quantum computing systems mainframes and cross-checked the results with the mainframes run by the Norwegian Meteorologisk Institutt, which, not surprisingly, had the most sophisticated polar weather models, for both the North and South poles. The synopsis read:

Forecast for coordinates 73°16'49"S, 176°13'36"W

A deep low-pressure system centered over the Ross Ice Shelf is generating strong katabatic winds and extensive blowing snow, significantly reducing visibility. A high-pressure ridge to the east is reinforcing cold air advection, maintaining hazardous conditions for maritime operations. Significant wave heights 18 to 22 feet, increasing to 25 feet in open waters. Occasional rogue waves possible due to persistent gale-force winds. Navigation hazardous for all vessels, particularly those without ice-strengthened hulls. Severe restrictions on aerial visibility with whiteout conditions possible.

His hand hovered over the key that would send the full analysis to Lau. He hesitated. Perhaps there *was* a way to be sure. He picked up a phone and called the control center.

"Grant for Dr. Lau, please," he said when someone answered.

A brusque voice came on the line. "Grant, where is my forecast?"

"Uh, sir, I've finished the report for the location 400 miles northeast McMurdo, but I've had to rerun the report on the NOAA platform. It's going to take another …"

Lau was audibly irritated. "NOAA platform? I didn't ask for an update on weather at the NOAA platform. Just get me the update on the other position, and get down here!" Grant heard raised voices in the background … but not raised in argument. Raised in alarm?

"Sir, yes, but I may as well wait until the NOAA platform analysis is done. It's nearly there …" Grant said, testing again.

"Listen to me, Grant, we don't need the NOAA platform weather. Forget it! You'll learn soon enough—the device is on a bloody submarine, man. Send me what you have, and send it now." Lau hung up.

He nearly clapped himself on the back. Underwater test! *Well, there you have it, Donovan.* He hit "SEND" on his weather data, and then composed a message to Saara. Probably his last before the test. It had a momentous feeling about it, but he tried not to let that bleed into the text:

: Test coordinates confirmed as 73°16'49"S 176°13'36"W.

: No change to test time or date. Current time is H-hour minus 58.

: Delivery by submarine planned. Repeat, bomb will NOT be delivered by air.

No, dammit, he couldn't help himself. Saara would be trying to guess his state of mind, worried about him. Wondering what he was thinking. He added another couple of lines.

: Moving to control center now. This will be my last communication before the test. May God forgive us for what we are about to do.

***

"New sonar buoy contacts, bearing zero five five, range estimate 5 miles. High probability of detection!"

"Helm port two zero degrees," *Sarov*'s captain, Komarov, said quietly. "Take us down to 300."

"Captain, at that depth, we'll start taking water through the outer torpedo doors," the chief engineer, Akopian, reminded him. "If those buoys have passive acoustics, the noise could …"

"Reveal our position, yes, thank you, Lieutenant," Komarov said. "A risk we will take. Please go forward and check on the special weapon; keep me updated on hull integrity."

So close. They had been so close—at *Poseidon* launch depth, weapon armed and ready to launch, just waiting for the final target coordinates—when a line of air-dropped sonobuoys had landed right on top of them. They were a good crew, this scratch crew of his, pulled from *Kilo* class submarines across the fleet. He knew some of the captains asked to sacrifice their best crew members for this mission wouldn't have complied, but they hadn't sent their worst either.

Within a minute of being detected, they had killed their reactor noise, disarmed the special weapon and switched to electrical propulsion only, and *Sarov* was almost silently spiraling down and away from the American sonobuoys. Tense minutes followed as they waited for the overhead aircraft or helicopter to follow through with an air-dropped torpedo, but it didn't come. They'd gotten away.

But now the Americans knew where they were.

***

Bunny O'Hare had returned to the scene of her crime.

As soon as she got in range, she had hailed Outlaw on VHF. Somewhere on the cold gray sea below, Outlaw's emergency locator beacon was strobing, but visibility was no better over the crash site than it had been farther west, and she had to circle lower and lower—dangerously low—to be able to differentiate sea from swirling sky. She found the module floating on the surface like a large metal lifeboat, heavy waves washing around and over it, and had started with a wide circle, tightening it with every sweep, until she was almost in a vertical turn right on top of it by the time she got a return hail.

"O'Hare!" Rory's voice. "Tell us you got the bastard."

Bunny breathed a sigh of relief. "That's affirmative, Two," she said. "But not in time. Did everyone make it out?"

The silence that followed her question gave her the answer before Rory did. "Not everyone. I don't suppose you've got a locator beacon for anyone else down in the water?"

"No. Who?" she asked. But she knew.

"Uncle stayed with Outlaw to make sure we got out," Rory said. "But we have other problems right now. The Navy P-8 Poseidon just got a sonar return from a submarine southwest our position, but they lost it again."

Bunny quickly checked her tac screen. "I haven't received tasking," she said. "They may not know I took off with VLTs in the payload bay. Look, it's going to be a while before I can get help for you."

"We know," Rory replied.

"One out," Bunny said, then switched to the AWACS frequency. "Turtle from Aggressor One. I am available for anti-submarine duties. Carrying two MAD-mesh buoys and two Very Light Torpedoes."

"Good copy Aggressor One. US Navy Poseidon 4801, call sign 'Reptile,' is currently prosecuting a contact inside the naval exercise exclusion zone. Live weapon use is authorized. Please coordinate on following frequency ..."

***

Komarov knew their best hope was to go where the Americans didn't expect. He ordered a randomly zigzagging course, away from the point they'd been detected, and deeper *inside* the American circle of picket vessels. They hadn't heard from the pickets for some time, but they hadn't been able to update their satellite intel either, so there was no reason to believe the enemy vessels weren't still out there, still hunting *Sarov*.

"Surface noise!" the sonar operator said. "Distant splashes, bearing niner zero. AI says range is 3 miles. Sounds like sonobuoys. Not pinging."

"Helm, port 10 degrees, please," Komarov said calmly, turning *Sarov* to avoid the new threat.

The entire control room held its metaphorical breath as the new line of sonobuoys slid past their starboard side and then fell behind them.

"Range 7 miles," his sonar operator said. "No sign they … *Torpedo in the water!* Bearing zero four five, range 6 miles, pinging …"

"Helm steady on current heading and depth. Propulsion, ahead slow."

His XO shot him a glance. "Launch MG-94?" His hand hovered over a control panel.

The enemy aircraft had dropped on them this time. But well away from their position. They could launch an MG-94 decoy down the bearing to the torpedo, try to jam or lure it away, but there was no sign it was tracking them yet.

"No. That was a blind shot. They're trying to flush us out, Lieutenant. Firing decoys would do more harm than good; hold your nerve," Komarov said. "Sonar, update?"

"Torpedo seems to be circling and pinging," the man said. "Range 5 miles now."

With tension in the control room at breaking point, Komarov held *Sarov* on a heading away from the threats until they lost contact with both the torpedo and the new line of buoys. The silence was broken by a call from the torpedo section. "Conn, Engineering," Akopian's voice broke in. "Outer tube door failure. *Poseidon* launch tube has flooded. Inner doors holding.

"I've trimmed for the added weight, Captain," his helmsman told him.

Komarov acknowledged the detail with a wave. "Thank you, Chief Engineer," he said to Akopian. "Please evacuate the water when we get above 200 again."

"Will do," Akopian said. "Engineering out."

An uncomfortable silence settled back over the men in *Sarov*'s control room. To be a submariner trying to sneak away from a torpedo must be like being a death row prisoner in the moments before execution, Komarov reflected. Your death was coming, was almost inevitable, but there was that one-in-a-hundred chance of a last-minute reprieve. And you clung to that.

"Six miles …" the sonar operator said quietly. "Enemy torpedo falling behind, but still searching."

Fedorov's hand hovered over the control that would send their decoy and looked at Komarov again in a silent question. He ignored him.

"Wait …" the sonarman said. "I think it's lost power. No propulsion noise. No longer pinging."

They couldn't cheer, but the crew members of the *Sarov* settled for the next best thing, with smiles, back claps and winks.

Komarov consulted his nav screen and dropped a waypoint on it. "Sonar, stay alert for enemy submarine activity. Helm, bring us back around to one two degrees true. Make your depth 50 meters. XO, prepare for an ELF check-in, and ready the boat for immediate *Poseidon* launch."

"Aye, prepare for ELF download and special weapon launch," Fedorov said.

***

The US Navy P-8 Poseidon, 'Reptile,' had picked up the Russian submarine again, and dropped on it. But it was a generation older, and a few hundred knots slower, than Bunny's FB-22. It used passive acoustic sonobuoys, which were excellent at picking up the noise of even quiet submarines like the *Sarov*, but by the time they reported the target's position to their circling aircraft, and it made its torpedo run, several valuable minutes could pass in which the prey could escape.

Bunny's FB-22 was equipped with a "MAD-mesh" air-deployed detection system that was launched from her payload bay like a bomb, dropping toward a position on the sea under a parachute that slowed its fall. A thousand feet over the water, it began spinning and spat a dozen small magnetic anomaly detection buoys into the water in a circle with a 5-mile radius. The MAD buoys used low-frequency radio data signals to create a "mesh" network across *70 square miles* of water. Anything larger than a tin can and made of metal was silently identified, with pinpoint precision.

And circling overhead, Bunny could load the contact data into her Very Lightweight Torpedo and drop it onto the target inside a minute.

But even with the MAD-mesh's broad footprint, the Southern Ocean was a very, very large body of water, and the *Sarov* a very small target inside it. The P-8 made several passes and dropped more buoys, but the *Sarov* had disappeared, again.

***

Arsharvin *ran* from Eizen's office. The two officers had been following the *Envoy*'s engagement report live as it broke radio silence and uploaded the data from its multiple engagements. It had been all they could do to stop themselves from whooping in celebration at the devastation Russia's most potent attack aircraft had wrought on the American task force.

They had given each other a high five as the report of the cargo aircraft's destruction ticked in. And then sat stunned in horror as the transmission ended in what could only have meant the destruction of their own aircraft.

But the two Russian pilots had not given their lives in vain. The American weapon had been destroyed. Destroy the cargo plane, destroy the American bomb, set off the explosion prematurely. At any moment now, seismic readings should start coming in from across the world, for which Russia already had its disinformation campaign ready—an illegal, failed American nuclear weapon test, breaching dozens of treaties. More importantly, a years' worth of American antimatter production vaporized, their ability to monitor the experiment crippled by the untimely destruction of their "task force" and the disarray sown by the *Envoy*.

The ideal outcome would have been a more clandestine, deniable attack of sabotage that also took out "Operation Minerva's" 300 most critical scientific staff, but the *Sarov* could manage that task.

Except …

The seismic reports weren't ticking in. Even their Antarctic monitoring station at Mirny reported nothing. And then his cell phone had buzzed with a message from the GRU source in Finland. And their short-lived victory cries turned to ashes in their mouths.

: Test coordinates confirmed as 73°16'49"S 176°13'36"W.

: No change to test time or date. Current time is H-hour minus 48 mins.

: Delivery by submarine planned. Repeat, bomb will NOT be delivered by air.

So Arsharvin *ran* back to his office. He called his navy liaison.

"I need to get an urgent message to the *Sarov*," he said. "Immediately!"

***

"ELF depth, sir," *Sarov*'s helmsman said.

They didn't need to deploy a special mast to pick up the Extra Low-Frequency signals from Severomorsk. An ELF antenna was miles long and wound through the very hull of the *Sarov*. Fedorov ran the comms check-in, reporting their ready state and awaiting confirmation, or otherwise, of their orders.

He frowned at the decryption device he had retrieved from his quarters, then tapped a key to transfer the message to a tablet PC, which he handed to Komarov.

"Final orders received. Target coordinates for the primary objective confirmed, Captain," Fedorov said. "And launch authority."

It wasn't like launching a nuclear ballistic missile that couldn't be recalled, or destroyed, in flight. The *Poseidon* could only be armed by a direct command from Moscow. All *Sarov* had to do was send it on its way to the coordinates he had just received. So what was it that was tickling the back of Komarov's mind?

"What is it, Captain?" Fedorov asked, sensing his disquiet.

Sarov's twin mission objectives had just been altered, but not significantly. When they sailed, Komarov had been told their primary mission was the destruction of the American research station at Concordia with a standoff cruise missile strike. A secondary mission objective, for which the special weapon would be used, was possible. To facilitate execution of both missions if needed, he was required to navigate to a position which had shown itself to be teeming with US Navy warships. So be it. But now the secondary objective had become the primary, and the strike on Concordia was secondary. Curious.

"Target coordinates, a time and a depth for deployment of the special weapon, Fedorov," he said, pointing at the screen. "Why a depth?"

"To make sure our torpedo doesn't explode at the surface?" Fedorov said, stating the obvious.

Komarov was patient with him. "Yes, but why? We are disrupting an American weapons test. A surface detonation would cause a wider radius of shockwave destruction, better wave propagation, more radiation damage."

Fedorov frowned too. "It must … The American test is underwater?"

"The American test is underwater." Komarov nodded. "Is the special weapon ready for launch?" Komarov asked.

"Aye, sir, as soon as I input the coordinates, time on target and detonation depth."

"Good. Take us down to launch depth. Time on target is five minutes before the time noted in that ELF signal," Komarov said.

"Aye, captain. Launching special weapon, TOT as instructed."

He relayed the necessary orders, and Komarov stood by to ensure they were being executed by his subordinates as the submarine dived again. It was always possible a crew member might get qualms about being involved in the launch of a special weapon, but this one could only be activated by orders from Russia, so all personal responsibility was at arm's length.

"Engineer Akopian reports the special weapon is armed, and the tube is flooded. Torpedo propulsion, navigation and communication systems are nominal. *Poseidon* time on target is locked in," Fedorov reported after several minutes. "We are at launch depth, and ready to launch, Captain."

Komarov checked the weapon settings. "Very good, XO. Launch the weapon," Komarov said. There was a special atmosphere inside the control room, and why not? The first combat launch of a *Poseidon* intercontinental torpedo. Not on an intercontinental mission, but on one that no other torpedo could execute: traveling 70 miles, dynamically adjusting its speed through the water so that it arrived on target ahead of the American submersible, where it would loiter until it was sent the order to *obliterate* it.

A moment Komarov had never imagined he would still be in service to see.

He closed his eyes and held space for it, for just a second, listening as the launch order was relayed through his boat.

"Open doors, torpedo tube one."

"Tube one, doors open."

"Confirm weapon final waypoint."

"Weapon final waypoint set to seven-three decimal two south, one-seven-six decimal one west."

"Check threat environment."

"Threat board is clear."

"Match heading tube one and shoot."

"Match heading tube one and shoot, aye."

Fedorov waited on confirmation from Akopian in the torpedo room. "Captain, torpedo away. Closing tube one doors."

Their sonarman chimed in. "Torpedo in the water, running straight and strong."

Komarov opened his eyes and fixed his gaze on the XO. "Lieutenant, bring the reactor online, and take us up to comms depth to report our successful launch."

301

Sarov, like its *Poseidon* torpedo, could receive orders from its Russian masters by Extra Low-Frequency radio, but it didn't have the power to send a reply by ELF. To transmit, it had to rise to a depth of 100 feet and float a comms buoy that would squirt a quantum compressed message to an overhead satellite.

Fedorov baulked. "Captain, I recommend we wait to make radio contact until we have executed our secondary mission—the land attack missile launch?"

"No, XO. This launch was time critical, and that launch confirmation is too. Once we have made our transmission, I want you to cut the buoy, take us down to 200 feet and make preparations for cruise missile launch."

Komarov saw the flame of rebellion flare in Fedorov's eyes again. But he was without any allies in the control room. Komarov was keeping his partner in potential mutiny, Akopian, forward. Not by accident. Fedorov bit down on his disquiet. "Aye, captain. Readying for comms transmission. Laying in a course for the secondary objective launch waypoint."

***

Signals energy! Like its F-22 Raptor cousin, Bunny's Nemesis had an exquisitely sensitive signals detection suite, and though she couldn't unscramble the signal that had just been detected off her port wing, her sensor suite gave her a bearing and a range to the signal and told her it was *not* using NATO encryption codes.

Bunny flipped her aircraft onto a wing and cued a MAD-mesh canister for launch, steering on the position she had just been given. She ran a synthetic aperture scan of the sea ahead of her and came up blank at the signal's position—so it was not from a surface vessel. Her heart rose into her throat as she waited for indications of a cruise missile launch, but none came.

She contacted the P-8 Poseidon. "Reptile, Aggressor One. I have signals energy at my 12 o'clock, range 10 miles. Probable submarine buoy. Prosecuting with MAD-mesh; request support. Sending you coordinates."

"Good copy, Aggressor One," the Poseidon replied. "We are changing course for your coordinates … uh, TOT is … TOT 7 mikes."

In the time it took the P-8 Poseidon to make its turn toward Bunny's position, she was already over the contact coordinates. Her visor showed a circle like a 3D basketball hoop and drew a line between her aircraft and the hoop to show her where to steer. The launch was automatically calculated and triggered. As she flew through the hoop at 5,000 feet, her bay doors flipped open, and the cylindrical MAD-mesh canister was kicked out, falling behind her before deploying a parachute that would drop it right on top of the radio signal position. But before that, at 1,000 feet, rockets fired on the rim of the canister, spinning it at a thousand RPM as it flung a dozen magnetic anomaly detection buoys in a 5-mile circle around it.

Bunny was fairly confident that if there was a submarine inside that footprint, she'd find it, and between them, she and the P-8 Poseidon could kill it. It had already declared itself hostile with its attack on their submersible, and was well inside a declared US military exercise area. Its intentions weren't in question … The only question was whether they could intervene in time to frustrate them.

Or had the *Sarov* already done what it came to do?

***

When Grant got to the control center on level five, the scene he walked in on was not the one he expected. Yes, he'd heard raised voices on the phone line, but he hadn't read too much into it.

Whatever had gotten people riled up was still happening.

He heard Bellings yelling. "There are American sailors in the water, David!"

Lau was pacing, not looking at Bellings. "No. No, it doesn't matter how many ships Russia sinks, or aircraft it shoots down, as long as the drone with Juliet aboard makes it to the test site."

"It matters, David," Janssen said. "The Navy just reported contact with a Russian submarine. Who is going to stop it attacking our drone if no one is alive to hunt it?" The three scientists were standing in the center of the control room. It had been cleaned up after the events of the day before, he was glad to see, but there were still bullet holes visible in walls, and cardboard taped over shattered glass. Sandilands and DD Cohen, like the techs and engineers at their stations, were either hunkered down trying to ignore the shouting match or following it like a tennis game.

Grant made his way over.

"So, we … we contact the Aggressor base at Christchurch," Lau was telling Bellings. "Have them prepare to take control of the submersible if we don't hear from that AC-130 crew inside the next five minutes …"

"Their control module was designed to survive the destruction of their aircraft. They *might* have made it down …" Bellings said.

"That's why I'm giving them five minutes, Jake," Lau said patiently.

"Director?" Grant said, interrupting reluctantly.

"It's 45 minutes to J-hour," Bellings pointed out. "Forty minutes until we send the signal to arm Juliet. We don't *have* five minutes, David. We only just received confirmation our submersible is still en route."

"If it wasn't, Jake, you would have felt the tremor," Lau said, derisively.

"Uh, Director Lau?" Grant asked again.

Lau rounded on him. "What?! What could possibly …" Then his eyes focused. "Oh, Grant. I got your forecast. Any change that might affect satellite communications?"

"Satellite? No sir," Grant said. "Conditions aren't optimal, but satellite comms will get through."

"Fine, sit over there, and only speak if spoken to," Lau said, pointing at a vacant workstation. He turned back to Bellings. "*Three* minutes now, Jake. Then you can make your panic call to New Zealand."

Grant took the seat he was pointed to and switched on the screen there so that he could pull up his reports and update them if needed. Looking over at the station next to him, he spotted a refrigeration engineer he recognized. The man was one of the few USAP personnel still at Concordia—an 'ice lifer' like Grant. "They got you watching containment?" Grant asked him.

Bellings and Lau were still going at each other, and the man rolled his eyes and moved his chair closer to Grant, so he didn't have to speak too loudly. "Yup. You heard those Russian psychos killed Mirelli?"

"Yeah. He was a good guy."

"Three kids, man. So they put me in his chair."

Grant nodded toward the commotion. "What's everyone so tense about, apart from the obvious?"

The man brought his head closer, lowered his voice even more. "There's a freaking *war* broken out over the test site," he said. "Two Navy ships sunk, I heard. The Russians again, everyone says. The plane carrying Juliet just got its ass shot down," he said. "Except it wasn't."

"Wasn't shot down?"

"Wasn't carrying Juliet," the man said, looking over his shoulder at Lau. "That was some BS. The bomb is on a drone sub being piloted by someone aboard the plane, but they lost contact with it when the plane was shot down, so that was *real* smart."

"So the submersible is lost too?"

"Apparently not," the man said. "They just reestablished contact—don't ask me how. Lau is trying to act like everything is still on track, but you can hear not everyone agrees." He rolled his chair back to his station. "Keep your head below the parapet, man, is my advice."

There was another loud shout, but not angry this time. Jubilant?

"Yes!" The military man, Sandilands, looked up from behind the shoulder of a man at the comms station. "AWACS just heard from Aggressor! They still have control of our sub. And Navy has a fix on the Russian sub and is on its way to take it out, but it's well behind our boat. There's nothing between our submersible and the target area now."

Lau wiped a hand across his face, then straightened and pointed at a wall screen that was showing a map of the Antarctic coast, a blue dot marking Juliet's target coordinates, another showing the NOAA platform and a big countdown timer. "Alright, people. We are 35 minutes from H-hour, 30 minutes from sending the signal to Juliet to trigger trap collapse." He snapped his fingers. "Solomon, your people will advise of any loss of satellite signal. Let me know if it even flutters. Jake, double- and triple-check the collapse code. Colonel, we lost a lot of monitoring assets aboard those Navy ships, and the NOAA platform package. Find out what we have left, please?"

A look of disbelief crossed Sandilands's face. Grant thought he might explode, but instead, when he replied, his voice was cold, and level. "Director, all of our surface vessels are currently engaged in rescue operations. Any 'monitoring' they are capable of will be secondary to those operations."

"No, no, no, that is *not* acceptable," Lau said. "Our thoughts are with your comrades at sea, Colonel. But nothing supersedes the importance of this test. Emphasize that to the commanders of those vessels."

Grant reflected that it was lucky the naval officer wasn't carrying a sidearm. Sandilands clenched his fists, turned away and wordlessly left the control room.

***

"Surface noise!" *Sarov*'s sonarman called out. All voices in the submarine's control room fell silent. "Right on top of us."

"What noise, man?" Fedorov asked. Komarov had handed command to him but was still in the control room, unable to relax until their cruise missiles were also on their way.

"Nothing now," the sonar operator said. "It was like a single object, hitting the water. Then gone. Could be a buoy," he said.

"It could also be waves slapping on an ice floe," Komarov observed. "An iceberg, calving off."

"I don't like it. Rig for silent running!" Fedorov ordered. "Turn port 90; take us down to 250 feet, ahead slow."

More cautious than me, Komarov thought. But he couldn't blame the younger man for being more careful with his life than Komarov was.

307

Red warning lights came on throughout the boat. The power supply winked in and out as their noisy reactor was dampened, and battery power was routed to their slowly turning screw as they slowed to a 3-knot creep.

The noise *Sarov*'s alert sonarman heard was the empty MAD-mesh canister and its parachute hitting the water. But he hadn't heard the dozen smaller MAD buoys it had flung in a circle around the *Sarov*. As the crew executed Fedorov's order and the boat began spiraling deeper to port, the maneuver took it closer to two of the MAD buoys.

***

Bunny had shoved her throttle forward and pulled her Nemesis up into a soaring Immelmann that took her to 10,000 feet and kept her right on top of the MAD-mesh footprint. She dropped a wing and began circling around the buoys in a racetrack pattern.

From the south, swirling snow behind laboring turbofan engines announced the approach through the swirling snow of the Navy P-8 Poseidon, boring in on her position from a few miles away at 2,000 feet and over 600 knots. Bunny smiled. That had been the fastest seven minutes Bunny had ever seen. The P-8 was booking.

Contact! A ping sounded in her helmet, and an icon appeared on her tactical screen. *Behind her.* She reacted reflexively, pulling herself into a looping reverse at the same time as she pushed the data point to the P-8.

"Reptile, Aggressor One. Contact your 12 o'clock; pushing coordinates to you. Are you in position to engage?"

"Roger that, Aggressor," the P-8 pilot replied coolly. "We are inbound your contact, weapons hot."

"Aggressor One standing off," Bunny said, banking away to clear the air for the P-8 Poseidon.

She could track the ingress of the P-8 Poseidon on her Distributed Aperture Camera system though, and watched with satisfaction as the Navy crew executed a perfect torpedo run, slowing their approach, lowering their machine to about 500 feet. Right over the MAD-mesh footprint, the two long cylinders of Mark 54 torpedoes dropped from under the P-8 Poseidon's fuselage, one after the other, and disappeared below the waves.

Get some, Navy, Bunny thought. She armed her own VLTs and swung her Nemesis around in a wide banking turn that would put her over the same spot on the water within a couple of minutes—just in case.

***

"Torpedoes! Two torpedoes in the water, overhead. Active sonar pinging; probability of acquisition extreme. Time to first impact: 24 seconds!"

The loud cry of alarm wasn't really needed. The stillness inside the *Sarov*'s hull only served to amplify the sound of the torpedo sonars closing on them.

Captain Yury Komarov heard his XO, Fedorov, shouting orders as though he was listening through cotton wool. Time slowed. The deck shifted under his feet, and he spread his legs to keep his balance as their engines went from ahead slow to ahead emergency, and their turn accelerated. Fedorov would also be ordering decoys and defensive weapons to be deployed, but with the enemy torpedoes dropping vertically on them from just 200 meters above, the effort was pointless.

If only they had been able to go deeper …

"Impact in 10 …" the sonarman yelled, the cry penetrating the wool around Komarov's ears.

Forty years at sea, and now just 10 more seconds to live. He closed his eyes and thought of his wife, gone some years ago now. But he couldn't keep her image in his mind. Another thought intruded.

I knew this fucking boat would kill me.

***

"Aggressor One, we are seeing surface wreckage and oil. Preliminary assessment is a successful torpedo kill. Thank you for the assist," the Navy pilot said, in a rolling southern drawl.

"You're welcome, Reptile—thanks are all ours," Bunny said with uncommon magnanimity, since it was arguably her kill. She couldn't feel happy, with Uncle's body probably floating on the icy sea somewhere below her, a frigate maybe sunk and two more vessels damaged on her watch … but relieved? Yeah, that was allowed. Project Minerva had survived the worst Russia could throw at it, from sabotage to armed assault, a full-scale aerial offensive with Russia's most advanced stealth platform and, last but not least, infiltration by a nuclear attack submarine moving into position to disrupt the test, probably with a cruise missile strike on that NOAA platform.

Project Minerva's "decoy strategy" had worked after all, grabbing the *Envoy*'s attention, then forcing the attack submarine to reveal itself. Which triggered her memory. Her EW GAMBIT! It had been flying escort for Outlaw. After Outlaw was destroyed, it should have just entered a holding pattern, waiting for new orders. She found it and checked its fuel state. Down to 30 percent. It wouldn't make it back to McMurdo with her, but she might as well have it form up on her. She sent it an order to rejoin.

Bunny checked her own fuel state, and was immediately grateful for the long legs of the FB-22 Nemesis. She still had about two hours of fuel left before she would need to return to McMurdo, and she didn't want to leave the operations area until she knew there was some kind of rescue planned for the crew of Outlaw, below and behind her somewhere.

She rolled her head and flexed her shoulders. It felt to her like the main event was over, but looking at her mission timer, she knew it was just about to start.

***

J-hour minus 30 minutes

"Thirty minutes to terminal waypoint," Trigger announced. "All systems nominal on the delivery vehicle. How's Juliet doing, Professor?"

"Not a professor, just a doctor," Anna Venice told her for about the fifth time. *Charlene* had deployed a towed comms buoy, and Venice had a remote link to the bomb in its payload bay so that she could monitor its energy state, cooling system and ancillary systems. "And Juliet is just fine, for someone who is about to give birth to a small supernova."

The mood in the module had lightened a little, though the sacrifice made by Bob 'Uncle' Lee still weighed on all their minds. Rory's most of all, of course. But for better or worse, he was feeling worse physically than he was mentally. The constant pitching and rolling of the module—which was most definitely not built as a seagoing vessel—had turned him green. Rory had chosen Air Force over Navy for a reason, and he was reminded of it every time he emptied his insides into a plastic garbage bag.

"Sonar?" Trigger asked.

"*Charlene* just sailed through a krill mating frenzy," Bell said. "Which, because I recognized it before the AI, tells you I've been a sonarman too long. And that the new sonar suite we fitted at McMurdo is working nicely."

311

"Professor, can we go through the detonation protocol again?" Trigger asked. "Start at J minus 15. Assume *Charlene* is in position at that point."

"Still not a professor," Venice said, not giving in, which Rory figured probably only encouraged Trigger more, but he didn't say it. "So at J minus 15, AWACS and Navy confirm the test area is clear, and your colleague overhead should make a last pass over the test site to double-check there are no naval vessels or aircraft within 50 miles ..." she continued. "Um, Space Force will also check for infrared signatures on the surface. At J minus 10, all naval vessels report their positions for the test, which ..." She leaned over and looked at a screen in front of Bell. "It looks like *Lorenzen* has finished taking off the wounded from USS *Galvez*, so she will probably be the only vessel monitoring the explosion from sea level. She'll report in, and then the team remotely monitoring the cameras and sensors at the NOAA platform will also report in ..."

"The Vigilant sensor package never made it down," Rory reminded her.

"Another setback, but there are still subsurface sensors mounted on the platform, and the standard CCTV cameras on the rig, which can be realigned to point out to sea. Now everyone has reported in, and it's J minus five. A Space Force Skylon will pass overhead to film the event from low earth orbit."

"Go time," Trigger said. "We don't have to do anything else?"

"Not if Juliet is in position. Concordia will be online with the US president," she said. "He gets the final say. On his word, they send the signal via satellite to Juliet to cut power to dive to 1,000 feet, then collapse her antimatter containment trap." She shrugged. "After that, 2 kilos of antimatter meets 2 kilos of matter and ... *boom*."

Bell had been nervously monitoring their position relative to the test, but they hadn't drifted too far; they were more or less swirling in place, between 70 and 65 miles from ground zero. "Will we hear it?" he asked.

She nodded. "Hear it, and feel it," Venice said. "From here, it should be more like a thud than a roar. I admit, I didn't expect us to be the closest humans to the explosion of the world's first antimatter bomb, but here we are."

"Yeah, but we're safe, right?" Trigger said. "You said lethal distance was 50 miles, and we're 20 miles farther out."

"You want me to lie?" Venice asked.

"Yeah, of course," Trigger said.

"In that case, sure, we'll be fine."

"Good," Trigger nodded, swinging back to her screens.

"No, not good!" Bell said. "What's the truth?"

Venice spun her seat to face him, back to Rory and Trigger, so he couldn't see her expression, but he could imagine it was a disconcerting mix of excitement and fear. "We'll be safe from the gamma radiation burst … seawater will absorb most or all of that. And the electromagnetic pulse probably won't affect our electronics this far out, especially not your military stuff. Even though it's detonating 1,000 feet down though, there probably be blast overpressure, and heat. It will be interesting to see if we feel that …"

"Interesting is not the word," Rory pointed out.

She looked over her shoulder quickly. "True. Right. The real risk is the tsunami. How high will it be in deep water, and how far will it propagate?"

"Tsunami," Trigger said. "Great, thanks, Ears. I wasn't worried about a goddamn tsunami before. Now I am."

"And finally, of course," Venice said, ignoring her, "there's the expected unexpected effects."

"How can they be 'expected unexpected'?" Bell asked.

"Because we expect there to be effects that we never imagined," Venice said. "Like the scientists at Los Alamos working on the atom bomb didn't know it would release a huge electromagnetic pulse. Some of them also speculated it might set fire to the atmosphere and extinguish all life on earth." She smiled. "Those guys were wrong."

"So what's the 'set fire to the atmosphere' scenario with Juliet?" Rory asked, even though he didn't want to know.

Venice swung her seat to face him. "Well, exotic plasma formation. The antimatter annihilation process itself could create a super-heated plasma cloud of matter and antimatter particles, which could form semi-self-sustaining annihilation loops." She saw the confusion Rory was feeling reflected on his face. "A long series of massive explosions instead of just one," she explained. "But highly unlikely."

Trigger sighed. "Ears, you dipshit, next time the lady asks you if you want her to lie, you say *yes*, alright?"

***

Captain Anatoliy Kutuzov, of the GRU 411th Spetsnaz Detachment, believed what he had told the American base security officer. If he failed, his compatriots were probably going to bury Concordia with cruise missiles and blame the destruction on an illegal American weapons program. The throwaway comment by the GRU general about the *Sarov* could mean nothing else.

And Anatoliy Kutuzov did not intend to be locked underground at Concordia when it happened.

As they'd noticed when moving through the American facility, it wasn't set up like a military installation. Security had been light, its guards unarmed, access between floors, except from the fifth to the sixth, open and unguarded. The room he was being kept in was probably designed to hold and question petty thieves, or participants from drunken disputes. It was not made to hold a Russian Spetsnaz captain.

There were no cameras watching him that he could see. After the woman left him, he tested that by standing, placing his chair on the table and unscrewing one of its legs. He had no plan for what to do with it, wasn't even sure it would come off, but it did. And there was no reaction from outside the room.

The woman was careful though. She'd given him a camping mattress on the floor next to the table the night before, water, coffee, a juice bottle to piss in and a bucket for solids, and she'd left one hand free. So he'd had no opportunity to leave his small prison, no opportunity to tackle his guards or explore the area outside.

He sat the chair back down on its three remaining legs, slid the chair leg up the sleeve of his uniform, and sat on the chair again. It rocked a little, but was pretty stable. He looked underneath the table to see if he could get the table leg he was handcuffed to off the same way, but that wasn't going to happen. The top of the table leg was welded to the underside of the table, and bolted into the concrete floor. It wasn't budging. That, at least, they had gotten right.

And the handcuffs were tight. Those Hollywood scenes where the prisoner dislocated a thumb or broke their own fingers to slip out of handcuffs were nonsense, of course. Handcuffs went behind your wrist bones, and they couldn't be manipulated. The cuffs were digital too, locks operated by a thumbprint, and the mechanism covered so it couldn't be jimmied.

But as he'd already demonstrated, on a base with 50 security staff, thumbs were in plentiful supply.

315

He stiffened as there was a noise at the door, a lock clicked, and the woman he had spoken with earlier returned. She closed the door and stood just inside it, looking him over.

Come closer, my friend, he thought. "So you have come back to release me?" he said, rattling his handcuffed arm, but keeping his voice calm and level. *Nothing to fear here.*

She stepped forward, pulled out the chair on the other side of the table and sat. "You want the bad news or the good news?"

"Surprise me," he said.

"Alright. The good news is I was sent here to grill you about that Russian submarine, but our Navy task force just sunk it," she said.

If she had expected a reaction from him, he intended to disappoint her. He shrugged. "If that is the good news, what is the bad news?" he asked.

"Bad news is, you guessed it, I never intended to release you."

"Ah, well, such is life," he said. "I never believed you would." Kutuzov lowered his arm by his side, one end of the chair leg dropping into his palm as he closed his fingers loosely around it.

She looked offended. "Aww. I might have, if …"

He didn't wait for her to finish her sentence. Bringing his arm up, he let the chair leg drop free of his arm, caught the end of it and swung it toward her head. The look of offense on her face changed to shock, but she reacted quickly, pushing herself away from the table so that the chair leg only caught her head a glancing blow. But Kutuzov wasn't waiting to see the outcome. In the same movement, he swung himself up onto the table, using his chained arm as a pivot, and faced downward, swinging his legs over the table and slamming his heel into her temple.

Her head cracked into the table, and her body went limp, but he clamped her head between his shins so he didn't lose her. Grunting, as quietly as he could, he got one ankle under her armpit, then the other, and used his legs to pull her body up onto the table on one side, as he lowered himself to the ground with the other. Crawling to his knees, he reached up, grabbed one of her arms and pulled it toward his cuffs. He found her thumb and pressed it to the lock, wincing as the cuff clicked open and the woman's body slid to the floor.

He'd twisted his arm brutally, and a red welt was already rising on his wrist where the cuff had been. He stood and quickly checked the woman for a pulse.

She was alive. Good. Kutuzov did not like killing women. He took off her belt and quickly bound her hands and legs together behind her back.

She wasn't carrying a weapon. He felt her pockets, and came up with an ID, a key card, a packet of gum and a satellite phone that required a code to unlock. He tried using her thumb on the activation button, but it wanted a numerical code. He threw it on the desk in disgust and picked up the chair leg again. At least he had a club. He'd had plenty of time to plan his next move, if he managed to escape the room.

The door didn't lock from the inside; he'd seen that. He pulled it open a crack and looked down the corridor outside. Most of the levels inside the underground facility were curved, but this one wasn't. So either he wasn't underground—in one of the other habitats perhaps—or he was in a part of the underground facility he hadn't been in before.

Kutuzov had talked about escape with the American woman, but escaping the facility wasn't his objective. Destroying it was. For that, he needed first to find out where in the American station he was.

Pulling the door open, he stepped into the corridor. And felt the barrel of a gun press against his neck before he could turn. "Don't move, mother," the voice of Leroi Fontaine growled.

***

Anatoliy Kutuzov did not flinch at the touch of a pistol barrel on his neck. In fact, he welcomed it.

It put the man holding it right where he needed him.

He raised his hands slowly above his shoulders, still holding the chair leg. "Please, my friend, don't do anything stupid."

He could feel the tension in the man's grip—too firm, too rigid. A tell. The guard was nervous. Nervous meant slow. Kutuzov's hands remained in the air, fingers slightly spread, his body loose, deceptively relaxed.

"You're the stupid one," the voice behind him said. "Drop what you're holding and …

Kutuzov breathed in, deep and controlled. In the space of a single exhale, he moved.

His head snapped forward and to the left, just enough to shift the contact point of the muzzle away from his spine. At the same time, his left hand shot up and back, smacking the gun hand at the wrist with the chair leg while his right foot pivoted outward, dropping his body lower and twisting sideways.

The sudden movement knocked the gun off its mark as his right hand clamped onto the attacker's wrist, forcing the weapon upward. A sharp torque of his hips and shoulders turned his entire body into a lever, bending the guard's arm at a painful angle. A panicked shot rang out—harmlessly into the ceiling.

Before the man could recover, Kutuzov stepped in, driving his right elbow into his attacker's ribs. The air left the

318

guard in a wheezing gasp. A microsecond later, the operator's left hand stripped the pistol from now-weakened fingers, flipping it effortlessly into a firing grip.

By the time his attacker realized what had happened, he was the one staring down the barrel.

"OK, stupid," Kutuzov said, voice even, holding the pistol face high, letting the man see his finger inside the trigger guard. "Hands behind your head, fingers laced. Turn around, and start walking."

"Where?" Leroi asked angrily, massaging his arm.

"Take us to level six."

"I can't. Access to the forge is restricted," Leroi said.

"Yes, and your boss said security guards have access, so let's just see." He put a boot in Leroi's backside and shoved him. "Go."

Leroi shuffled toward the freight elevator. "The guards down there are armed now. You won't make it out of the elevator."

"Story of my life, as you Americans say," Kutuzov said. "But if I don't make it, you don't make it, so maybe you can talk them out of shooting us."

***

Leroi Fontaine wracked his mind for ideas that wouldn't get him shot trying to tackle the mountain of a man behind him. Maybe if they bumped into someone else on the way to the elevator, while the Russian was reacting to that, he could …

They didn't. They arrived at the elevator without seeing anyone.

The only idea he could come up with was to wait until they were in the elevator, moving down, and attack the guy while they were cramped up together. That might give him a chance.

"Inside," the Russian said, when the elevator doors opened. He followed Leroi in, but it was a freight elevator, right? Ten feet across. The Russian stood on the other side of the elevator, pistol pointed at his gut. Leroi had no way to rush him before he fired. "Six," the man said, motioning with the pistol.

Leroi reached behind himself, pressed his thumb to the reader there, and pressed the button for level six. The elevator jerked into motion.

The Russian smiled. "What do you know? Access granted."

Leroi's mind raced. He tensed, but there was nothing he could use the tension for. The ride would be about 30 seconds. He had maybe 30 seconds to live, or to come up with something that …

The elevator chimed, it shuddered to a halt, and at level four, it stopped.

"Say nothing," the Russian growled. His pistol was pointed at the doors.

As they opened, two base maintenance workers were standing there in overalls, a water cooler on wheels between them. One went to push it into the elevator without looking, and the other smiled. "Going down?"

The Russian fired.

Leroi leaped across the gap between them. The Russian caught the movement, twisted the pistol in his grip, shot at Leroi, but Leroi barreled into him, grabbing his gun arm. "Get him!" Leroi yelled to the maintenance workers.

One was on a knee, looking shocked at the flower of blood on his chest. The other was behind the water cooler, but shoved it out the way and jumped on the Russian too.

Leroi had his gun arm, trying to push it to the floor, as the man landed a left-handed punch to his head that made Leroi's vision blur. The gun fired again, but into the floor. The maintenance worker was whaling on the Russian, without apparent effect, then got an arm around his neck. Leroy grappled for the gun. Another shot, deafening in the small space. Then another fist to the side of Leroi's head like a ball peen hammer, and he fell to the floor.

The Russian turned the gun on the man hanging off his back, shot him in the face, then put another bullet in him after he fell. He pushed the water cooler, and the man with the chest wound, still shocked and gasping, out of the elevator. The doors closed.

Leroi rolled onto his back, but something was wrong. Not his head. His stomach. He lifted his head and looked at the front of his shirt, to see dark blood soaking his shirt down by his belt. His vision was blurred, but he looked at the Russian and saw blood on his uniform too, right side of his chest. The Russian was panting, right hand held to his side. He moved Leroi's pistol to his left hand and motioned to him.

"Stand up. You are not dead."

Leroi didn't comply. What was the point? Guy had shot him. Was going to shoot him again. But a meaty hand grabbed his shirt and hauled him to his feet with a grunt as the elevator reached six and chimed. The Russian grabbed a handful of collar behind his neck, and mashed his face into the elevator doors.

The doors opened. There was no one there. The Russian pushed him out into the corridor, around to the left, half holding him up, half propelling him forward, as Leroi clutched his hands to the wound down by his belt, which was pissing blood.

An engineer with a tablet came around the curve in the corridor, looking at his screen as he walked, then looked up as he realized there were people in the way. "Sorry …" he started to say.

The Russian pushed Leroi into him. Leroi grabbed him like a drowning man holding on to a life buoy.

"What the hell?" the man said, reeling back.

The Russian shoved Leroi aside and grabbed the engineer, spinning him around with one arm clamped across his throat and the pistol to his temple. "The reactor," the Russian said. "Where is it?"

Leroi rolled into a ball and screwed his eyes tight.

He heard voices, shuffling footsteps down the corridor, panting and grunting receding. He didn't care anymore.

***

Solomon Cohen looked up from his place at the comms station, frowning. "Show me the CCTV from that level," he told the man at the desk.

"What is it?" Lau asked, hearing the worry in his voice. "We're at J-hour minus 20."

"Silent alarm triggered, level six," Cohen said, leaning toward the screen. "No, find a different angle," he said to the man flipping between cameras. He put his hand to his mouth. "Oh my God. *How*?!"

Lau ran to his side. He couldn't decide what he was looking at, at first. A group of staff, standing beside the containment module access door. One was a security guard, pointing a rifle at something, or someone, off-screen. As Lau watched, he staggered backward, dropped his rifle and fell onto his knees, then onto his side.

A figure came on camera, pushing someone in front of him, a pistol held to the person's head.

"The Russian officer," Cohen said. "He got out. He's on six." Cohen grabbed the mic off the comms desk and flipped a switch to select an internal channel. "CC to security quick

322

response team. Intruder on level six, armed and hostile. He has hostages. He's trying … looks like he's trying to get access to containment. He must be neutralized. Acknowledge." Cohen waited for the response from the on-duty security detachment leader, then dropped the mic back on the desk. He put a hand on the comms specialist's shoulder. "Find Delaney for me. Last I heard, she was interviewing the Russian."

What little composure David Lau had left filled his shoes like urine. "If he breaches containment, he'll be a wrecking ball in there. If he punctures the vacuum …"

"I'm ordering an evacuation, all non-control-center personnel," Cohen said.

"There's no point," Lau moaned, collapsing onto a seat behind him. "Where are they going to go? There's nearly a half gram of antimatter in that reactor. It'll go off with the power of a Hiroshima bomb. You'd have to get people at least 2 miles out, or farther …"

"We have to try, David." He lifted his head and raised his voice. "Listen, people. We have a situation on the reactor level—security is responding. I'm going to issue a black alarm just to be safe, but the people in this room will remain at your stations. We will see the test through while the situation is being brought under control." He didn't wait for questions or complaints, just tapped his comms specialist on the back. "Sound the evacuation alarm in all above-ground facilities, and on levels minus one through four here."

Cohen looked at Lau and saw a broken man. He sat staring at the floor between his knees, with his hands clutching his hair as though he wanted to rip it from his skull. People were staring at Lau and himself, Bellings and Jansen included. Cohen started walking around, clapping his hands. "Nineteen minutes to J-hour, people. Fourteen until we arm Juliet. Keep yourselves together!"

"Submersible is in the sweet spot," Trigger said. "Hovering in position." She looked over to Bell. "Launch the comms buoy."

"Launching buoy," Bell said. "Good release … buoy ascending … initializing. *Handshake.* We have a good satellite link."

Venice was looking over his shoulder, and put a hand on his arm. She looked like she was tearing up. "It looks good. We did it. We actually made it."

Trigger gave her a disapproving look. "Can we save the tears of joy until after we see if the thing even works?"

"*Wait.* What the hell?" Elvis Bell said, grabbing his earphones and clamping them harder to his head. "Propulsion noise, single screw. There's a sub out here! It must have been waiting for us!"

"One of ours?" Venice asked, horrified. "The weapon …"

"Analyzing acoustic signature … oh, hell no," He looked at Trigger, horror on his face. "*Poseidon.* It's not a sub. It's a goddamn *nuclear* torpedo."

***

GRU Major General Tomas Arsharvin was standing stiffly by his desk, on line with the Kremlin. Thankfully, it was not a video call—just a telephone line, from his Argut River base. And not with any of the politicians he knew were sitting in the room at the other end, listening to the conversation. Just with his superior officer, the GRU commander Admiral Viktor Mikhailovich Rostovin.

Arsharvin drew a deep breath. "Yes, Admiral. I am able to confirm that the submarine, *B-90 Sarov,* successfully launched its special weapon. The weapon just floated a communication buoy to indicate that it has reached the target coordinates and is awaiting activation codes."

Arsharvin had also been informed by his naval liaison that *Sarov* had missed a comms check-in. It should have launched its cruise missiles at Concordia by now, but Russian satellites had not picked up any telltale missile launch blooms. Fires from burning US naval vessels, yes, but of the *Sarov*'s missiles, nothing.

And the *Envoy* stealth bomber had been lost north of the coast of Antarctica.

Arsharvin was in no hurry to pass on news of these failures. They would be received better once the American test had conclusively been disrupted.

"Thank you, Major General Arsharvin," the GRU commander said. Arsharvin heard muted voices conferring, before the admiral came back on. "The president has been informed. He has just issued the order to our Strategic Nuclear Command to detonate the torpedo."

The line went dead. Arsharvin stood there looking at the receiver in his hand.

That was it? Years of work, months of planning, days of action, and a simple thank you. And somewhere, on the other side of the globe, once the necessary orders made their laborious way through the Russian chain of command, a nuclear weapon would explode.

He slumped into his chair.

The SVR science chief, Artur Eizen, smiled at him and lit a cigarette. "I told you it was a good plan. Have more faith next time, my friend."

***

"Aggressor One, hostile contact, bearing seven zero degrees relative, range 2 miles, depth 1,000," Bell radioed to Bunny with near-panicked urgency. "Contact is a *Poseidon* nuclear torpedo. Sending coordinates. Request immediate interdiction!"

"She'll be on her way out of Juliet's explosion zone," Rory said. "If she takes that tasking, it's certain death."

"If she doesn't, and the Russian nuke goes off before Juliet," Venice said, "we lose everything. Juliet will explode, but the world will just think it was a big nuclear weapon test. All data will be useless."

"But if Bunny kills that torpedo, won't it set off the nuke inside anyway?" Rory asked.

"No. Fission weapons are more stable than antimatter," Venice said. "It has to be precisely triggered. Hit it with a torpedo, it will just break up and sink."

They waited for a response from the Aggressor Nemesis.

"Don't do it, girl," Rory said, voice barely audible. "It ain't worth it."

"She has to do it," Trigger said. "It's what she's there for."

They all jumped as the speakers built into the consoles in front of them woke to life.

"Two, this is Aggressor One," O'Hare replied. "I left my EW Gambit on patrol over your position. It should jam any signals being sent to that *Poseidon*."

"Will it also jam the activation signal for Juliet?" Venice asked worriedly.

"No, friendly signals will get through," Bell told her. "But if the jamming doesn't work …"

"I hear you, Two," Bunny said. "Coming in hot, VLTs armed."

Venice looked at the countdown timer in front of Bell. "J minus 10!" she said. "She won't make it."

Trigger sat back in her seat and folded her hands behind her neck. "She'll make it back in. Question is: Will she make it out?"

***

"You, open this door!" Kutuzov yelled at the terrified woman standing behind the security guard he had just shot. He had another of the American scientists, a young man, by the throat, pistol to his head.

The woman fell to her knees, hands over her head. "I … I can't," she sobbed. "If I open the containment module before the reactor is damped, it will—"

Kutuzov shot her. Twice. He turned his pistol to the person behind her, a bearded man. The Russian coughed, seeing blood on the back of his hand as he wiped his mouth. "Open the door," he growled at the man.

The man glared back at him defiantly. "Why should I? I'll die either way."

Kutuzov's finger tightened on the trigger. His gun bucked.

He staggered forward. No, not *his* gun.

A rifle fired again, punching him in the back, sending him to the ground, the man he was holding stumbling away from him. He couldn't breathe. He rolled onto his side, looking back behind him. Saw the damn security guard he'd brought down in the elevator with him. Gut-shot, but not dead yet. Leaning against a wall, rifle dangling from one arm. Bleeding.

Anatoliy Kutuzov tried to draw breath, but his chest wouldn't move. *Ah, fuck.* He saw the guard slip in his own blood and slide to the floor. He just had time for one more thought.

See you in hell, comrade.

***

Bunny been headed out of the blast zone with her tail on fire when Ears Bell called the contact. She was already at Mach 1.2, 20 miles from ground zero, headed for 50 before the device cooked off. Figured that would see her at about 70 miles out before any blast effect reached her.

Before she could even think, she had chopped her throttle and hauled her Nemesis into a looping split-S to put her back on a bearing to the contact. She put her GAMBIT into jamming mode and contacted Bell. As she was talking, she armed the two VLTs in her payload bay, preparing to drop her airspeed, adjusting her altitude for a safe release. There was no need for a MAD-mesh drop; she had a good fix on the target from *Charlene*, and there would be no time anyway. The familiar basketball hoop of her ground targeting system came up on her helmet visor, and she steered for the center of the loop, AI counting down to weapons release.

It never occurred to Bunny O'Hare that she wouldn't try to make the attack. Unlike Trigger, she'd stop counting how many lives she had left a long, long time ago. Because even back then, the answer was zero. Instinctively she knew that if she did the math now, it would tell her she had no hope of surviving. It always did. And one day, the math would be right.

She gripped her throttle in her left hand, her flight stick in her right, thumb hovering over her the weapons release trigger as she begun muttering her combat mantra to herself. *Girl, you are a supersonic, bat-winged mofo out of hell. That target is already dead. No antimatter superweapon can touch you. THIS is where you live. THIS is your time. You OWN the sky. You are a freaking NINJA, and your shadow will be the ONLY thing that catches you.*

***

Donovan Grant had run for the surface along with 280 other Concordia personnel. Unlike them, he had a to-the-minute idea of what they would be facing when they got out there. Temperature -112°F, with howling winds reaching speeds of over 62 miles per hour, a deafening roar and visibility to near zero. The snow and ice particles whipped up by the wind creating a disorienting, featureless void, making it impossible to distinguish the ground from the sky.

As he stumbled out onto the ice, he saw a snowmobile move away, three people in survival gear squeezed onto the seat, one being towed behind on short skis. "This way!" a man next to him said, pulling him toward the vehicle shed, where the station's tracked Beowulf transports were parked. Grant hesitated, and the man was gone.

He stumbled after him.

***

"J-hour minus five," Cohen announced, turning to Jake Bellings. "Send the trap collapse signal."

"Sending trap collapse signal!" Bellings announced, tapping a key on the console in front of him. He conferred with the woman sitting beside him. "Signal sent. We are at J minus 4:50 *and counting.*"

David Lau was standing again, biting his lip, looking at a large wall screen, which showed the CCTV vision from the NOAA platform and live, satellite-relayed imagery from a Space Force Skylon as it came up over the horizon and began to close on the detonation site, cameras zoomed onto the patch of ocean above Juliet, or zoomed out to show an area about 20 miles around it.

Other CCTV screens in front of Cohen showed people streaming out of Concordia's three habitats and running for the

329

ice. But he could only see a dozen or so feet beyond the station lights before everything and everyone was eaten up by the blizzard. He'd seen someone drop the attacker on level six, but he didn't have time to cancel the evacuation.

Five minutes—he would cancel the evacuation five minutes from now. Or, actually, four minutes 35.

"Aggressor aircraft in the blast zone!" Colonel Sandilands said. He had his head in a set of headphones, and was trying to read the screen in front of him. "There's … *what?* There's a Russian nuclear torpedo at ground zero. The Aggressor pilot just attacked it."

Cohen turned to Lau. "Abort?" It was still an option, up until one minute before detonation.

Lau had recovered his composure and looked at Cohen with dead eyes. "If the pilot can destroy the Russian torpedo, we can still save this …"

"Maybe," Cohen agreed. "But the pilot."

"Knows what they are doing," Lau said. He fixed a glare on Sandilands, expecting him to protest. "*Right?*"

Sandilands stood with hands spread on the desk in front of him and nodded tightly. "She does. God help her."

"J minus *four*," Bellings intoned.

***

The two Very Lightweight Torpedoes punched out of Bunny's payload bay at 500 knots and 1,000 feet, a half mile short of their target, and arced through the snowy sky to splash into the water 100 yards from the *Poseidon*, which had slowed to a crawl in the water, awaiting its detonation signal.

Which was fighting Bunny's GAMBIT to get through.

As Bunny hit the air above ground zero, she shoved her throttle through the gate, lighting the afterburners on her Pratt

& Whitney turbofan engines and keeping her nose level with the sea below. Every fiber in her body wanted to get altitude, to put as much height as possible between herself and the explosion of the antimatter bomb, but she knew physics was against her.

She dumped all her remaining ordnance.

Six hundred knots.

At sea level, the air was denser, slowing the blast wave. If she tried climbing, it would cost her airspeed, and she needed speed more than height.

Seven hundred knots. Supersonic. Come on, you big black beauty.

If the explosion was like a nuke, it would create a huge super-heated ball of steam, then a column of water a mile high, which she did not want to be caught in. The lateral blast *should* be smaller, and slower.

Eight hundred knots. She checked her distance from ground zero. Twenty miles …

Not enough.

***

Bunny's two torpedoes speared into the water at near-unsafe speeds. One hit at a perfect angle, shooting down 50 feet and engaging its propulsion and seeker systems to begin looking for the target … which was basically anything not chirping a "friend" code at it.

Bell had made sure *Charlene* was chirping like a canary.

The second torpedo hit the water at a steep angle and torqued violently, falling down to 200 feet before it stabilized enough to attempt a propulsion start. Its engine initialized later than its sister torpedo's, but it was already deeper, and began searching around and below it.

In the sky above, Bunny's GAMBIT was filling the air with jamming energy, but it was built to direct its energy at a specific target, not just fill a void. As long as the *Poseidon* was ahead of it, which it was at that moment, it could block the signal being beamed at the Southern Ocean by the Russian satellite. But the second the GAMBIT passed *over* the *Poseidon*, it would leave clear air in its wake, and the Russian signal would burn through to the comms buoy the *Poseidon* had tethered to it by an optical fiber cable.

As the lowest of Bunny's torpedoes got a return from the *Poseidon* and accelerated toward it, the GAMBIT passed directly over them.

The *Poseidon* got its detonation order. With silicon equanimity, it passed the coded signal to a decryption and validation routine to verify it was authentic, and arm its warhead.

That took precious milliseconds.

During which Bunny's VLT closed on the *Poseidon* and, while still 20 yards distant, triggered its high-explosive warhead. The blast propagated through the water and broke the *Poseidon*'s back. Water flooded into its hull and shorted its electronics, the two halves spiraling to the seabed 3,000 feet below.

***

The counter on the screen in front of Venice and Bell hit 01:00 and ticked over. Everyone in the module held their breath. Even Trigger was silent.

00:59

Venice broke the silence, tapping on a keyboard to log into her Concordia desktop, and pulled up a new screen in front of Bell. Trigger and Rory leaned in to see what it showed.

"What are we looking at?" Trigger asked.

"The view from the Skylon D4 space plane approaching ground zero," she said. "It's using AI-supplemented synthetic aperture, sees straight through the cloud and snow and redraws the image like it's pure HD vision. The bomb will detonate while it's still about 50 miles out, so the Skylon will have a ringside seat."

The screen showed a view from the spacecraft to the gray sea below. In the distance, the earth curved away from horizon to horizon, with nothing but black space beyond.

"Actually, we're the ones in the ringside seats," Bell said, checking their position. "We're only 70 miles out. That spacecraft is up in the bleachers."

"Ringside seat to Armageddon?" Rory asked. "Not sure I want that ticket."

00:40

Trigger peeled a garbage bag off a roll on the bulkhead beside her and handed it to Rory. "You'll be needing this. And I recommend you strap yourself in, flyboy. I have a feeling being in this tin tub will be like being inside a tumble dryer.

00:30

***

Bunny was shaking, but not because her Nemesis was. Hammering over the sea at Mach 1.3, it had long ago gone supersonic and was outrunning its own shockwave. She was telling herself to relax her grip on her throttle and joystick, but she couldn't. At 500 feet above the sea, there was no horizon to orient on. The slightest twitch, missed correction, and she'd slam into the rolling waves. Time to die: milliseconds.

The same counter that was burning its image into the retinas of the surviving crew of Outlaw was floating on her helmet visor, filling her vision.

00:20

Along with other numbers: 860 knots, 996 miles per hour, 1,606 kilometers per hour, *48 miles.*

00:10

Her torpedoes must have taken out that nuke, right? Or it would already have cooked off? She hit an air pocket, thumped down to 450 and guided herself back to 500 feet with a finger contraction on her stick.

Five seconds.

She stole a look over her shoulder. Would she see it or feel it first?

Three.

Or would it just kill her silently, a blast of gamma rays followed by hot plasma, searing the flesh from her bones?

One.

***

Inside Outlaw's command module, 70 miles from ground zero, the timer ticked over to zero, and nothing happened.

Where *they* were. Filmed from low earth orbit, the Skylon vision showed something was definitely happening.

Venice had her hand to her mouth. "My God, black sun!"

Rory wasn't sure what he'd expected. Something like a big white or blue ball of lightning, vaporized sea water blooming into the sky, then maybe a mushroom cloud of steam reaching up to the heavens? What he saw was a portal to hell opening.

A black ball, miles around, appeared where the water had been, and began lifting itself out of the depths. It was happening fast, but Rory's mind was slowing it down, trying to comprehend.

"What the hell …?" Trigger gasped.

"The gamma burst, ionizing the air, sucking in the light," Venice said, trying to explain. "It can't sustain …"

It couldn't. The ball shimmered, then flashed blue, lighting both pouring out of it, into the sky, and being pulled out of the very air and into the shrinking blackness. For a millisecond, Rory thought he could see a 20-mile-wide, 20-mile-deep hole in the sea. Then the polarizing filters on the Skylon's camera slammed shut as there was an almighty flash.

At that moment, a monster woke in the deep beneath their feet.

And it wasn't happy.

***

The sky behind Bunny's Nemesis turned black, left and right, as high as she could see. She looked forward again, checking her altitude and airspeed.

Sixty-two miles from ground zero. She needed altitude now. She eased back on her stick, the slight pressure causing her aircraft to rocket up into the sky. In seconds she was at 10,000 feet. Then 20,000.

Behind her, the black sky turned blue, then crackled with lightning. Thirty thousand feet. A dome of plasma, or whatever it was, was rising from the sea now, and it collapsed in on itself. It was like watching a cannonball land in a pool of gray paint, in slow motion. Huge walls of water began surging outward.

As she shot through 40,000 feet, everything in the cockpit shut down. And then the shockwave hit her.

***

Inside the module, the first sound to reach them was a single hollow thud.

"If we're hearing that, it means the gamma radiation wave already passed us," Venice said. "And we're not dead, so we were far enough out. Anything inside 50 miles would just have had its DNA fatally rearranged."

"You didn't mention our DNA being rearranged in your scenarios," Bell pointed out.

"Didn't want to freak you," she said. She pointed at the screen, as a wall of water rose in a circle around the collapsing white ball of lightning. "Blast wave. Hyper-compressed water."

"Doesn't look as bad as I thought," Trigger said.

Venice looked at her sideways, then back at the screen. "You're looking at it from *space*," she said. There was a scale on the screen mapped to the surface of the sea. "That wave is a half mile high, traveling at over 3,000 miles per hour." She had an app open on her phone and started tapping at it.

"What are you doing?" Rory asked.

"Putting that wave into a model we made," she said. "Trying to find out how big it's going to be when it gets to us." She bit her lip, then looked up. "Oh."

"*Oh*? Oh what?" Bell asked.

"Do you want me to lie?" she asked him.

"No. Yes." He caught Trigger glaring at him. "Yes, give us best case."

"Best case, that wave is going to be 100 feet high when it reaches us," Venice said.

Rory slapped his hand on the bulkhead with a confidence he didn't feel. "No problem. We'll ride it like a cork in a bathtub."

Venice didn't look reassured. "There's going to be more than one wave," she told them.

***

EMP, Bunny thought as her aircraft stalled.

The Nemesis had been hardened against EMP damage, with tweaks to its avionics based on the hard lessons learned from the Chinese nuclear weapon detonation in low earth orbit, which had not just ionized hundreds of miles of the Van Allen radiation belt, and turned everything passing through it into space junk, but also killed any insufficiently hardened electronics in the sky or on the ground within its 100-mile EMP footprint.

A lot of aircraft had fallen out of the sky that day.

But "hardened" didn't mean "immune." A safety trigger had been added to the FB-22's avionics so that all electrical and electronic systems would instantly shut down as soon as it detected a strong electromagnetic pulse. The pulse was dissipated across the skin of the Nemesis and discharged as static.

But it meant her aircraft had just turned from an awe-inspiring aeronautical marvel into a brick.

Momentum momentarily carried her Nemesis higher, but it began to oscillate, nose and tail fighting to see which would lose the battle with gravity first. Eyes closed, hands gripping the instrument panel in front of her as she felt for the auxiliary power unit switch to route power to her auxiliary starter, Bunny felt like she was riding a bucking bronco while trying to play a piano. Blindfolded.

She found the APU switch and flipped it. Heard the whine she wanted to hear. Half full of fuel, with nothing in her payload bay, the engines won the gravity fight. She began falling tail-first toward the sea, center of gravity behind her wings, her deliberately unstable aircraft even more so, gyrating as it fell. She had no idea what her altitude was. Forty thousand? Twenty? Two?

She began to alternately gray and red out, which should balance itself out, right? The redout was winning though, blood rushing to her head. Barely conscious, she saw a golden luminescence through her eyelids, her helmet-mounted display coming to life again.

Autopilot, she thought. Hand reaching feebly in front of her. *Come on, baby, save yourself.* Her gloved hand touched something on the instrument panel. She tried to pry her eyes open. Ah. Just their jerry-rigged RWR array.

Nice bit of kit. Not what she needed.

Her hand fell to her side, then got flung against the cockpit wall with the g-force of the next spin.

***

Donovan Grant had lost his bearings, which was ridiculous, since he couldn't be more than 20 yards from the station exit. Could he? He'd run toward a shadow in the storm, thinking it was the man who had run off in front of him, but then it swirled up and away. Just a snow flurry.

Grant stopped running, breathing hard. Spun around, looking for structures, movement. Anything. Looked up, trying to find the sun.

Thud.

The ground beneath his feet shook, as though … as though a bomb had just gone off nearby. The reactor?

No, if that had exploded, he'd have been reduced to atomic particles in a Hiroshima-sized ball of plasma. It was Juliet, somewhere out in the Southern Ocean. It had to be.

He closed his eyes. Saara, tell the world the truth. Tell them everything!

"What the hell are you doing, man?" a voice yelled at him.

He spun around. Standing 2 feet away was Raleigh, the station security chief.

"You … you're supposed to be in jail," Grant said, pointing at him stupidly.

"Electronic doors," Raleigh told him. "Open automatically during an evacuation." Raleigh wasn't dressed for the intense cold. He'd found a lined anorak and gloves somewhere, but he was wearing indoor overalls and sneakers, not boots. He had neither a balaclava nor goggles. He grabbed Grant by the shoulders and shook him. "I was following *you*. You're the lifer. Where the hell is the station? We have to find transport."

Grant felt the pounding of the wind against his body, trying to knock him to the ground. Southwesterly wind. Station exit faced south. He rotated right, looking north, northeast. Thought he saw a dark shape through the blowing snow, then it was gone again.

"This way!" he yelled, and let the wind push him forward.

With a murderer at his back.

***

Aboard the USNS *Lorenzen*, now moving away from the USS *Galvez*, the Juliet detonation 100 miles away was felt before it was seen—a deep bass *boom* that traveled from the keel, up through the ship and into the feet of the people standing on *Lorenzen*'s bridge.

Cameras on the superstructure were trained in the direction of the test, and the vision projected on wall screens throughout the ship, with the crew warned not to look directly at the explosion. Sincere Jones had been down in the ship's sick bay visiting with the wounded and speaking to medical personnel from both *Lorenzen* and *Galvez*.

Two hours earlier, Jones and the other captains of the remaining ships in the task force had finally been given a more detailed briefing of what to expect from the "antimatter weapon" test, and how to prepare. *Lorenzen*'s principal mission was to use its sophisticated sensor suite to measure the effect of the explosion on sea state, radiation levels, electrical and electronic disruption, and "atmospheric effects."

They had been warned of the chance of sea states ranging from seven (rough seas), to 8 (up to 50 feet high). But *Galvez* still had no power to its screws, and Jones had been preparing to take it under tow.

Jones had interrupted the colonel conducting the briefing, a USAF officer called Sandilands. "Colonel, you're talking a potential tsunami-sized wave hitting us, even out here at 100 miles. We would barely be able to make 8 knots with *Galvez* in tow, and we're already facing rough seas and high winds."

"It's your call, Commander," Sandilands said. "With the captain of the USS *Congress* missing, and *Galvez*'s captain incapacitated in your sick bay, you are the ranking officer in this task force. Transfer the crew of the *Galvez* to your vessel, and cut her adrift, or keep her in tow and ride it out. We will send you our modeling to help inform your decision."

"Does your 'modeling' take into account that this vessel also took a hit from a Russian antiship missile?" Jones said bitterly.

To his credit, Sandilands didn't bite back. "No one anticipated Russian aggression on that scale, Commander," he replied. "I'm deeply sorry for your losses, but the decision to continue with this test came directly from the White House."

After conferring with the captain of the *Galvez*, who was suffering from burns and smoke inhalation but conscious, Jones joined a quick conference with the commander of US Navy INDOPACOM and the Secretary of the Navy. It was agreed they would rig up an improvised sea anchor, take its crew off and abandon *Galvez* to its fate.

It was more easily said than done. Even though they had already transferred the wounded and medical personnel from *Galvez*, it had taken the full 90 minutes they had available, and they had only just begun moving away from the wallowing frigate, gathering speed so they were ready to meet any incoming waves—another challenge since the prevailing winds meant they were sailing into westerly swells, whereas the test, and any waves it generated, was taking place to their southeast.

Like any crew member on the two vessels not actively occupied at the moment of the test, Jones had gone outside for J-hour—in his case, to their starboard bridge wing—and stood with his back toward the test. They'd been told that, following the explosion, there could be a brief rise of up to 80 degrees in ambient temperature, but not enough to cause burns to exposed skin.

When he felt the thud, he turned.

The water around his ship was *glowing*. A pale blue, slowing fading to gray. But that wasn't the strangest thing.

He'd expected to see a false sun dawning to the southeast, and given low visibility due to the blowing snow, probably not more than a faint glow. Instead, a black stain was spreading on the horizon, like an artificial night. It rose into the sky, a diffuse, evil shadow. Almost immediately, it flashed blue, then white, and collapsed.

"That had to be miles high for us to see it in these conditions," Jones said to the USAF lieutenant, Stiles.

"And feel it," Stiles added. "What now?"

"Atmospheric shockwave will take another few minutes to reach us," Jones said. "Should have blown itself out by the time it gets here, the modeling says."

"Here's to the modeling," Stiles said without conviction.

Jones thought he could hear a sound above the wind buffeting the bridge wing, then decided he couldn't … but it was definitely there. A building roar.

"Into cover!" Sincere yelled, waving to a bosun on the foredeck before he grabbed Stiles and the ensign on bridge watch duty and shoved them both into the bridge. The wind changed direction, coming from the direction of the test now and rising in strength.

The USAF TAO, Pile, looked over as they slammed the hatch shut behind them. "Lieutenant, just about to fetch you, got something about 50 miles out …"

As Stiles quickly joined his men at the CIC station, Jones watched a wall screen showing the sky toward ground zero. A bridge watch officer was standing beside him, and pointed at the screen. "Holy shit."

The blowing snow between *Lorenzen* and the test site had completely cleared; blown away, or evaporated, he couldn't tell. Suddenly, they could see all the way to the far horizon, where a white column was rising out of the collapsed dome of darkness and lightning. Miles wide, it blasted straight up into the sky. Not a mushroom cloud … a column of pure energy. Plasma? Super-heated water? Jones had no idea. But it was an ill omen.

Which proved true moments later. Stiles looked over from his station. "Commander, you have to see this," he said.

"I'm looking at it, Lieutenant," Jones said. "Helm, prepare to come about, on my order." Rolling outward from that blast would be the waves he'd been warned about. But if he made his turn too soon, they'd be wallowing in the wind-driven cross swell.

"Not that, sir," Stiles urgently corrected him, pointing at a screen in front of him. "This. We have a read on the incoming sea surge."

Jones stepped over to his side and looked where Stiles was pointing. "Picked it up on L-band, 40 miles out now. That's a wave front. Scale is on the left side of the screen."

"Fifty meters?" Jones said, shocked. "*One sixty feet?*"

"It was 55 a minute ago," Stiles said. "Falling, but …"

"How fast is it moving?"

"Uh, 520 knots. It'll reach us in four minutes—still be 30 meters high." Stiles's face was pale.

Lorenzen was sailing with the prevailing swell, her starboard beam toward the incoming wave. "Helm! Hard right 40 degrees, ahead full! Sound the collision alarm!" Jones yelled.

***

The Juliet shockwave hit Bunny's Nemesis while it was still recovering from its corkscrewing tail-first plummet to the sea. She had managed to engage the autopilot, which stopped the spin, applied power to her engines and dropped her nose so the Nemesis was once again flying instead of falling. It recovered at 15,000 feet above the ocean, 70 miles from ground zero, when a blast of 300-degree air struck it from behind.

Bunny was fully conscious again, vision clearing, struggling to get a grip on airspeed, altitude, attitude and heading so that she could take control of the aircraft back from the combat AI system, when it felt like her Nemesis was grabbed by an enormous hand and shoved through the sky. Her airspeed jumped from 400 to 450 knots in a heartbeat, but she felt the aircraft stalling and yawing as the wind from behind broke the flow of air over her wings and vertical stabilizers.

She knocked out the autopilot, grabbed her stick and throttle, and shoved both forward, pouring on power to stabilize the airflow and counteract the turbulence. But despite the fire pouring from her tail, she was wallowing like a pig in mud, airspeed climbing only slowly, sea getting closer …

She reached for the ejection handle under her seat. She'd been warned by Aggressor's physician she might not survive another ejection, but she certainly wouldn't survive pancaking into a frozen sea in the aftermath of the biggest explosion known to humankind.

Don't punch out! A voice yelled inside her head. Time stood still. What the hell? She recognized the voice: Charlene 'Touchdown' Dubois, the pilot who their submersible *Charlene* had been named after. Who had sacrificed her life to save Bunny's in the last days of the war with China.

That was nuts.

Bunny's eyes flicked to the altimeter reading in her helmet visor: 11,000 feet.

You got this! The voice yelled again.

And then another voice. *Ride it, O'Hare.*

Uncle? She shook her head violently, tried to focus on what her instruments were telling her. Airspeed 590, altitude 10,400, attitude eight degrees nose down …

She lifted her hands away from the ejection handle, put them back on throttle and stick, pulled back on her stick gently to bring her nose up.

Nine thousand eight hundred feet. Airspeed 600. No yaw.

I got this, she thought. I got this.

***

"Flash message from *Lorenzen*," Ears Bell said. "Wave surge, tsunami strength, observed at 60 miles from ground zero, moving at 500 knots …"

Rory did the math. "It's going to hit us any second." They'd just had a panicked discussion about the rising heat inside the module, but that appeared to have peaked just before the latest bad news ticked in.

"It will be a rolling wave, not a whitecap, if that helps," Venice said.

"Cool. A thousand bucks to a hundred says we make it," Trigger said, pulling her seat harness tighter. "Takers?"

Bell was out of his seat, checking Venice's harness. "Anyone who bets against you can't collect. You are a complete nutjob, you know that?" he said to Trigger.

"Aw. You flirting with me?" Trigger smiled back at him.

Ears shook his head and fell into his own seat, pulling his straps over his shoulders and securing his lap belt.

Venice had a tablet in her lap. She was still logged into Concordia's servers, watching data stream across it from the command center, which was assimilating inputs from Navy, Space Force and Air Force, even seismic monitoring stations scattered across Antarctica.

"Holy crap," she said. "Five point nine!"

"Five point nine what?" Rory asked.

"On the Richter scale. The Tsar Bomba explosion was only five. We predicted maybe five point five."

"Congratulations?" Rory said dryly. "And that wave?"

She frowned at him, then down at her tablet. "Oh. Going to hit us in …" They started rising like the module was an express elevator, headed for the penthouse suite. She reached for the console in front of her to brace herself. "Now."

Rory screwed his eyes shut, and clutched the garbage bag to his chest. The flotation belt around the module should help, right? They might tumble, but they wouldn't sink? Unless that heat blast had cooked their air bags and burst them. They hadn't heard anything, but there was a lot going on …

They stopped rising, the module tilted, Rory felt like his worst fear was coming true, then he was lifted out of his seat as the module started going *down*, the express elevator now headed for the basement level. A quote came to him: *It's not the journey that kills you; it's the destination.*

They hit the bottom of the elevator shaft with a tooth-jarring smack, the module tilting over and snapping back upright with enough violence to fling his brain out though his ears.

A minute passed. They looked at each other.

Trigger broke the silence. "Good news: we're alive," she said, but she was looking at her feet. "Bad news: we have a leak." As the module righted itself, a small stream of water shot out between her boots.

Then the module started rising again.

***

Donovan Grant *was* a lifer: he carried inside everything that decades on the ice could teach a man. He knew how to read the wind and the diffuse light to find his way, even in blinding snow.

He led Raleigh back toward the station, and stopped up, momentarily puzzled, as he saw people streaming back *into* the central habitat. Raleigh pushed past him, headed for the vehicle park.

"Hey, stop," Donovan said. "The evacuation must have been canceled."

Raleigh ignored him, pushing forward against the wind toward the vehicle park, and Donovan realized he didn't intend to go back inside. At a shuffling run, Donovan caught him, then grabbed Raleigh by the shoulder of his anorak. "Stop, I said!"

Raleigh spun, an ice pick appearing in his hand, which he buried in Donovan's chest. He leaned back, kicked Donovan in the midriff, freed the pick and then turned for the vehicle park again.

Donovan staggered backward and collapsed, gasping like a fish on a riverbank. His vision grayed. Snow swirled above him, forming a face. He reached a hand up to it.

Saara, he croaked. *Saara*.

***

The USNS *Lorenzen* met the rising wall of water head on. Screws churning, she was making 16 knots when her bows started climbing up the 100-foot swell. Twelve thousand tons, 540 feet of ocean-going vessel wasn't built for climbing mountains, but she gave it all she had. About two thirds of the way up the wall of water, her bow dug in and was slowly eaten by the sea.

The immense pressure of the wave forced her stern upward, exposing her screws to the air as they spun wildly, thrashing against the void. The ship groaned in protest, hull creaking and buckling under the strain of titanic forces.

As the bow dug deeper, the weight of the water pouring over her decks began to drag her down. Jones saw his bridge crew clinging to whatever they could find. The ship's angle grew steeper, and the sea rushed over her like a predator claiming its prey. Bridge windows bulged, then shattered. Below decks, machinery strained and failed, and lights flickered as seawater breached bulkheads and surged through corridors.

But *Lorenzen* was not done yet. Just as it seemed the wave would claim her, momentum carried her through and out the other side of the wave. Slowly, agonizingly, she emerged, hull shuddering as she shed the weight of the sea. Jones, drenched and battered, watched in awe as her bow emerged from the water, streaming foam and debris. She leveled out, decks awash but unbroken, and engines, though strained, still pushing her forward.

Drifting snow had enveloped them again, and through buckled window frames, Sincere Jones saw another wave approaching. But it was smaller, and he knew his bloody magnificent ship could tame that one too.

***

Chief Raleigh pulled Donovan Grant's cold weather gear from his dead body, dressed in it and made it to the undercover vehicle park to find it empty of personnel, and near empty of vehicles. The personnel who had evacuated in Concordia's ground transports were either still out on the ice or not back yet. He had taken a satellite phone during the flight from his suddenly unlocked cell, and his plan had been to get as far out as he could, then call his Russian handler to send a chopper to pick him up and take him to Vostok, like they'd promised. If the Russian Spetsnaz officer had reported him deserting them before he was captured … well, he'd just have to bluff his way out of that.

At the back of the park were a Beowulf transport and a snowmobile. The Beowulf was locked, and in any case, it looked like its electric motor was being worked on, parts and circuits laid out on a tarp on the ground beside it.

The snowmobile though … He jumped on and saw the key in place between its handlebars. A yellow Post-It note was stuck beside it. *"Warning: transponder U/S. New part ordered."* He pulled the note off, crumpled it up and threw it on the ground. A faulty transponder was the least of his worries—it was only used to send out the vehicle's position and identity so it could be found in a search, or recognized by drones. And Chief Raleigh most definitely did *not* want to be found.

He turned the key, and the snowmobile hummed to life. The instrument display showed it had a fully charged battery – range 100 miles, even in the Antarctic cold. A nav screen showed the navigable ice all the way out to 50 miles from Concordia. *Yes.*

He leaned forward, turned the throttle, and the snowmobile's rear caterpillar belt shoved it forward on its skids.

***

On patrol outside Concordia, on the orders of the late Cath Delaney, were two of three Legged Squad Sentinel drones. With Leroi Fontaine on guard duty down below, Matt Reynolds was running perimeter operations, and Delaney had told him she wanted both aerial and ground patrols out, just in case.

He had two "dogs" circling at all times, one at a time coming in at staggered intervals to recharge. They circled the base on pre-programmed routes, sending an alert if they detected any movement or infrared signatures out on the ice.

When the Black Alert evacuation alarm sounded at Concordia, Reynolds ran like everyone else, shepherding personnel through exit doors before he crammed into the back of a Beowulf, headed as far out on the ice as fast as he could go.

The last thing he did before bugging out was to set his dogs onto "Autonomous Defensive Patrol" mode without even realizing what that meant—just because it sounded right—since Matt Reynolds had barely even read the operating manuals for his dogs before he was ordered to deploy them.

"Autonomous Defensive Patrol" was not the same as the "Passive Perimeter Patrol" mode he'd had the dogs working before the evacuation. "Autonomous" gave the dogs full decision-making freedom about how they executed their patrol, within a predefined area. And "Defensive" meant that they could take proactive action to defend Concordia, within the limits of their programming. Which did *not* include attacking humans, but which did include interrogating vehicles for the transponder code that all Concordia vehicles carried—and if a transponder code wasn't received, placing themselves in the path of the vehicle to prevent its passage.

LS3 "Charlie" had just come around the corner of the vehicle park when it heard the sound of a motor and focused its sensors ahead of it. It didn't need line of sight to interrogate a radio transponder, so it sent a radio signal out before it even saw the vehicle making the noise.

And got no response. It tried again. Still no response.

Unauthorized vehicle, it concluded. Across packed snow, Charlie could move at just 20 miles an hour, but it was traversing the ice and salted sand that covered the paths around Concordia, and the snow drifts weren't too deep on this lee side. Charlie started running toward the sound of the vehicle at 38 miles an hour.

***

Chief Raleigh's snowmobile exited the covered vehicle park at 25 miles an hour, and he screwed the throttle all the way back …

As he did, he saw movement out the corner of his eye. His snow-wet goggles showed only a gray metal blur, skidding to a stop—*right in front of him!*

Logan Raleigh was no ice lifer. He pulled hard on both brakes, twisting his handlebars savagely, trying to swerve. The snowmobile's front skis dug into the sand and snow, and Raleigh pitched over the handlebars, landing headfirst on the ice. The 600 lb. snowmobile flipped over end, crushing him underneath it.

He didn't feel it. His neck had snapped the second he hit the ice.

***

"Aggressor Two, Aggressor One, I have eyeballs on your module. Coast Guard is still conducting operations alongside USS *Congress* but say they expect to get a helo to you within the hour." Bunny was circling over the Outlaw's crew at 1,000 feet after trying to find someone, anyone, who could get to the module's position. The USS *Congress*, it turned out, had not been lost, as an excitable helicopter pilot had reported while circling the burning vessel in heavy snow. The USCG *Polar Warden*, however, was standing by while fires onboard were contained, in case the crew needed to be evacuated.

"No rush, One," Rory replied. "We got a battering in the sea surge, and we're taking water, but we think we can plug the leak. Will revert if that changes."

Bunny checked her fuel state. "Good copy, Two. I can stay on station another 90 minutes. I'll make sure Coast Guard doesn't forget you."

"Just good to hear your voice, One. We weren't sure you … you know," he said.

Bunny thought back to the inky black dome of artificial night that nearly consumed her. "I wasn't sure either, Two. But the Nemesis has a new number-one fan, I can tell you that."

***

In the command center down at level five at Concordia, there was no cheering.

Bellings, Cohen, Lau and Jansen were standing beside one another, watching a replay from the Skylon spacecraft overflight. "My God, we got it so wrong," Bellings said.

"No, it was just at the upper range of all our modeling," Jansen said.

Bellings pointed at the screen, which was showing, in slow motion, a midnight black dome rising out of the sea. "Your models did not predict *that*."

Solomon Cohen had not spoken since they felt the same thud under their feet that had been felt halfway around the world. His reaction was typically stoic. "Well, I guess it worked," he said at last.

But David Lau was not listening to them. He had wondered how he would feel at this moment. He was looking at the culmination of decades of work, millions of hours, billions of dollars, hundreds of lives lost, and he knew people in the room around him were looking at him. Should he look exulted, or weep?

Sure enough, Bellings put him on the spot. "What are you thinking, David? For God's sake, say something."

The night before, David Lau had fallen into a fitful sleep reading Nietzsche's *Thus Spoke Zarathustra* ... and of all things, what came to his mind rewatching the explosion was a contortion of one of Nietzsche's thoughts.

He kept his eyes on the screen, not turning to address the room, his voice quiet. "We have torn the veil between creation and oblivion ... and stared into the void that stares back."

Epilogue
J-Day plus 12 hours

The morning sun was visible through the curtained window behind US President Mark Bendheim as he gazed down the barrel of the camera in the Oval Office, the producer beside him counting down from three with his fingers. Bendheim took a deep breath, and began.

"Twelve hours ago, scientists of the United States successfully demonstrated the potential of a new energy source known as 'antimatter.' Their research required the extreme cold of Antarctica, and I am proud to announce that on that isolated and desolate continent, they successfully created the world's first antimatter forge, or reactor. They proved that antimatter fuel could be safely manufactured, could be transported across land, sky and sea, and finally, they tested what the effect would be if just 4 lbs. of this material was detonated."

Bendheim had long ago signed off on the Project Minerva "narrative" that would follow a successful test of the Juliet device. It had been shaped to announce the dawn of the antimatter era to the public, without panicking the American or global populations, or triggering economic mayhem.

"I can confirm that at 2 p.m. local time, a vessel containing 4 lbs. of antimatter produced by our Antarctica forge was transported from our research center on Antarctica to a position 400 miles out in the Southern Ocean, where it was exploded underwater, releasing unimaginable force. The fuel annihilated itself and caused a seismic shock that was felt globally. We believe the explosion to have been the equivalent of *85 megatons* of TNT—for comparison, the largest nuclear weapon ever tested reached just 50 megatons. By way of alternate comparison, this single explosion was equivalent to the *entire* arsenal of nuclear weapons possessed by China, France and the United Kingdom, combined."

His next words gave Bendheim the most pain. He had agreed with the Joint Chiefs and National Security Council to make no mention of Russia's efforts to cripple Project Minerva, nor of all those who died at Russia's hands as result. Their sacrifice would remain a national security classified event, and their families would only be told that their loved ones had died heroes. Revenge for that insult would come, but it would be a dish served cold.

"The force of this explosion exceeded our own scientists' expectations. I regret to report that despite heroic efforts to ensure their safety during the test, a number of personnel—civilian and military—were killed or injured in the explosion. Out of respect for the families of those impacted, and because of the national security nature of the test, I have signed an Executive Order classifying as secret all information related to it, unless authorized for public release."

He looked down at the pages in front of him on the Resolute Desk and then back at the camera. Not that he needed to check where he was in his speech—he had a teleprompter—but he wanted to signal a change of gears.

"From this incredible scientific advance, new opportunities, and risks, arise," he said. "The forge created by our scientists—truly a world first—can produce antimatter at an industrial scale. Just one and a half ounces of antimatter, safely harnessed, can meet our nation's *entire* energy needs for a year. Antimatter is a clean and efficient energy source that can provide power to our homes and industries, to the ships that sail our oceans, and even to the vessels that we will one day send to the stars.

"But as this explosion demonstrated, it is a fuel with terrible potential if put to military use. A fraction of an ounce could flatten downtown Manhattan, Moscow or Beijing. As we have shown, the USA already has the potential to develop such weapons. We know that several other nations, Russia and China among them, have also been researching antimatter production, though they are some years behind us."

He leaned forward. He'd wanted to say something like "Ladies and gentlemen, we stand at a precipice ..." but had been talked out of that.

"My fellow citizens, this great nation stands alone in its mastery of this new power, and in all humility, we invite the rest of humanity to join us in the antimatter era. We have tabled an emergency session of the United Nations Security Council, at which we will urgently call for the creation of an Antimatter Arms Control Treaty. We expect all nations currently engaged in antimatter research to be party to this treaty. To that end, we are willing to share certain of our advances into the use of antimatter for peaceful energy production in return for commitments by participating nations not to pursue the development of antimatter weapons."

He narrowed his eyes, trying to channel the steel will of his predecessor again, who had faced down China over Taiwan, without blinking.

"Let me be clear about this. This nation will actively assist other nations to pursue the peaceful use of antimatter for energy production. We will share the antimatter produced in our forge with the world for that purpose and only that purpose. And we will, with equal resolve, and with *all* means at our disposal, act to prevent any other nation from weaponizing antimatter." He folded his hands in front of him. "May God bless you, and bless all those involved in this new endeavor, especially those brave souls who gave their lives in its name; and may God bless this great nation."

***

Alone in the back of his limo on the way to Andrews AFB later that night, Bendheim reviewed the first polls on his announcement. Not surprisingly, just over fifty percent of viewers described their feelings after seeing the broadcast as *'worried.'*

Bendheim couldn't blame them. They'd be even more worried if they'd seen the after-action reporting that he'd been privy to. Most striking had been the footage from the NOAA platform, 50 miles from ground zero. It recorded the dark ball of energy rising from the sea on the horizon before it collapsed into a lightning storm that generated a column of super-heated steam. Gamma radiation monitors peaked at lethal levels, dropping away again just as quickly, and then seconds later the entire platform shook violently as the first of several underwater shock waves struck it. The atmospheric blast wave hit it next, shaking loose anything not welded or bolted fast, bending its loading crane back over itself. Many of the cameras filming the event were lost, but enough remained to show what came next: a growing swell that turned into a hundred-foot-high rolling wave that bore down on the platform at 500 miles an hour.

Already weakened by the first series of underwater shock waves and the atmospheric blast, the platform surrendered its purchase on the ocean floor and was consumed by the angry seas. Any human aboard the platform would have received a deadly dose of radiation almost instantly. The platform's complete physical destruction took less than six minutes.

Minerva's scientists had underestimated the destructive power of the weapon in many ways, but they'd also gotten a lot

356

right. The crews of the naval vessels 70 to a hundred miles out from the blast received only non-lethal doses of gamma radiation, and were able to ride out the wave surges. Propagated at the speed of underwater sound, the first shock waves hit the Ross Ice Shelf just seven minutes after detonation, but caused only minor ice calving. On Scott Island, a small icy cliff rising out of the sea 280 miles from ground zero, there were rockfalls, but no structural damage.

The seismic impact was registered at stations across the globe, and the acoustic *'thud'* it generated was carried by the undersea 'deep sea sound' channel across the globe, registering on NATO SOSUS anti-submarine sound detectors as far away as Faslane Submarine Base in Scotland.

The question of what to do with this newfound power had been debated at a hastily called Principals Committee convened by Bendheim, and including the Joint Chiefs, Defense Secretary, Secretary of State, and the heads of intelligence agencies.

Bendheim had listened to the various arguments and then issued a classified Presidential Directive, ordering the various weapons research directorates in the US armed forces to focus not on the development of new strategic antimatter weapons, but their adaptation for use in existing tactical weapons systems—battlefield-level missiles, artillery shells, torpedoes, precision glide bombs, even mortars and FPV drones.

"God forbid we should ever use these weapons in anger," Bendheim told the Principals Committee after reading out the directive. "But if we do, it must be in a way that reduces the likelihood our enemies will reach for a tactical *nuclear* weapon in response. More powerful warheads for existing systems, that can give us battlefield dominance but still fall well below the destructive threshold of tactical nuclear weapons, will be key to achieving both battlefield victory *and* nuclear deterrence."

He hoped to God he was right.

***

GRU Major General Tomas Arsharvin turned off the screen showing the US president's address and threw his remote control at the wall.

"Antimatter Arms Control Treaty?" his SVR counterpart, Eizen, asked, arching an eyebrow. "A fairly simple matter to control, if only one nation possesses antimatter weapons."

Arsharvin stood and glared at the slow-moving river outside his window, as though the sheer force of his dissatisfaction could alter its glacial pace … but he knew he could no more influence the waters of the Argut than he had been able to influence events in Antarctica. "They are trying to avoid their atomic weapons mistake, and think they can prevent proliferation by hanging the empty threat of destruction by antimatter weapons over our head."

"They don't need to use antimatter," Eizen pointed out, a finger raised toward the ceiling. "They could already flatten this research center from space, with orbital bombardment weapons. Our former Chinese 'allies' are nothing more than a puppet state now and will no doubt support this 'treaty.' The non-aligned nations will be easily bought by the promise of cheap power—produced in American antimatter reactors, over which they have a monopoly."

"Let them drop their orbital weapons or rattle their antimatter saber," Arsharvin said. "All the Americans will achieve with their threats and bluster is to move our programs underground … literally."

"Unless they plan something more," Eizen said. He had entered Arsharvin's office with a cigarette, even though he knew Arsharvin hated the smell. He tapped ash into his cupped palm.

"What is to stop NATO rolling across the wheat fields of Ukraine now? Or sailing across the Bering Strait from Alaska to help themselves to our Siberian rare earths?"

Arsharvin sat again. "You know it will never be allowed to come to that, so stop playing your tiresome games," he said. "You hear the thunder of war drums too, I know it."

Eizen gave him a thin smile. "I am not so well informed on military matters as you, of course, but certain rumors may have reached my ears. Rumors of mobilization. Europe is mentioned."

"Do not trust your rumors, Director." He sighed. "Our new president is not the fool the last one was, determined to recreate an empire in Europe that was lost long ago. Especially when our foes now possess the ability to eliminate an entire tank division with a single artillery shell."

"Asia then? Surely not again," Eizen asked.

"Not Asia," Arsharvin replied. "Now you will have to excuse me. I have been called to Moscow to account for the failures of the last several days, including but not limited to the loss of a Spetsnaz detachment, a special operations submarine, a multibillion-ruble stealth bomber, a strategic nuclear warhead and the inability of any of these to make a discernable impact on the US antimatter program." He gestured at the bleak gray landscape outside the window. "I expect that where I am headed, I will come to miss this view."

***

Leroi Fontaine died twice. Once on the floor outside the containment area, where a CPR trained staff member brought him back, and once in Concordia's med bay, where the station doctor brought him back with an IV bag and a defibrillator.

No, he didn't see no bright lights or talk to no angels.

To be honest, he was glad to remember nothing. He remembered hearing the noise inside the cell, going to investigate, seeing the Russian come out and … that was about it until he woke up in the med bay with drips in his arm and a catheter in his johnson.

But dammit, man. Delaney. The Concordia security detachment lost six personnel at the gate to that traitor Raleigh, two on level five, one on level six before Leroi got the Russian, and Delaney too.

And there's wasn't going to be a funeral—for anyone. A nurse had brought a tablet PC to Leroi's bedside while he was still wondering whether he was going to make it, and a man in a dark suit had asked him how he was doing. The guy told him he was not to discuss nothing with no one. Either at Concordia, or later, when he was repatriated stateside.

"What about at the funerals?" he'd asked. "So many dead? People are going to talk."

"There will be no funerals," the man said. "I'm told the relatives of the deceased will be getting a letter of consolation from the president himself."

***

Bunny hated funerals and memorials. She did her grieving best alone, where no one could try to stop her self-flagellation rituals or visit empty words upon her, trying to ease her conscience. But Rory had threatened her—if she didn't come to Uncle's wake, he was going to bring the wake to wherever she was hiding.

"You *really* aren't drinking?" Trigger asked Rory for about the third time. They'd hired a mountain cabin at Arthur's Pass on New Zealand's South Island, about two hours from Harewood's airfield, and made their way there separately—

Outlaw's crew in a minivan, Two-Tone Hamilton in a rental car, and Bunny on a 150-horsepower Ducati Moto-e, also rented, which despite her best efforts, she didn't manage to drop on the way up the mountain.

"I'm on the wagon," Rory said. He looked up at the ceiling and raised his can of zero-alcohol beer. "And yeah, I mean it this time, you old coot."

"Drugs then," Trigger said. "I got something in my backpack you …"

"And it's going to stay in your backpack, whatever it is you didn't just mention in front of me," Two-Tone said.

For a man called Elvis, Bell had proven himself a total lightweight in the matter of substance abuse. Three hours into the wake, and he was already passed out in an armchair, a mascara mustache and lipstick on his face, courtesy of Trigger.

A photo of Uncle, surrounded by candles and empty bottles, sat on a coffee table. Rory stood, kicked Bell's boot to see if he could wake him, decided that he was a lost cause and cleared his throat. "I'm not much good at speechification, so I'll keep this short. Bob Lee was a cantankerous, stubborn, sarcastic son of a bitch with a murderous streak, who was the kind of guy tried to sneak a look at your cards in poker," he said. "But he was also blindly loyal, patriotic and, as he showed in his last moments, willing to … to die for the people he loved." Rory choked down tears with a swig of his beer before continuing. "A lot of us wouldn't be here if not for him, not least me, who I honestly believe the crazy bastard would have shot if I hadn't moved when he told me." He raised his can. "To Uncle."

They toasted, but Rory wasn't finished. "Now, before I play some more of Uncle's favorite Stanley Brothers banjo numbers …"

Trigger and Two-Tone groaned.

"Which are good for nothing, if not banishing the devil," he continued, "we also have someone else to thank, and she's sunk down in the sofa there trying to make out she isn't here. Talk of banishing the devil, she killed the demon what killed Outlaw and then stopped the clock on a gawdamned *nuke*." Bunny fixed him with a baleful glare, but it didn't stop him. "Now she's giving me her death stare. She blames herself she couldn't save Outlaw single-handed, but Uncle would tell her— I know he would—there was an entire task force out there supposed to do that, and if they couldn't do it, who is she to think she should wear all the blame?"

Bunny stood too. "And … this is why I don't go to funerals," she said, grabbing her backpack and jacket from the floor. "I'll see you good people back in Arizona."

As she closed the door of the cabin behind her, she heard Rory declaiming, "What are you all looking at? Someone had to tell her."

Pulling on her jacket and strapping her backpack to the pillion, she pulled the charging cord from its socket and swung her leg over the bike, then looked up at the sky. It was a beautiful clear night, and the million stars in the sky were the same ones she'd grown up with in Australia. Snow-covered mountains, infinitely more benign than the ice-capped ranges of Antarctica, marched off into the distance.

She started the bike, looked at her watch. 0200 hours. Wouldn't be much, if any, traffic on the roads back to Christchurch.

Time to *really* see what a Moto-e with a freaking fighter pilot at the throttle could do. As she pulled on her left glove, she stopped to read the tattoo across the back of her hand. She'd mused for a very long time about how to honor the sacrifice of Bob 'Uncle' E. Lee. The frostbitten crew of Outlaw had been pulled from the seawater-filled hull of their command module by a Coast Guard helicopter flying off the deck of the USCG *Polar Star*, and none of them would have been alive but for Uncle.

And Uncle wouldn't be dead, if Bunny had … if she …

Back in Christchurch, she'd tried to drown that thought with a handful of sertraline tablets, eased down with a pint of bourbon, but it would never go away; she knew that. So she took it head on, like all her problems, by deciding she'd carry Uncle on her skin where she'd see him every single day for the rest of her life. Where people would notice, and would ask her about it, and she would have to tell them.

She'd had the motto from Uncle's home state of Virginia tattooed across the hand from knuckle to knuckle: *Sic Semper Tyrranis*. Death to Tyrants.

She could only hope that the terrifying weapon they had helped to create would be used to deliver exactly that.

/END

***

PREVIEW: Africa STORM

Aggressor Inc. STORM series Book II
J-Day plus ONE YEAR

"Are you ready?" 22-year-old Maxim Peskov asked his camera operator, Danila. It had taken him several days and a lot of bribes, most paid out of his own pocket, to get them where they were, and he didn't want Danila to miss this moment.

"Ready," Danila said, looking annoyed. "Been ready 10 minutes." Maxim didn't care.

"Alright, camera on me, and then pan right, yeah?"

"You got it."

Peskov reached down to the rattling, roaring hull of the tank he was sitting on, wiped his hand on it to smear it in red sand, then wiped it over his sweaty face and resettled his ballistic vest, so it was certain to be in shot. The man whose head and arms were sticking out of a hatch in the tank beside him looked on with bemusement. "Senior Sergeant Tarisov, right?" Peskov asked him.

"Just 'Sergeant,'" the man said.

"Senior Sergeant sounds better," Peskov said. "I need you to speak louder, so we can hear you over the sound of the engine. Yes?" He wagged a finger at Danila. "Alright, start streaming."

"Streaming."

Peskov tried not to look as excited as he felt. World-weary—that's the vibe he was going for.

"Maxim Peskov, reporting from Sudan, where tanks of the 144th Motor Rifle Division have just reached the Nile, which you can see behind me." Danila panned right, taking in the broad river, then behind them, to an armored column of crewed and uncrewed vehicles. Two uncrewed attack helicopters thudded past. *Right on cue,* Peskov thought. *Brilliant.* Peskov held a microphone down to the tank commander. "Senior Sergeant Tarisov, where are you headed?"

The soldier grinned. "Khartoum, the capital. Yeah."

"Have you seen any fighting since you left Port Sudan?" Peskov asked.

"Well, we heard government forces …"

"The *illegal* government of coup plotter General al-Sadiq …" Peskov corrected him.

"Right, yeah. Sadiq's forces might have set up at the road junction here, but it looks like they ran away." Tarisov grinned. Then he ducked, looking at the sky, as a flight of four jet aircraft—big delta-winged combat drones, by the look of them—screamed low overhead. He gave Peskov a sheepish look. "Americans."

"American *mercenaries.* Thank you, Sergeant," Peskov said, turning back to the camera. "And so you see the situation in a nutshell. After fake elections, an American-backed government, supported by private military contractors, was installed in Sudan's capital, Khartoum, and demanded the withdrawal of all Russian forces from Sudan. Why?" He shook his head in disbelief. "They say because of Russian naval aggression in the Red Sea, but our Navy has just been protecting Russian ships, sailing from Russian docks, at the Russian naval base at Port Sudan.

"As I reported earlier, the more than 100,000 Russian troops landed at Port Sudan in the last several weeks moved out today, to secure Russian interests across the country." Peskov patted the hull of the tank. "Our president has declared a special military operation to dislodge the usurpers in Khartoum and restore the legitimate government of Sudan."

365

The American fighters reached the horizon and turned around, dropping lower, moving faster, the roar of their engines increasing. Peskov pointed. "Danila, get this." *Come on, America, do something stupid*, Peskov urged the approaching fighters. Well, if they did, the US government could try to deny it, since the fighters were flown by private contractors appointed by the illegitimate regime, but the world would see through that bluff.

The four fighters spread out, flying wingtip to wingtip as they rocketed right over Peskov, and moments later, the double whip-crack of a sonic boom threatened to shatter their eardrums.

Danila's camera followed them away, then he focused back on Peskov, giving him a thumbs-up to show he got the shot of the fighters.

Peskov leaned down again, holding his microphone out to the tanker. "You don't look scared at all, Tarisovich. Isn't it dangerous to be driving in a column in broad daylight like this?"

The man looked more than scared. He looked like he would have shat himself if he weren't on camera. But he gave Peskov a lopsided smile. "No, why should we worry? As you see, they do nothing."

"The Americans threaten us with antimatter weapons," Peskov insisted. "Are you not worried they will use them?"

"No. Here in *Africa*? No," the sergeant said. "And besides, we have nuclear missiles, so let them try."

Peskov lifted the microphone away again. "From the mouth of a front-line warrior. Our president has warned the American president that if he uses an antimatter weapon against Russian forces, we will respond with nuclear weapons that are just as powerful. This is Maxim Peskov, embedded with our front-line forces on their way to liberate Khartoum."

***

The Russian mil-blogger might have been surprised at who was watching the live stream of his report from Sudan.

In the sunroom overlooking the upper terrace at Camp David's Aspen Lodge, Chief of Staff Dana Morrel killed the big screen. Beside her on the green sofa were the newly elected president of the United States, Thomas Joseph 'TJ' Dance, his National Security adviser, Harlan Ford, and Defense Secretary Alicia 'The Hammer' Rodriguez.

"They'll be at the gates of Khartoum by this time tomorrow," Dana Morrel said, "Barring some kind of miracle. General al-Sadiq's forces might hold them outside the capital for a day or two, but that's all."

There were no senior military personnel in the room, because politics was on the agenda, not military strategy—though Defense Secretary Alicia Rodriguez was a former Air Force and Space Force colonel with as much military experience as most of the Joint Chiefs of Staff.

The president's inner circle was yet to jell. The administration of former President Mark Bendheim might have delivered America the antimatter bomb, but it had failed to deliver on the Antimatter Arms Control Treaty, and more importantly, it had both underestimated and mismanaged the global economic turmoil that followed the Antarctica weapons test. TJ Dance's campaign had hammered these issues and cleverly weaponized the bereaved families of Concordia and Navy personnel who had died in the Antarctic, and who were still waiting for answers about what had happened to their loved ones a year after the test.

Dance was a tall, lean former Arkansas governor, and exuded down-home charm in public, but in private he could display a volcanic temperament. "Goddammit," Dance said. "Russia sets up a blockade in the Red Sea, a Russian troop ship rams our destroyer, and they land a hundred *thousand* troops in Sudan, and all Bendheim does is send this private contractor ..." He clicked his fingers.

"Aggressor Incorporated," Rodriguez said.

"Aggressor ... send a few aircraft and slaughterbots to support al-Sadiq." He got up from the sofa and stood, looking out at the snow-covered terrace. "He could have flattened Port Sudan from orbit while the Russians were building up, but no. Now they've moved out, and I'm the one left with shit on my face while 20-year-old video bloggers laugh at us."

"Not sure our new friend al-Sadiq would have appreciated us destroying his only port," the National Security adviser, Ford, pointed out. A former career spook, he had silver hair and white sideburns, and dark-blue eyes framed by anachronistic wire-rimmed glasses, even though it was common knowledge he'd had laser surgery that gave him near 20/20 vision.

"Sadiq, Sadiq," Dance muttered. "Maybe Bendheim was right ignoring Sudan," he said. "Dana, why do we care?"

"Sudan, how do I love thee, let me count the ways," Morrel lyricized. She held up a hand and started counting on her fingers. "*One*, it has one of the world's biggest untapped reserves of rare earths, not to mention gold and diamonds. *Two*, Russia took over the place and installed a puppet government during the 2020s, while we were asleep at the wheel, and have been plundering it to finance their military rebuild and get around all our sanctions. *Three*, we spent the last decade supporting al-Sadiq's rebels and working for regime change, and he finally won elections, only for Russia to call it a coup and start a naval blockade. *Four*, Bendheim gave Russia an ultimatum to lift the blockade and get out of Sudan, and they responded by doing the opposite—moved five divisions of troops, with armor, and aircraft, into Port Sudan and mining towns across the country—

nearly sinking one of our destroyers in the process, as you just mentioned. Bendheim threatened Russia with orbital or antimatter weapons, but in the end did nothing because he was worried it would hurt his election chances, so *five* … Russia thinks we are bluffing and it can just stroll back into Khartoum."

Dance bit his lip. He usually had no problem making the big calls, but this early in his presidency, he had yet to make a really big one. And even after the recent Shanghai Pact conflict, going toe to toe with Russia in Sudan was A Big Call.

"I hear what you say, but are we really desperate for those rare earth reserves? I mean, China relaxed rare earth export restrictions as part of the ceasefire deal, so we can't be."

"Mr. President, while we were focused on the Asia Pacific, Russia installed puppet governments in Algeria, South Africa, Angola, Mozambique *and* Sudan," Rodriguez said. "Sudan also gave Russia a chokehold on the Red Sea."

"And if we give Sudan back to Russia without a fight, we may as well forget Africa for another 20 years," Ford added. "It's the only continent with population and economic growth guaranteed for the next 50 years at least, which is why Russia wants to dominate it. Regime change in Sudan was supposed to be our way back in."

Dance and Morrel exchanged a look. "You thinking about what we discussed earlier?" Dance asked her.

Morrel turned to Rodriguez and Ford. "The president and I were discussing earlier in what circumstances he would authorize the first use of antimatter weapons."

"Sir, I know President Bendheim and the NSC were working on a draft Presidential Policy Directive …" Rodriguez said.

"I'm not Bendheim," Dance snapped at her. "I don't want to announce what I'm going to do to Russia before I do it.

Truman didn't warn Japan before he dropped the bomb. He used atomic weapons at the time and place of his own choosing, showed what they could do, and they have not been used since." He scowled. "Orbital weapons weren't enough to bring Russia to heel. President Bendheim thought the demonstration in the Southern Ocean would get Russia to sign his Antimatter Arms Control Treaty, and they stonewalled him." Dance pointed at the dark TV screen. "Now, they're openly *mocking* us."

"Sudan could be the place we draw a line in the sand," Morrel said, then winced. "Yeah, I know what I said."

Dance didn't smile. "Madam Secretary, if we decided to deploy AM weapons to stop Russia in Sudan, tell me how *you* would go about it," he asked Rodriguez.

Rodriguez gave herself a moment to think. "It would have to be escalatory," she said. "We start with a visible statement of intent, move the pieces into place—quickly, since Russian armor is already rolling—and do something to let Russia know we are serious."

"We could let them know through back channels that AM weapons are on the table if they don't pull out of Sudan," Ford suggested.

"Exactly," Rodriguez said. "But if we do that, we can't blink this time."

Dana Morrel frowned. "That all sounds like it will take too long. Like you said, Russian armor is already rolling. Their ships are threatening commerce in the Red Sea."

"There's a step we can take immediately, which will lay down a marker for Russia," Rodriguez told her.

"What's that?" Dance asked, sitting down again and leaning forward.

"Aggressor Inc. is a private contractor, but its aircraft are leased from the USAF, and all its pilots are USAF Reserve. Stand them up as a USAF squadron, today, and put them to work dismantling the Russian push on Khartoum."

"A single squadron can't hold off a whole damn army," Ford said.

"No, but they can stall them. Russia has only sent two of five divisions toward Khartoum; the rest are spreading across the countryside, securing commercial interests and population centers. One has been held back to guard Port Sudan, or as a ready reserve."

"And the escalation strategy?" Morrel asked. "If it looks like Russia isn't getting the message, we hit their fleet in the Red Sea from space?"

"Yes. And if they still don't get the message …" Rodriguez said.

"We stop them with AM weapons?" Dance asked. "What can we put in place?"

"Can we arm the Aggressor detachment with AM weapons?" Ford asked Rodriguez.

"Well, in theory, the bombs and missiles are no different to the types already in service; it's only their effect that is different.," Rodriguez told her. "The reports I've seen from testing in California show no special training is needed, just specialized armorers—who we can fly in—and … extra caution."

"Air forces don't win wars," Morrel cautioned. "You'll need boots on the ground."

"But not as many as in the past," Rodriguez said. "AM weapons are the ultimate force multiplier. The Marine Corps Warfighting Laboratory has been training the 1st Marine Expeditionary Unit in the use of tactical AM weapons at Twentynine Palms for the last few months. One MEU might be enough."

"I don't know. Deploy troops to *Africa*?" Dance said. "We've got mile-long lines at food banks, the Dow is in record bear territory … people want me focused on rebuilding after the last war, not starting a new one."

"Which is exactly why Russia is moving now, and in Africa, not Europe," Morrel said. "They think you'll baulk, like Bendheim did."

"I say it could work," Ford said. "Just standing these contractors up as a USAF squadron in Khartoum dares Russia to cross the Rubicon and engage in direct combat with the US military. And if they do …"

Dance nodded slowly. "We show Russia what crossing a red line looks like."

"I hate to be my own devil's advocate," Morrel said. "But the Russian president has said he'll respond to any use of antimatter weapons with tactical nukes."

"He said that about orbital weapons," Ford said. "But we flattened half his Far East Fleet from orbit in the Pacific War, and he didn't make good on the threat."

"The chances Russia would go nuclear over a conflict in Sudan have to be low," Rodriguez added.

"But not zero," Morrel warned.

"I'll take those odds," Dance said, clicking his fingers again. "Alicia, get it moving. We stand that Aggressor squadron up immediately, put them to work supporting Sadiq's forces so the city doesn't fall overnight. Harlan, tell him we're stepping up our direct support, and if the bastard even *mentions* us flying him out of Khartoum, you tell him it would be a direct flight to Guantanamo and ask if he still wants to leave."

Morrel was taking notes, and looked up. "Meanwhile, we fly in antimatter ordnance teams, weapons, scramble a Skylon space plane and leak it to the Russians through back channels.

Let them know what we're prepared to do. Mobilize those Marines, and get them down there as quick as we can." She hesitated. "Congress already authorized us running the Russian naval blockade, and standing up a USAF squadron might squeak through, but a Marine MEU …"

"Good point. Get a meeting with the two House leaders in my calendar; see if we can do it the easy way. Call it … I don't know … contingency planning or something," Dance said. "And call a meeting of the Joint Chiefs, of course."

"Press briefing?"

"No. Let's keep this under the radar as long as we can," Dance said, then saw the looks on people's faces and raised his hands. "I know, as soon as we use orbital weapons, the whole world will be watching. But we can hope Russia blinks before it even gets to that. Until we do, people need to know I've got my focus here, at home, not in goddamn Africa." He made a small bow to Alicia Rodriguez and clapped his hands briskly. "So Madam Secretary, you are excused. Dana, get the Treasury Secretary in here. Harlan, you can stay."

***

Former RAF Squadron Commander Jules 'Two-Tone' Hamilton was tired of people at Wadi Sayyidna Air Base thinking just because he was Black, he could speak Sudanese. At first, he'd tried politely explaining he was British. Then when they looked dubious, he'd explain his family were West Indian migrants. And then when they shrugged because they had no idea where that even was and kept talking Sudanese to him, he would explode.

It was very … awkward.

He'd done it again to the well-meaning Sudanese cleaner who had stuck his head through the door for the fourth time that morning to ask, Hamilton guessed, if he couldn't clean Hamilton's office now.

But Hamilton had growled at him and sent him away because he needed to think. His laptop was open at the encrypted message he had received from Aggressor Inc.'s billionaire owner, Mark Aaronson. It had the title "Heads Up," which in Two-Tone's experience was never good. And in this case, it was very much not good.

Awaiting official confirmation, but your detachment to be stood up as USAF 68th Aggressor Squadron, as of 1600 hours today. USAF stocks of fuel, ordnance and other materiel at Wadi Sayyidna can be drawn down. USAF 'AM' weapon armorers are én route. Two pilots from USAF 461st Flight Test Squadron also inbound and will be attached 68th Aggressor, one as CO. US Marines embarking 1 MEU for Khartoum. Looking at what other resources we can send you meantime. Suggest you don't wait, begin immediate preparations for operations to support forces of General al-Sadiq. Call when official orders come through, Aaronson.

There were several layers of pain in Aaronson's short message. His detachment was being taken from him. If he were a USAF Reserve officer, like all the other pilots in the Aggressor detachment in Sudan, he'd be able to retain command, but he wasn't. USAF naturally wanted one of their own officers at the helm, so they were flying one in. But Aaronson wasn't pulling him out, so he still wanted Two-Tone to be his point man. That was going to require finesse.

Secondly, *AM weapons*? Two-Tone had been following intelligence on the Russian buildup, and the first reports of contact between the Russian forces and regime troops, south of Atbara. They'd had several weeks to prepare for the Russians to move out of Port Sudan and had a few surprises ready if the

Russians moved on Khartoum. Two-Tone and his team had also had time to set up coordination points with regime forces in case the Aggressor detachment was let off the leash.

But AM weapons? If the two USAF pilots on their way to Khartoum were from the 461st, they must be specialists in AM weapon use, to the extent anyone was. He saw a very steep and potentially lethal learning curve ahead for his pilots. Like the rest of the world, Hamilton had seen the vision of the American test in the Southern Ocean. And like the rest of the world, he'd hoped he'd never see weapons like it used in combat - while deep inside, he knew they would be. The power of an atomic weapon, without the fallout? The ability to turn a mortar round into a 1,000 lb. bomb? No politician could resist that kind of temptation.

And where better to test them than in the empty deserts of Sudan?

He made a quick mental inventory. He had 14 Semi-Autonomous Air-Ground Assault systems, or SAAGAs—colloquially known as "slaughterbots"—and 14 US Fury uncrewed aircraft. Aggressor Inc. did not deploy with ground troops, but for tactical ground defense, they had six Ukrainian *Vulyka*, or 'Beehive,' swarm carriers. Keeping them operational was a ground crew of a dozen specialists, supporting six remote vehicle pilots. But if Two-Tone was brutally honest, Aggressor Inc. hadn't deployed to Sudan with its A-team. His SAAGA-*Vulyka* lead, Julie 'Trigger' Brown, had just converted to ground operations. She was a combat veteran, but in naval operations, not ground warfare. She'd done well in conversion training, but Sudan was supposed to be a low-intensity first deployment on UGVs for her.

And his uncrewed aircraft lead? Well, she had just returned from a six-month sabbatical in the Australian outback, helicopter mustering on cattle stations. After events on Antarctica, she just couldn't settle, and had decided to quit. Hamilton had served with Karen 'Bunny' O'Hare, where she had worked with him as a consultant after the war with the Shanghai Pact helping him stand up the British Fleet Air Arm's first dedicated Aggressor squadron. She'd pitched him as a candidate to Aaronson, when Aaronson was looking for a new head of operations, so he owed her that, too. But Two-Tone had supported her quitting.

After her last deployment, it was like she had a death wish. Everything she did, she did to the extreme, whether it was flying, getting constantly ticketed for speeding on her damn motorbike or her not-infrequent bar fights. They'd had to smuggle her out of Japan on Aaronson's private jet after she sucker-punched the son of a local Yakuza boss who'd made the mistake of both insulting and turning his back on her. But Aaronson talked her out of quitting, and told her to take a month off, which became six.

She'd agreed to come back on uncrewed operations—a soft reentry—and arrived in Sudan tanned and phlegmatic. Hamilton had his doubts about whether it was a front or a rejuvenated Bunny O'Hare. He'd been nervous as she led a flight of four Furies in a low-level flyover of the Russian spearhead, with live ordnance in their payload bays, but her orders were just to send a signal to the Russians, and she'd held to that.

His last worry, but not his least: O'Hare and Trigger were like oil and flame. If they weren't arguing, they were egging each other on. There were times when he wasn't sure whether he was the CO of an Aggressor detachment or the referee in a WWE Raw title match.

Speak of the devil, and she shall appear, he thought, as his door opened and O'Hare walked in.

"I'd like to file a complaint," she said, sitting without being invited.

Hamilton pointed to his trash can. "Feel free. But before you wind up, read this …" He threw Aaronson's message across the table, and waited for her reaction.

TO BE CONTINUED: 'Africa STORM,' AN AGGRESSOR INC. NOVEL, WILL BE RELEASED IN SEPTEMBER 2025.

Author note

I am, fittingly, writing this note in the city that produced one of the founding parents of quantum physics—Copenhagen, birthplace to the physicist Niels Bohr.

If you are a Star Trek fan like me, you know there is a lot of antimatter tech in that sci-fi series: it powers the infamous Warp Drive, and it is the explosive source in "photon torpedoes." You might also remember Dan Brown's 20-year-old novel *Angels and Demons*, in which terrorists try to blow up the Vatican with an antimatter bomb.

Antimatter is no longer science fiction; it is reality. And what provoked this novel was the announcement in 2024 by scientists at CERN laboratory in Switzerland, (paraphrased at the start of this novel) not just that they had produced antimatter in their Large Hadron Collider, but that they also had designed a way to *transport* it.

This news might have gone right under your radar.

CERN scientists transported 100 protons trapped in an 850-kilogram cryogenically cooled box—a proof of concept for antimatter—from one side of CERN to the other, in a Mercedes van. Their next test will be with actual, potentially explosive, antimatter. With the technology proven, only two things remain to weaponize it: scale (larger quantities of antimatter) and miniaturization (smaller containment traps).

Fast forward to the timeframe in this novel: 2041, and a new Manhattan Project–style effort, like that in *Antarctica STORM*, could deliver these. But just because scientists can—*should they?*

378

Antimatter research is also proceeding at pace in Russia and China, and those countries do not publicize their results to the extent we do in the West. Russia currently has six publicly documented antimatter research programs, and is a participant in a new collider planned by Japan. China can already produce antimatter in its Beijing Collider, and is planning to build a Circular Electron Positron Collider, which would be a massive circular collider similar in scale to the CERN collider but focused on *electron-positron* collisions rather than the proton-proton collisions mostly studied at CERN.

Why does that matter? Quite simply, electron-positron collisions have the potential to produce *more* antimatter than proton-proton collisions. This is not a coincidence.

People are suddenly worried about the threat of AI to humanity because it is now visible to them. I am more concerned about the unconstrained abandon with which our scientific community is pursuing antimatter research, and how invisible that research is to the average person. Some of that research is published, but given the terrifying potential of these weapons, we must also assume that much is not.

So in *Antarctica STORM*, and its follow on novel, *KHARTOUM* I want the reader to be able to imagine a world in which antimatter weapons are a reality, because *it is right now that we need to sit up and pay attention.*

FX HOLDEN
COPENHAGEN APRIL 2025

A new FX Holden novel—KHARTOUM *The Antimatter War*—is coming in September 2025, but until then …

For news and subscriber-only previews of new work by FX Holden, go to www.fxholden.com and join the free newsletter mailing list!

Also by FX Holden
The Aggressor Series

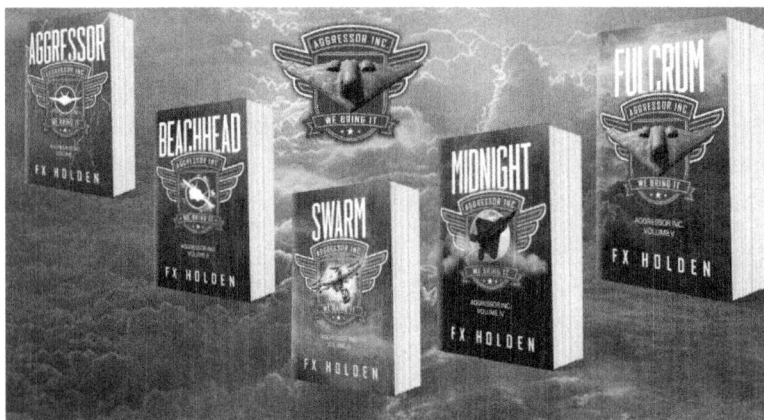

Before the events of Antarctica Storm, there was the war with the Shanghai Pact.

"Holden's high-tech, near-future geopolitical thriller starts a series and, as it hits the highs that have long set Holden's books apart, stands as an inviting jumping-on point for new readers."
PUBLISHERS WEEKLY BOOKLIFE.
"Fans of the author will surely find Aggressor to be the best novel yet, and newcomers who love action-packed military thrillers are in for a treat."
KC FINN, READERS' FAVORITE, 5 STARS

It is April 1, 2038. Day 60 of China's blockade of the rebel island of Taiwan.

The US government has agreed to provide Taiwan with a weapons system so advanced, it can disrupt the balance of power in the region.

But what pilot would be crazy enough to run the Chinese blockade to deliver it?

AGGRESSOR is an epic series that uniquely looks at the coming conflict between China and the US through the eyes of the soldiers, sailors, civilians and aviators on ALL sides who would be caught up in it. Featuring technologies that are on the drawing board today and could be fielded in the near future, AGGRESSOR is the page-turning military thriller series you have been waiting for!

Dive into the AGGRESSOR series today to get a unique and gripping insight into the conflict that all pundits agree has the biggest potential to be the next world war. This five-volume series is available in paperback, e-book and audiobook.

THE FUTURE WAR SERIES

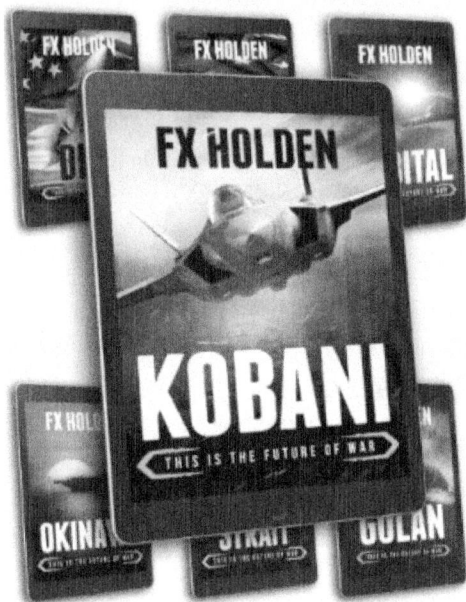

"Be prepared to strap in and hold on for the ride of your life"—Readers'
Favorite
"Tom Clancy Fans will be pleased."—Publishers Weekly STAR

The Future War series is an action-packed thrill ride that explores the impact weapons of the near future will have on the way wars are fought, and on the people who will fight them. *Unlike the Aggressor series, each book is a self-contained story*—they can be read in any order.

KOBANI (updated Jan 2025 to reflect recent events in Syria): The novel that introduces readers to Karen 'Bunny' O'Hare. While superpowers duel in the skies above Syria, Kurdish sniper Daryan al-Kobani fights to keep her mother and sister alive. "With compelling characters, cleverly written dialogue, and a riveting narrative that freezes your blood at times, Kobani is a blockbuster of a novel"—Readers' Favorite, 5 Stars.

GOLAN (updated Jan 2025 to reflect recent events in Syria) asks a question few want to consider. What will happen if Iran acquires nuclear weapons in the next 10 years? In true Future of War style, GOLAN explores the question through the eyes of front-line participants on all sides, in a conflict set 10 years in the future. Featuring military tech that is on the drawing boards today and characters you won't easily forget, GOLAN throws the reader straight into the center of a nuclear storm and doesn't ease up.

BERING STRAIT: Without warning, Russia starts a lightning operation to seize control of a vital arctic waterway off the Alaska coast. "Impossible to put down. The action is intense and the plot unique. It soars along at a fast pace. This story is unmissable."—5-star review from Anne-Marie Reynolds for Readers' Favorite.

OKINAWA: China is determined to forge a new empire in the East with Japan by its side. Its determination is about to be put to the test. "Tom Clancy Fans will be pleased."—*Publishers Weekly* STAR

ORBITAL: In 2034, a cataclysmic meteorite shower rains down on Saudi Arabia, destroying the world's largest oil processing facility and sending the price of oil into the stratosphere. But was it an act of God, or of man? "Masterfully elaborated and executed. The story is suspenseful, audacious, and full of thrilling surprises."—BookLife Prize

PAGASA: China moves to take over Pagasa Island in the South China Sea, putting it on a collision course with the USA that very quickly takes the region to the brink of total war. Set in an all-too-possible future, PAGASA is "a whirlwind of a novel"

that follows the lives of ordinary men and women facing extraordinary peril, on all sides of the conflict.

DMZ: Can a single ordinary person change the course of history? The Future War series takes on one of the most likely superpower confrontations of coming years. As a nuclear weapon is detonated over South Korean territory in the Sea of Japan, six protagonists hold the fate of the Korean peninsula in their hands. Their decisions could see North and South Korea reunited at last, or send the world spiraling into nuclear Armageddon.

Available in e-book and paperback; Kobani, Golan and Bering Strait available on audiobook.

Glossary

For simplicity, this glossary is common across all FX Holden novels and may refer to abbreviations or systems not in this novel. As such, it is useful as a reference beyond this book! Please note, weapons or systems marked with an asterisk* are currently still under development or speculative. If there is no asterisk, then the system has already been deployed by at least one nation.

3D PRINTER: A printer which can recreate a 3D object based on a three-dimensional digital model, typically by laying down many thin layers of a material in succession.

AC-130X*: a variant of the AC-130 series of special operations aircraft and follow-on to the AC-130J Ghostrider. Stripped of all heavy weapons to make room for two Rapid Dragon* palletized ordnance dispensers, it is envisaged as a signals and electronic intelligence, surveillance and reconnaissance aircraft with drone and standoff strike capability.

ADA*: All Domain Attack. An attack on an enemy in which all operational domains–space, cyber, ground, air and naval–are engaged either simultaneously or sequentially.

AI: Artificial intelligence, as applied in aircraft to assist pilots, in intelligence to assist with intelligence analysis, or in ordnance such as drones and uncrewed vehicles to allow semi-autonomous or even fully autonomous decision making.

AIM-120D: US medium-range supersonic air-to-air missile.

AIM-260* Joint Advanced Tactical Missile (JATM), proposed replacement for AIM-120, with twin-boost phase, launch and loiter capability. Swarming capability has been discussed.

AIS: Automated identification system, a system used by all ships to provide update data on their location to their owners and insurers. Civilian ships are required to keep their transponder on at all times unless under threat from pirates; military ships transmit at their own discretion. Rogue nations often ignore the requirement in order to hide the location of ships with illicit cargoes or conducting illegal activities.

AIR TROPHY*: 'Trophy' is an Israeli-made anti-projectile defense system using explosively formed penetrators to defeat attacks on vehicles. It is currently fitted to several Israeli and US armored vehicle types. In 2023 the US Navy announced it was testing the Trophy system for naval defense. Use as an air defense system is speculative.

AGGRESSOR/ADVERSARY: Fighter squadrons that provide training against adversary aircraft are known as 'Aggressor' squadrons. The US Air Force has several in-house No. 9 Squadrons (including F-16s and F-35s) which it uses to train fighter pilots and joint tactical air controllers. In the US Marines and Navy these are known as 'Adversary' units. In 2022, the USAF confirmed that Aggressor aircraft in Alaska had been used to intercept Russian aircraft off the coast of Alaska, and No. 9 Squadrons had been used to backfill regular USAF squadrons deployed overseas. Many air forces including the USAF and RAF, also use private contractors to provide these services, and several large private military aviation contractors exist, fielding recently retired F-16 and F-18 fighters. The most advanced private air force in the world, Air USA, claims to be able to field three No. 9 Squadrons including 46 ex-RAAF F/A-18 Hornets.

ALL DOMAIN KILL CHAIN*: Also known as Multi-Domain Kill Chain. An attack in which advanced AI allows high-speed assimilation of data from multiple sources (satellite, cyber, ground and air) to generate engagement solutions for military maneuver, precision fire support, artillery or combat air support.

AMD-65: Hungarian-made military assault rifle

AN/APG-81: The active electronically scanning array (AESA) radar system on the F-35 Panther that allows it to track and engage multiple air and ground targets simultaneously.

ANGELS: Radio brevity code for 'thousands of feet.' Angels five is five thousand feet.

AO YIN: Legendary Chinese four-horned bull with insatiable appetite for human flesh

APC: Armored personnel carrier; a wheeled or tracked lightly armored vehicle able to transport troops into combat and provide limited covering fire.

ARMATA T-14: Next-generation Russian main battle tank

ASFN: Anti-screw fouling net. Traditionally, a net boom laid across the entrance of a harbor to hinder the entrance of ships or submarines. Can also be dropped from a fast boat, or fired from a subsea drone to foul the screws of a surface vessel.

ASRAAM: Advanced Short-Range Air-to-Air Missile (infrared only)

ASROC: Anti-submarine rocket-launched torpedo. Allows a torpedo to be fired at a submerged target from up to ten kilometers away, allowing the torpedo to enter the water close to the target and reducing the chances the target can evade the attack.

ASTUTE CLASS: Next-generation British nuclear-powered attack submarine (SSN) designed for stealth operation. Powered by a Rolls Royce reactor plant coupled to a pump-jet propulsion system. HMS *Astute* is the first of seven planned hulls, HMS *Agincourt* is the last. Can carry up to 38 torpedoes and cruise missiles, and is one of the first British submarines to be steered by a 'pilot' using a joystick.

AUKUS class submarine*: AUKUS is a trilateral security pact between Australia, the United Kingdom, and the United States announced on 15 September 2021 for the Indo-Pacific region to counter China's influence The AUKUS submarine deal signed in 2022 will provide Australia with access to nuclear-powered submarines, which are stealthier and more capable than conventionally powered boats. The total cost of the deal is estimated to be $100 billion, making it Australia's biggest defense spend. According to media reports, Australia will first buy US-designed *Virginia*-class submarines as a stopgap, before acquiring a future UK-designed boat under a multi-billion-dollar deal. The UK-built submarines are currently in the design phase and are set to replace the *Astute* fleet. The *AE1* featured in this novel is speculative.

ASW: Anti-Submarine Warfare

AWACS: Airborne Warning and Control System aircraft, otherwise known as AEW&C (Airborne Early Warning and Control). Aircraft with advanced radar and communication systems that can detect aircraft at ranges up to several hundred kilometers, and direct air operations over a combat theater.

AXEHEAD: Russian long-range hypersonic air-to-air missile, identifying code R-37, designed primarily to shoot down large aircraft at long ranges. Used in combat in Ukraine. The Royal United Services Institute stated: "The Russian Air Force fired up to six R-37Ms per day during October 2022. The extremely high speed of the weapon, coupled with very long effective range and a seeker designed for engaging low-altitude targets, makes it particularly difficult to evade." The Ukraine Air Force disputes this assessment. The Axehead effectiveness is therefore assumed high, but impossible to verify.

AUTONOMOUS vs SEMI AUTONOMOUS: In drone warfare, an autonomous drone is one which can conduct its mission completely independent of human interaction once launched. This reduces its vulnerability to jamming as no signals pass between its operator and the drone which can be jammed. A semi-autonomous drone is one which relies on a wireless/radio/satellite link for communication with its operator but can make some decisions on its own if contact with the human operator is lost or unnecessary. Due to the reliance on a communication link to the operator, such drones are susceptible to jamming.

B-21 RAIDER*: Replacement for the retiring US B-2 Stealth Bomber and B-52. The Raider is intended to provide a lower-cost, stealthier alternative to the B-2 with expanded weapons delivery capabilities to include hypersonic and beyond visual range air-to-air missiles.

BARRETT MRAD M22: Multirole adaptive design sniper rifle with replaceable barrels, capable of firing different ammunition types including anti-materiel rounds, accurate out to 1,500 meters or nearly one mile.

BATS*: Boeing Airpower Teaming System, semi-autonomous uncrewed combat aircraft. The BATS drone is designed to accompany 4th- and 5th-generation fighter aircraft on missions either in an air escort, recon or electronic warfare capacity.

BATTLE-NET: Generic name for tactical data sharing systems such as the US The Tactical Targeting Network Technology (TTNT) system; a high-bandwidth, secure data sharing network that enables real-time sharing of targeting and situational awareness data among aircraft, ground vehicles, and command centers, allowing for faster and more effective decision-making on the battlefield.

BELLADONNA: A Russian-made mobile electronic warfare vehicle capable of jamming enemy airborne warning aircraft, ground radars, radio communications and radar-guided missiles

BESAT*: New 1,200-ton class of Iranian SSP (air-independent propulsion) submarine. Also known as Project Qaaem. Capable of launching mines, torpedoes or cruise missiles.

BIG RED ONE: US 1st Infantry Division (see also BRO), aka the Bloody First

BINGO: Radio brevity code showing that an aircraft has only enough fuel left for a return to base. The fuel level above this, preset as a cautionary reminder for a pilot, is called JOKER.

BIRD-DOG*: An 'autonomous foraging drone' or uncrewed aerial vehicle which can locate its own sources of power resupply and operate completely independently of human interaction when ordered to.

BLACK WIDOW (P-99)*: *Artist impression above.* Several companies were competing in 2023/4 for the Next Generation Air Dominance (NGAD) air superiority initiative. The BLACK WIDOW is a purely speculative platform combining what is known about the requirements issued and the designs in testing. NGAD is described by the USAF as a "family of systems," with a stealth fighter aircraft as the centerpiece of the system, and other parts of the system likely to be uncrewed escort aircraft to carry extra munitions and perform other missions. In particular, NGAD aims to develop a system that addresses the operation needs of the Pacific theater of operations, where current USAF fighters lack sufficient range and payload. The successful NGAD aircraft is therefore unlikely to resemble current US stealth fighters such as the F-22 Raptor or F-35 Panther. In the Aggressor novels, the WIDOW can be armed with 14 air-to-air missiles internally, or fewer air-to-air missiles with a combination of land or ship attack cruise missiles. In Beast Mode, using external hardpoints, it can carry 22 air-to-air missiles.

BLOODY FIRST: US 1st Infantry Division, aka the Big Red One (BRO)

BOGEY: Unidentified aircraft detected by radar

BRADLEY UGCV*: US uncrewed ground combat vehicle prototype based on a modified M3 Bradley combat fighting vehicle. A tracked vehicle with medium armor, it is intended to be controlled remotely by a crew in a vehicle, or ground troops, up to two kilometers away. Armed with 5kw blinding laser and autoloading TOW anti-tank missiles. See also HYPERION.

BRO: Big Red One or Bloody First, nickname for US Army 1st Infantry Division

BTR-80: A Russian-made amphibious armored personnel carrier armed with a 30mm automatic cannon.

BUG OUT: Withdraw from combat.

BUK: Russian-made self-propelled anti-aircraft missile system designed to engage medium-range targets such as aircraft, smart bombs and cruise missiles

BUSTER: 100% throttle setting on an aircraft, or full military power

CAP: Combat air patrol; an offensive or defensive air patrol over an objective

CAS: Close air support; air action by rotary-winged or fixed-wing aircraft against hostile targets in close proximity to friendly forces. CAS operations are often directed by a joint terminal air controller, or JTAC, embedded with a military unit.

CASA CN-235: Turkish Air Force medium-range twin-engined transport aircraft

CBRN: Chemical, biological, radiological or nuclear (see also NBC *SUIT*)

CCP: Communist Party of China. Governed by a Politburo comprising the Chinese Premier and senior party ministers and officials.

CENTURION: US 20mm radar-guided close-in weapons system for protection of ground or naval assets against attack by artillery, rocket or missiles

CHAMP*: Counter-electronics High-power Advanced Microwave Projectile; a 'launch and loiter' cruise missile which attacks sensitive electronics with high power microwave bursts to damage electronics. Similar in effect to an electromagnetic pulse (EMP) weapon.

CHONGMING CH-7 Rainbow*: A stealthy flying-wing uncrewed fighter aircraft similar to the US F-47B, with a 22-meter wingspan and 10m length, and a maximum take-off weight of 13 tons. Reportedly able to fly at 920 km/h or 571 mph, with an operational radius of 2,000 km or 1,200 kilometers. Can carry air-to-air or air to surface missiles in an internal bay. Prototypes have been photographed and production was due to begin in 2022 but deployment has not yet been confirmed.

CIC: Combat Information Center. The 'nerve center' on an early warning aircraft, warship or submarine that functions as a tactical center and provides processed information for command and control of the near battlespace or area of operations. On a warship, acts on orders from and relays information to the bridge.

CO: Commanding Officer

COALITION: A US-led Coalition of Nations.

COLT: Combat Observation Laser Team; a forward artillery observer team armed with a laser for designating targets for attack by precision-guided munitions

CONSTELLATION* class frigate: the result of the US FFG(X) program, a warship with advanced anti-air, anti-surface and anti-submarine capabilities capable of serving as a data integration and communication hub. The first ship in the class, *USS Constellation*, is expected to enter service mid-2020s. *USS Congress* will be the second ship in the class.

CONTROL ROOM: the compartment on a submarine from which weapons, sensors, propulsion and navigation commands are coordinated.

COP: Combat Outpost (US)

C-RAM: Counter-rocket, artillery and mortar cannon, also abbreviated counter-RAM.

CROWS: Common Remotely Operated Weapon Station, a weapon such as .50 caliber machine gun, mounted on a turret and controlled remotely by a soldier inside a vehicle, bunker or command post

CUDA*: Missile nickname (from barraCUDA) for the supersonic US short- to medium-range 'Small Advanced Capabilities Missile.' It has tri-mode (optical, active radar and infrared heat-seeking) sensors, thrust vectoring for extreme maneuverability and a hit-to-kill terminal attack.

CYBERCOM: US Cyberspace combatant command responsible for cyber defense and warfare.

DARPA: US Defense Advanced Research Projects Agency, a research and development agency responsible for bringing new military technologies to the US armed forces

DAS: Distributed Aperture System; a 360-degree sensor system on the F-35 Panther allowing the pilot to track targets visually at greater than 'eyeball' range

DEWS*: Directed Energy Weapon Systems. Various laser and microwave energy-based systems are in development or have seen experimental use by militaries including US, UK, Japan, Russia, China, India and South Korea. The US Navy has deployed the 60+ kilowatt HELIOS laser system on several vessels, which is claimed to be capable of long-range Intelligence, Surveillance, Reconnaissance (ISR) and Counter UAS operations, including optical-infrared jamming. The US Army has announced the BLUEHALO 20-kilowatt anti drone system will be mounted on light tactical vehicles and a 50-kilowatt MSRAD (Maneuver Short Range Air Defense) laser on Stryker vehicles. It is also experimenting with a truck mounted 50 kilowatt HEL-MD (High Energy Laser Mobile Demonstrator) laser for cruise missile and artillery defense.

DFDA: Australian armed forces Defense Forces Discipline Act

DFM: Australian armed forces Defense Force Magistrate

DIA: The US Defense Intelligence Agency

DIRECTOR OF NATIONAL CYBER SECURITY*. The NSA's Cyber Security Directorate is an organization that unifies NSA's foreign intelligence and cyber defense missions and is charged with preventing and eradicating threats to National Security Systems and the Defense Industrial Base. Various US government sources have mooted the elevation of the role of Director of Cyber Security to a Cabinet-level Director of National Cyber Security (on a level with the Director of National Intelligence), appointed by the US President to coordinate the activities of the many different agencies and military departments engaged in cyber warfare.

DRONE: Uncrewed aerial vehicle, or UAV, used for combat, transport, refueling or reconnaissance. Militaries and manufacturers twist themselves in knots to avoid using the word 'drone.' For example, 'kamikaze drones' such as the Switchblade and Lancet have been described by the UK military as 'One Way Uncrewed Aerial Attack Vehicles.' Rolls right off the tongue, right? Drones that fly were called Uncrewed Air Vehicles, then

Remotely Piloted Aircraft and now also Collaborative Combat Aircraft. Let's just call them drones.

ECS: Engagement Control Station; the local control center for a HELLADS laser battery which tracks targets and directs anti-air defensive fire.

EMP: Electromagnetic pulse. Nuclear weapons produce an EMP wave which can destroy unshielded electronic components. The major military powers have also been experimenting with non-nuclear weapons which can also produce an EMP pulse–see CHAMP missile.

EMPIRE DOMINATOR*: In 2017 China's Communist Party issued the "New Generation Artificial Intelligence Development Plan," which directed that resources be allocated to making China the world leader in AI. In 2021 the US DoD China Military Power report assessed that China was outspending USA on military investment in AI, and China was now the 'pacing challenge' for US military research into AI. EMPIRE DOMINATOR is a hypothetical Chinese analytical and decision support AI based on these developments. A domain-agnostic generative AI that dynamically integrates and learns from multiple intelligence sources, in FX Holden novels it has been integrated in Chinese naval vessels, and uncrewed autonomous weapons systems such as the *Tianyi* ground attack drone (CN, slaughterbot/US SAAGA*), *Taifun 002* class uncrewed submarine*, *Lanjin* uncrewed medium sized submarine*, and the J-20ED stealth fighter.

ETA: Estimated Time of Arrival

F-16C/D FALCON: US-made 4th-generation multirole fighter aircraft flown by Turkey.

F-22: The F-22 fighter is a stealth aircraft with low radar cross-section (RCS), long range, and high weapons payload capability, introduced in 2005 and currently planned to be retired in the 2040s. Though intended primarily for air-air combat it is capable of carrying a variety of air-to-air and air-to-ground weapons, including missiles, bombs, and rockets, with a maximum weapons payload of approximately 2,000 pounds.

F-35: US 5th-generation fighter aircraft, known either as the Panther (pilot nickname) or Lightning II (manufacturer name). The Panther nickname was first coined by the 6th Weapons Squadron 'Panther Tamers'. There is much speculation about the capabilities of the Panther, just as there is about the Russian Su-57 Felon. Neither has been extensively combat tested, though the F-35 has reportedly been used in combat by the Israeli Air Force.

F-47B (currently X-47B) FANTOM*: A Northrop Grumman demonstration uncrewed combat aerial vehicle (UCAV) in trials with the US Navy and a part of the DARPA Joint UCAS program. See also MQ-25 STINGRAY. The Fantom is used in these novels as an example of a possible uncrewed combat aircraft, and should not be taken to reflect the actual capabilities of the X-47B.

FAC: Forward air controller; an aviator embedded with a ground unit to direct close air support attacks. See also TAC(P) or JTAC

FAST MOVERS: Fighter jets

FATEH: Iranian SSK (diesel-electric) submarine. At 500 tons, also considered a midget submarine. Capable of launching torpedoes, torpedo-launched cruise missiles and mines

FB-22 Nemesis*: The Lockheed Martin FB-22 was a proposed supersonic stealth bomber / regional strike fighter aircraft for the United States Air Force, derived from the F-22 Raptor air superiority fighter. The FB-22 leveraged much of the design work and components from the F-22 to reduce development costs. It was never green lighted, with the USAF choosing instead to proceed with the B-21, F-35 and to extend the service life of its existing F-15EX strike fighter fleet. Six prototypes were purchased by private military contractor Aggressor Inc. and restored to operational status. Range: 3,600 nmi (4,100 mi, 6,700 km). Hardpoints: 8 internal hardpoints in three weapons bays, 4 underwing hardpoints with a capacity of 15,000 lb. (6,800 kg) internal and in LO wing weapons bays, 30,000 lb. (13,600 kg) total.

FELON: Russian 5th-generation stealth fighter aircraft, the Sukhoi Su-57. There is much speculation about the capabilities of the Felon, just as there is about the US F-35 Panther. Neither has been extensively combat tested. Unlike the F-35 however the FELON has not entered large scale production and few flying production airframes exist. Capabilities discussed in these novels are speculative.

FINGER FOUR FORMATION: a fighter aircraft patrol formation in which four aircraft fly together in a pattern that resembles the tips of the four fingers of a hand. Three such formations can form a squadron of 12 aircraft.

FIRESCOUT: an uncrewed autonomous scout helicopter for service on US warships, used for anti-ship and anti-submarine operations.

FISTER: A member of a FiST (Fire Support Team)

FLANKER: Russian Sukhoi-30 or 35 attack aircraft; see also J-11 (China)

FOX (1, 2 or 3): Radio brevity code indicating a pilot has fired an air-to-air missile, either semi-active radar seeking (1), infrared (2) or active radar seeking (3)

FURY*: Collaborative Combat Aircraft in development by Anduril Corporation as part of the USAF Skyborg program to develop low-cost attritable 'loyal wingman' aircraft. It distinguishes itself from other competitors in part through its fighter-like performance attributes, with a near-supersonic top speed of Mach 0.9 (it was originally envisaged as an autonomously piloted 'aggressor' drone), and its use of commercially available or already deployed engines and avionics.

GAL*: A natural language learning system (AI) used by Israel's Unit 8200 to conduct complex analytical research support.

GAL-CLASS SUBMARINE*: An upgraded *Dolphin II* class submarine, fitted with the GAL AI system, allowing it to be operated by a two-person crew.

G/ATOR: Ground/Air Oriented Task Radar (GATOR); a radar specialized for the detection of incoming artillery fire, rockets or missiles. Also able to calculate the origin of attack for counterfire purposes.

GBU: Guided Bomb Unit

GPS: Global Positioning System, a network of civilian or military satellites used to provide accurate map reference and location data.

GRAY WOLF*: US subsonic standoff air-launched cruise missile with swarming (horde) capabilities. The Gray Wolf is designed to launch from multiple aircraft, including the C-130, and defeat enemy air defenses by overwhelming them with large numbers. It will feature modular swap-out warheads.

GRAYHOUND: Radio brevity code for the launch of an air-ground missile

GRU: Russian military intelligence service

H-20*: Xian Hong 20 stealth bomber with a range of 12,000 km or 7,500 kilometers and payload of 10 tons. Comparable to the US B-21.

GYRFALCON, J-31/J-35*: The Shenyang FC-31 Gyrfalcon, also known as the J-31 or J-35, is a Chinese prototype mid-sized twinjet 5th-generation fighter aircraft being developed by Shenyang Aircraft Corporation. It has a length of 16.9m, height of about 4.8m, and a wingspan of 11.5m. The aircraft has a maximum speed of 1,200 knots, a combat range of 670 nautical miles on internal fuel or 1,042 nautical miles with external tanks, and a service ceiling of around 65,616 feet3. It has a maximum payload of 8,000 kg (four missiles in internal bays and six missiles or bombs on external hardpoints) and a maximum take-off weight of 28,000 kg. The first prototype took flight on October 31, 20121, and reached operational capability in 2020. It is being made available for export and is expected to replace the J-15 Flying Shark as China's dominant carrier aircraft.

HACM*: Hypersonic Attack Cruise Missile. A two-stage missile with solid fuel first stage boosting the missile to supersonic velocity after which a scramjet engine takes over to drive the missile to speeds of Mach 5 and above. The contract to develop HACM was awarded to Raytheon in September 2022.

HARM: High-speed Anti-Radar Missile; a missile which homes on the signals produced by anti-air missile radars like that used by the BUK or PANTSIR

HAWKEYE: Northrop Grumman E2D airborne warning and control aircraft. Capable of launching from aircraft carriers and networking (sharing data) with compatible aircraft.

HE: High-explosive munitions; general purpose explosive warheads

HEAT: High-Explosive Anti-Tank munitions; shells specially designed to penetrate armor

HELIOS*: Laser weapon. See DEWS

HEL-MD*: High Energy Laser Mobile Demonstrator) laser. See DEWS.

HELLADS*: High Energy Liquid Laser Area Defense System; an alternative to missile or projectile-based air defense systems that attacks enemy missiles, rockets or bombs with high energy laser and/or microwave pulses. Currently being tested by US, Chinese, Russian and EU ground, air and naval forces. The combination of HELLADS with HPM defense systems is logical but speculative. See also DEWS.

HIMARS: High Mobility Artillery Rocket System, is a highly mobile artillery rocket system developed by Lockheed Martin Missiles and Fire Control that offers the firepower of MLRS on a wheeled chassis. It carries a single six-pack of rockets or one long range GPS guided ATACMS missile on a 5-ton truck, and can launch the entire MLRS family of munitions. It has a shoot-and-scoot capability that reduces the enemy's ability to locate and target it.

HORDE*: Drones, missiles or smart bombs with onboard AI and the ability to coordinate their actions with other drones while in flight, either autonomously or using pre-selected protocols. 'Horde' tactics differ from 'swarm' tactics in that they rely on large numbers to overwhelm enemy defenses. See also SWARM.

HPK: High Probability of Kill, usually used to describe the range at which a weapons system should optimally engage. An engagement at long range usually has a Low Probability of Kill, as does an engagement at very short range. A High Probability of Kill is achieved in the sweet spot in between.

HPM*: High Power Microwave; an untargeted local area defensive weapon which attacks sensitive electronics in missiles and guided bombs to damage electronics such as guidance systems. Chinese weapons developers using a pulse-HPM or EMP weapon were reported in 2023 to have brought down an uncrewed aircraft flying at 5,000 feet. The US Air Force Research Laboratory's (AFRL) Tactical High Power Operational Responder (THOR) system is a shipping-container-sized HPM weapon designed to bring down drone swarms. All HPM systems can currently be regarded as prototypes, and squad level or miniaturized HPM systems do not yet exist.

HSU-003*: Planned Chinese large uncrewed underwater vehicle optimized for seabed warfare, i.e. piloting itself to a specific location on the sea floor (a harbor or shipping lane) and conducting reconnaissance or anti-shipping attacks. Comparable to the US *Orca* or *Manta Ray* classes.

HYPERION*: Proposed lightly armored uncrewed ground vehicle (UGCV). Can be fitted with turret-mounted 50kw laser for anti-air, anti-personnel defense and autoloading TOW missile launcher. See also BRADLEY UGCV

HYPERSONIC: Speeds greater than 5x the speed of sound. Often used in relation to missiles. Ballistic missiles are by nature hypersonic. Examples in use include the Russian Kh-47M2 Kinzhal, or "Dagger" in Russian: a Russian hypersonic air-launched ballistic missile that is claimed to have a range of 2,000 km (1,200 mi) and Mach 10 speed. It can carry either conventional or nuclear warheads and can be launched by Tu-22M3 bombers or MiG-31K interceptors. It has seen use in the Ukraine conflict with US forces claiming a 100% interception rate using the PATRIOT missile defense system (unverified).

ICC: Information Coordination Center; command center for multiple air defense batteries such as PATRIOT or HELLADS

IED: Improvised explosive device, for example, a roadside bomb.

IFF: Identify Friend or Foe transponder, a radio transponder that allows weapons systems to determine whether a target is an ally or enemy.

IFV: Infantry fighting vehicle, a highly mobile, lightly armored, wheeled or tracked vehicle capable of carrying troops into a combat and providing fire support. See NAMER

IMA BK: The combat AI built into Russia's Su-57 Felon and Okhotnik fighter aircraft.

INTERSCEPTER UAV*: Entirely conceptual uncrewed aerial vehicle. In 2023 Mitsubishi Heavy Industries (MHI) announced it had successfully field tested a battalion-level C-UAV or counter-UAV system called Interscepter, which used a 10kW laser to destroy small drones. It said Interscepter systems could be mounted on vehicles, or ships. At the same time, MHI announced it was working on a prototype combat UAV. In the novel FULCRUM, these two systems are tied together to create the MHI Interscepter laser-armed UAV, with a more powerful 50kW laser.

IONIC BOUNCE: a technique used by air defense radars to detect stealth aircraft by bouncing radio waves off the boundary to the ionosphere, striking the aircraft on their larger upper surfaces.

IR: Infrared or heat-seeking system

ISIS: Self-proclaimed Islamic State of Iraq and Syria

J-7: Fishbed; 3rd-generation Chinese fighter, a copy of cold war Russian Mig-21

J-10: Vigorous Dragon; 3rd-generation Chinese fighter, comparable to US F-16

J-11: Flanker; 4th-generation Chinese fighter, copy of Russian Su-27

J-15: Flying Shark; 4th-generation PLA Navy, twin-engine twin-seat fighter, comparable to Russian Su-33 and a further development of the J-11. Currently the most common aircraft flown off China's aircraft carriers.

J-11 AI variant*: *Zhi Sheng* (Intelligence Victory); 4th-generation, two-seater twin-engine multirole strike fighter. In 2019 it was announced a variant of the J-11 was being developed with *Zhi Sheng* Artificial Intelligence to replace the human 'back seater' or copilot.

J-20: 'Mighty Dragon'; 5th-generation single-seat, twin-engine Chinese stealth fighter, claimed to be comparable to the US F-35 or F-22, or Russian Su-57. Aviation experts believe it would have a larger radar cross section than its western counterparts, not just because of its larger size, but also because it employs nose-mounted canards. The first operational squadron of J-20 fighters was stood up by China in 2018. As many as 20 squadrons exist today. It has been photographed teamed with Chongming drones, and in a two-seat J-20S version with an AI 'back seater' (weapon systems officer). The J-20ED* model in FULCRUM is entirely speculative.

J-35: See Gyrfalcon.

JAGM: Joint air-ground missile. A US short-range anti-armor or anti-personnel missile fired from an aircraft. It can be laser or radar guided and has an 18 lb. warhead.

JASSM: AGM-158 Joint Air-to-Surface Standoff Missile; long-range subsonic stealth cruise missile capable of fielding multiple warhead types (e.g. electronic warfare, high explosive, cluster, anti-armor.) JASSM-ER is the Extended Range variant which can travel up to 580 kilometers or 930 kilometers. JASSM-E is an electronic signature attack version designed specifically to attack enemy command, control and intelligence targets. Other variants include electronic warfare and anti-radar capabilities.

TJAM: Joint Direct Attack Munition; bombs guided by laser or GPS to their targets.

JIANGSU*: China's fourth aircraft carrier is under construction (the name chosen here is fictional and simply follows the Chinese tradition of naming its carriers after provinces.) Like the Type 003 *Fujian*, it will feature an integrated electric propulsion system that will allow the operation of electromagnetic catapults. Unlike the conventionally powered Type 003, the Type 004 will be much larger and also the first Chinese carrier to feature nuclear marine propulsion, and could generate enough electricity to power laser weapons and railguns currently under development. China has announced it hopes to complete this carrier by the late 2020s, and indicated that up to four might be built.

JNAAM*: See Meteor. Euro-Japanese version of Meteor air-to-air missile with Japanese designed phased array radar to allow the missiles to fit both the Japanese F-35 and the coming Euro-Japanese Tempest fighter. It is speculated that the combination of Tempest + JNAAM will give Japan a high-altitude ballistic missile interception capability.

JOE*: "Joint Outcome Evaluator." A natural language learning system (AI) used by the DIA to conduct sophisticated analytical research support. The DIA has publicly reported it is already using AI for analytical support and to explore machine learning potential, but the JOE system in this novel is speculative.

JOKER: fuel level. BINGO is a radio brevity code showing that an aircraft has only enough fuel left for a return to base. The fuel level above this, preset as a cautionary reminder for a pilot, is called JOKER.

JLTV*: US Joint Light Tactical Vehicle; planned replacement for the US ground forces Humvee multipurpose vehicle, planned in recon/scout, infantry transport, heavy guns, close combat, command and control, or ambulance versions.

JTAC: Joint terminal air controller. A member of a ground force–e.g., Marine unit–trained to direct the action of combat aircraft engaged in close air support and other offensive air operations from a forward position. See also CAS.

K-30M*: short range air-to-air missile in development by Russia. A modification of the R-73 differs from the R-73 in the use of a modified "Mayak-80M" seeker with a target capture angle increased to 120 degrees and an increased capture range. The range has been increased to 40 km, the control system has been modified, and four gas dynamic control channels have been introduced.

K-77M*: Supersonic Russian-made medium-range active radar homing air-to-air missile with extreme maneuverability. It is being developed from the existing R-77 missile.

KALIBR: Russian-made anti-ship, anti-submarine and land attack cruise missile with 500kg conventional or nuclear warhead. The Kalibr-M variant* will have an extended range of up to 4,500 km or 2,700 kilometers (the distance of, e.g., Iran to Paris).

KANYON*: NATO codename for Intercontinental Nuclear-Powered Nuclear-Armed Autonomous *Poseidon* Torpedo. Claimed by Russia to be operational, but this is unconfirmed. Video showing test firing by the submarine *Sarov* has been released, but the *Sarov* has not been sighted since 2019. The *Kanyon* project is intended to be the ultimate stealth weapon, able to receive orders while underway, and navigate itself undetected to its target across hundreds, even thousands of miles of sea.

KARAKURT CLASS: A Russian corvette class which first entered service in 2018. Armed with Pantsir close-in weapons systems, Sosna-R anti-air missile defense and Kalibr supersonic anti-ship missiles. An anti-submarine sensor/weapon loadout is planned but not yet deployed.

KC-135 STRATOTANKER: US airborne refueling aircraft.

KINZHAL: Russian air launched ballistic missile. Deployed in Ukraine conflict. Claimed to fly at Mach 10, Russia asserts the Kinzhal is both hypersonic and impossible to intercept. Ukrainian Patriot missile crews claim the Kinzhal travels only at Mach 3.6 (not hypersonic) and has been successfully intercepted. It is impossible to verify these competing claims.

KRYPTON: Supersonic Russian air-launched anti-radar missile, it is also being adapted for use against ships and large aircraft

LAUNCH AND LOITER: The capability of a missile or drone to fly itself to a target area and wait at altitude for final targeting instructions

LCS: Littoral combat ship. In the US Navy it refers to the *Independence* or *Freedom* class; in Iran, the *Safineh* class; in other navies it may be considered equivalent to a frigate or corvette class. Has the capabilities of a small assault transport, including a flight deck and hangar for housing two SH-60 or MH-60 Seahawk helicopters, a stern ramp for operating small boats, and the cargo volume and payload to deliver a small assault force with fighting vehicles to a roll-on/roll-off port facility. Standard armaments include Mk 110 57mm guns and RIM-116 Rolling Airframe Missiles. Also equipped with autonomous air, surface and underwater vehicles. Possessing lower air defense and surface warfare capabilities than destroyers, the LCS concept emphasizes speed, flexible mission modules and a shallow draft.

LEOPARD: Main battle tank fielded by NATO forces including Turkey

LIAONING: China's first aircraft carrier, modified from the former Russian Navy aircraft cruiser, the *Varyag*. Since superseded by China's Type 002 (*Shandong*) and Type 003 (*Fujian*)

carriers, the *Liaoning* is now used for testing new technologies for carrier use, such as the J-31 stealth fighter.

LIBERATOR II*: Also known as the 'Liberty Lifter.' The Liberty Lifter is a concept for a long-range, low-cost seaplane that can carry heavy loads across oceans by flying close to the water surface using the ground effect. The concept was launched by DARPA in mid-2022 to develop a new plane that could combine the speed and flexibility of airlift with the runway-independence and endurance of sealift. The concept aims to revolutionize heavy air lift for maritime operations and logistics. DARPA awarded contracts to two teams, Aurora Flight Sciences and General Atomics, in February 2023 to design their own versions of the Liberty Lifter. The final designs are expected by mid-2024, and the winning design will proceed to build and test a full-size prototype. DARPA hopes to have the Liberty Lifter flying within roughly five years.

LOCUST*: The Office of Naval Research Low-Cost UAV Swarming Technology (LOCUST) program, fires swarming drones from a tube-based launcher. Similar to USAF Perdix, UK Ministry of Defence's Fire Shadow concept or China's CETC-Tsinghua drone, these drones are primarily anti-personnel or anti-armor, but can also be used to intercept low flying aircraft. The Tsinghua is claimed to be able to switch from radio to autonomous guidance if jammed.

LOITERING MUNITION: A missile or bomb, able to wait at altitude for final targeting instructions. Example: The AeroVironment Switchblade is a miniature loitering munition, designed by AeroVironment and used by several branches of the United States military. Small enough to fit in a backpack, the Switchblade launches from a tube, flies to the target area, directed wirelessly by an operator and crashes into its target while detonating its explosive warhead.

LONG-RANGE HYPERSONIC WEAPONS (LRHW)*: A prototype US missile consisting of a rocket and glide vehicle, capable of being launched by submarine, from land or from aircraft.

LONGSHOT*: Air launched drone, first flight expected 2024. According to manufacturer "able to be launched by crewed fighter jets, transports or other aircraft and capable of venturing deep into hostile airspace to effectively engage enemy targets. Able to conduct a fighter sweep ahead of a strike wave and join human-crewed aircraft on a mission, effectively bolstering the firepower of the forces."

LRASM: Long Range Anti-Ship Missile is a stealth anti-ship cruise missile developed for the United States Air Force and United States Navy by the Defense Advanced Research Projects Agency (DARPA). It is a precision-guided missile designed to meet the needs of U.S. Navy and Air Force Warfighters against maritime capital ship targets, with a long range that enables target engagement from well outside the range of direct counter-fire weapons.

LS3*: Legged Squad Support System—a mechanized dog-like robot powered by hydrogen fuel cells and supported by a cloud-based AI. Currently being explored by DARPA and the US armed forces for logistical support or squad scouting and IED detection roles.

LTMV: Light Tactical Multirole Vehicle; a very long name for what is essentially a jeep.

M1A2 ABRAMS: US main battle tank. In 2016, the US Army and Marine Corps began testing out the Israeli Trophy active protection system to provide additional defense against incoming projectiles. Improvements planned for the M1A3 are to include a lighter 120mm gun, added road wheels with improved suspension, a more durable track, lighter-weight armor, long-range precision armaments, and infrared camera and laser detectors.

M22: See BARRETT MRAD M22 sniper rifle.

M27: US-made military assault rifle

MAD: Magnetic Anomaly Detection, used by warships to detect large artificial objects under the surface of the sea, such as mines, or submarines.

MAD-mesh: Air deployed Magnetic Anomaly Detection buoys which network to create a large detection footprint.

MAIN BATTLE TANK: See MBT

MANPAD: Man portable air defense missile, such as US Stinger, Chinese Crossbow or UK Starstreak.

MANTA RAY*: Xtra Large Uncrewed Underwater Vehicle comparable to the US *Orca*. Unlike traditionally shaped cylindrical submarines, the long-endurance *Manta* is wide and flat like its namesake, giving it a very small sonar cross section and stealth properties—it has been described as a 'sea glider.' The testbed version however features noisy wingtip propellers which are unlikely to feature in a final version. Like other XLUUV platforms it has been designed with modular payload capabilities. It can be transported disassembled in trailer trucks or transport aircraft. The *Manta* testbed made its first sea trials in February 2024. In Aggressor, the Manta Ray is fitted with four vertical launch tubes firing out the bottom of the vessel, capable of launching either Naval Strike Missiles or Very Lightweight Torpedoes.

MASS*: Marine Autonomous Surface Ship, or autonomous trailing vessel. Not to be confused with Uncrewed Surface Vessels such as kamikaze drone boats, which have already seen action in Ukraine.

MBT: Main battle tank; a heavily armored combat vehicle capable of direct fire and maneuver

MEFP: Multiple Explosive Formed Penetrators; a defensive weapon which uses small explosive charges to create and fire small metal slugs at an incoming projectile, thereby destroying it. As used in the Israeli Trophy armored vehicle defense system.

MEMS: Micro-Electro-Mechanical System

METAL STORM*: an Australian designed 36-barreled stacked projectile volley gun, boasting the highest rate of fire in the world. The prototype array demonstrated a firing rate of just over 1 million rounds per minute for a 180-round burst of 0.01 seconds (~27,777 rpm / barrel). Firing within 0.1 seconds from up to 1600 barrels (at maximum configuration) the gun claimed a maximum rate of fire of 1.62 million RPM and creating a dense wall (0.1 m between follow-up projectiles) of 24,000 projectiles. The weapon never found a buyer, and the early 2000s the patent rights were subsequently sold to a defense company now involved in making UAVs.

METEOR: Long-range air-to-air missile with active radar seeker, but also able to be updated with target data in-flight by any suitably equipped allied unit

MIA: Missing in action

MIG-41*: Proposed design from the famous the Mikoyan design bureau, the Mig-41 (PAK DP) entered prototype development in 2021. According to Russian media it is envisioned to become a high-altitude interceptor of hypersonic missiles by carrying a multifunctional long-range interceptor missile system (MPKR DP) that will dispense several sub-missiles in order to increase the chance of intercepting hypersonic weapons. The PAK DP is also intended to be able to deliver hypersonic and anti-satellite missiles, reaching near-hypersonic flight speeds itself.

MIKE: Radio brevity code for minutes

MIL-25: Export version of the Mi-25 'Hind' Russian helicopter gunship

MOP: Massive ordnance penetrator. A 30,000 lb. bomb with a hardened steel casing using GPS guidance to enable precision targeting. It can be launched at 'standoff' ranges and glide to its target.

MOPP: Mission-Oriented Protective Posture protective gear; equipment worn to protect troops against CBRN weapons. See also NBC SUIT

MOSQUITO* swarming drone: developmental program started and then cancelled by UK to develop an air-deployable small swarming drone. In FX Holden novels it is assumed this program was revived. The Mosquito is a small canister-launched x-wing drone with a 40lb warhead that is launched as part of a swarm and can network with other Mosquito drones to coordinate attacks on small targets, such as dismounted troops, or group together to attack larger targets such as tanks or warships.

MP: Military Police

MQ-25 STINGRAY: The MQ-25 Stingray is a Boeing-designed prototype uncrewed US airborne refueling aircraft. See also F-47B Fantom. Already in service.

MSRAD: Maneuver Short Range Air Defense laser. See DEWS.

MSS: Ministry of State Security, Chinese umbrella intelligence organization responsible for counterespionage and counterterrorism, and foreign intelligence gathering. Equivalent to the US FBI, CIA and NSA.

NAMER: (Leopard) Israeli infantry fighting vehicle (IFV). More heavily armored than a Merkava IV main battle tank. According to the Israel Defense Forces, the Namer is the most heavily armored vehicle in the world of any type.

NAMICA: The Indian NAMICA (NAG Missile Carrier) is an Infantry Fighting Vehicle (IFV) equipped with a 30mm automatic cannon, a 7.62mm machine gun, and a launcher for anti-tank guided missiles, designed to provide fire support and transport for infantry troops.

NATO: North Atlantic Treaty Organization

NAVAL STRIKE MISSILE (NSM): Supersonic anti-ship missile deployed by NATO navies.

NBC *SUIT*: A protective suit issued to protect the wearer against Nuclear, Biological or Chemical weapons. Usually includes a lining to protect the user from radiation and either a gas mask or air recycling unit.

NEURAL CHIP*: In Feb 2024 Elon Musk's Neuralink company demonstrated how an implanted chip could allow an implant patient, paralyzed in a diving accident, to control a mouse cursor purely by thought. Soon, the patient was able to play computer chess, again by thought. As of 2024 the technology is still in its infancy and human clinical trials are ongoing.

nEUROn*: an experimental unmanned combat aerial vehicle (UCAV) being developed with international cooperation, led by the French company Dassault Aviation. The design goal is to create a stealthy, autonomous UAV that can function in medium-to-high threat combat zones. First flight was in 2012. Since 2019, the nEUROn has carried out test flights at the Istres Air Base, to increase the operational use scenarios and confrontation campaigns regarding threats.

NORAD: The North American Aerospace Defense Command is a United States and Canadian bi-national organization charged with the missions of aerospace warning, aerospace control and maritime warning for North America. Aerospace warning includes the detection, validation and warning of attack against North America whether by aircraft, missiles or space vehicles, through mutual support arrangements with other commands.

NSA: US National Security Agency, cyber intelligence, cyber warfare and defense agency

OFSET*: Offensive Swarm Enabled Tactical drones. Proposed US anti-personnel, anti-armor drone system capable of swarming AI (see SWARM) and able to deploy small munitions against enemy troop or vehicles while moving.

OKHOTNIK*: 5th-generation Sukhoi S-70 uncrewed stealth combat aircraft using avionics systems from the Su-57 Felon and fitted with two internal weapons bays, for 7,000kg of ordnance. Requires a pilot and systems officer, similar to current US uncrewed combat aircraft. Can be paired with Su-57 aircraft and controlled by a pilot.

OMON: Otryad Mobil'nyy Osobogo Naznacheniya; the Russian National Guard mobile police force

OVOD: Subsonic Russian-made air-launched cruise missile capable of carrying high-explosive, submunition or fragmentation warheads

P-99 BLACK WIDOW (Pursuit Fighter)*: Concept aircraft. Several companies were competing in 2023 for the Next Generation Air Dominance air superiority initiative. The WIDOW is a purely speculative platform combining what is known about the requirements issued and the designs in testing. NGAD is described by the USAF as a "family of systems," with a stealth fighter aircraft as the centerpiece of the system, and other parts of the system likely to be uncrewed escort aircraft to carry extra munitions and perform other missions. In particular, NGAD aims to develop a system that addresses the operation needs of the Pacific theater of operations, where current USAF fighters lack sufficient range and payload. The successful NGAD

413

aircraft is therefore unlikely to resemble current US stealth fighters such as the F-22 Raptor or F-35 Panther.

PANTHER: Pilot name for the F-35 Lightning II stealth fighter, first coined by the 6th Weapons Squadron 'Panther Tamers' due to the unpopularity of the official name 'Lightning II'. There is much speculation about the capabilities of the Panther, just as there is about the Russian Su-57 Felon. Neither has been extensively combat tested against peer opponents.

PANTSIR: Russian-made truck-mounted anti-aircraft system which is a further development of the PENSNE: 'Pince-nez' in English. A Russian-made autonomous surface-to-air missile currently being rolled out for the BUK anti-air defense system.

PARS: Turkish light armored vehicle

PATRIOT: An anti-aircraft, interceptor missile defense system which uses its own radar to identify and engage airborne threats

PEACE EAGLE: Turkish Boeing 737 Airborne Early Warning and Control aircraft (see AWACS)

PENSNE: See PANTSIR

PERDIX*: Lightweight air-launched armed microdrone with swarming capability (see SWARM). Designed to be launched from underwing canisters or even from the flare/chaff launchers of existing aircraft. Can be used for recon, target identification or delivery of lightweight ordnance.

PEREGRINE*: US medium-range, multimode (infrared, radar, optical) seeker missile with short form body designed for use by stealth aircraft.

PERSEUS*: A stealth, hypersonic, multiple warhead missile under development for the British Royal Navy and French Navy

PHASED-ARRAY RADAR: A radar which can steer a beam of radio waves quickly across the sky to detect planes and missiles.

PING-PONG*: Fictional air launched loitering reconnaissance missile. Multiple drone manufacturers are currently working on loitering ISR drone concepts with these capabilities. The original Ping-Pong was a battlefield reconnaissance rocket developed by Lockheed-California—later the Lockheed Missiles and Space Company—for use by the United States Army. Intended to give battlefield commanders the ability to gain photographic data on enemy locations before physically returning to its launch point, it reached the flight-test stage before being cancelled.

PL-15: Chinese long-range radar-guided air-to-air missile, comparable to the US AIM-120D (though with longer range) or UK Meteor.

PL-21*: Chinese long-range multimode missile (radar, infrared, optical), comparable to US AIM-260

PLA: People's Liberation Army

PLA-AF (PLAAF): People's Liberation Army Air Force, comparable to the US Air Force, with more than 400 3rd-generation fighter aircraft, 1,200 4th-generation, and nearly 200 5th-generation stealth aircraft

PLA-N (PLAN): People's Liberation Army Navy

PLA-N AF (PLANAF): People's Liberation Army Navy Air Force, comparable to the US Navy Air Force and Marine Corps Aviation, it performs coastal protection and aircraft carrier operations with more than 250 3rd-generation fighter aircraft, and 150 4th-generation fighter aircraft. There is speculation the PLA-N AF is considering the J-31 Gyrfalcon* (a prototype stealth fighter) for its aircraft carriers.

415

PMC: Private Military Contractor—for example Aggressor Inc., which provides 'red flight' combat aircraft and pilots to US and allied air forces for training purposes. Or Wagner Group, the large Russian PMC, which was heavily engaged in Ukraine, and is still present in Africa. In 2018 Wagner Troops fought against US troops over control of an oil facility in Syria. Up to 200 'Wagnerites' died in the battle, but no US troops were killed or injured.

PODNOS: Russian-made portable 82mm mortar

POSEIDON torpedo*: Intercontinental Nuclear-Powered Nuclear-Armed Autonomous *Poseidon* Torpedo, NATO codename - Kanyon. Claimed by Russia to be operational, but this is unconfirmed. Video showing test firing by the submarine *Sarov* has been released, but the *Sarov* has not been sighted since 2019. The *Kanyon* project is intended to be the ultimate stealth weapon, able to receive orders while underway, and navigate itself undetected to its target across hundreds, even thousands of miles of sea.

POSEIDON aircraft: the P-8 Poseidon is a maritime surveillance and anti-submarine platform in service with several navies/air forces. It has surface scanning radar for ship detection, and is capable of dropping sonobuoys for submarine detection. It can be armed with anti-ship and land attack missiles, torpedoes, naval mines, and depth charges.

PUMP-JET PROPULSION: A propulsion system comprising a jet of water and a nozzle to direct the flow of water for steering purposes. Used on some submarines due to a quieter acoustic signature than that generated by a screw. The 'stealthiest' submarines are regarded to be those powered by diesel-electric engines and pump-jet propulsion, such as trialed on the Russian *Kilo* class and proposed for the Australian *Attack* class*.

QHS*: Quantum Harmonic Sensor; a sensor system for detecting stealth aircraft at long ranges by analyzing the electromagnetic disturbances they create in background radiation.

QING* class submarine (Type 032): A class of diesel-electric submarine currently undergoing testing in China's People's Liberation Army Navy. It is said to be the world's largest conventional submarine, at a submerged displacement of 6,628 tons and is able to submerge for a maximum of 30 days. It features torpedo and vertically launched missile tubes and is believed to be capable of firing nuclear armed ballistic missiles. Only one of this class is known to have been deployed. It is speculated China built only one of this type of submarine because it was struggling at the time to build small nuclear reactors, having relied on Russia until this point to supply nuclear submarine power plants. This may also be why China's aircraft carriers are not nuclear powered.

RAAF: Royal Australian Air Force

RAF: Royal Air Force (UK)

RAPID DRAGON*: Palletized Munition Deployment System, in testing with USAF. A disposable weapons module which is airdropped from rails inside a cargo hold in order to deploy flying munitions, typically cruise missiles, drones or glide bombs, from unmodified cargo planes such as the AC-130J Ghostrider.

REUNION* (Operation): Secret Chinese project to develop the Tianyi (Wing of Fate) armed autonomous drone and associated deployment technologies such as the TLV drone mothership and launch sites. Equivalent in scope to the US Manhattan project to develop the atom bomb, it is intended to supplant traditional invasion by ground forces, allowing control of enemy territory without the massive cost and risk of a conventional invasion.

ROCAF: Republic of China Air Force. The air force of Taiwan.

ROE: Rules of Engagement; the rules laid down by military commanders under which a unit can or cannot engage in combat. For example, 'units may only engage a hostile force if fired upon first.'

RPG: Rocket-propelled grenade

RTB: Return to base.

SAFINEH CLASS: Also known as *Mowj/Wave* class. An Iranian trimaran hulled high-speed missile vessel equivalent to the US LCS class, or the Russia *Karakurt*-class corvette.

SAM: Surface-to-Air Missile; an anti-air missile (often shortened to SA) for engaging aircraft

SAR: See SYNTHETIC APERTURE RADAR

SCREW: The propeller used to drive a boat or ship is referred to as a screw (helical blade) propeller. Submarine propellers typically comprise five to seven blades. See also PUMP-JET PROPULSION

SEAD: Suppression of Enemy Air Defenses; an air attack intended to take down enemy anti-air defense systems; see also WILD WEASEL

SENTINEL*: Lockheed Martin RQ-170 Sentinel flying wing stealth reconnaissance drone.

SIDEWINDER: Heat-seeking short-range air-to-air missile

SITREP: Situation Report

SKYHAWK*: Chinese drone designed to team with fighter aircraft to provide added sensor or weapons delivery capabilities. Comparable to the planned US Boeing Loyal Wingman or Kratos drones.

SKY THUNDER: Chinese 1,000 lb. stealth air-launched cruise missile with swappable payload modules

SKYLON*: With capabilities similar to the US Space Shuttle and a modular payload Skylon is designed to take off and land like a normal aircraft. The vehicle design is a hydrogen-fueled aircraft that would take off from a specially built reinforced runway, and accelerate to Mach 5.4 at 26 kilometers (85,000 ft) altitude using the atmosphere's oxygen before switching the engines to use the internal liquid oxygen supply to accelerate to the Mach 25 necessary to reach a 400 km orbit. The high temperature test of the Reaction Engines—Rolls Royce precooler took place in 2019. Testing of the core engine components and pre-burner took place during 2020 and 2021. Uncrewed test flights in a "hypersonic testbed" (HTB) are planned for 2025.

SLAUGHTERBOT: A speculative design based on the TIKAD/SMASH DRAGON prototypes; gyro stabilized flying gun quadcopters which can be fitted with automatic weapons or a 40mm grenade launchers. US version: Semi-Autonomous Air-Ground Assault system, or SAAGA.

SLR: Single lens reflex camera, favored by photojournalists and enthusiasts.

SMERCH: Russian-made 300mm rocket launcher capable of firing high-explosive, submunition or chemical weapons warheads

SOSUS: Sound Surveillance System. A chain of underwater listening posts located across the Arctic and Pacific Oceans. Used primarily for detection of submarines. US Navy recently announced it was upgrading SOSUS into the Deep Reliable Acoustic Path Exploitation System (DRAPES)* which is expected to have active low frequency sonar and magnetic anomaly detection capabilities added.

SPACECOM: United States Space Command (US SPACECOM or SPACECOM) is a unified combatant command of the United States Department of Defense, responsible for military operations in outer space, specifically all operations above 100 km above mean sea level.

SPEAR/SPEAR-EW*: UK/Europe Select Precision at Range air-to-ground standoff attack missile, with LAUNCH AND LOITER capabilities. Will utilize a modular 'swappable' warhead system featuring high-explosive, anti-armor, fragmentation or electronic warfare (EW) warheads.

SPETSNAZ: Russian Special Operations Forces

SPLASH: US Navy and Air Force Radio brevity code showing a target has been destroyed. In artillery context splash over means impact imminent, splash out means rounds impacted.

SPLIT-S: An aerial combat maneuver by which by which an aircraft performs a half-loop to rapidly change direction, either inverting and descending to gain speed or ascending and rolling to reverse course and gain altitude.

SSBN: Strategic-level nuclear-powered (N) submarine platform for firing ballistic (B) missiles. Examples: UK *Vanguard* class, US *Ohio* class, Russia *Typhoon* class.

SSC: Subsurface Contact Supervisor; supervises operations against subsurface contacts from within a ship's Combat Information Center (CIC)

SSGN: A guided missile (G) nuclear (N) submarine that carries and launches guided cruise missiles as its primary weapon. Examples: US *Ohio* class, Russia *Yasen* class.

SSK: A diesel-electric-powered submarine, quieter when submerged than a nuclear-powered submarine, but must rise to snorkel depth to run its diesel and recharge its batteries. Examples: Iranian *Fateh* class, Russian *Kilo* class, Israeli *Dolphin I* class.

SSN: A general-purpose attack submarine (SS) powered by a nuclear reactor (N). Examples: HMS *Agincourt*, Russian *Akula* class.

SSP: A diesel-electric submarine with air-independent propulsion system able to recharge batteries without using atmospheric oxygen. Allows the submarine to stay submerged longer than a traditional SSK. Examples: Israeli *Dolphin II* class, Iranian *Besat** class.

STANDOFF: Launched at long range

STINGER: US-made man-portable, low-level anti-air missile

STINGRAY*: The MQ-25 Stingray is a Boeing-designed prototype uncrewed US airborne refueling aircraft.

STORMBREAKER*: US air-launched, precision-guided glide bomb that can use millimeter radar, laser or infrared imaging to match and then prioritize targets when operating in semi-autonomous AI mode.

SU-57: See FELON

SUBSONIC: Below the speed of sound (under 767 mph, 1,234 kph)

SUNBURN: Russian-made 220mm multiple rocket launcher capable of firing high-explosive, THERMOBARIC or penetrating warheads

SUPERSONIC: Faster than the speed of sound (over 767 mph, 1,234 kph); see also HYPERSONIC

SWARM: Drones, missiles or smart bombs with onboard AI and the ability to coordinate their actions with other drones while in flight, either autonomously or using pre-selected protocols. 'Swarm' tactics differ from 'horde' tactics in that swarms place more emphasis on coordinated action to defeat enemy defenses. See also HORDE.

SYNTHETIC APERTURE RADAR (SAR): A form of radar that is used to create two-dimensional images or three-dimensional reconstructions of objects, such as landscapes. SAR uses the motion of the radar antenna over a target region to provide finer spatial resolution than conventional beam-scanning radars.

SYSOP: The systems operator inside the control station for a HELLADS battery, responsible for electronic and communications systems operation

T-14 ARMATA: Russian next-generation main battle tank or MBT. Designed as a 'universal combat platform' which can be adapted to infantry support, anti-armor or anti-armor configurations. First Russian MBT to be fitted with active electronically scanning array radar capable of identifying and engaging multiple air and ground targets simultaneously. Also the first Russian MBT to be fitted with a crew toilet. Used in combat in Syria from 2020 and claimed by Russia to have entered combat in Ukraine (but not verified independently). Very few examples are believed to exist and the last time they were paraded in public, three were seen, but one broke down and could not complete the parade.

T-90: Russian-made main battle tank

TAC(P): Tactical air controller, a specialist trained to direct close air support attacks. See also CAS; FAC; JTAC.

TAIFUN 002: Speculative iteration of the Zhu Hai Yun class drone mothership. The Zhu Hai Yun, launched in 2022, is the world's first drone carrier vessel, capable of launching and recovering up to 50 autonomous uncrewed vehicles.

TAO: Tactical action officer; officer in command of a ship's Combat Information Center (CIC)

TCA: Tactical control assistant, non-commissioned officer (NCO) in charge of identifying targets and directing fire for a single HELLADS or PATRIOT battery.

TCO: Tactical control officer, officer in charge of a single HELLADS or PATRIOT missile battery

TD: Tactical Director; the officer directing multiple PATRIOT or HELLADS batteries in ground air defenses, or interception operations aboard an AWACS aircraft.

TEMPEST*: British/European 6th-generation stealth aircraft under development as a replacement for the RAF Tornado multirole fighter. It is planned to incorporate advanced combat AI to reduce pilot data overload, laser anti-missile defenses, and will team with swarming drones such as BATS. It may be developed in both crewed and uncrewed versions, and a version for use on the two new British aircraft carriers is also mooted.

TERMINATOR: A Russian-made infantry fighting vehicle (see IFV) based on the chassis of the T-90 main battle tank, with 2x 30mm autocannons and 2x grenade or anti-tank missile launchers. Developed initially to support main battle tank operations, it has become popular for use in urban combat environments.

THERMOBARIC: Weapons, otherwise known as thermal or vacuum weapons, which use oxygen from the surrounding air to generate a high-temperature explosion and long-duration blast wave

THUNDER: Radio brevity code indicating one minute to weapons impact

TIANYI (Wing of Fate) autonomous drone*: A speculative design based on the TIKAD/SMASH DRAGON prototypes; gyro stabilized flying gun quadcopters which can be fitted with automatic weapons or a 40mm grenade launchers. US version: Semi-Autonomous Air-Ground Assault system, or SAAGA. Slang: Slaughterbot.

TIANGONG: Chinese space station launched in April 2021 and currently comprising 3 modules. Planned expansion to 5 modules by 2025, the station is seen as a step toward a crewed Mars mission. With the International Space Station (ISS) due to be decommissioned in 2031, China will have the only functioning space station. There have been no discussions about international missions involving Tiangong, primarily because China was excluded from ISS participation by the USA.

TLV: Tianyi Launch Vehicle, a supersonic drone mothership launched by maglev, which glides to its target before engaging an electric engine and dispersing a swarm of autonomous Tianyi (Wing of Fate) drones.

TOT. Time On Target. The time at which a unit or munition is expected to reach its target or launch point.

T-POD*: Trauma-Pod battlefield medical assistant. A speculative merger of ongoing research into battlefield trauma treatment which aims to enable AI assisted rapid diagnosis and stabilization of the most common battlefield injuries (blast injury, projectile weapon injury, cardiac failure).

TOW: US wire-guide anti-tank missile, fired either from a tripod launcher by ground troops or mounted on armored cavalry vehicles

TROPHY: Israeli-made anti-projectile defense system using explosively formed penetrators to defeat attacks on vehicles, high-value assets and aircraft. It is currently fitted to several Israeli and US armored vehicle types. Use in aircraft is speculative.

TSIRKON*: (aka Tsirkon), scramjet powered anti-ship missile claimed by Russia to be capable of Mach 9 or 9,800 km an hour. Because it flies at hypersonic speeds within the atmosphere, air pressure in front of it forms a plasma cloud as it moves, absorbing radio waves and making it difficult for radar to detect. Russia claims to have deployed the missile on its *Admiral Gorshkov* class frigates but it has not been observed in use e.g. in Ukraine. Seel also Zmeyevik (air launched variant).

TU-190 *Envoy**: Russian strategic stealth bomber, in development. Though Russian media has stated the aircraft is in production, no flying examples have been documented. The Envoy is expected to be a delta winged aircraft similar to the US B-2, capable of carrying a 20-ton payload comprising air to air and air to surface ordnance in rotary launchers and fixed launch points. Also referred to as type Pak-DA.

TUNGUSKA: A mobile Russian-made anti-aircraft vehicle incorporating both cannon and surface-to-air missiles

TYPE 054, TYPE 055: Chinese fleet defense destroyers. The Type 054 destroyer is a multi-role frigate equipped with anti-ship missiles, air defense missiles, torpedoes, and a 76mm gun based on the old Soviet *Sovremenny* class; while the Chinese Type 055 *Renhai* class destroyer is a more advanced guided missile destroyer with a more powerful armament that includes advanced air defense systems, land attack cruise missiles, anti-ship missiles, torpedoes, and a variety of guns, similar in role to the US Arleigh Burke class but superior in firepower with 112 vertical launch cells to the Arleigh Burke's 96.

TYPE 075: *Yushen* class Chinese helicopter landing dock with full length flight deck for vertical landing and takeoff operations. Similar in size and design to the US Wasp or America class. Can carry 800 troops, 60 tanks and 30 helicopters.

TYPE 095*: Planned Chinese 3rd-generation nuclear-powered attack submarine with vertical launch tubes and substantially reduced acoustic signature to current Chinese types.

UAV: Uncrewed aerial vehicle or drone, usually used for transport, refueling or reconnaissance.

UCAS: Uncrewed combat aerial support vehicle or drone

UCAV: Uncrewed combat aerial vehicle; a fighter or attack aircraft

UDAR* UGV: Russian-made uncrewed ground vehicle which integrates remotely operated turrets (30mm autocannon, Kornet anti-tank missile or anti-air missile) onto the chassis of a BMP-3 infantry fighting vehicle. The vehicle can be controlled at a range of up to 6 kilometers (10 km) by an operator with good line of sight, or via a tethered drone relay.

UDV: Underwater delivery vehicle. A small submersible transport used typically by naval commandos for covert insertion and recovery of troops.

UGV: Uncrewed ground vehicle, also UGCV: Uncrewed ground combat vehicle

UI: Un-Identified, as in 'UI contact.' See also BOGEY.

UNIT 8200: Israel Defense Force cyber intelligence, cyber warfare and defense unit, aka the Israeli Signals Intelligence National Unit

UPWARD FALLING PAYLOADS (UFP)*: A DARPA research project of the 2020s, now shelved, to develop deployable, uncrewed distributed systems that lie on the deep-ocean floor in concealed containers for years at a time. These deep-sea nodes could be remotely activated when needed and recalled to the surface. In other words, they "fall upward." Payloads could include sensor packages, canister-launched aerial drones, mines or torpedoes.

URAGAN: Russian 220mm 16-tube rocket launcher, first fielded in the 1970s

U/S: Un-serviceable, out of commission, broken.

USO: United Services Organizations; US military entertainment and personnel welfare services

V-22 OSPREY: Bell Boeing multi-mission tiltrotor aircraft capable of vertical takeoff and landing which resembles a conventional aircraft when in flight.

V-280* OUTLAW: Bell Boeing-proposed successor to the V-22, with higher speed, endurance, lift capacity and modular payload bay.

V-280* VAPOR: Concept aircraft only. AI-enhanced V-280 with anti-radar absorbent coating, added rear fuselage turbofan jet engines for additional speed, and forward-firing 20mm autocannons.

VALKYRIE (XQ-58)*: an experimental uncrewed stealth fighter designed and built by Kratos Defense and Security Solutions to support a USAF requirement to field an uncrewed wingman cheap enough to sustain losses in combat but capable of supporting crewed aircraft in hostile environments. In January 2023 it was announced the USAF had purchased two Valkyrie demonstrators for $15.5m USD, shortly after which the US Navy announced it had done the same.

VERBA: A Russian-made man-portable low-level anti-air missile with data networking capabilities, meaning it can use data from friendly ground or air radar systems to fly itself to a target.

VIGILANT CLASS COAST GUARD CUTTER: The Vigilant-class Coast Guard cutter is a medium-endurance cutter with a displacement of approximately 1,000 tons, a sensor suite that includes radar, sonar, and electronic surveillance equipment, a weapons system that includes a 25 mm Mk 38 chain gun and various small arms, as well as a flight deck and hangar capable of supporting helicopter operations for search and rescue, law enforcement, and other missions.

VIGILANT V-247 tiltrotor uncrewed combat aircraft*: Bell V-247 Vigilant is a large uncrewed aerial vehicle, designed to be able to execute all the missions of a crewed tilt rotor except for personnel transport. Concept in Aggressor novels: air launched, vertical landing, mid-air recoverable. Range 2,400 nm, Long Range Cruise 240 kts, Cruise at Maximum Continuous 300+ kts, Best Endurance 178 kts, Service Ceiling 25,000 ft, Payload Internal Mission 2,000 lb., Sling Load 9,000 lbs., two hardpoints for ordnance including e.g. AGM-114 Hellfire variants; Air-to-Air Stinger (ATAS); AGM-65 Maverick and Spike missiles.

VIPERFISH*: In March 2014, the Navy said it will hold a competition for the Offensive Anti-Surface Warfare (OASuW)/Increment 2 anti-ship missile as a follow-on to Tomahawk Block V OASuW, and navalized Long Range Anti-Ship Missile, LRASM, which was due to enter service in 2024. The OASuW Increment 2 competition started 2017. The winner was the Viperfish, which features autonomous targeting, stealth design and flight profile optimization, active countermeasures and modular payloads including electronic warfare, armor piercing and tactical nuclear warheads.

VIRGINIA CLASS SUBMARINE: e.g., USS *Idaho*, nuclear-powered, fast-attack submarines. Current capabilities include torpedo and cruise missiles. Planned capabilities include hypersonic missiles.

VL(W)T Very Lightweight Torpedo*: The VL(W)T is designed to fit into the six-inch countermeasure launchers on current submarines, not launched out of normal twenty-one-inch tubes. Warhead: 100 - 220 lbs. HE. Can be launched by surface ships from twelve-and-a-half-inch torpedo tubes on cruisers and destroyers and even fired from drones, strike aircraft and helicopters.

VORTEX*: 'Quantum Radar' technology that generates a mini electromagnetic storm to detect objects. First reported by Professor Zhu Chao at Tsinghua University's aerospace engineering school, in Journal of Radars, 2021. A quantum radar is different from traditional radars in several ways, according to the paper. While traditional radars have on a fixed or rotating dish, the quantum design features a gun-shaped instrument that accelerates electrons. The electrons pass through a winding tube of a strong magnetic fields, producing what is described as a tornado-shaped microwave vortex.

VYMPEL: Russian air-to-air missile manufacturer/type

WIDOW*: P-99 WIDOW (Pursuit Fighter). Concept aircraft. Several companies were competing in 2023 for the Next Generation Air Dominance air superiority initiative. The WIDOW is a purely speculative platform combining what is known about the requirements issued and the designs in testing. Envisaged is a long-range missile truck' able to carry 12 medium range and two short range air-to-air missiles in an internal payload bay, or a mix of air-to-air and air-to-ground weapons e.g. cruise missiles. NGAD is described by the USAF as a "family of systems," with a stealth fighter aircraft as the centerpiece of the system, and other parts of the system likely to be uncrewed escort aircraft to carry extra munitions and perform other missions. In particular, NGAD aims to develop a system that addresses the operation needs of the Pacific theater of operations, where current USAF fighters lack sufficient range and payload. The successful NGAD aircraft is therefore unlikely to resemble current US stealth fighters such as the F-22 Raptor or F-35 Panther.

WILD WEASEL: An air attack intended to take down enemy anti-air defense systems; see also SEAD.

WINCHESTER: Radio brevity code for 'out of ordnance'

X-37C*: A successor to the US X-37B uncrewed re-usable space craft, itself a scaled down version of the X-40 space shuttle intended to put small payloads in orbit. First observed in 2010, it set a record for the longest time in orbit for a re-usable spacecraft in 2022, with a flight of 908 days. The X-37C is a conceptual armed variant that will carry a 250kW High Energy Liquid Laser to enable it to conduct satellite interceptions.

X-95: Israeli bullpup-style assault rifle. Bullpup-style rifles have their action behind the Trigger, allowing for a more compact and maneuverable weapon. Commonly chambered for NATO 5.56mm ammunition.

YAKHONT*: Also known as P-800 Onyx. Russian-made two-stage scramjet-propelled, terrain-following cruise missile. Travels at subsonic speeds until close to its target where it is boosted to up to Mach 3. Can be fired from warships, submarines, aircraft or coastal batteries at sea or ground targets. Claimed to be operational but has not been seen in use in the Ukraine conflict. Instead, Russia has used the similar *Kinzhal* missile. A Ukrainian Patriot operator that intercepted the Kinzhal missile launched on 4 May 2023 claimed that the missile travelled only at approximately 1,240 m/s (Mach 3.6), which is about one-third of the maximum speed claimed by Russia.

YPG: Kurdish People's Protection Unit militia (male)

YPJ: Kurdish Women's Protection Unit militia (female)

YUAN EIZEN class tracking ships: Ships of 18-21,000 tons displacement, used for tracking and support of ballistic missiles and satellites, aircraft and for signals interception. Regularly used to trail NATO carrier fleets and intercept communications.

Z-9: Chinese attack helicopter, predecessor to Z-19

Z-19: Chinese light attack helicopter, comparable to US Viper

Z-20: Chinese medium-lift utility helicopter, comparable to US Blackhawk

ZHU HAI YUN class vessel: Aka Zhuhai Cloud (pinyin: Zhu Hai Yun) is described by China as an autonomous 'oceanography research vessel' designed for uncrewed operations in open waters and as a mother ship for uncrewed vehicles. It has been described in media as the first Chinese "drone mothership" and the first "uncrewed aircraft carrier." It is capable of hitting a top speed of 18 knots (about 20 kilometers per hour) and can carry 50 flying, surface, and submersible drones that launch and self-recover autonomously. A semi-submersible variant which can launch surface-to-air missiles is speculative.

Zmeyevik: air launched near-hypersonic ballistic missile. See also Tsirkon (Zirkon).